CONQUERING SPACE WILL CLAIM THE ULTIMATE
SACRIFICE FROM TOMORROW'S PIONEERS,
AS A WORLD MUST BE WON
WITH VALOR AND BLOOD

America 2040—Volume 3
CITY IN THE MIST

CAPTAIN DUNCAN RODRICK—
He has built a new settlement from the untamed land, but
now he faces the supreme test of a leader's training and a
man's courage—he must wage war against a terrifying
enemy . . . and as his own heart battles with a secret
passion, his decisions will send his soldiers to victory or
death.

LT. JACQUELINE RODRICK—
The Captain has made her his wife, but not the keeper of
his heart. In passion and rage, she will plan a dangerous
gamble that will either win his love . . . or lose him
forever.

MANDY MILLER—
Sole survivor of an attack by alien beings, she will volunteer for a risky mission to try to forget her nightmares . . .
and her dreams of forbidden kisses from a man she can
never have.

more . . .

America 2040—Volume 3
CITY IN THE MIST

SAGE BRYSON—

Most beautiful of all the women in the colony, her exquisite loveliness may spell her doom as she is chosen to be consort to a royal alien.

PRINCE YANEE—

As handsome as a Greek god and as careless of human life, his perfect face is a mask that hides an awesome cruelty as his race claims this planet for their own . . . at any cost.

DEXTER HAMILTON—

Former President of the United States, his vision sent a mission into space . . . but will he have the courage to himself board a second ship and become a pathfinder to the stars?

CLAY GIRARD—

An orphan stowaway who has grown into young manhood on his adopted world, his outstanding skill as a pilot will be all that stands between destruction and victory.

more . . .

America 2040—Volume 3
CITY IN THE MIST

CINDY McRAE—

Vibrantly sixteen and irrepressible, she will prove herself a woman with a daring act of courage . . . and an act of love.

ASTRUD CABRAL—

Anthropologist aboard a Brazilian starship, she will be torn as she watches an old history of conquest and cruelty carried out in a new world . . . and she will be faced with a shocking choice.

LYTHE—

Proud warrior of the people called Caan, he will fight lasers with a sword, pit good against evil, and risk his planet's future by giving his heart to a woman who can save them . . . or destroy them.

BABY—

The playful dragonlike creature who has become a mascot of Rodrick's settlement, she will prove her true worth when a planet's secret turns into a deadly threat.

AMERICA 2040
Volume 3

CITY
IN THE
MIST

Evan Innes

Created by the producers of
**Wagons West, White Indian,
Wolves of the Dawn,** and
Children of the Lion.

Book Creations Inc. Canaan, NY • Lyle Kenyon Engel, Founder

BANTAM BOOKS
TORONTO • NEW YORK • LONDON • SYDNEY • AUCKLAND

AMERICA 2040: CITY IN THE MIST

*A Bantam Book / published by arrangement with
Book Creations, Inc.*

Bantam edition / April 1987

*Produced by Book Creations, Inc.
Founder: Lyle Kenyon Engel*

ISBN 0-553-26204-1

Published simultaneously in the United States and Canada

*Bantam Books are published by Bantam Books, Inc. Its trademark,
consisting of the words "Bantam Books" and the portrayal of a
rooster, is Registered in U.S. Patent and Trademark Office and in
other countries. Marca Registrada. Bantam Books, Inc., 666 Fifth
Avenue, New York, New York 10103.*

PRINTED IN THE UNITED STATES OF AMERICA

O   0 9 8 7 6 5 4 3 2 1

CITY
IN THE
MIST

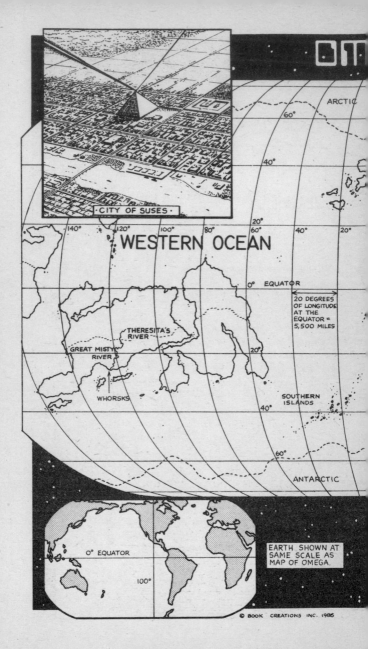

CITY OF SUSES

ARCTIC

60°

40°

20°

WESTERN OCEAN

140° 120° 100° 80° 60° 40° 20°

0° EQUATOR

20 DEGREES
OF LONGITUDE
AT THE
EQUATOR =
5,500 MILES

THERESITA'S
RIVER

GREAT MISTY
RIVER

20°

WHORSKS

SOUTHERN
ISLANDS

40°

60°

ANTARCTIC

0° EQUATOR

100°

EARTH SHOWN AT
SAME SCALE AS
MAP OF OMEGA.

© BOOK CREATIONS INC. 1985

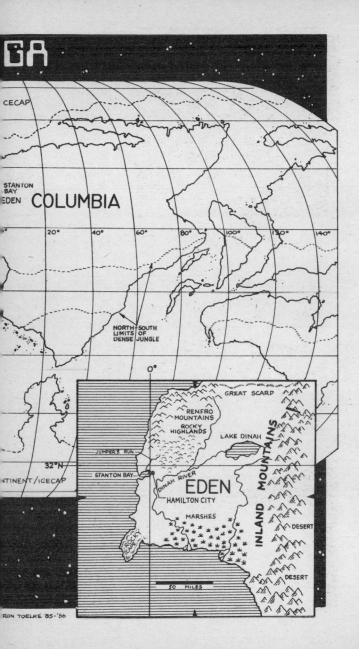

CECAP

STANTON
BAY
EDEN COLUMBIA

20°   40°   60°   80°   100°   120°   140°

NORTH-SOUTH
LIMITS OF
DENSE JUNGLE

0°

32°N

NTINENT/ICECAP

GREAT SCARP

RENFRO
MOUNTAINS

ROCKY
HIGHLANDS

LAKE DINAH

JUMPER'S RUN

STANTON BAY

DINAH RIVER

EDEN

HAMILTON CITY

MARSHES

ROCKY

INLAND MOUNTAINS

DESERT

DESERT

50 MILES

RON TOELKE '85-'86

PROLOGUE

*From the journal of Evangeline Burr,
official historian, the* Spirit of America

In the brief time that we have been on our
new planet, the odd and wonderful Omega, so
much has happened that I have fallen behind in
keeping my records. It has been a time of hope
and disappointment, of bizarre discoveries and
terrible tragedies.

Our new world presented a kind face to us
at first. In Eden, the committee-chosen name for
the area of land we have made our own, the
climate was mild and the wildlife posed no threat.
The only visible predator, a small, lionlike cat,
liked to have his tummy scratched, and the bees
did not have stingers. That Omega might have
hidden perils was made clear to us when we lost
a woman to a giant worm similar to a slug, later
to be called a miner because of the beast's ability
to burrow deeply into solid rock.

Our commander, Captain Duncan Rodrick,
became seriously concerned when a mineral exploration party led by Stoner McRae discovered
an ancient city built of stone. We still do not
know who built the city, where they are now, or
why they abandoned it. How far might that civi-

1

lization have progressed since the time when the city was built—if the culture still survives—and does it pose a threat to us now?

But our greatest tragedy to date, one that not even Rodrick's care could have prevented, was sadly unnecessary and came as the result of the dissatisfaction of the egotistical first officer, Rocky Miller. Commander Miller stirred the fires of a dissident group of scientists and led a party of ninety families, some two hundred men, women, and children, into a deadly ambush staged by one of the indigenous intelligent life forms, the insectlike Whorsk. Dr. Mandy Miller, the commander's wife, was the only survivor of the Whorsk attack.

Aside from the hostility of the Whorsk, our most serious challenge is the lack of heavy metals in Omega's crust. Without rhenium, the metal that fuels our starship, Captain Rodrick would never be able to complete his mission to take the Spirit of America back to Earth with a cargo of Omega's fine food plants, which have great potential for making the arid areas of the Earth green again. The lack of heavy metals is now being overcome with the help of the giant miners. They trade the metallic ores they have extracted from far beneath the surface for a synthetic lubricant we manufacture for their boring teeth.

We've had a number of births and several weddings, the most notable of which was the double ceremony of Captain Duncan Rodrick and Lieutenant Jackie Garvey, and Chief Engineer Max Rosen and Dr. Grace Monroe. And although it does not make up for our losses, one person has been added to our little colony. She's a former marshal of the Soviet Union, no less. Theresita Pulaski was the only survivor of the great starship Karl Marx. She survived an incredible epic journey through Omega's jungles to be taken captive by the Whorsk, later to be rescued by Jacob

West, a scout-ship pilot and Apache Indian with a PhD in physics.

We're still mystified by Theresita Pulaski's experiences, for, although it is biologically impossible for Whorsk and humans to interbreed, it has been discovered that Theresita is pregnant. Under drugs and hypnosis, she can vaguely remember—almost as if it were a dream—making love with a very handsome and very human man. This could only have happened during the time she was recovering from being seriously mauled by a large predator along the Great Misty River, so our investigations are concentrated on that river. If there is a life form on Omega so similar to humans that interbreeding is possible, we all want to know about it. However, every surveillance flight of that area is fruitless because of a thick mist that hangs over the entire river valley. It cannot be penetrated by our detection instruments.

And our main worry still plagues us: Was the Earth destroyed in a nuclear holocaust after our takeoff? We didn't know whether to be disappointed or relieved when we discovered that Theresita Pulaski did not have the answer either. Although the Karl Marx left Earth after the Spirit of America, she too lost her communications with Earth. Thus it was that Theresita will remain as ignorant as we, about whether the Earth's leaders blundered into a final nuclear war, until we can accumulate enough rhenium to send the Spirit of America back through space.

Meanwhile, life is good in Eden, although the work hours are long and our ability to establish the kind of technological civilization necessary to continue our space travel has been severely impaired by the deaths of many skilled people. I am confident, however, that with God's help we will overcome and that soon our great ship will roar upward on her rockets to return to the

Earth and there discover whether we are the last representatives of the American nation left alive.

On a personal note, I am quite far along in my study of Portuguese. I've had a chance to practice my Russian with Theresita, and she says my accent is improving. I think I'm adequate at Portuguese since it is so similar to Spanish, and, should we ever contact the Brazilian expedition into space, aboard the Estrêla do Brasil, *I will be able to converse with them.*

I

WARNINGS FROM A
SPACE BEACON

ONE

Jennie Hamilton had become a morning person since having left the turmoil and daily crises of her role as America's First Lady. Living now with her husband, ex-President Dexter Hamilton, in western North Carolina, she liked to watch her peaceful, private world brighten before the sun burst over the mountain to the east. On a morning when spring had definitely established itself against any vagrant urge by winter to make one final assault, she clasped her coffee mug in both hands, sat sidesaddle on the railing of the eastern balcony of a house she had come to love, and watched the glory of rhododendron blooms emerge from the predawn darkness.

The house had been built by an industrialist of the old school, and it was shamefully extravagant in an age when rat-pack cities sprinkled the nation like algae on a stagnant pond, ever growing. Behind her was one of the few remaining wilderness areas and to the east an unbuildable, steep, seemingly bottomless chasm and a sheer mountain. At night, however, the glow of light from the metro sprawl of Asheville dimmed the stars.

Jennie did her best thinking in the early morning. The habit had grown from an inability to sleep, and then it had become a curative process, which over a period of months began to soothe her resentment and frustration about the way the so-called pundits and political writers had handled the retrospective assessment of her husband's presidency. It had all been rather terrible.

They were calling Dexter Hamilton's two terms in the White House the most disastrous eight years in American history. Republicrats were blaming the growing isolation of the United States on Dexter, but in view of recent events, more and more people were beginning to question the Republicrats' attempt to blame their failures on Dexter's Conservative administration.

More and more common people in the overpopulated cities were beginning to remember that Dexter Hamilton had at least made a stand. He had fought the Russians in South America, and he had destroyed Soviet power in the Western Hemisphere, even if the victory had been pyrrhic, with crippling losses to America's air and sea power.

The people of the United States were frightened. The country was becoming an isolated island of democracy in a hostile world. One by one the smaller nations of South and Central America had deserted their alliances with the United States to cast their lot with fascist Brazil—a political giant equal to the Soviet Union and the United States, with a nuclear arsenal comparable in destructive power to that of either of the aging superpowers and a space program second to none.

For the first time in modern history, the United States was fighting a border war. Mexico was in turmoil, torn between the last-surviving Communist party in the Americas and the Brazilian-backed nationalists. The civil war spilled over the border with both right-wing and left-wing guerrilla groups bringing death and terror from the Gulf of Mexico to the Pacific.

That situation could not be blamed on Dexter Hamilton. In a recent interview, he had stated, "It is time for the Republicrat administration to mobilize the reserves and to establish law and order on our southern border, even if it means we have to march all the way to Mexico City."

Jennie and a precious few others knew that it was unfair to blame the uncontested, swift, and devastating Russian conquest of Europe on the Hamilton administra-

tion, but the political writers were all in agreement that if
Hamilton had not forced the showdown in South America
with the Russians, they would have been content to leave
Western Europe nominally free . . . although the Western
European countries had long since fallen into the Soviet
orbit.

It was a frightening world. In all of Europe only
Switzerland had sovereignty over its affairs, because, Western cynics explained, even Soviet strongmen needed secret Swiss bank accounts. The exhausted English had at
long last granted total independence to Scotland and Ire-
land, and oddly enough the three nations were working
more closely than ever, for only their frail lifeline extending across the Atlantic Ocean to the United States protected them from becoming yet another Soviet province.

Japan was still independent, in spite of being sur
rounded by the Communist horde. The old men who
ruled in the Kremlin following the assassination of Premier Yuri Kolchak had realized that the industrial capabilities of Japan and the United States were so meshed that a
Soviet attack on Japan would force the United States into
war, most probably with the use of nuclear weapons.

Australia and New Zealand, awash in a Red sea, were
hardly worth the effort of conquest, and there was a risk to
the Soviets because of Australia's and New Zealand's ties
with their English-speaking American allies. South Africa,
that nation of mad dogs, glowered from behind its ramparts at Communist black Africa and was left alone, for the
men in the Kremlin *knew* that the nukes would fly from
South Africa at the first sign of an attack, and that tiny tip
of the continent was not worth the loss of a dozen or more
Russian cities and a good portion of Africa.

Although the Republicrats tried to blame it all on
Dexter Hamilton, the facts that had led to the South
American war were still classified as top secret. Only a few
knew that Hamilton had had no choice, save surrender, in
the face of Yuri Kolchak's threat to have a Red world or a
dead world before he died of his incurable disease.

Jennie Hamilton knew that historians, if there were
to be any, would state that Dexter Hamilton had shown

great bravery and love of freedom and that he had stopped the surge of communism in the Western Hemisphere. At first the barrage of criticism had bothered her, but now she was at peace. She knew what her husband had faced and what he had accomplished. His record in world affairs would eventually stand on its merits.

However, there was another area of criticism, which was for months the heaviest of all. It came from the spokesmen and -women for the eighty percent of the population who lived on government money, either a federal or state paycheck, or one of the multiple forms of welfare. What Hamilton considered to be his greatest achievement, the building of the *Spirit of America*, was viewed by most as an egghead experiment that had wasted billions of dollars, which should have been spent on the masses. He had sent an untested ship into space, and that was, they accused, his worst folly.

There would have been heavy criticism of the *Spirit of America* even if it had been a success. But when communications were lost with the ship before it reached the point of lightstep, when it was evident that all aboard were dead, the voices of the masses rose to near hysteria.

Even Jennie had her doubts about the *Spirit of America*. She tried, but she could not share Dexter's optimism about the ship. Harry Shaw, builder of the starship and the inventor of the rhenium-powered drive that had made interstellar travel possible, had tracked her past the far orbit of Pluto, but he had no evidence that anyone was alive aboard her. There had been a tiny disturbance on a recording tape, enough to make Shaw and Hamilton hope and pray that the ship had used her rhenium drive; but at that great distance the ship was only a tiny mote in space, and the disturbance on the tape could have been, as the cynics said, a glitch in the electronics. The ship, most people felt, was a dead hulk, speeding away from the solar system at sublight speed to travel forever into the depths of space.

Now the sun was up, and an hour later, so was Dexter Hamilton. A maid served breakfast on the balcony. Hamilton did not look like a reviled and defeated man;

only in his late fifties, he was youthful, vibrant, and energetic. He made many public appearances and spoke often on the viewscreen, for, after all, he was the only living ex-president, and Americans honor their past presidents regardless of their actions in office. Hamilton was writing his memoirs. He worked well at Starview—that was the name Jennie had given to the estate in the North Carolina mountains—and he enjoyed the privacy. He was near enough to Asheville to look in now and then on the construction of the Hamilton Presidential Library, and he had an old friend in residence most of the time at Starview. Oscar Kost, former scientific adviser at the cabinet level and still complaining of his aching neck, had his own suite of rooms in an isolated wing of the huge house, from which he ventured out now and then to have a bourbon on the balcony or to make lecture appearances at various universities.

Hamilton was having his second cup of coffee and enjoying the view—the beauty of both the mountain spring and his wife—when his secretary brought a cellular telephone to the table and said, "It's Harry Shaw, Mr. President."

Jennie didn't get much from the conversation. Hamilton's end of it was brief, consisting of affirmatives and a final, "That's great, Harry." Then he smiled at her and said, "He wants to come down and bring a couple of friends."

"It'll be nice to see him again," Jennie said.

Harry Shaw had left government service. After the apparent failure of the *Spirit of America*, all space development funds had been cut. The government was pushing hard to turn Shaw's invention of the century, perhaps of all time, into a weapon. Harry Shaw had made it possible for a spaceship to travel faster than the speed of light, but all the Pentagon in Washington could think of was the explosive potential of antimatter-bombarded rhenium. Shaw had wanted no part of that. With enough nuclear warheads in place to demolish the Earth ten times over, who needed a doomsday machine? Shaw felt that his invention, transformed into a weapon, could not only split the Earth into small asteroids but destroy nearby planets and affect the life cycle of the sun itself. There were times when he wished he had never started working with the peculiar properties of rhenium.

A man has to live, and a man of Shaw's character has to work. He had taken private employment with Transworld Robotics, where Dr. Grace Monroe had developed the computer brain that had made android construction possible. Transworld Robotics had allowed Shaw to write his own contract, given him almost unlimited funds, and allowed him to pursue any line of research he chose. For a long time he had ignored his work with rhenium, for even to think of it put pictures of failure, devastation, and death aboard ship into his mind. He knew that he was expected to explore further the properties of rhenium—and to his surprise Transworld had provided him with a couple of pounds of that rarest of metals—but for long months he continued to resist all efforts to get him talking about the Spirit of America project. Then, one day when his current speculation had led him into a dead-end box for the thousandth time, he punched up the lightstep file, mused through it, then sat up with a jerk. He did some swift calculations, walked the floor for a while, sat down at the computer terminal, and repeated the calculations a half-dozen times, then requested a line to the office of Brand Roebling.

Roebling's voice was crisp. "Yes, Harry?"

"If you have time, I'd like to see you in my lab," Harry said. He was not much on protocol. During Project Lightstep he had been the boss.

"I'll be there in five minutes," Roebling said.

Brand Roebling was the great-grandson of Brandon Roebling, the founder of Transworld Robotics. He liked to tell people that he could trace his ancestry to John Roebling, who had invented wire rope and used it to build the Brooklyn Bridge, an edifice that was still standing in New York, although no vehicular traffic was allowed on it. Brand had sprung from a long line of achievers, and he himself had not depended on family wealth. He had developed his own electronics company, and it had not been family money but his own that he had used in the corporate takeover of Transworld, thus regaining control of the company lost by his father. Not yet sixty-five, he had accumulated one of the largest private fortunes in the world. He was absolutely disgusted by the events of recent decades, events he saw as the total loss of American power and prestige. He saw no future for his son, in his midthirties, and daughter, in her early twenties, as long as the country was in the hands of the fumbling, cowardly Republicrats.

Harry Shaw was seated, his feet on his desk, when Roebling was admitted by Shaw's private security guard. Shaw merely nodded and waved a hand at a chair in front of his desk as if he were the boss instead of Roebling.

Roebling looked at Shaw's face, seeking a clue to what was obviously a summons, but saw only a small, dark, pleasant-faced man apparently completely at ease. Shaw was his kind of man. Their relationship had not become intimate because Roebling was a busy man and Shaw a private one, but Roebling had enjoyed Shaw's company the few times they had talked.

Before Roebling could speak, Shaw said, "Damn, I was stupid."

"Wrong, maybe. Stupid, no. But I do admire modesty in scientists."

"We wasted tons of the stuff," Shaw fumed.

"That's interesting," Roebling said, not having the slightest idea of what stuff Shaw was talking about.

"You can get the same power out of a couple of ounces as you can out of two tons," Shaw said, rubbing his wide forehead.

Roebling felt a prickle go up his spine. He was very familiar with Project Lightstep, and there were interesting implications in Shaw's revelation. If the *Spirit of America* had not been destroyed or damaged beyond function, there was going to be a wait of years before the world would know the results of the expedition because the ship had not carried enough rhenium to make a return trip.

"I'd like to borrow a rocket," Shaw said simply. "A

Truman I.C.B.M. will do. And there's a lightstep probe engine sitting in a shed down at Vandenberg Air Force Base. Do you think you could get your hands on it?"

"I can twist a few arms," Roebling replied. He was persona grata at the Pentagon because he had simplified Grace Monroe's admiral design, taking out some of the sophistication that had made the admiral so human but leaving the android all his fighting skills and military sense. "Am I to understand that you want to send out a lightstep probe?"

"Got a couple of things I need to check out," Shaw said.

"I might have a little trouble," Roebling said. "You know how this administration feels about new space ventures. It'll be hard to sell anyone on the idea of spending money on a project that won't reach critical point for two years after launch." He was talking about the long trip out of the solar system, which had been required for the *Spirit of America* before her lightstep engine could be engaged.

"Two hours, not two years," Shaw said.

Roebling rubbed his forehead. He was balding, and the length of forehead made his narrow face look longer. "All right, Harry, maybe you'd better stop speaking in shorthand and tell me what's on your mind."

"That I'm damned stupid," Harry repeated. "It was there right in front of me all the time."

"Are you saying that you can engage a lightstep engine inside a planet's gravity well without causing the king of all explosions?"

"Yes. It happens so fast," Harry explained, "that the reaction takes place and the ship is gone before the field it generates leaves the vehicle. We can go lightstep from Earth orbit, and we can do it with two ounces of rhenium. We've got two pounds of it here. We could make sixteen jumps, of any chosen distance, with two pounds. With the tons of stuff on the *Spirit*, they could have explored the universe."

Roebling was deep in thought. "If I understand you, we could take a shuttle vehicle and go to the stars."

Shaw nodded. "But a shuttle wouldn't carry enough rocket fuel and oxygen for much exploration."

"But we wouldn't need something as big and as complicated as the *Spirit of America*."

"Nope." Shaw let his feet crash to the floor. "Stupid, stupid, stupid. We could have been moving colonists all this time." He looked at Roebling. "Do you think there's any chance of getting government help on this?"

"Two chances—slim and none."

"We've got to do it, Brand," Harry said.

"Let me give it some thought, Harry. I'll get back to you."

Roebling made no commitment until several weeks later, when Harry Shaw pushed a button and a rocket that had been built to carry multiple nuclear warheads deep into the Soviet Union lifted off from Vandenberg Air Force Base and, closely tracked by Brazil and the Soviet Union as well as by Shaw's own instruments, reached for orbit. There, as far as the Brazilian and Soviet observers were concerned, it malfunctioned and exploded. Only Shaw's team knew that the explosion had been a dummy and that the third stage of the Truman I.C.B.M. had winked out of existence and emerged over eleven light years away. Within hours the third stage was back, just another piece of space debris, which was recovered by a shuttle chartered by Transworld and later delivered to Harry Shaw's lab.

Brand Roebling was there when Shaw removed the information-gathering instruments from the vehicle. The tapes projected a picture of a sun with a family of planets, 61 Cygni A, the *Spirit of America*'s prime landing objective.

Roebling was silent but awed. It was difficult to believe that he was seeing pictures that had been made so far away; the light captured on the tapes would not reach the Earth for over eleven years. Shaw was tense as he watched the results of measurements of the sun's planets. He grinned when he saw the data on the third planet—a planet of water and free oxygen and green growing things.

"If they made it, they're there," Shaw said. "On that planet."

"Any indication?" Roebling asked.

"Hold one. We're scanning all wavelengths." Shaw pushed buttons and heard only the static of space for a long moment as the instrument scanned the recordings; then his eyes went wide as a human voice spoke, the words swimming in space static.

"All ships, all ships," the voice said in the calm, measured tones of a space jock. "The *Spirit of America* has diverted to 61 Cygni B. Do not attempt landings on the third planet of 61 Cygni A. Repeat, do not attempt landings on the third planet of 61 Cygni A. All ships, all ships—"

They listened to it for a second time, and then Shaw turned it off. "They made it!" he said, his face beaming. "They had some kind of trouble on the A planet and left a space beacon to warn us, but they made it."

"There's no assurance that they found anything better in the other system," Roebling said.

"No, and that's why we've got to go out there," Shaw said with great intensity. "If they didn't find a habitable planet in the 61 Cygni B system, they're stranded. All we have to do is get a ship out there and tell them what we now know, and we can use the *Spirit* to explore the galaxy." He leaned forward. "We owe it to them, Brand. I don't care what it takes, we owe it to them. And we owe it to ourselves, to humankind. We could have the means now to relieve all the overpopulation of the world. Hell, we could move the total population of the United States to other planets and let the Brazilians and the Russians have this one."

"It takes money, Harry."

"Not nearly as much as it took the *Spirit of America*. We won't need all the extensive life-support systems because we won't have to spend years in space. We can be at 61 Cygni in hours. We can explore a dozen or more star systems in a month."

Roebling rose and paced the floor. "Have you seen the news lately?"

"No. I've been too busy."

"The Brazilians are moving into Mexico. Washington is making a lot of noise about it but doing nothing concrete. Brazil has her nuclear forces on full alert. The Russians are yelling about overt aggression against the last Communists in the Western Hemisphere, and they're threatening to move on Japan to 'secure their Asian flank.'"

"So we have our little problems," Shaw said, with a cynical smile. "So what makes this series of crises different from any of the others of the past decade or so?"

"Harry, you know and I know that sooner or later some fool is going to push the little red button."

Harry nodded in silence, remembering the tense times late in Dexter Hamilton's second term when it seemed that the rockets would fly and the bombs would start falling from the space stations at any moment.

"That's another reason why we have to go," Harry explained. "I'd like to be sure that Dexter Hamilton's dream isn't dead. It's almost as if we've been given a second chance. We can take a ship out there for a fraction of what it cost to take the *Spirit*. We could even move a colony group, just like the one on the *Spirit*, and have enough rhenium to assure that we'd find a habitable planet this time."

Roebling was deep in thought. He saw images of his beloved son and daughter, Derek and Jean. He saw the bombs going off, leaving a cold and lifeless world.

Brand Roebling was not a Republicrat, but he was not without influence in Washington. At midmorning the next day he was seated across the desk from a small, nervous man who could not meet his eyes. It made Roebling even more uneasy to see that the man who was President of the United States had lost—or was in the process of losing—his nerve. He stated his case quickly, and for the first time the President looked him in the eye.

"There will be no money poured down the rat hole of space during my term in office," the President said.

At the Pentagon Roebling was told, "Brand, I wish we could do something. But we're not even sure those people on the *Spirit of America* are alive. After what Hamilton did with the contingency funds, we have no money squirreled away. I can't even buy myself a new staff car. Maybe things will change after the next election. Let's keep it in mind."

Roebling flew back to Transworld Robotics, and there, where the communications system was a bit more secured against electronic surveillance than even that of the Pentagon, he began to make calls. He awoke Harry Shaw at three in the morning. "Harry," he said, "I think you'd like to go out to the Cygni system."

"Even at three o'clock in the morning," Shaw said, all symptoms of sleepiness washed quickly away.

"I'm going to have a few friends over to the house tomorrow night," Roebling said. "We'll eat at eight. See you there."

TWO

Brand Roebling's personal aeroyacht was a converted multipurpose attack bomber. As one of the more important military-industrial contractors to the Pentagon, he had certain privileges and the money to pay for turning a deadly weapon of war into a means of private transportation. The yacht could go ballistic on its rockets and circle the globe in mere hours, or it could land in an area just large enough to accommodate its length and wingspan. The hover jets of the yacht hissed and roared, sending crashing echoes bouncing in three directions around Starview, and then, as it touched down on the pad carved from the side of a mountain, there was quiet disturbed only by the startled cries of crows as they fled the area.

Dexter Hamilton was standing in the shelter beside the pad. He walked out as the jets whined down into silence, saw a delighted Harry Shaw appear in the hatch, and raised his hand in greeting. He recognized the others who followed Shaw from the yacht, and although his face continued to show a smile, he was startled. The people with Shaw represented great power and wealth, and in the past that power and wealth had contributed to several Dexter Hamilton campaigns. He walked rapidly forward to meet his guests, shaking hands one by one.

There was plain, old Bill Farlock, the farmer. That was the way Farlock thought of himself, although in reality Farlock, in his mideighties, had amassed the largest land-holding ever put together under the free-enterprise system. If all his hundreds of thousands of acres in several states could be combined, Farlock Farms would represent the second-largest green area in America, bettered only by the National Park and Wilderness holdings. Farlock Farms produced a significant percentage of all the fresh vegetables, fruits, and grains that made up the American diet. Farlock was lean and wrinkled, scorning the available wrinkle removers and the surgeons who could make the old look young. His nose showed sunburn under his wide-brimmed straw hat, and his hands were the rough hands of a working man.

The attractive woman was Maryann Ward, daughter of the founder of Synthafoods, Inc., the firm that had put artificial protein on American tables in a form that replaced the eating of fatty, unhealthy animal flesh. Under her control, Synthafoods had become one of the most powerful conglomerates in the nation. Tall, elegant, and energetic, she had the look of a woman who has the self-esteem to be at her best at all times—a woman in her prime late fifties.

White-maned Karl Zeitz, the eldest of them, was a cantankerous man who preferred the company of his computers to that of any human being. His hair hung in a mass to his eyes, as if he wanted a curtain to hide behind from the rest of the world. Although he was almost one hundred years old and a bit paunchy, he walked with the strength of a man of fifty, and his handshake was firm.

The last passenger off the yacht was Brand Roebling, and he completed an impressive foursome. Dexter Hamilton could not even guess at the number of billions of dollars in assets represented by the four industrialists who joined him in the short walk from the landing pad to Starview's small lawns and overhanging balconies.

Jennie met the group at the main entrance and was her usual charming self, quickly putting even the misanthropic Karl Zeitz at ease. Of course everyone knew everyone. Jennie offered them a chance to refresh themselves, and Zeitz rumbled, "I'm not tired. Any of you monkeys tired?"

"I gather you'd like to get right down to the business that has brought you here," Hamilton said.

"If that's all right with you, Mr. President," Harry Shaw replied.

"Fine with me," Dexter said, as Jennie took Karl Zeitz's arm and led them into a large, sunken seating area with a glass wall and a spectacular view of the gorge below.

"Since we're in the South, Jennie," Zeitz said, "a tad of bourbon and branch water might loosen our tongues a little."

Jennie touched a hidden signal button with her toe, and a maid quickly came to stand in the doorway. Even before the group had found seats, the maid was rolling a portable bar into the room, and in a few minutes, everyone was holding a cool glass except Harry Shaw, who sat on the edge of his seat impatiently. Farlock and Maryann Ward were looking out the window and commenting on the view.

Shaw spoke over the low voices. "Mr. President—"

Hamilton held up one hand. "Harry," he said, "that 'Mr. President' stuff is fine for public appearances and shows respect for the office, but I'd appreciate it if you'd just call me Dexter."

"All right," Harry agreed, but he could not think of Hamilton in any other context, so he would just refrain from using any title when he spoke to the ex-President. "I wanted to tell you as soon as we knew," he said, "but I didn't know how secure your communications are here. I'm very pleased to tell you that we have positive proof that the *Spirit of America* went lightstep and reached the 61 Cygni system."

"Thank you, Lord," Hamilton said, looking up. He sprang to his feet to seize Shaw's hand and pump it. "Harry, those are the sweetest words I've heard since Jennie said she'd marry me."

It took a few minutes to brief Hamilton on Shaw's recent discoveries about the Shaw Drive—as the engine using rhenium and antimatter for fuel was called by most— and then there was a pause. Hamilton was pacing the carpet in front of the glass wall, his hands behind his back.

"We rushed you too much, Harry," he said finally.

"No blame can be attached to you," Harry soothed. "You had a pretty sizable gun, megatons of nuclear gun, at your temple. The thing is, we're now in a position to gain from our past mistakes. We can send another ship out there, Mr.—" He paused.

Hamilton stopped his pacing and looked at each of his visitors, one at a time. "The Republicrats won't fund one dollar for space," he said. "To do so would be to admit that their criticism of Project Lightstep was in error. It would be praising me and the last administration, and they're not going to do that with midterm elections coming up and control of the House in doubt." He mused for a moment, then picked Brand Roebling for his question. "Brand, quite a pool of money is represented in this room. I suppose there's a reason for this gathering of industrial eagles."

"There is, Dexter," Roebling answered. "But before we talk about that, we'd like to hear your opinions on the state of the nation."

"Well," Hamilton said, "I'm still briefed now and then by the National Security Council, and I have my own sources. Let me see . . . do you want the pessimistic version or the optimistic version?"

"We get the optimistic version from the administration," Bill Farlock grumbled.

"To narrow the question down a bit," Roebling said, "how long do we have, in your opinion, before we blunder into another war with either the Brazilians or the Russians, with the possibility of the use of nuclear weapons?"

"The way you state the question, Brand, you seem to think that nuclear war is inevitable," Hamilton said.

"Don't you?" Karl Zeitz growled.

"I don't know," Hamilton admitted. "When I was eyeball to eyeball with Yuri Kolchak and he told me he was going to nuke us unless we gave him South America, I believed him, but on some level I still didn't believe it would ever happen." He held up a hand to stop Zeitz from interrupting. "Things aren't good, that's for sure. The terrorist raids on our southern border are inspired by both the Russians and the Brazilians. The Russians are trying to use their dwindling cadre of dedicated Communist guerrillas to force us into a war over Mexico with the Brazilians, and the Brazilians are sending their nationalists after our people for God only knows what reason, unless that idiot da Lisboa's Napoleonic delusions actually extend to a military conquest of the United States and Canada. He'll take Mexico in a year unless Washington does something. That last is not likely, because they're trying to put a press lid on the obvious fact that da Lisboa has terror squads operating right here in this country, killing off Mexican patriots and Brazilian defectors."

"We need you back in the White House, Dexter," Maryann Ward said.

"Well, I appreciate that, Maryann," Hamilton said, "but it's not likely. I don't think Jennie would let me run again."

Jennie made a moue.

"As far as nuclear war is concerned," Hamilton continued, "I think the greatest danger comes from Brazil. They've never seen the results of a nuclear bomb used on a city. There are Russians of high rank who were in the field during that nuclear exchange with South Africa. Carlos da Lisboa is also a dictator in the old-fashioned sense, with total personal power. In the Kremlin they haven't developed a strong leader since Yuri Kolchak's death, and since the decision-making process there is divided among several people, it would take longer for them to do something stupid, like invade Japan or the British Isles. Da Lisboa could push the button in an instant, without consulting anyone. There's the danger."

"Would you say there is a high probability of nuclear war?" Roebling asked.

"Well, if we let da Lisboa have Mexico, he'll want Texas and California," Hamilton said.

"You're not going to commit yourself, are you?" Maryann Ward asked.

"Let me say only this," Hamilton said. "Our forces have been living on yellow alert for months, and we've gone to red three times."

Jennie shivered. She liked it best when they were alone at Starview, when there was no one to discuss the serious dangers facing the world, when Dexter was working on his memoirs and she was coordinating.

"If the *Spirit of America* found a life-zone planet at 61 Cygni B," Harry Shaw said to Hamilton, "you've accomplished your purpose of continuing the American tradition, regardless of what happens on Earth. But if they didn't, they're orbiting some lifeless world with no fuel to search for another star. We want to assure that your dream has been realized. We want to send a ship out there, with enough people and material on it either to assist the *Spirit of America*'s mission or take it over if something has happened to the *Spirit*."

"Well, I'd go along with that," Hamilton said, "and gladly. I assume that you're contemplating the use of private funds, which is why we have such distinguished company."

"Private funds," Karl Zeitz confirmed.

"You're all very wealthy," Hamilton said, "but it'll take more than you four to do it. Hasn't Harry told you what the *Spirit of America* cost?"

"The new ship won't have to be as self-sufficient as the *Spirit*," Shaw said. "We won't have to spend years in space. We can explore dozens of star systems for a good planet in the time it took the *Spirit* to reach Pluto's orbit. She'll be bare bones, a utilitarian ship with just one purpose—to set a new colony of one thousand Americans in place with enough equipment to insure its survival. In contrast to this ship, the *Spirit* was a luxury vessel."

"No-frills flying," Hamilton said. "All right. But why have you come to me? I'm not in the same financial class with you folks."

"We want you to use your influence in getting strategic materials and to convince the administration to lease the Utah facilities at Desert Haven to us at a reasonable figure," Shaw explained. "And we want you to head up the project, Mr.—Dexter."

Hamilton began pacing again. Something was bothering him, cutting into the pleasure he felt at having been given a second chance to establish the American tradition among the stars. It took him a minute or two to isolate it. He stopped pacing and looked into Karl Zeitz's pale gray eyes.

"Karl," he said earnestly, "you've been a good friend, and you've always been generous with your money at campaign time, but I won't be a part of a lifeboat project for aging billionaires."

Bill Farlock laughed heartily. "That's why he became president instead of secretary of state."

"Don't get your bowels in an uproar," Zeitz said grumpily.

"The people for this ship will be selected much as we selected the complement of the *Spirit*," Shaw said.

"Then none of you want to go?" Jennie asked.

"I will reserve two berths on the ship," Roebling said, "for my son, Derek, and my daughter, Jean. They won't be deadweight. Maryann's daughter, son-in-law, and two grandchildren will go. The son-in-law will be a valuable asset, since he's a synthetic-food expert."

"I have two sons," Bill Farlock said. "Only one, the younger, wants to go. He's a farmer like me. Can grow anything anywhere, so he'll carry his own weight."

"And what about you, Karl?" Hamilton asked.

"I'm giving my seat to a monkey," Zeitz said sourly, "to remind everyone on board that they're not so smart, after all."

"Harry?" Hamilton asked. "I think you ought to go this time."

"Yes," Shaw said. "Since we won't have help from the military, I'll be ship's commander and pilot." He rose, went to the bar and refilled his glass, and turned to face Hamilton. "Well? What say you?"

"I can get the Utah base. I still have men in Washington who owe me."

"I mean about being a passenger. We want you and Jennie on board," Shaw said softly, looking at Jennie.

Jennie went pale. Hamilton went to her quickly and took her hand. "Well, Jennie," he said, "why not? We've been tossed out on the dung heap to die, and we've got a lot of years left, so maybe we should see a little bit more of God's universe."

"But why us?" Jennie asked, overwhelmed. "We have no scientific skills."

"When we come back," Shaw explained, "the world will listen to Dexter Hamilton. When he describes the good planets waiting out there for settlement, when he tells the world that out there, in space, we'd have the chance to relieve overpopulation and eliminate the age-old battle for Earth's scarce resources by spreading our population throughout the galaxy, people will listen, and that might save all of us."

"This is so sudden, it's difficult to think clearly. But I still remember how I felt when the *Spirit* lifted off. It was so magnificent, so exciting." She turned to her husband. "You want to go, don't you, Dexter?" she asked, looking at him as if they were the only two people in the room.

"Yes, I do, Jennie," Hamilton said, his blue eyes bright.

"All right," she agreed quietly. "I've learned to listen to my instincts, and they're telling me to start packing."

Bill Farlock rose. "I've got work to do," he said in a tone that left no doubt that he was ready to leave.

"Can you stay here, Harry?" Hamilton asked. "Oscar will be back tomorrow."

"I'd planned to stay for a couple of days," Shaw said.

The discussion lasted a few minutes longer. Then the three of them, Hamilton, Jennie, and Shaw, watched the aeroyacht rise on its jets and blast away rockets for the cloud-studded sky. Hamilton and Shaw then went to Hamilton's office.

"Well, Harry," Hamilton said, "it's been a long time since I had a project of this magnitude to organize. Where do we start?"

"With the Utah facility."

That was simple. It took only a telephone call to the General Accounting Office, whose personnel were happy to lease the unused construction site of the *Spirit of America* to the private sector for a low fee, with the condition that upkeep would be paid by the leaseholder. The rest of the day was spent in beginning to compile a list of key people for the complement of the ship.

Oscar Kost came back to Starview the next day. Kost had been Dexter Hamilton's university professor over forty years earlier, and their fast friendship had been a moving force in the concept and construction of the *Spirit of America*. Harry Shaw was pleased to note that Kost looked as if he had not aged a day since Shaw had last seen him—gaunt, stooped at the shoulder, wearing a cervical brace, and complaining of a stiff neck. He forgot his aches and pains, however, when he heard the news. "If you don't offer me a part in this, I'll demand it," he threatened.

"Oscar, we couldn't have built the *Spirit* without you," Harry said, laughing, "so how do you think we could build *this* one without you?"

"Oscar, I'd like you to take over the selection process," Hamilton said. "We've already got a few people on the list, so you can start with them and maybe draft one or two of them to help you out. We'll be taking a thousand passengers. I think we'll be able to operate with a bit more security than when we built the *Spirit*. Private-industry security has always been better than government security. We'll need a security force out in Utah. We'll leave that up to you, too."

Kost knew just the person to head his security team. Her name was Leslie Young, and he had worked with her during the construction of the *Spirit* when she had been a member of the National Service Corps and in charge of guarding the base during the *Spirit*'s construction.

"Brand Roebling is going to send us a couple of Transworld Robotics's Skydarts tomorrow morning," Hamilton continued. "I'll need one of them for a while, but when the first one gets here, you can have it to take a look at the Utah site, to get things organized there."

The first Skydart, with a pilot in Roebling's employ, left Starview the next day with a single passenger, Oscar Kost. Soon he was looking down on the arid and inhospitable desert, then landing in a swirl of dust. He was pleased to see that the desert crawler coming toward the aircraft was driven by Leslie herself.

Leslie's khaki uniform was dusty, but there was a twinkle of delight in her brown eyes when she recognized Kost. She ran forward and gave him a very informal hug, and then said, "You're the last man I expected to see here."

"Let's get out of the sun," Kost said, taking her elbow. "I'm going to offer you a job."

Things had not been going well for Leslie Young. She had originally joined the National Service Corps because she loved the outdoors and wanted to help preserve the few remaining wilderness areas in the United States. The *Spirit of America* project had been a highlight of her career, although she had become a part of it by circumstance. She had been assigned to guard a nuclear waste dump in the badlands of Utah, and when that area had been chosen as the construction site of the *Spirit*, she had instantly become an important person. Leslie had done an excellent job, even finding cleverly concealed surveillance apparatus planted by the Russians or Brazilians in a sand dune.

When the *Spirit* had lifted off and the Utah site deactivated, Leslie's new prestige enabled her to get a choice post in Yellowstone National Park, and for a while she loved it, spending her time learning every hiking trail and getting on a first-name basis with the few remaining animals in the park. Then the new administration had appropriated park acreage for underprivileged-citizens' housing, to be inhabited mostly by people who were part of the eighty percent of the population on the welfare roles. Once that precious Yellowstone wilderness had been gobbled up by the demands of overpopulation, Leslie Young knew there would be no getting it back, so she had raised a fuss that reached all the way to Washington and resulted in her being sent back to guard the Utah site. The most exciting event in a year had been the arrival of a hot core from a dismantled nuclear generating plant, but at least she had no regrets.

Leslie had watched the *Spirit of America* lift off on her bellowing rockets, and she had wished that she were aboard. Now, over a cool drink, when Oscar Kost said that they were going to build another ship, that they would need good security while it was under construction, and that the ship would need a good security officer when it lifted off, Leslie leaped from her seat, planted a warm, wet kiss on his cheek, and said, "Oscar, you've saved my life."

She was out of the National Service Corps uniform within two days, just as soon as her formal resignation was acknowledged and her small crew of National Service Corps people were given reassignment orders. Professional private security guards from Transworld Robotics began to arrive, and then shipments of material, and once again the Utah desert came awake to the sounds of urgent and vital activity.

Oscar Kost was having dinner with Hilary Diaz, the daughter of Maryann Ward. Two well-behaved children, Susan, nine, and Mark, seven, ate politely and listened. The conversation had been all small talk, but over coffee, after the two children had excused themselves, Hilary looked directly at Kost and asked flatly, "Well, Dr. Kost, do you like what you see?"

"Very much," Oscar answered. Hilary Diaz was a tall woman, her dark hair fashionable, her finely sculpted face perfectly cared for. He smiled. "You're a very attractive woman. I see a lot of your mother in you."

Hilary tossed her hair, and an expression of displeasure momentarily crossed her perfect face. "You know what I mean. You're here to assess the progeny, to see if I measure up to the standards."

"Not at all," Kost responded, sitting back comfortably. "That's all been decided."

"My mother's influence," Hilary said. "Oh, I want to go. I'd do anything to get my children off this rotten planet before some maniac starts hurling bombs, but I'd be more pleased if I felt I could earn my way aboard this ship."

"But your husband is very well qualified," Kost said. "I'm sure he'd be selected as the synthetic-food expert even if he weren't Maryann Ward's son-in-law."

"He wouldn't have been in Mother's graces a few years ago," Hilary said. "Hilary Ward, marrying a Mexican."

Kost covered his lack of an answer to that statement by hiding his face behind his coffee cup. He had talked with Roberto Diaz in Roberto's office, and he had found Diaz to be an outgoing, impressive man who would fit in well. It was Hilary Ward Diaz who was giving Oscar pause. He knew that for four years Roberto and Hilary had been on the brink of divorce. That fact had not been difficult for his investigators to uncover. And the dissatisfaction in the marriage seemed to emanate totally from Hilary's side. Roberto Diaz was a workaholic, and Hilary wanted a proper home and a full-time father for her children. The grandmother of the children, Maryann Ward of Synthafoods, Inc., wanted Susan and Mark to grow up free, on a new world—so Oscar Kost was saddled with an estranged couple. He was not happy with the situation, but there was nothing he could do about it since Maryann Ward's contribution of over a billion dollars was vital to the project.

"I do have some talent to contribute. . . ." Hilary said.

"I've admired your work for years," Kost told her. "And I stopped by the gallery on the way to your husband's office. I was very impressed. Your technique is quite innovative."

"But there's not much use for an artist aboard a spaceship," Hilary replied, averting her eyes.

"On the contrary. We're trying to take a representation of all aspects of Earth's culture, as well as our scientific knowledge."

"Well, at least Roberto won't be able to go to the office while we're on board," Hilary said.

Oscar Kost's next stop was at the apartment of Derek Roebling, thirty-five-year-old son of the owner of Transworld Robotics. Derek was a cultured, likable man who had specialized in educational problems, and an investigation of his qualifications had quickly convinced Kost that Derek would be a valuable addition to the ship's roster, for the establishment and maintenance of an educational system for the young had been of prime importance on a new planet. Kost assumed that Betsy McRae, *Spirit*'s school-teacher, would appreciate Derek's help and expertise. Oscar felt lucky with regard to Derek Roebling, for he was the quality of man who would have been chosen without his family connection to Brand Roebling.

Kost spent a couple of interesting hours with Derek discussing a computer-assisted teaching program to encourage faster learning in very young children. Kost got the idea that Derek was not overly enthusiastic about going but would do so mainly to please his father.

Derek Roebling's sister, who lived in a penthouse apartment in New York, was a direct opposite. After thirty minutes with Jean Roebling, Kost felt as if he had been dipped repeatedly into fluffy feathers coated with whipped cream. Beautiful she was, and young and vibrant, but her head was as empty as the space that she enthused about, telling Kost how wonderful it all was and what a great adventure it would be and how she was so pleased to be able to go to tell all those who had preceded her on the *Spirit of America* about the latest fashion trends on Earth.

James Farlock was running one of his father's large farm holdings in the green belt in central Alabama, where he had been born and from where he was reluctant to leave—for any destination other than a new planet. He was quite young, in his midtwenties, but the health and vigor of the farms he managed spoke of his agricultural ability. He, like Derek Roebling, might have been selected even if his father's billions had not bought him a berth.

There was one more passenger to be seen before the main selection process began. Kost flew to the giant complex that was Transworld Robotics and was escorted by Brand Roebling into the bowels of the Earth, far below the complex, into the same simulated combat area where, years ago, the admiral had demonstrated his abilities to Captain Duncan Rodrick under the direction of Dr. Grace Monroe.

Kost was familiar with the type of android manufactured by Transworld for military use, and he had admired the admiral. He knew that the current combat androids had been modeled after the admiral but had not been given the admiral's capacity for original thought. Instead they were workaday models designed to do one thing—kill enemy soldiers or androids. Therefore, he was not sure why Brand wanted him to see an android. It just did not seem necessary. When he entered a room and a very sturdy figure in combat gear snapped to attention, heels together, hand flashing up in a salute, however, Kost knew that this one was no mere combat android.

"Sergeant York, sir, ready for duty," the android snapped, dropping his salute smartly.

"Very good, Sergeant," Brand Roebling said. "This is Oscar Kost. You'll be working with him."

"My pleasure, sir," the sergeant said.

"Sergeant York trains the combat models," Brand explained.

"I see," Kost said. There was a definite gleam of intelligence in the sergeant's eyes.

"Sergeant, perhaps you'd like to tell Dr. Kost about your qualifications," Brand suggested.

The sergeant stood at attention. "Sir," he said, "I am the latest model, based on the work of the great Dr. Grace Monroe, who produced the brain that made me possible. Under Mr. Roebling's direction, however, we've made some improvements over primitive models, such as the one called the admiral. The admiral, of course, was somewhat of a scientific marvel, but he is now hopelessly outdated. For example, in single combat, because of my improved reaction time, the older model would be overwhelmed. In addition, I have added memory capacity, so I can store much more data than the admiral."

"Very impressive," Kost said, nodding.

"As for my rank, sir," the android continued, although Kost had not even thought about it, much less mentioned it, "I felt, after studying all possible data on this so-called admiral, that it was a bit pretentious to wear brass. It is we sergeants who keep things running smoothly in the army, and it is we sergeants who, in combat, are on the front line. I think, sir, that you will find me much more responsive to orders than someone with an artificially elevated rank."

"I think we'll get on fine, Sergeant," Kost said. "Are you ready to travel?"

"My weapons and gear are packed, sir," the sergeant assured him.

"Good. Then you'll come with me to Utah. There you'll be working with our chief security officer, Leslie Young."

The sergeant's face showed question, and Oscar said, "Have you a question?"

"May I ask, sir, if Leslie is a male or female name?"

"Well, it can be both," Oscar said, "but in this particular case it's female."

The sergeant's face froze. "Very well, sir."

"You seem disturbed to know that you'll be taking orders from a woman," Kost said.

"Not at all, sir," the sergeant replied, with a completely impassive face. "There are some very fine female officers in the army."

"Miss Young is a civilian," Kost corrected.

The sergeant blinked, then said, "Very well, sir, I will consider myself on detached duty. Rest assured that I will cooperate to the fullest, for the sake of the project." And, he was thinking, to have a chance to meet the brass-happy, overly glorified admiral. Then they would see who was the better man.

Alone with Brand, Kost asked, "Think he'll be able to handle taking orders from a civilian woman?"

"Sure," Brand said. "He's a bit young, and he's having an identity crisis as far as females are concerned."

"He's not at all like the admiral," Kost said. "That one was open, confident without being egotistical, and very eager to please."

Brand smiled wryly. "We've found that the final product of a Monroe brain is a bit unpredictable. They all have different personalities. But the sergeant's a good man. He'll obey orders."

THREE

There were no bloodsucking insects on Omega, not even in the dense equatorial jungles, and the bees did not have stingers, but Dr. Amando Kwait, the colony's African agricultural expert, was finding that there were some Omegan insects that were as pesky as an Earthside boll weevil or the Mediterranean fruit fly. Kwait had begun his carefully controlled experiments in growing Earth produce in the rich Omegan soil, and the lush crops of tomatoes, lettuce, okra, and squash had attracted a variety of crawling and flying things, which apparently chortled and leaped for joy at finding this new and different source of food.

Kwait was a man who had seen his beloved native Africa fall not only to communism but to starvation and near genocide. He had seen the last remaining herds of Africa's wild animals slaughtered by starving people. He had seen the results of overgrazing on fragile lands by domesticated animals and developed such hatred for the goat—that prime destroyer of the scattered vegetation that had once kept vast areas of Africa from turning into desert—that he had hidden the frozen sperm and eggs that could produce breeding pairs of the various types of goats far back in the *Spirit of America*'s deep-freeze cabinets and had even considered destroying them.

On Earth, insects had, of course, been a major problem, and Amando was familiar with the history of man's battle against them. In Africa itself, large areas of

34

potential croplands had been abandoned because of tiny biting black flies, carriers of onchocerciasis, or river blindness. Continued exposure to the bite of the flies had caused apathy, general deterioration of health, and then total blindness. Kwait had also seen the results of attempts to eradicate the flies. Using potent chemicals, those attempts had done more damage than had the insect itself. The insecticides had to be introduced into streams in order to kill larvae clinging to rocks under the river rapids. A total fish kill had resulted, and near extinction of several varieties of birds. It had seemed that the World Health Organization, totally controlled by the Communist bloc of nations, had forgotten the terrible lesson of DDT—a colorless, odorless chemical that accumulated in ecosystems with devastating results.

Although Amando had insecticides at his disposal, he was very reluctant to poison Omega's virgin soil and atmosphere with artificial chemicals. But something would have to be done about the crop-ravaging insects if the colony was going to add familiar Earth produce to its diet. After considerable soul-searching he came to a decision and requested an appointment with Duncan Rodrick.

Rodrick was a busy man, but he made time to listen to the problems of the various department heads in the colony. If he had been asked to place Amando Kwait's problem with Omegan insects on a priority list, it would have fallen far below other issues that occupied his mind, but he told him he would stop by the experimental farms within the hour. He found Kwait standing hip deep in a tomato patch. The tomatoes were just beginning to turn red, and it did not take a trained eye to see that most of them were damaged.

Rodrick was soon looking at a bright-red little worm that seemed happy to curl up in Amando's palm. "That's the little beggar," Kwait said. "He's really an amazing specimen. In his natural form he's deep green and ekes out a living by eating one particular weedy plant that grows rather sparsely among the native grass. When I planted tomatoes and they started to ripen, he found a worm heaven. He thrives on the acidity of the tomato and has very quickly developed the ability to turn red to match the tomato's color. He eats only the outer skin of the fruit, but he does a thorough job."

Kwait dropped the worm, squashed it with his foot, and picked a tomato that was rotting on the vine. A full seventy percent of its outer skin had been eaten away, leaving no protection for the ripening pulp.

Duncan Rodrick had great respect for the big black man. He knew that Kwait had not asked to see him just to show him a rather pretty little worm, so he waited patiently.

"I could kill them with chemicals—" Kwait said.

"But you don't want to," Rodrick finished for him.

"No. I'd like to keep this planet unpolluted as long as possible."

"Well, Amando, you're the doctor in this field. Whatever you want to do is all right with me," Rodrick said.

Kwait looked moodily at the rotting fruit and then threw it away. "Back in the mid-twentieth century, entomologists tried seriously for the first time to control an insect pest without the use of poisons. There was a fly that laid its eggs in open lesions on the hides of cattle, and the resulting larvae, the screwworm, was a serious problem, capable of wiping out the cattle population in an infested area. The entomologists released male flies, which were made sterile in the laboratory, and controlled this screwworm by simply halting the fertilization of female flies."

"I think I see where you're going," Duncan said. "Genetic engineering."

"Yes."

"We're still technically under the laws of the United States, Amando," Rodrick reminded his colleague.

"The early methods of genetic engineering encouraged swift mutation," Kwait said patiently, gazing earnestly into Rodrick's face. "There were mistakes."

"The cotton plant that mutated into a poisonous, rapidly growing horror," Rodrick commented. "Had to use flamethrowers on hundreds of thousands of acres in the South."

"Yes, yes," Kwait said, "and unless you've made a thorough study with access to secret files, you have no idea of the things that were produced in labs. If some of them had gotten into the environment—" He shrugged. "But Stamler's work in the early part of this century eliminated the tendency for gene tampering to cause swift and often unfortunate mutation."

"What do you propose to work on, the plants or the insects?"

"Both," Kwait said. "We have an expert in the field among us, you know."

"No, I didn't."

"Dr. Dena Madden. Before the small and frightened minds outlawed genetic engineering in most of the world, she did some outstanding work in Australia."

Rodrick turned away to walk down a row and look at Kwait's devastated tomato crop. Kwait walked silently behind him. At the end of the field Rodrick turned and said, "We do have a certain freedom of action."

"Yes. It would not make sense to try to apply all of Earth's laws to a new planet."

"I want it kept under strict control, Dr. Kwait. Before you release anything into the environment, or put one engineered plant into the soil, I want it reviewed by our scientific board."

"That is agreeable. I have your permission, then, to proceed?"

"In the lab," Rodrick said.

"I would ask one more thing. I would like to have Dr. Madden assigned to me."

"What's her section?"

"Biochemistry."

"I'll speak with Dr. Miller, and if Dr. Madden can be spared, she's yours."

"Thank you," Kwait said simply.

Dena Madden was thirty-five, small, dark of hair, and brown of eyes. A combination of Oriental racial strains blended with the blood of a British grandfather to make her one of those increasingly rare Eurasian beauties. She spoke with a broad Australian accent and was not above using some choice Aussie profanity in times of adversity. When Dr. Mandy Miller, head of the Life Sciences sec-

tion, found Dena in her lab and told her that if she had no
objections she was going to be loaned out to the Agricul-
ture section to work with Dr. Kwait, she had objections.

"I am not yet finished with my work on the blood
analysis of the various Omegan animal forms," Dena said.

"Doctor, it'll be a hundred years or more before we
finish analyzing everything about Omega," Mandy replied.
"Dr. Kwait has requested you, and it's been approved by
Captain Rodrick. We all feel that the work you'll be doing
with Dr. Kwait is important."

Dena made no further protest, but she whispered a
few fine Aussie oaths under her breath as she slammed
around the lab, bringing her current work to a halt and
cleaning up after herself. From the Australian home-in-
exile of her parents—they never came to terms with having to leave the Philippines in the face of Communist
brutality—she had watched the so-called Third World countries desert freedom and ally themselves one by one with
the Communists. Time and time again she had heard the
tales of Communist murder and repression in her own
native country. To say that Dena Madden was violently
anti-Communist would have been a total understatement.

She did not perceive herself as being bigoted, but it
was, she felt, indicative of national and racial character
that the darker the skin of a race, the quicker it had
turned to communism. Of course there were many other
contributing factors, such as the lack of an educated elec-
torate in Africa and the other Third World nations, but in
spite of her own mixed blood, she had come to associate
darker skin with weakness, ignorance, and the lack of
understanding of true freedom. In Africa, Dr. Amando
Kwait's native land, communism had taken control behind
the guns of a tiny minority, and now the millions who had
survived the famines and genocides lived in the same
abject poverty that they had known for hundreds of years
and did not even have the freedom to practice their tribal
customs.

So it was that Dena strode into Amando Kwait's office
thinking that her new boss was one of the weaklings of the
world, a member of a race that had given in to commu-

nism without a fight, with cheers and rejoicing in many cases, and had not made even a halfhearted attempt to regain freedom since the entire continent, with the exception of South Africa, went Communist.

It was not Kwait's racial characteristics that made her wary and contemptuous, for she thought that he was rather a handsome man, a powerful man, and there was no hint of blackness in his speech. He was in his fifties, she knew, but looked much younger. His skin was relatively light, considering his country of origin, and because he was slim, he looked taller than his actual six-foot, one-inch frame.

"Dr. Madden," Dena said, introducing herself and taking a seat. "I'm interested in learning just what sort of work you have in mind, Dr. Kwait."

"You and I are going to mount a war on bugs," Kwait said, with a wide, white-toothed smile.

Oh, terrific, Dena thought. *He's going to have me spray his tomato plants.*

Kwait picked up a sheaf of computer printout sheets. "I've been reading your monograph on altering DNA patterns in influenza virus," Kwait said.

"Genetic engineering's single triumph," Dena said, showing a bit more interest.

"We all owe the Stanford team a debt of gratitude for that work, and I've never had a chance to thank anyone associated with it. Now I have a chance. Thank you."

"I had only a small part in it," she said.

"That's not what the reference material says," Kwait replied with a smile. "At any rate, I do thank you. I can still remember the miseries of the flu."

"It was an interesting project," Dena said, warming to the subject. "We were trying to develop a serum that would be effective against all strains—"

"And the virus kept mutating so swiftly, you couldn't keep up," Kwait said.

"So we concentrated on the little beggar's ability to make rapid changes and came up with a juice that stopped its mutating ability."

"I love that scientific jargon," Kwait said, and this

time Dena smiled with him. She was accustomed to having to omit scientific terminology from her conversation when explaining genetic engineering. It would be nice to be able to talk with someone without having to simplify.

"What does my genetic engineering work have to do with growing vegetables?" she asked.

"I don't want to start using pesticides."

"Ah," she said, sitting up on the edge of her chair. "We have permission to attack the problem at its source?"

"Our work will be reviewed by the scientific board."

"Bully," she said. "We'll be controlled by physicists and astronomers who don't know diddly."

"We'll use the lab on board the *Spirit*," Kwait said, not addressing her concern. They would deal with the review board when the time came. "Once you have taken a look at it, let me know the things you'll need."

"I won't know what I'll need until I know what we're going to do," she said.

Kwait fingered his mustache. "I was thinking of moving in one of two directions: either to alter the offending insects or to alter our produce so that they don't like to eat it."

"In what way?" she asked.

"We could engineer a tough outer skin on all our threatened fruits and vegetables. A 'sepraskin,' as it were, which could be acidic or alkaline, as dictated by the appetite of the pests. A skin that could be removed easily by humans once the produce is ripe."

"*Hmmm*," Dena said.

"And while we're at it, we can do some work on a dream I've had for years. The climate of Omega will allow it. I've always dreamed of doing something about the one-crop-per-year limitation of many fruits and vegetables. I see no reason why we couldn't develop a perennial tomato tree, for example, with a continual ripening process, with new fruit coming along throughout the year. This alone would solve most of the Earth's food problems."

"Could be tough on the soil," Dena remarked.

"Yes, but we have thousands of years worth of accumulation of the best natural fertilizer I've ever seen in the

elimination dumps of the miners," Kwait said. "And tomatoes wouldn't be the only perennial. When the *Spirit of
America* goes back to Earth, she can carry perennial fruit
and vegetable plants, along with some Omegan plants that
will make the deserts green again."

"A big dream," Dena said. She nodded. "But it can be
done if we're given a free hand and if the bleeders don't start
worrying that we're going to engineer a doomsday gene."
She rose. "Okay, let's get off our buns and get to work."

The town of Hamilton was undergoing a gradual
change. Because of the scarcity of metals in the crust of
the planet Omega, the light metal alloys in the dwelling
cubicles that had been removed from the *Spirit of America*
were being melted down for reuse, and those portions of
the colonists' homes on Stanton Bay were being replaced
by spacious rooms built from the smart plastic, which
offered a wide choice of colors and removed heat from the
outside air for interior warmth in winter and vice versa in
summer—a function once expensively performed by heat
pumps.

The smelter on the Dinah River was working full-
time, for Stoner McRae's section was delivering iron ore
now. An aluminum-processing plant was almost ready to
start utilizing the bauxite deposits discovered by the admiral in the Renfro Mountains. The hydrogen diffusion plant
kept the colony's vehicles in fuel, and Max Rosen was
supervising the construction of a plant to begin the manufacture of rocket fuel for the *Spirit of America's* lift-off.
The only source of heavy metals continued to be the
miners, and although the underground beasts were eager
to trade ores for the synthetic lubricants they needed for
their drill-like snouts, heavy metals were so rare on Omega
that less than half an ounce of rhenium had been accumulated.

In contrast to the dearth of metals, the colony's kitchen
tables groaned under a burden of plenty. So much of
Omega's native fruits had been found to be edible and
quite healthy that the colony could have lived well without transplanting Earth's food-producing plants, but even

when one was stuffed with the sweet fruits of the tropic South and with delicious nuts and tubers and fresh fish from Stanton Bay, there was still a memory of red, ripe tomatoes, golden-baked squash, an okra gumbo, a fresh salad.

Although the colony was shorthanded after the loss of the dissident faction led by Commander Rocky Miller, Duncan Rodrick had issued strong suggestions that all personnel schedule some recreation time. The temptation was, for most, to utilize the extra ten minutes in each of Omega's hours to put in a ninety-hour workweek, and Mandy Miller had voiced fears to Rodrick that sooner or later the stress would begin to affect even the dedicated scientists who wanted nothing more than to unravel all of Omega's mysteries in the next twenty-eight hours.

She was indeed a bountiful and generous and hospitable planet. Her orangish sun, her accentuated colors, her vivid sunsets, her oceans blue to near purple, her pure air and untainted water all made the name they had given that squarish peninsula on which they had settled, Eden, seem very accurate.

Dr. and Mrs. Jacob West had built their cottage on the long slope to the north of Stanton Bay, outside the town proper.

The marriage of Jacob West and the big, well-formed, Polish-born Theresita Pulaski had not been a big affair. "I don't want everyone snickering at me, you wild savage," Theresita had protested to her Apache husband. "Look at me."

"With pleasure," Jacob had replied, but he understood, for Theresita's protruding stomach held one of Omega's most amazing mysteries, a baby that seemed to be the impossible child, even, perhaps, an immaculate conception.

Theresita did have vague memories of being in bed with a handsome man after having been savagely attacked by an Omegan lion on the continent shaped like a diving duck in the Western Hemisphere. But she had been kept—by something or someone—in a heavily drugged condition, so clear memories were locked inside her subconscious. Dr. Miller wanted to use chemicals and hypnosis on Theresita in an effort to enable her to remember what had happened while in that drugged stupor.

Theresita kept regular appointments with Dr. Robert Allano, who was both a psychiatrist and an ordained minister, but to date their work had been relatively unsuccessful. In fact, the entire period following her being mauled by that Omegan lion had been wiped from her mind. There was no memory of pain, although some faint scars showed where the Omegan cat had severely clawed her and where its teeth had torn her flesh. The scars showed no stitch marks, although the extent of her injuries would have demanded stitching. One thing was for certain: The insectlike Whorsk—in whose primitive village she regained consciousness after her convalescence—had no such medical skills.

During Theresita's stay with the Whorsk she had gotten the idea that a priestly caste of Whorsk lived along the Great Misty River, under the protection of a thick fog bank that could not be penetrated. That still seemed to be the best explanation, but it did not explain Theresita's pregnancy. Blood tests on the fetus showed nothing abnormal.

Jacob, while wishing that it was *his* child that his wife was carrying, was as puzzled as the others but not traumatized. He left the decision whether to abort the fetus entirely up to Theresita, and she had procrastinated so long in trying to decide, that the idea of terminating a pregnancy already four months along was emotionally unacceptable.

Theresita had never given much thought to having children. For most of her adult life she had been an army-career woman in Russia, climbing to the post of marshal, second in power only to the Premier, in spite of her handicap of being Polish in the Soviet Union. Her career had occupied all her thoughts, had taken all her energy and ability. It was surprising to her to learn that she had deep maternal feelings for this unborn child with an unknown father. To think of killing the baby misted her eyes, and she clung to Jacob while he soothed her, told her it was all right, that it would be their child, not just hers.

The medical scientists, Mandy among them, were elated that Theresita would carry her baby to term. There would be much to learn about the planet by studying the fetus, then the child. When Theresita told Mandy that she had made just that decision, Mandy embraced her but released the hug quickly, a bit embarrassed by her emotion.

"I've been thinking," Theresita said. "You remember that I told you about the mud along the river where my pod ship crashed? How it healed my wounds?" She laughed. "Maybe that mud had some other magical properties. Maybe I've been impregnated by something in the mud."

Mandy knew that Theresita was joking, even if it was not very funny. Theresita, with an Eastern European sense of humor, thought the entertainment robot, Juke, which had been programmed with all the jokes of hundreds of old Earth comedians, was hilarious. But, reminded of the healing mud, Mandy expressed a renewed interest in having samples of it.

"Hey, savage," Theresita said to Jacob over dinner, "Mandy wants some of that river mud. Want'a go for a boat ride?"

"Not if it involves getting anywhere near a jungle," Jacob answered.

"A little honeymoon," Theresita suggested, "before junior gets so big you can't reach some of my more interesting body areas?"

"You could talk me into that," Jacob said, grinning.

But first Jacob had other work to do. He and another scout pilot, his Mescalero friend Renato Cruz, were working with Sage Bryson installing test instruments on his scout ships. Sage was an expert in electrical-field theory. She was also outstandingly beautiful. Her dark hair was pulled into a loose bun at the nape of her neck, and, as usual, her almond-shaped green eyes were without makeup. Sage did not need cosmetics. Her complexion had a natural golden glow, and her full lips had a deep pink blush. To all outward appearances, Sage had recovered from her mental breakdown and seemed to be enjoying her work with Jacob and Renato. She appeared in the scout-ship park in shorts and halter and worked alongside the men, even flirting back when Renato made admiring remarks about her appearance. This was a true sign of mental health, since the sexual abuse she had suffered as a child had worked to isolate her from men.

The two scout ships lifted off on hydrogen thrusters, engaged rockets, and took a ballistic arc across the vast Western Ocean. Previous flights to the Great Misty River on the far Western continent had produced little information. The mist appeared to be—and tested to be—ordinary fog. Why such a solid bank of fog should be permanent in the middle of a desert and why it should follow the course of the Great Misty River exactly were two of the questions that needed to be answered.

Earlier surveillance flights had increased the mystery, for certain instruments did not function if a scout ship lowered itself into the thick fog. The life-detection instruments, for example, would not penetrate to ground level. Radar drew a blank. This failure of usually reliable instruments had been the reason for Jacob's work with an electrical-field expert, and Sage's new instruments, mounted on Jacob's *Apache One*, would, they hoped, answer some interesting questions.

Jacob used his retro-jets, slowed the ship in multiples of Mach, and lowered it slowly down into the fog bank at a point near the mouth of the river. Renato Cruz flew above the fog, trying to keep in touch with *Apache One* by radio.

It wasn't too pleasant flying blind with unreliable, fog-affected instruments, so Jacob just hovered the ship and lowered it slowly, slowly, until he seemed to be surrounded by cotton. He stayed there long enough for Sage Bryson's instruments to make their observations, and then he lifted the ship, found clear air, and saw *Apache Two* circling overhead.

"Let's go home," Jacob said into his communicator.

Sage was waiting at the scout park. She began to remove the information capsules from the instruments she had installed. "Want to come to the lab and see what we've got?" she asked.

"Try to keep me away," Jacob replied.

"I'm scheduled for mapping duty," Renato said, but he accompanied Jacob and Sage until their paths separated.

"Tell me about the fog," Sage said, as she walked by Jacob's side.

"It's thick. As thick as any fog I've ever seen. Zero visibility. The instruments go more haywire the closer the scout gets to the ground. Also, I felt a prickling sensation on my skin. I don't know whether it was caused by sheer fear or something else. Hard to tell inside the suit."

"I've discussed the problem with some of the others," Sage said ruefully. "They laughed. They don't believe a society as primitive as that of the Whorsk could produce any kind of an electrical field."

Since Sage carried all the information capsules, Jacob opened doors, and then they were in Sage's lab aboard the *Spirit of America*. She hummed to herself as she began to work. Jacob, meanwhile, helped himself to a cup of coffee from the lab's coffee maker and watched over her shoulder. She reviewed the data in each of the capsules. Then she turned off the equipment with the snap of a main switch and looked at Jacob, her face grave.

"It's one of the strongest electrical fields I've ever measured," she said, "and it has characteristics that puzzle me."

"The people who said it wasn't possible must have forgotten that the Whorsk use helium in their lighter-than-air craft," Jacob said.

"I think we'd better inform Captain Rodrick," Sage decided.

Rodrick listened to Sage's report, his face growing more grim. "What puzzles you about the field other than the fact that it exists?" he asked.

"Give me some time to study the data, Captain," she requested, "and I'll prepare a full report, including unanswered questions."

"Could it be of natural origin?" Rodrick wanted to know.

"If it were in the upper fringes of the atmosphere, I'd

say possibly," Sage replied. "Or if there was an active volcano on the river."

Rodrick turned his eyes to Jacob. "Any turbulence in the cloud?"

"Seemed to be dead calm, Captain. No visible currents in the fog, no buffeting of the ship."

Rodrick mused for a moment. "Get back to me as soon as you've finished your examination of the data, Sage."

"It'll take a day or two to do all the analyses I want to do," she said.

"Any reason to send other ships out?" Rodrick asked, glancing at both of them.

"Not unless you want to find out what's under that fog the hard way," Jacob answered. "It's like trying to fly through a thick, white gravy as far as visibility is concerned, and the instruments are useless."

"If you were going to send a ground expedition to the river, where would you start?" Rodrick asked.

"Well, not near the delta," Jacob said. "The parts of the river Theresita saw were enclosed in high cliffs. That was upstream from where the fog bank begins."

"Well, we won't do that immediately," Rodrick said.

Sage and Jacob rose. "We'll get to work."

"Stay a minute, Jacob," Rodrick said. Jacob sat back down. "I have a request from Dr. Miller for mud samples on Theresita's River."

Jacob rolled his eyes.

"Mrs. West says she's willing," Rodrick said with a grin, knowing that Jacob was not overly fond of jungles. The last time he had visited the jungle, he had brought back Baby, a multihued dragon . . . but not before Baby's mother took a chunk of flesh from Jacob's rump.

"All right, all right," Jacob said. "I know when I'm outmaneuvered."

"Allen Jones will lend you a boat. He's getting it ready now. Lift it onto the river with a scout and get some samples, and then we'll pick you up."

"Well, as long as I'm going to be forced to go for a boat ride on a jungle river," Jacob said, "I've got some leave time coming. How about we take a few days and cruise down the way Theresita drifted on her raft? I'd like to see what she saw."

"Permission granted," Rodrick said. "Have a nice vacation, Jacob."

"Theresita says there are things in that river with teeth a foot long," Jacob muttered. "Maybe I ought to take Mopro."

Rodrick laughed, thinking of the huge Mobile Overt Protection Robotic Operator squeezed into a boat. "Too big for the boat," he said. "Take any weapons you care to draw from Paul Warden. The boat itself is armed with lasers and projectile weapons."

FOUR

Jennie Hamilton had gone to work. Closing down her North Carolina mountain home had been traumatic, but after spending a few weeks there alone—with Dexter away on the business of organizing the space flight—except for a few hours one weekend, she had decided that it was time to cut all ties with the past. An auctioneer moved the contents of the house to a sales warehouse in the New York megapolis, and people paid astounding prices to own a piece of furniture or a decorative item from the home of the only living ex-President. Since money was not to be of any use in space, Jennie contributed the proceeds of the sale to the Hamilton investment in the new ship. Compared to the contributions of the principal backers, all industrial billionaires, the Hamilton fund was tiny, but it gave both Jennie and Dexter some satisfaction to know that they had contributed everything they had.

Jennie had traveled to some odd places during Dexter's long political career, but seldom had she ever seen so desolate a spot as the Utah construction site, Desert Haven. Dexter had an apartment in the temporary quarters. Living in an area with a total of four hundred square feet of space took Jennie back to her youth, to the time when she and Dexter were fresh out of college and just getting started. At first it was almost like a second honeymoon. Dexter took some time to be with her during what he looked on as her adjustment period, and then he was back at work, which took him all over the country.

"Give me something to do," Jennie demanded after a couple of weeks in Utah.

"We can always use help," Dexter said. " 'Matter of fact, I have had something in mind for you. We have our selection board, of course, to choose the people who'll go on the ship, but just checking people's scientific qualifications and running them past a few psychiatrists to get a psychological profile don't give me a full picture. If you'd put your intuitive people knowledge to work, it would be a big help. You can talk with people, get to know them a little, and give me the rundown on them."

Without knowing it, Jennie had already started on the assignment. Even while the hull skeleton of the new ship rapidly took form, specialists had begun to arrive in Utah to begin work that would be integrated as various phases of the ship's construction were completed. Among the first to arrive was the Diaz family. Jennie fell in love immediately with the two well-behaved Diaz children, felt that Roberto was charming, and noted that Hilary seemed a bit tense.

Derek Roebling was also an early arrival. He had been asked to set up a temporary school system for the children of the starship's builders. The site was so remote that, as during the construction of the *Spirit of America*, a complete city had to be assembled, with all the basic services available.

Jennie was assigned a Skydart and a pilot. Soon she was putting in more air miles than Dexter himself, and she found meeting the people who were being handpicked to build a new life on another world to be very stimulating but hectic. During one of her weekends at Desert Haven, she received an invitation to dinner from Hilary Diaz. Since Dexter was in Washington, she called Derek Roebling and asked him if he would like to escort an older woman. She and Derek had become friends almost instantly.

Hilary was dressed in an elegant hostess gown that had cost, most probably, three months' welfare payments for a family of four in one of the government city-warrens.

She greeted them warmly, but her smile, to Jennie, seemed forced. Jennie soon knew why. The table had been set for four, but there was no sign of Roberto Diaz.

"Rob had to cancel out at the last minute," Hilary said, and Jennie could see a whiteness around her lips. "So we'll just be three."

"Lucky me," Derek said. "Two beautiful women all to myself."

"Where are those lovely children?" Jennie asked.

"I'm going to feed them in the kitchen," Hilary answered.

"Oh, no," Jennie said. "Let's put another plate at the table and let them eat with us."

"Are you sure you don't mind?" Hilary asked. "They'd love it. They're so fond of you, Jennie."

"Bring on the brats," Derek said, with a smile, for he too was fond of the Diaz children. Nine-year-old Susan was, in fact, his prize student, with a strong aptitude and interest in mathematics and a determination to master computer science.

Mark, seven, led the way into the room where Jennie and Derek sat, cool drinks in hand. "It's so nice to see you, sir," Mark said, offering his hand to Derek in quite a grown-up way. He smiled at Jennie and was less formal. "Hi, Miz Hamilton."

The presence of the children at the table seemed to put the smile back on Hilary's face. She had given them a nod, letting them know that it was all right to participate in the adult conversation. At first the talk was about progress in construction.

"My dad is back East," Mark said, "putting the finishing touches on the synthafood plant we'll carry along. It can take any basic carbon and turn it into protein, such as synthasteak."

"It's good to know we won't go hungry," Jennie replied.

"I wish the ship were ready to go right now," Susan said.

"Susan is looking forward to meeting Dr. Grace Monroe," Mark explained to Jennie. "Dr. Monroe is her role model."

"I've never met her, of course," Susan said. "I was quite young when the *Spirit of America* left."

"I knew her," Derek said. "She was a remarkable woman."

"I haven't yet figured out how she miniaturized components to the point of being able to construct an intelligent computer," Susan said.

Derek laughed. "I'm sure she'll be happy to clarify it for you when we get out there."

It was a delicious meal, and the atmosphere had been lightened by the cheerful children. When they had excused themselves and gone off to bed, Hilary served afterdinner coffee and brandy. As Derek raved about Susan's remarkable understanding of subjects that should have been far beyond her age abilities, Jennie saw the tautness return to Hilary's face.

Derek checked his button-watch. "Ladies, I'm sorry, but I have to go. I'm booked on the dawn shuttle flight to San Francisco, and I'm a fellow who needs his sleep."

"You go ahead, Derek," Jennie said. "I'll stay and help Hilary clean up."

With the dishes washed and put away, Jennie and Hilary sat at the kitchen table for one last cup of coffee.

"I'm sorry Rob wasn't here," Hilary said.

Jennie had read the files on the Diaz family and was aware that there had been problems between Roberto and Hilary. She mused into her cup for a moment. "There's an excellent child-care center here."

"Yes, I know," Hilary said. "I left the kids there last week while I flew into Denver for some shopping. They enjoyed it." She laughed. "My little girl-woman said that it gave them a chance to meet and study the thinking patterns and life-styles of other people their own age."

"How would you feel about leaving them there for days at a time?"

Hilary looked up quickly.

"I took on a job for Dexter," Jennie explained, "and I'm finding it's too much for me. I'm spending too much of my time keeping records of what I've done and am thinking of taking on an assistant." She knew how limited life at Desert Haven was. She knew that Roberto Diaz would not be able to spend more time with his family during construction of the ship, even if he wanted to. And it was her opinion that most of Hilary's discontent stemmed from Roberto's work habits. Giving the woman something to do, something important, might just solve the problem. Jennie explained what she was doing.

"It will require being away from Desert Haven most of the week," she said. "But I think you'll find it fascinating, and it'll give you a head start toward knowing the people we'll be living with on our new world."

"Jennie," Hilary said, "I'm embarrassed to admit that I've never worked."

"You can operate a recorder and a word processor, can't you?"

"Yes."

"That's all you'll need to start. You record and then transcribe the pertinent information. I'll dictate my personality profiles, and you put them on paper for Dexter."

Hilary sat back and folded her arms across her chest.

"I'm tempted, but I've never been away from the children."

"I'll tell you what—let's put the question to *them*. Let's ask them if they'd like to have their mother participating in the project."

"Well, all right," Hilary said doubtfully.

"That's a wonderful idea," Susan enthused when they talked with her in her bedroom. "You should definitely do it."

"Find some people with boys my age," Mark requested, "and not too many girls, please."

On the first flight, Hilary's luggage filled the baggage compartment of the Skydart, but she quickly found that traveling light was preferable. She took to the work, listening with great interest as Jennie interviewed prospective fellow passengers.

"It's as if we have a chance to choose our companions

for a desert island, isn't it?" Hilary asked, after a week of flying all around the country.

"A thousand of them," Jennie said. She was pleased with Hilary so far. She had been quite efficient in transcribing pertinent information, using a small keyboard and doing the work in the evenings, after they had checked into a hotel.

The next Monday, when the Skydart soared upward from the Desert Haven pads, Hilary happily said, "This job isn't having the negative effect on the children I had feared. I spent most of the weekend with them, and we seemed to appreciate each other more, having been separated for a few days."

Now the weeks, and the months, seemed to scurry by. In the huge underground cavity, the ship, smaller than the *Spirit of America*, was taking shape. All the construction problems had already been solved in building the first ship. There was no complex life-support system to be installed. Production facilities were still in place from the *Spirit of America* project, and many of the skilled workers were called back. Soon the ship was hulled in, the multiple rockets were being installed, and the Shaw Drive put in place.

And all over the country, people who had received word of their final selection were winding up their affairs, selling property, terminating research projects, and taking trips to have one last look at a favorite place.

Hilary had blossomed into a different person. She had gradually begun to participate in the interviews, and she and Jennie made a good team. In California, while talking with a handsome and charming heart specialist, Hilary demonstrated an insight into people that pleased Jennie.

"What a fine man," Jennie said, as they walked away from the doctor's office after what Jennie felt was a perfectly satisfactory interview. She noted a perplexed look on Hilary's face. "You don't think so?"

"Oh, yes, he's very charming, but—"

"But?"

"His application says that he's a bachelor."

"So? We need a few single men. There are going to be single women among us."

"He just doesn't have the look or the actions of an unmarried man," Hilary said. "If you don't mind, I think I'll do some discreet inquiry."

When Hilary didn't join her for dinner in the hotel dining room, Jennie called her room and got no answer. Hilary came to Jennie's room a couple of hours later. Jennie had bathed and was in her gown and robe.

"The charming doctor is married, has a house, a wife, and two children," Hilary reported. "It's supposed to be a happy marriage."

"How did you find out?" Jennie asked, amazed.

"Occasionally Mother's firm uses a private detective in Los Angeles. I just dropped in and asked for a favor. It didn't take him an hour to find out all about our charming doctor friend. In addition to his wife, he has a mistress in a North Hollywood apartment. Apparently he's tired of both wife and mistress, or, the detective suggested, things are getting too hectic or too expensive for him. He's trying to do the most complete husband-disappearing act of all time, all the way to the stars. We don't need people like that."

"Definitely not," Jennie said, and the women re-worked their schedule to find a suitable heart specialist.

The last few months of the construction period were not hectic for just Jennie and Hilary. As stores were being loaded, the rocket-fuel bins filled, various systems aboard ship being tested, the one thousand passengers selected to ride the great ship began to arrive, and none of them attracted as much attention as Derek Roebling's sister, Jean. She came to Utah in a cargo plane and imperiously demanded that her belongings be transferred to the ship. When a harried man tried to explain that each passenger was limited to a definite weight and bulk of personal items, she said, "Do you know who I am?"

Leslie Young happened to be in the security office when the call came in. "There's a woman here who says she's Jean Roebling. She has a planeload of stuff and insists on talking to Dexter Hamilton."

Leslie took an all-terrain crawler over to the landing pads to see a very attractive young woman in the latest New York fashions pacing beside the cargo plane.

"Another hired hand?" Jean asked scornfully when Leslie introduced herself.

"Miss Roebling, if you'll come with me and let me show you your quarters aboard ship, I'm sure you'll understand why we must limit the personal possessions of all passengers."

"That won't be necessary," Jean said. "Just take me somewhere where I can call my father. After all, he's paying for a good portion of this fantasy."

"All right," Leslie said politely. "Come with me, please."

"On that?" Jean asked, pointing to the crawler.

"Unless you prefer to walk," Leslie said.

Jean climbed into the crawler, her face set as if in stone. Leslie pushed the vehicle to top speed and took grim satisfaction in seeing Jean's expensive hairdo well windblown on the ride to the security office.

There was a wait of some twenty minutes before the call could be completed because Brand Roebling was in conference. Then his face appeared on the screen.

"Daddy," Jean complained, leaning forward to put her face in close focus on Brand's screen, "these people won't let me take my things aboard ship."

Brand Roebling shook his head and smiled. Jean had been the first girl born into his family in three generations. She had been the most beautiful girl in the world and could still melt him with one of her smiles.

"What are you trying to take aboard?" Brand asked.

"Well, my clothes, of course. And a few personal items. My paintings, and—"

"Paintings?" Brand asked. "You're trying to take your entire collection?"

"Well, for heaven's sake, we're going to a world where there's *nothing*. It'll be good for everyone to have a collection by good artists."

Brand Roebling grasped the situation completely. "Is that Leslie Young I see looking over your shoulder?"

"Yes, it is, Mr. Roebling," Leslie said.

"Let me speak with Colonel Young for a moment, honey," Brand said.

Leslie stepped defiantly in front of the screen, prepared to fight this all the way to the top if Roebling insisted on making exceptions for his daughter.

"I like the new uniform," Brand said.

"Thank you. It's standard ship's issue. Easy to make, easy to maintain. We'll all be wearing it for a while—until we're able to make our own clothing on the new world."

"You expect me to wear that?" Jean asked, from the side.

"Colonel Young," Brand said. "And Jean, I want you to listen to this. Colonel Young, I have read the regulations drawn up for this expedition by Dexter Hamilton. While the ship is in space and until a colony is firmly settled, the regulations, as I understand them, call for a quasi-military organization, with the captain as the final and absolute authority. Am I right?"

"That's right, sir," Leslie said.

"I was willing to trust the affairs of my country to Dexter Hamilton," Roebling said. "I am willing to entrust my daughter and my son to him. There will be no exceptions made for either of them, not under any circumstances. Is that clear?"

"Daddy," Jean wailed.

"I understand that the ship is equipped with a confinement room?"

"Yes, sir," Leslie said.

"If my daughter gives you any trouble or if she tries to leave the site, confine her."

"I hope that won't be necessary, sir," Leslie said, glancing sideways at Jean.

Jean pushed Leslie aside and leaned in toward the screen. "Daddy, all my beautiful clothes! My art collection! My lovely things! You can't do this."

"Jean, just send it all back here, and we'll put the

paintings into a museum and give your clothing to the Salvation Army."

"Daddy," Jean wailed again, but the screen was dead.

Leslie was ready to meet any resistance when Jean turned to face her, frowning. But then a gamine smile lit Jean's face. "Well, you can't say I didn't try."

"You tried," Leslie agreed.

"You won't have to lock me up," Jean assured her. "You're about a size eight, right?"

"Ten," Leslie said.

"Well, in designer clothes, you can usually wear one size smaller. Good for the ego. I understand that there are community-building social occasions here for the passengers. I have a blue dress that would look wonderful on you. We might as well get some use out of it before I donate it to the Salvation Army."

The quick turnaround was a bit suspicious, but Jean's smile was warm. "My brother says that you're a super person and that I should get to know you. May I?"

"I didn't think so at first," Leslie confessed, "but I'm beginning to think I'd like that. We have a band flying in for a dance tomorrow night."

"Good, we'll go together, you in blue, and me in white. We'll knock these yokels on their butts."

Dexter Hamilton flew back to Desert Haven late in the day. As the Skydart dropped, it fell from the glow of the sun into the shadows of evening. Hamilton was weary. He had been in Washington not on his own business, but at the request of the current secretary of state, who had wanted his opinion of the events in Mexico. Hamilton had known that things were serious, but he had not realized how serious. The Brazilian-backed rebels had surged northward all the way to the Rio Grande, and only Mexico City, an embattled pocket, still stood against them. Captured leftist and Communist troops, with their families, were being executed by the thousands. That was bad enough. But what was worse was that the Republicrat administration and the Congress were considering going to the aid of the Mexican government with an active invasion.

"They're mad," Hamilton told Oscar Kost. "Absolutely mad. They sat on their thumbs and let the whole Mexican nation go down the drain, and now when it's too late they want to send in an army?"

"What about the Canadians?" Kost asked.

"They want nothing to do with it," Hamilton said.

"What would it take to push the Brazilians out of Mexico?"

"Total mobilization. Six million soldiers under arms. A buildup of all the hardware—planes, ships, tanks, everything. We have ten divisions of ground troops at the moment, Oscar, and those fools are moving them to the Mexican border. That's not all bad, because we'll need at least that many men down there to stop the hit-and-run terrorist raids, but to go into Mexico with ten divisions—madness. Carlos da Lisboa has thirty divisions in Central America, with the capacity to airlift them, ten divisions at a time."

"Well, Dex," Kost said, "in a few more weeks we won't have to worry about all that."

"Won't we?"

"Well, we will, but there will be nothing we can do about it."

"I feel like I'm running out on my country," Hamilton admitted grimly.

"Now you don't really feel that you have an obligation to die in a nuclear war brought on by Republicrat stupidity—"

"But people still listen to me, Oscar."

"They will listen with both ears, and with their hearts, when we come back here with the holopictures of new, virgin planets, when we can offer them an escape from overcrowding, shortages, continual war."

Hamilton sighed. "I know, Oscar. I know." He rose. He had stopped by Oscar's quarters immediately upon arriving in Desert Haven, needing his old friend's ears and understanding in the face of what he had learned in Washington. "Do you happen to know if Jennie is here?"

"She's here, and my bet is that you'll be going to a dance tonight."

"Oh, Lord," Hamilton complained, but he smiled.

"Well, I guess I can handle that. Jennie's the only woman in the world who can stay with my two left feet. See you there?"

"I will have a very pretty young woman on my arm," Oscar said.

"Good for you."

Leslie Young and Jean Roebling waited until the recreation room was filled with people and the band was in full cry. At first, as they entered, there was only the noise of the crowd, the beat of the music. Then Oscar Kost saw them from his table near the bandstand and stood up and waved to them. Others, seeing Oscar wave, looked to see whom he was waving at, and soon three hundred people were looking toward the raised entrance to the room to see two very beautiful women—one with dark hair and one with blond, dressed dramatically in blue and in white.

The band wound down to the end of the number and stopped. There was a hush in the room. Leslie could hear her heels clicking on the wooden floor.

"It's like an old movie," she whispered out of the side of her mouth.

"Enjoy it," Jean said. "We'll be looking just like all the others in uniform soon enough."

Oscar met them a few steps from the table, took both by the arm, with one on either side. "You two know you look good, don't you?" he remarked.

"Thank you," Leslie replied.

"You bet your sweet ass," Jean said, with a crooked little smile.

It took only thirty seconds for the first of the single men to put in an appearance at Oscar's table, asking for an introduction.

FIVE

After only two days of searching, Theresita and Jacob West located the Russian pod ship at the bottom of Theresita's River. The idea of salvaging the ship had come jointly to Jacob and Theresita, but for different reasons. Theresita, reminded of the ship and its contents—the remains of a Russian comrade—suggested that it would be fitting to recover what was left of the spaceman for a decent burial in the cemetery near Hamilton City. Jacob, when she reminded him of the ship, thought of metal. Any metal was valuable on Omega.

Jacob had decided to photomap the entire length of the river that, at its southern end, was known as the Great Misty River and, above the tremendous waterfall that was the dividing point between semiarid uplands and desert, Theresita's River. The river ran approximately down the center of the larger of the twin western continents that lay with their northern tips just above the equator. This single continent was larger than the entire Eurasian land mass on Earth. Mountainous on its northern and western fringes, it made for a watershed extending thousands of miles from the northern mountains to the southern sea.

Theresita could only estimate the point of the crash of the Russian pod ship, so Jacob had to fly low, using the ship's detection instruments, for a distance of hundreds of miles before the mass of metal made a sharp *ping* on the ship's detector. Once the ship was located, Allen Jones,

the underwater expert, was contacted to bring in a team of
divers and the boat Jacob and Theresita would use during
their mud-gathering mission. Because of the menace of
the underwater beasts, which had been seen many times
by Theresita during her journey down the river, the salvage operation was performed by a semi-intelligent underwater robot. Lines were attached to the Russian two-
passenger pod ship, which was hoisted easily to the surface underneath a hovering scout ship piloted by Chief
Scout Jack Purdy, with Apprentice Scout Clay Girard in
the right-hand seat operating the winch controls.

What was left of the Russian spaceman—nothing more
than bare bones—was still strapped into the pilot's seat.
The skeleton was removed by a team from the Life Sciences section at Hamilton. Instead of staying on the river
and beginning their vacation, Theresita asked Jacob to
take her back to Hamilton so she could attend the Russian's funeral.

The ceremony attracted every resident of the colony
who was not out on a mission. The memorial service made
Theresita moody. During the months of being alone in the
jungle and on her raft, she had not mourned her comrade.
Perhaps that was because she felt that she was the only
human being on the huge world, and all her energy and
concentration were given over to the problem of her own
survival. But now, as Juke, the entertainment robot, used
his speakers to send the impressive strains of the Soviet
national anthem soaring and reverberating through the
warm summer air, she felt tears form. She had been fond
of the man. He had been a fellow fighter in the mutiny
aboard the *Karl Marx*, and the sight of the casket and the
memories of young Ivan brought home to her the absolute
tragedy of the *Karl Marx*. The loss of the ship had probably been unavoidable, for the final titanic explosion had
come when the fields generated by the Shaw Drive affected stored rhenium near the drive room, but the killing
and the death that had gone on before, *that* had been
totally senseless.

Theresita knew in that solemn time that she might
well be the last Russian subject, the last Soviet citizen

alive, for, knowing the mentality of the rulers of the Soviet Union, she could easily believe that they had stumbled into the last war on Earth.

She was thankful when the commemorative service was over and she and Jacob were in *Apache One*, driving a long ballistic arc to the southwest, to slow over the north coast of the continent shaped like a diving duck. They were in no particular hurry, so they dawdled around in the mountains of the north, some of which lay directly on the equator. It was odd to see dense jungle rise in convoluted hills and then in mountains, to fade through various types of trees into permanent snowcaps.

The river had several sources, which began as small streams cascading down from the snowmelt and growing as the jungle rains fell. Two main branches of the river angled off to the east and southeast, and for a long time the river was not all that impressive, often hidden from aerial view by the overhanging canopy of trees that grew to a height of four hundred feet. Then, a few hundred miles north of the crash site, two smaller streams joined Theresita's River, which broadened to a width of miles and became more sluggish.

The boat, lowered by Allen Jones's crew, was floating on the river, moored to a permanent marker to designate the crash site. There was not much danger of its being stolen, since the Whorsk did not seem to penetrate into the dense jungles from their settlements on the south coast. But the Whorsk coveted metals as intensely as anyone else on this planet, so Jack Purdy and young Clay Girard had been left behind to guard the boat. Jacob and Theresita photomapped the river all the way to the northern edge of the fog bank and then rocketed back to the marker to hand the scout over to Jack and Clay.

Soon Theresita and Jacob were standing on the deck of the boat, listening to the fading sound of the scout's jets as Clay and Jack returned to Hamilton City. Now Jacob heard only the lap of water against the hull of the boat, a distant splash, and the cry of a bird or a treetop animal from the near shore. Theresita had disappeared below while he was inspecting the boat, and a half hour passed while he familiarized himself with the boat's controls and safety equipment. He heard a sound behind him and turned to see Theresita's face peering up from the steps leading into the craft's cabin.

"I have a small problem," she said.

"Don't worry," Jacob answered, his dark eyes shining. "Chief Sky Flyer handles all challenges."

"If you laugh, I will beat you severely about the head and ears," Theresita threatened, emerging onto the enclosed bridge. She had maintained the deep tan she had gotten on the river. She was rather spectacular, topside, in a skimpy halter, and downright beautiful in the long, exposed legs. The problem was at the midsection, where her stomach protruded significantly over the bottom of a brief bikini.

"Why would I laugh because my squaw has a little pleasure belly?" Jacob asked tenderly, cupping his hands over her stomach.

"I remember how pleasant it was in the sun," she said. "I wanted to just bask on the deck, but I can't—not looking like this."

"Well, squaw, we can fix that easily," Jacob said. "It is the look of the bikini bottom that bothers you?"

She did not answer. When he grabbed the bikini bottom and pushed it down to her knees, she tried to seize it, but he was too quick. And then the skimpy material was at her feet.

"When I first saw you, you looked like this," he said, removing the halter.

"So you want me to be a shameless nudist all by myself?"

"Well, if you want company—" He was out of his own clothes in seconds. As they walked onto the deck, Jacob felt rather exposed. But, he reminded himself, they were alone—so alone that the nearest pair of curious human eyes was thousands of miles away. The boat did not leave its mooring at the permanent marker until early the next morning. Then Jacob eased it to the bank and waded into the marshy fringes to take mud samples for Mandy Miller.

Duncan Rodrick was finding that married life with the

slender, beautiful Jackie had good aspects that he had not anticipated. For example, breakfast had become one of the high points of his day. Jackie, needing less sleep than he, was always awake first, and usually he was awakened gently, to the sound of music, the scent of Jackie's perfume, and the aroma of good food coming from the kitchen.

Rodrick had been married once before, when he was a brand-new Space Service Academy graduate. The differences between his first wife and Jackie were astounding. Ellen, the daughter of a Space Service admiral, believed that the world owed her endless leisure and riches that were beyond the reach of a brand-new two-stripe officer. Jackie, on the other hand, had the discipline of the service combined with an endless store of energy. She ran the Rodrick home, cooked most meals, and performed her job as communications officer with ease. Another of the very good things about being married to Jackie was lovemaking, which was prompted and powered by her own feminine sensuality.

On the other hand, Jackie was almost too perfect, too eager to please. That her love for him bordered on worship made Rodrick edgy, for his attraction was, and had been from the moment he saw her, for Mandy Miller. But Duncan Rodrick was a man to see things through, and Jackie was the woman he had married. He felt a genuine fondness and respect for her and would never intentionally cause her pain. It was Rodrick's hope that his love for Jackie would develop in time and that the strong magnetism he and Mandy felt for each other would eventually fade.

Rodrick's custom of having captain's breakfasts aboard the *Spirit* suffered during the first few months of his marriage. Now it was a rare occasion for him to notify selected individuals that the captain's table invited their presence. When such invitations came, as they did one morning to Max Rosen and Grace Monroe, Mandy Miller, Sage Bryson, and Paul Warden, each of them knew that the captain had serious business to discuss.

Jackie did not wait to be asked. She simply assumed

that she was included when Rodrick told her, as they went to bed, that he would eat aboard ship next morning.

The natural order of life aboard a service vessel had changed since the *Spirit* landed on Omega. With the colony shorthanded, Rodrick could not afford the luxury of taking the ratings away from important work to act as servants. So it was that food servos were activated in the captain's mess to serve the breakfast—but not always from the left, as a rating trained for the job would have done.

Max Rosen looked sleepy. His gray-shot black hair was unruly, and as always, he had a dark stubble on his cheeks and chin. On the other hand, his wife, Grace Monroe, looked immaculate and radiant. The conversation as they ate was small talk, and then, over coffee, Rodrick said, "Max, you've been doing the job, but I think we'd better make it official. Jackie, will you please enter into the log that the chief is now first officer?"

"Consider it done," Jackie said.

Max growled and started to say something, but Grace winked at him. "Don't fuss when your true abilities are recognized," she ordered.

"Hell, I'm a civilian," Max said.

"So you're a civilian first officer," Rodrick said. He was about to speak further when the door to the mess burst open, and Juke, the entertainment robot, rolled in, a red mouth with a white smile painted on his metal face.

"Good morning," Juke chirped cheerily. "I just heard that there was to be a captain's breakfast, and I'm here to volunteer to serve."

"Good timing, Juke," Lieutenant Commander Paul Warden said. Paul was an armaments expert and built like a professional wrestler.

Juke turned his head on its well-lubricated swivel and surveyed the table. "Sorry," he said, "but I'll be glad to clear away."

"Thank you, Juke," Grace said. She knew that her robot was at loose ends. With everyone so busy, there was little demand for his time and talents. Now everyone had a terminal in his home connected with the main library computer, and Juke's portable terminal was not used much.

"And since I'm here," Juke continued, "would you like some music? A brief travel film just processed from the cameras of *Apache One*?"

"No, thank you, Juke," Rodrick said.

"Wait in the kitchen, Juke," Grace told him.

"I'll be very quiet," Juke pleaded. "I'm so lonely, I can't even eat."

"Not now, Juke," Max said, recognizing a lead-in for one of Juke's jokes.

"And it makes me nervous," Juke complained. "What's the right wine to go with fingernails?"

Jackie giggled, which was more than enough to encourage Juke.

"I was just reading the story of Michelangelo, you know, the Italian painter who spent seven years painting the ceiling of the Sistine Chapel? He spent five years locating all the numbers and two filling them in."

"The kitchen, Juke," Rosen said.

"Just think," Juke went on, "seven years to get a ceiling painted! They must have had the same landlord I had back on Earth."

"Good-bye, Juke," Grace said.

"After seven years he crawls down from the scaffold— seven years of painting, painting, painting. He looks up and says, 'Well, what do you think?' and this big, ghostly voice says, 'Mike, I've changed my mind. Make it plain blue.' "

"Juke—" Grace began firmly.

"Okay, okay, I'm going," Juke said, rolling into the kitchen, trailing maniacal giggles. Grace, who had tried to hide her amusement from Juke, chuckled until Max looked at her with one bushy eyebrow raised, and then she laughed outright.

"She hid this side of her character from me until she had me hooked," Max said, just as Juke, having heard the sound of laughter, which was, to him, like a magnet, banged back through the kitchen door.

"Then there's the *Mona Lisa*," Juke said. "That's the picture that looks like your wife when you tell her you had to work late at the office."

Jackie's hoots were now joining Grace's outright laughter.

"A lot of people say the reason for the popularity of the *Mona Lisa* is that sly, questioning smile. Big deal. I see that every year on the face of my tax examiner."

The laughter was contagious. Paul Warden barked out a laugh, and then the others joined in.

"Now you take my wife," Juke said.

"I don't *want* your wife," Sage Bryson gasped through laughter. "*You* take her."

"She's an expert on family planning," Juke said brightly. "The day after we got back from our honeymoon, half her family moved in with us, and the other half is planning to."

Juke's photobeam eyes were glowing with pleasure. He rolled around in a tight circle, giggling to himself. He recorded the sound of laughter, and when it began to fade, he gave a mechanical sigh and rolled into the kitchen where he played the recorded laughter back, for his ears only, over and over.

"*She* programmed that stuff into him," Max hissed, leaning over and wrapping his hands playfully around Grace's neck. "That's *her* sense of humor. And *I* have to live with it. Last night she gave me a bowl of fruit with shaving soap on top instead of whipped cream."

He grinned, the closest he ever came to laughter.

"Don't laugh," Rodrick warned, himself laughing, and pointed toward the kitchen, "or he'll come back."

Rodrick waited until Jackie had stifled her last giggle; then he started to speak, laughed again, wiped his eyes, and said, "I don't want to get serious—"

"What's on your mind, Captain?" Max Rosen asked.

"Well, I guess you can call this a council of war," Rodrick said. The mood of the group quickly sobered. "We all know that our truce with the Whorsk holds because we've got them outgunned, so that's not what I'm concerned about. But have you all seen Dr. Bryson's report on the test reading that Jacob made in that cloud of fog?"

He didn't have to tell them which cloud of fog. They all knew. Paul Warden nodded his head.

"It looks as if we're going to have to go in on the ground to find out what's under the fog," Rodrick said. "Anyone who can set up an electrical field like that poses a potential threat to the safety of this colony. But before we make that decision, I want to know all we can know about it. For example, Mandy, have you studied Sage's report?"

"Yes, I have," Mandy said. She had felt Rodrick's eyes on hers for a moment, and in spite of herself she felt the same old thrill.

"What effect would this sort of electrical field have on a man exposed to it for a relatively long period?" Rodrick asked.

"None, at the intensity Jacob measured from the scout ship," Mandy replied. "If it were intensified—it'd have to be increased in strength, say, by a factor of one hundred—it could cause nerve irritation, possibly even an interference with the proper functioning of the body, such as the pacemaker mechanism of the heart."

"I can't imagine what kind of power source might be on the river that would create this sort of field," Sage Bryson said in a calm, sure voice.

She had recovered well, Paul Warden was thinking, from her mental trauma. He had difficulty keeping his eyes off her, even when others were talking. She had been his first choice, and the fact that her rejection of him had been fueled by events in her childhood did not make him feel any better about it. Recently, though, he had come to feel that she was not, perhaps, the woman for him after all. Even now she was cool to him—friendly, but cool. His self-image was good enough to prevent him from believing that it was his looks that prevented Sage from reciprocating his feelings, even if some did call him the no-neck monster because of his well-developed athlete's body.

"What about the effect it has on a ship's instruments?" Rodrick asked. "Could it be made strong enough to mess up anything that depends on electronics or electricity?"

"Possibly," Sage replied.

"How about the hydrogen engine of a crawler or a scout ship?"

"I don't think so," Max Rosen said. "It takes more than an electrical or magnetic field to stop hydrogen combustion."

"So if we did send in a ground expedition, we could be reasonably sure that the crawlers would remain functional?" Rodrick asked.

"Some of the fire-control mechanism might be affected," Warden said, "but we could always operate the weapons manually."

"Max," Rodrick said, "send out a couple of scouts, just to confirm the original readings. Tell them not to take any risks, not to try to be heroes, but go just deep enough to confirm that the field gets more intense with a decrease in altitude."

"There is one thing," Grace Monroe told him. "You won't be able to take any of the robots along. That field would play havoc with their brain mechanism."

Rodrick frowned. He had been counting on having the admiral and the big defense robot, Mopro, on any expedition to the Great Misty River. Mopro's firepower was more deadly than that of a standard company of men.

"Is there any way we could develop some sort of shield for them?" Rodrick asked.

"Maybe after a few years of research," Grace answered.

"Well, I'm in no big rush to send men over there," Rodrick said, "but I don't think we can wait for years. Paul?"

"Yes, sir," Warden said, jerking his eyes away from Sage's calm, beautiful face.

"When I send an expedition, it looks as if you will be honcho for it. You might start thinking about whom you'd like with you. We'll discuss numbers later." That was going to be one hard decision. If he sent too few into the unknown and they encountered hostility, he might lose them all; but if he sent a large force and the opposition was still too powerful, the colony would be depleted of defenders.

"Right," Warden agreed. "We'll be ready when you say go."

"Okay," Rodrick said. "That's all I have to say. Anyone have questions or anything to discuss while we're here?" He looked around, and no one spoke. "Oh, there is one thing, Max. Should we give D.C. the title of chief engineer?" D.C. Broadfoot was Max's second engineering officer.

"He's a good man," Max said. "He's working with Makeitdo a lot." Makeitdo was another of Grace's "boys," a robot with an ingenious collection of tools and instruments built in. Makeitdo was programmed with all the systems aboard the *Spirit of America*, and there were few things he could not repair. "That frees most of the engineering crew for other duties."

"It's settled then," Rodrick said.

"Titles don't mean much out here," Max grumbled, "but I'll give him the word."

Paul Warden followed Sage from the room and caught her in the corridor. "You're looking good," he said.

"Thank you. I feel good."

"Interesting work on the electrical field, huh?"

"Yes, very."

"If you need any help, a strong back or something—"

"Thank you, Paul."

She had turned into a side corridor toward her lab, and the others had followed the main corridor, so she and Paul were alone. The ship, gutted of all the colonists' cubicles and emptied of equipment and people, seemed lonely. She took Paul's arm and pulled him to a halt.

"Paul, I haven't really had a chance to say thank you."

"For what?" he asked, his face going red.

"For standing by me. For being my friend."

"Listen—"

She put her hand over his mouth. "No, you listen," she said. "I was sick, Paul, and I didn't even know I was sick. It wasn't just you I hated—it was all men, and I didn't even know why. I know now, but I've got a long way to go."

"I've got plenty of time," Warden said, hope springing up in him.

"No, no," she whispered. "Don't think that way, Paul. The things that happened to me while I was a child—well, I'm not like—I'm not—Oh, hell."

"We don't have to talk about it now," he said.

"But I want to. I want to tell you, Paul, that I'm very fond of you. I want you to continue to be my friend, but that's all it can ever be. Can you please understand that and not hate me?"

Warden swallowed. Something in him told him that he had known that all along. It was just that she had never put it into words before.

"All right, friend," he agreed, forcing a grin and holding out his hand. She shook it solemnly.

She smiled. "There's at least one woman in this colony who has good sense," she said, and when he looked blank, she added, "Been to the library lately?"

He flushed again, for of late he had been going to the library a lot, and the librarian had been in his mind many times when he did not go to the library. "I go there now and then," he said sheepishly.

She started walking. "As a matter of fact, I have some material in the lab that needs to be returned. And since it's on your way—"

"Playing cupid?" Paul asked, a bit of resentment in his voice.

"You could do a lot worse, dummy," Sage said, her smile taking the edge off the word.

Yeah, he thought as he carried the tapes toward the ship's library, *I guess I could*.

School, that age-old thief of the prime hours of childhood and adolescence, had been keeping Cindy McRae from her favorite pastime, playing with the multicolored Omegan dragon, Baby. And since Cindy's mother, Betsy, was one of the colony's teachers, there was no way to avoid getting an education. Baby was reaching her full growth now, standing tall on long, seemingly fragile legs. She had shed again, giving the colony a large stock of the scales that hardened into jewels that, when polished and cut, were spectacular.

Baby had the freedom to roam throughout the colony. She had been taught from the first to stay out of Amando Kwait's fields and gardens, and her main problem was finding someone to play with while the young ones were in classrooms. She had learned which house might have an open window and a friendly person inside to hand out a tasty bit of food, and if a dependable window happened to be closed, Baby would stand outside, making a plaintive wail just a few decibels short of an alarm siren, until it opened. Usually there was a small, black dog with her, unless Clay Girard had managed to snag some solo time in a scout ship, in which case Jumper the dog was riding in the right seat, next to his master.

Clay, sixteen now, was, as the scout pilots said, a natural flyer. He loved nothing better than to be allowed training time, without any assigned chores, in a scout. There was plenty of fuel, so his training time was limited only by the demands on the available ships. A geological survey of the planet was nearing completion, with infrared and other types of specialty photography being used from low orbit to seek out likely mineral deposits anywhere on Omega, and there was always a list of requests for survey and exploration flights from the various scientific departments. Usually when Clay flew he had to follow a set course with cameras running, instead of hotdogging it, doing acrobatics, or just free-lancing in low flights over the Columbian continent. He flew to the dead city in the rocky highlands as often as possible, since he was the one who had seen it first from the air and later had led Stoner McRae to it. The archaeologists had just about finished their excavations there, finding nothing to dispute the theory that the city had been built by ancestors of the Whorsk before the development of lighter-than-air craft freed the insectlike stickmen to roam the planet at will.

Between his classroom work and his scout training, Clay did not see much of Cindy anymore, except at the McRaes' table and in the evenings. He missed her. Not too many years ago—although it seemed to be ages since they had been cooped up on the *Spirit* in deep space, not knowing how long it would be before they would breathe fresh air again—he and Cindy had pledged themselves to be lifelong friends. Now it was more than that. Every time Clay saw her and realized that she was a young woman, he felt warm all over.

When he got kicked out of his favorite scout ship, Jack Purdy's *Dinahmite*, early one afternoon, he had a good idea where to find Cindy. He whistled Jumper to heel, which, for Jumper, was a point about ten feet ahead, and headed for Jumper's Run, the small, bubbling, rocky stream to the north of the town. He heard mighty splashing even before he could see Baby rolling happily in a pool, with Cindy wading nearby. Jumper announced their presence with a happy yip and dashed to join Baby in the water. The huge dragon was very careful not to crush the little dog as they rolled and yapped at each other in the cool water.

"Hi!" Cindy yelled.

Clay broke into a trot and then sat down to remove his shoes quickly.

"The water's delicious," Cindy said as he waded in. "Did they take your flying toy away from you?"

"Knock it off," Clay said, secretly pleased that Cindy was jealous of the time he spent flying. "Feel like going up to the falls?"

"Sure," she answered, turning to whistle to Baby.

"No, let's walk," Clay said. "I need the exercise."

They waded when the water was shallow, finding interesting rounded stones in the streambed, being splashed by both Baby and Jumper, and bumping into each other now and then with a soft shock for Clay. The falls—low, clear, and beautiful—were about a mile upstream. They made a pleasant muttering water sound, and there was a mossy bank on the eastern side, glowing dark green in the afternoon sun. Clay threw himself down on it, put his hands behind his head, and watched as Cindy capered in the falling water with the two animals. She came to the moss bank soaking wet, her shirt clinging, showing her neat, growing breasts.

"Wow," she said, as she threw herself down beside him, the one word expressive of everything—the purple beauty of Omega's sky, the color-tinted summer clouds, the pleasant warmth of summer. They lay there for a long time without speaking. It was Clay who broke the silence.

"Cindy, remember when we were with the admiral up north and the Whorsk attacked, and we were running out of ammunition?"

"Do I! That was the most frightened I've ever been."

"Remember what we did?"

She raised herself on one elbow and looked into his handsome young face. He was blushing. "Are you referring to the fact that you kissed me?"

"Well, yeah," he said, his face burning. Funny, they were so close that there were absolutely no secrets between them, as close as two friends had ever been. But when he started thinking of her as a *girl*, he got a case of the abysmal dumbs. It made him a little nervous, too, because he had promised Stoner McRae that he would never, never touch Cindy like *that*.

"Do you want to kiss me again?" she asked, smiling a cheery smile. She leaned closer and brushed back a lock of his straight black hair. "You haven't done it since then, you know."

He couldn't speak.

"Well?" she demanded. "Do you?"

"Yes, I *guess* so," he said.

"You *guess* so?" She beat him on the chest with her fists. "You guess so?" She started tickling him, and he grabbed her wrists, and she was breathing fast and looking down at him, and it happened, just like that, his lips on hers, and her body feeling so soft and hot through her wet clothing.

"You're getting me wet," he said when he felt that things were going a little too far.

"Too bad," she laughed, kissing him again. He pushed her off and stood up quickly.

"What's wrong?" she asked, sitting up.

"I feel funny."

"Well, so do I." She giggled. "Mother says that when we can't stand it anymore, we can get married."

"What?" he yelped.

"Don't you want to?"

"S-s-sure," he stammered. "But—"

"I know, we're only sixteen, but Mother says this is a new world, and since we're eventually going to get married anyhow—"

He felt his legs go weak, and he sank to the moss. She scooted over, put her head in his lap, and smiled up at him. "Well, what do you think?"

"I think—" What he was thinking was so new to him, he could not tell even his best friend and the girl he loved.

"Let's see how much we can stand," she whispered, running a finger under his chin.

"I don't know," he croaked, then tried hard to swallow.

"Mother says I shouldn't have children until I'm at least eighteen, maybe twenty."

He took one finger and traced the shape of her cute little nose. Everything about her, he decided, was cute and little. Then he was thinking that he had come a long, long way from being an orphan in a foster home, and later a stowaway on the *Spirit of America*. He kissed her, and then he said, his voice very firm, "I've decided that I can't stand much more."

"Good," she whispered.

II

THE
CONQUISTADORES

SIX

Astrud Cabral had spent her life studying humankind and its prime method of communication: the spoken word. She had acquired this interest early in life as she grew up among the few remnants of Brazil's once numerous Indian clans in that giant wilderness called the Mato Grasso. She was proud of the fact that she was a *pardo* woman and refused to accept any shame in that word, which described a person of mixed races—with a skin more brown than that of the peoples of Brazil's teeming cities.

Her father, a self-styled backwoodsman, a *caboclo*, had been her sole source of education during her preteen years. Pedro Cabral was self-reliant and well educated, even if most of his knowledge was self-taught. In short, Cabral was a self-made man. He was content with his accomplishment of having carved out a sizable holding from the wilderness, with the virgin jungle falling to his ax and saw. But he was forced to fight continuously to retake the land he had cleared from the jungle Indians.

He accomplished all this without the support of the politicians in the coastal cities. Government help had been available, for even before Carlos da Lisboa's military take-over of the Brazilian government, the policy had been either to exterminate or civilize the jungle Indians, and Pedro Cabral was in absolute opposition to that policy. Pedro prided himself on his native Indian blood, and he was careful to instill that pride in his one chick, his daughter, Astrud.

Astrud had carried her father's fierce independence to the university in São Paulo, where she had found that compromise was required if she was to realize her goal of being the first in her family to hold a college degree.

Carlos da Lisboa had seized power while Astrud was completing her PhD in anthropology. He had gained the support of the masses, even though there had been opposition and some bloodshed in the major cities during the takeover. Astrud was among those young people who were drawn to da Lisboa by his fervent patriotism. She did not realize until years later that da Lisboa's views were quite jingoistic. Brazil, Astrud and the young university students felt, had too long been thrust aside from major world decisions by the two nuclear giants, the Soviet Union and the United States. Da Lisboa's promise to make Brazil a power second to none appealed to pride, and Brazil's glory seemed more important than the socialistic, humanistic approach of the deposed government.

"We will build our strategic industries," da Lisboa preached, "and our growth will eliminate poverty. When we have secured our place as a superpower, there will be funds and time to educate the masses, and they will be eager to take their rightful places in the structure of our new nation."

Fifteen years of da Lisboa's dictatorship had seen the accomplishment of his number-one goal, for Brazil was no longer weak. She had a nuclear arsenal equal to or, since it was more modern, perhaps superior to those of the old nuclear superpowers. The Brazilian air force had the planes and the men to sweep away *all* opposition . . . or so it was felt. The navy was a growing baby giant.

Since Carlos da Lisboa was an autocrat, he was solely responsible for devising Brazil's foreign policy. When it became apparent that the smaller countries of South and Central America were being squeezed between the Soviet Union and the United States, the dictator seized the opportunity. One by one the smaller countries began to cast their lot with Brazil, sheltering themselves under Brazil's nuclear umbrella.

The South American War, which saw the total destruction of the Soviet Union's Pacific Fleet and the crippling of the home fleets of the United States, gave da Lisboa his greatest opportunity. His treaties with Argentina could be compared with Adolph Hitler's takeover of Austria in the early twentieth century. Peru and Chile, drained, impoverished, bled by years of internal war against the Communist rebels, rushed to link themselves with the growing Brazilian Empire, selling their independence for Brazilian money and raw materials. Smaller nations, such as Uruguay and Bolivia, were swallowed by the Brazilian colossus without so much as a burp, and then da Lisboa's juggernaut rolled north, creating a union with the northern South American nations, then those of Central America. Next the Caribbean had become a Brazilian lake, with only Cuba putting up armed resistance. Only strife-torn Mexico—where the last organized Communist party in the Western Hemisphere fought against hopeless odds—stood between Brazil and dominance of every inch of land south of the Mexican-United States border.

Da Lisboa had no illusions about seizing the entire United States. He knew that the defenses of the Yankee giant were too formidable, that the land mass was too great ever to be totally occupied by an invading power—in spite of the fact that Brazilian army orbiters rose on wings of fire from the Galapagos and the Falklands to add even more power to Brazil's outposts in near space. But he felt that the steady pressure being put on the United States from the Soviet Union would, within a very few years, allow him to force agreements down Washington's throat that would make the United States a second-rate power firmly within Brazil's sphere of influence. Then, with the nuclear power of the combined Western Hemisphere pointed at Moscow, that nonsense started by Lenin early in the twentieth century would be ended.

Astrud Cabral's mental union with the ambitions of the dictator had ended long before she had been selected for the anthropological team on board Brazil's starship,

Estrêla do Brasil. And by the time the ship made planetfall in the area of the bright star Pollux, much farther from Earth than the 61 Cygni system where the Americans had landed, Astrud was at philosophical odds with the purpose and the mission of the *Estrêla do Brasil.*

The Brazilians had not been handicapped by a lack of rhenium, as had the United States. They did not make the mistake of storing spare fuel pellets near the drive room, as had the Russians. They had methodically and patiently sent out probe after probe, delaying their departure for months after the crisis moments during the South American War. They had thus been able to target three different planets shown by the probes to have the proper distance from a suitable sun to allow water to exist in a fluid state.

Pollux, one of the brighter stars as seen from the Earth, was 10.8 parsecs away. Distance, of course, made no difference in travel time once the starship went into lightstep, as long as the proper destination was programmed into the ship's computer. The giant Pollux had two companion stars, and one of these, the G-type star, had a family of planets, one of which was very much like Earth, with a water-oxygen atmosphere very well suited for human life.

The *Estrêla do Brasil's* voyage to a point almost eleven parsecs from Earth, about three-and-a-quarter times farther from home than the destination of the *Spirit of America,* was a smooth one. There were no near brushes with disaster—as there had been aboard the *Spirit,* when sabotaged retro-rockets could not prevent the vessel's inexorable drift toward a sun—and so the quite capable engineers aboard the Brazilian ship did not make the discovery made by Max Rosen, that a small amount of rhenium supplied just as much power as did a ton of the scarce metal. Nor did the Brazilians have need to defy Harry Shaw's warning not to activate the Shaw Drive within the gravitational influence of a cosmic body.

During the long cruise to the fringe of the solar system, Astrud Cabral had spent her time in interdisciplinary studies, for she was ever curious and did not want to be a specialist confined to her two chosen fields. She had kept her social life to a minimum. She was not antimen or antilove. She had done the usual college-type experimentation, and she had had more than one satisfactory relationship since college. She simply did not want to complicate her life.

She had accepted the invitations to have meals at the captain's table when her rotation for that honor came around, and she felt that the captain, Gilberto Francisco da Lisboa, liked her. On first meeting her he had insisted that she call him Gilberto. He had invited her to his cabin at a time when his wife was engaged in duty, and she had politely made excuses based on her workload.

There had been quite a bit of talk at first about the fact that the captain of the ship was the nephew of the dictator, but it soon became evident that Gilberto's selection had not been mere nepotism. He was a very capable man. He had a secret mission, which had been laid down quite exactingly by his uncle, the dictator: simply to return treasure, in whatever valuable form it came, to Brazil. The opportunity was taken to send along colonists, since the ship was going anyway, but a colony in the stars was a secondary goal for both the dictator and his nephew.

The da Lisboa family was an ancient one. Gilberto could trace his heritage back to the time of the original settlement of Brazil, when his remote ancestors, wielding swords and muskets, overcame the defenses of a native Indian population. Uncle Carlos had no children, and since Gilberto was the only son of the dictator's only sibling, Gilberto da Lisboa looked upon his trip into space as merely another training mission in preparation for assuming the power of the ruler of half the world when his uncle died. Gilberto would let nothing stand in his way of a successful mission, meaning that the *Estrêla do Brasil* must go back to the Earth laden with gold, jewels, or some heretofore unknown but very valuable alien commodity.

When the initial scout-ship reports indicated that the *Estrêla's* chosen planet had a native race that was quite humanoid, Gilberto da Lisboa was surprised, as were most, but not deterred from his mission. The fact that the natives wore heavy ornaments of gold brought a glad smile to his face. When all the reports were in and tests had shown that the planet would be habitable for human life, he called a conference of all department heads. Astrud Cabral was there in her capacity as chief linguist.

"By now you know," Gilberto da Lisboa said in his cultured, pleasant voice, "that history is repeating itself, even here in the depths of space."

Gilberto was a very handsome man, in his midforties, trim, tall, and clean shaven. His favorite uniform was black, as black as the depths of space, and it complemented his air of charismatic leadership. He knew he cut a splendid figure, and he liked to have the opportunity to exercise his effective, informal way of speaking to small or large groups.

"When the first da Lisboa landed on the Brazilian coast, he met much the same conditions," he said, hugely pleased. "An indigenous, hostile population threatened death by violence . . . but he and those with him recognized the opportunity, the duty to bring the gift of civilization and true religion to a heathen land."

Astrud, all too familiar with Brazilian history and with South American history in general, felt a cold shiver go up her back at da Lisboa's words. She considered South American and Mexican history to be the story of greed, hypocrisy, and horror. There had been well-developed societies, especially in Mexico and Peru, and the Spanish conquistadores had destroyed them—looting, killing, even obliterating the history of the Aztecs and the Incas as being the blasphemous prattling of heathens.

"When we land on this planet," da Lisboa continued, "we will offer peace to the natives, but we will be ready, for the pictures we have taken from heights show that they are well armed."

With Stone Age weapons, Astrud thought to herself.

"I am giving instructions to offer peace, but not to risk one single Brazilian life in hesitation if the natives prove to be hostile," da Lisboa said. He pushed a button and a newly made map of the coast of the main land mass on the planet was shown on a screen. "We will land here," he said, pointing to a beach near a major city.

Astrud wanted to protest. By looking at the walls of the city and the arms carried by all the males of the native race, any fool could see that war was a common thing among them, and that the landing so near a major population center would undoubtedly be construed by the natives as being a provocation, a threat. It was almost as if Captain da Lisboa wanted a confrontation early on to show the superiority of the Brazilians' weapons and instill fear in the natives.

Since the dictator of Brazil did not have to clear his expenditures with a congress, the Brazilian space effort, which was the dictator's favorite program, had never had to skimp for funds. The hydrogen-powered scout ships carried by the *Estrêla do Brasil* were large, plush, and heavily armed. Each could carry ten armed men in addition to the two-man crew. Even then it would take some time and all of the scouts working together to land a respectable force. The first group of ten scout ships to go down swiftly off-loaded a hundred soldiers, and that trained force immediately threw up a defensive perimeter around the landing site on a broad, white-sand beach.

The first incident occurred after the landing of the first hundred men and before the arrival of the second group of scout ships. Two natives, awed and curious, peered over the oceanside dunes. A young Brazilian crew member, so young that he had not seen combat in any of Brazil's recent wars, opened fire with a projectile gun, killing one of the natives and wounding the other. The wounded native managed to run away, trailing very humanlike red blood.

By the time the second group of one hundred men were landing, a noncommissioned officer was bellowing orders to attack, forming the men into marching wedges, with some heavy firepower at the point of the wedge. As the leading element responded to the orders and marched forward, hundreds of natives leaped to the top of the dunes and, with a concerted cry of war, launched arrows, spears, and a unique throwing weapon at the invaders.

The Brazilians wore body armor, thin mesh overshirts that covered vital organs from neck to groin, and the mesh deflected arrows and spears. Nevertheless, Brazilian soldiers went down with native weapons embedded in their legs, arms, and in a few cases, heads and throats. The lead element of Brazilians opened fire with small, hand-carried rocket weapons and blew huge gaps in the line of natives atop the dunes, while others fell to the sand or knelt to bring their shoulder-fired projectile and laser weapons to bear.

It was, of course, a slaughter. The Brazilians took enough casualties to anger them—eleven dead and more wounded—and the officers could not stop the enraged men, intent on avenging their fallen friends, from charging the dunes to face a weapon unlike any ever seen on Earth.

It took a strong being to use the weapon. It consisted of an odd, long metal chain on which were strung a dozen spiked metal balls about six inches in diameter. Each of the balls had twenty sharp spikes radiating from its center. At the time deemed proper by the wielder of the weapon, he slung the long chain into a circle over his head, whirling like an Earthside discus thrower to add speed to the whirring chain with its spiked balls, and then, with a precision that indicated long training, a trip wire released all twelve balls instants apart. The effect was a barrage of metal balls with sharp spikes flying at a tremendous speed through the air, their staggered release spreading them over a front of some twenty feet. The balls flew off the chain with so much centrifugal force that the long spikes did what a bullet could not do—pierce the Brazilian body armor. Before the ball throwers were exterminated by massive fire, twenty-four Brazilians lay dead or dying, for the spikes, it was later determined, had been dipped in a poison only slightly less toxic than cobra venom.

"So be it," said Captain Gilberto da Lisboa when he had heard the reports from the landing party. "We have come in friendship, but now we will return in war."

This time, to prevent any further Brazilian casualties, the *Estrêla do Brasil* was taken down to the surface,

landing in a grassy plain where the nearest native settlement was ten miles away. Da Lisboa had picked the spot
for its defensive characteristics. The natives would have to
charge across open spaces, under the fire of the main
batteries of the ship. There was good water at the site in
the form of a slow-running but clear stream, and the sea,
where the larger cities sprawled along the shore, was also
only ten miles away.

The captain had put a military force on alert, so they
were ready to set out not a half hour after the *Estrêla do
Brasil* had landed. Once their all-terrain crawlers had
surrounded the nearest native village, the officer in command called out in Portuguese for the inhabitants of the
village to throw down their weapons and surrender. When
a hail of arrows met his demand, the heavy lasers on the
crawlers opened fire, and within minutes there was only
smoking refuse on the village site. The gold salvaged with
the aid of gold detectors was, in some cases, slightly
melted. From a large hut at the center of the village, the
troops collected gold estimated to weigh at least fifty pounds,
with the major piece being taken from a stone altar. It was
crafted in a humanoid shape, but the head of what everyone considered to be an idol was snakelike.

Gilberto da Lisboa was in his quarters with his military leaders, looking over quickly made aerial maps of the
main land mass, when a delegation of department heads
from the scientific community asked to see him.

"Tell them I'm busy," he said to the rating who had
announced the would-be visitors.

"Captain," said the Brazilian army officer in charge of
the ship's complement of troops, "I have talked with some
of the scientists. They feel that an effort should be made to
contact the natives in order to prevent further bloodshed."

"I will prevent Brazilian bloodshed by killing as many
of the savages as I can," da Lisboa stated flatly.

"Captain," the officer said, "you are going back to
Earth soon. I am going to have to stay here and live and
work with these colonists. Perhaps we should hear them."

Da Lisboa shrugged. "Send them in."

The delegation, da Lisboa saw, was led by that attractive Cabral woman who had politely refused to join him in his bed while his wife was at her duties. "Dr. Cabral," he said, "we have only a little time. Please be brief."

"Captain," Astrud said, "if we are to live and work on this planet, perhaps we should try to do so in peace."

"My sentiments also," da Lisboa responded. "But have we a choice when the savages attack us?"

"I ask, sir, that I be allowed to establish communications with the people of this planet," Astrud said. "We are an enlightened people. We have experience in dealing with races of the Stone Age cultural level, having had our own Indians with us in Brazil. Would it not be better to live in peace?"

Da Lisboa was about to refuse the request when a signal told him there was a call from the bridge. He pressed a button and the face of the duty officer appeared on a large screen. "Captain, there are six natives approaching the ship at a distance."

"Put them on the screen," da Lisboa ordered, and then there was a gasp and a snicker or two, for, their images enlarged on the screen, six of the natives were, indeed, approaching the ship. It was the method of their approach that caused surprise there in the captain's quarters.

"What in the hell—?" someone said.

The six natives were nude, and they were walking backward, heads turned sharply to look over their shoulders.

"Witch doctors? Trying to cast a magic spell?" asked da Lisboa, looking toward Astrud, the expert on the often peculiar behavior of the race of man.

"I'd say it's more likely a peace gesture," Astrud said. "Look, all of them are healthy specimens, well muscled. They carry no arms. I believe that this is their version of a white flag, that they're asking for a talk with us."

For a few minutes, as the natives came nearer, da Lisboa was silent. "All right, then," he said finally, "we'll talk. I assume, Dr. Cabral, that you, as our oral-communications expert, will want to go out to meet these savages."

"Yes," Astrud answered eagerly.

The army officer laughed. "And will you strip naked, Dr. Cabral?"

"I don't think that will be necessary," Astrud replied coldly.

Within minutes she was going out a hatch, with two scientists who had volunteered to go with her. She walked until she was out of the shadow of the ship and halted. The natives were about a hundred feet away. They had halted, their backs still toward the ship. Astrud waited, and the natives did not move. "Turn around," she told the two men with her, and when they all three turned and gave the natives their backs, looking over their shoulders, the natives began to move toward the ship again. They halted about ten feet away.

One of the natives spoke. The sounds were definitely humanoid, the language a melodious one, full of long vowel sounds. Astrud answered, "Greetings, my friends. We come in peace."

There was a muttering among the six natives. Astrud's neck was getting tired from being twisted to look over her shoulder. She spread her arms out from her sides, palms out, and slowly turned to face the natives. The six men whispered, then, imitating her arms-wide stance, turned. Astrud let her arms fall slowly.

"All right, my friends," she said, "let me hear some more of your speech."

The tallest of the natives, a man—she could think of him in no other way—said something in his soft, musical language.

Astrud was having trouble keeping her eyes on the eyes of the speaker. He was tall, over six feet, and he had the chest and muscles of an athlete and the sexual organ of a well-developed man. He showed no self-consciousness about his nakedness.

She thought she was beginning to hear a pattern in the language, but it would take some time to begin to understand. "My friend," she said, when the speaker fell silent, "this is going to take a while, isn't it? Let's see how you do with sign language." She pointed to her own chest and said, "Human." She pointed upward toward the sky and made a motion like a flying bird with her hands, "From the sky." She held both hands in front of her heart. She pointed to the natives and then spread her hands in friendship. "No kill," she said, stabbing an imaginary spear at one of the scientists, shaking her head no, crossing her hands repeatedly in front of her. "No kill. Want peace."

The tall man, whose eyes were black, as were the eyes of all six of the men, nodded and smiled. He pointed to Astrud and the ship and spoke. He made a motion of carrying a load on his shoulder, pointed to the west and drew the shape of a native house in the air, pointed to a gold ring on his finger. Astrud heard him repeat a word, pointing to the golden ring. "*Ond, ond,*" he said.

"He's saying we carried gold from the village we destroyed," she told the two men who stood nervously on either side of her.

The native was making other motions. He used Astrud's way to illustrate "kill," shook his head.

"You don't kill us," Astrud translated, "and we will bring you much *ond,* much gold."

The other scientists exchanged glances.

"Yes, yes," she said, nodding her head and smiling. "We no kill. You no kill us."

The native smiled, nodded, made the motions for "We no kill. You no kill us." He turned, waved, and a small group of men with a heavy burden appeared, on the top of a slight rise in the distance.

"Now don't panic, friend," Astrud said, "I'm just going to speak to my captain."

The natives started when da Lisboa's voice came as if by magic from Astrud's belt radio. "Captain," she said, "they want to give us gold, and they want peace."

Was there, she wondered, just a bit of disappointment in da Lisboa's voice? "That is good, Dr. Cabral. But have no fear, we will be alert in case that burden being carried toward us is not gold."

It was gold. It was two hundred pounds of gold in the form of lovely objects, drinking cups, and interesting eating utensils with two prongs and a blade on the other end, odd-shaped medallions, and small statues. When it was spread on some sort of animal-skin blankets on the grass, it made a gleaming, golden display that caused da Lisboa, who was watching on the *Estrêla*'s screen, to stop breathing for a moment or two, and aroused a hint of avarice even in Astrud.

The tall native stepped forward and extended both hands toward Astrud. She extended her hands, and he locked his hands around her elbows and moved her arms back and forth gently, smiling, saying something in that soft, beautiful language.

"Yes, we will be friends," Astrud said, and when he released her arms she made motions from the heart, smiled, and repeated his arm-clasping. "Now," she said, "I will learn your language, my friend." She pointed to her mouth, to his mouth, then to her head. She held up one hand and pointed to her one ring. *"Ond,"* she said. Then she repeated the other gestures.

He nodded.

"I go with you," Astrud said, making the appropriate motions. The native raised his eyebrows, then nodded in agreement.

"Permission to go with the natives, Captain," Astrud said into the radio.

"Are you sure you know what you're doing, Dr. Cabral?"

"Yes, sir, I believe I do," she said.

"I can't risk men coming to your rescue if you get into trouble," da Lisboa warned.

"Captain," she said, "I think that in three to four days I can learn enough of the local language to begin basic communication. Will you refrain from any further actions until I have that chance?"

"I will give you four days," da Lisboa agreed. "Then we will start to explore this country in force."

Safely beyond the crest of a rise in the plain, the native men halted to retrieve their colorful clothing and weapons from several others, who had been waiting for them. Then the party started out at a trot, and Astrud soon realized that she had not been getting enough exercise, but she managed to keep up. About three miles later, they slowed, walked up a long ridge through the beginning of a stand of strange, twisted trees, and then she looked down into a beautiful green valley divided by irrigation canals.

The sight that took her breath was the city. It was surrounded by a cyclopean wall formed of huge, cut slabs of stone, and behind the wall soaring, graceful stone structures gleamed in multicolor paints.

The tall native had halted, as if to let Astrud have time to appreciate the sight. "Beautiful," she whispered. When the native showed question in his expression, she pointed to her eyes, smiled, held her hands over her heart to indicate, "What my eyes see pleases my heart." The native nodded and smiled.

Once in the city she saw many things that pleased her heart. She saw beauty and riches. She saw a healthy, happy, smiling people. The similarity to Earth's life astounded her. Their civilization could have developed somewhere on Earth, perhaps on the shores of the Mediterranean Sea, the mother of civilization. These people could have been mistaken for one of the ancient civilizations of Earth. There were, of course, alien differences. She was, after all, at a distance from the Mediterranean that most men could not even conceive, but it was as if she had been taken back in time to those strange and glorious days when the developing race of humans had first begun to realize its potential. She had been returned to the Bronze Age, and here was a race in the stage of development called the monumental stage, to indicate that they had developed the capability to build with stone and, as if to challenge the gods or to come closer to them, raised their buildings and temples as high toward the sky as their skills and tools and labor supply would allow.

She felt that she would have seen similar sights had she been able to visit ancient Mycenae, or the Crete of King Minos, or—and this was closer to her knowledge— the stone cities of the Aztec or the Inca. And she hungered to *know,* to learn all there was to learn about this impressive race of alien people with their tall, handsome men and their smiling women and boisterous children.

Her eyes could not drink in enough. She noted the bronze axes and bronze-tipped spears and arrows of the warriors, the well-made pottery that stored liquids and foodstuffs in a street market, the exacting cuts of the stones of the buildings, the bright array of colors in clothing to indicate that the natives had developed many different dyes.

She saw alien animals, and again the similarity to Earth was amazing, for although there were different shapes and colors and many subtle differences, she could compare these animals to horses or donkeys, dogs and cats, and there was, in the market, even a snake charmer working with five of the most deadly looking reptiles she had ever seen, things of such evil that she shuddered.

Absorbed in trying to drink in all the sights and sounds of the city, she forgot the *Estrêla do Brasil* and her captain for the length of time it took to walk through the teeming streets to a large, impressive building with triangular columns supporting a pediment crammed with beautiful, realistic statuary. The forms were men and animals, some of the animals eerily strange in form, and all were painted in lifelike colors. The entire city was a blaze of color, a thing of such beauty that quite often she had to brush away tears of sheer appreciation.

And yet she was so far from Earth that it would be over half a century before any Earthside telescope could record the light currently being emitted by the planet's sun.

As she stood in front of the gleaming building, she remembered the words of Ovid, who had lived at the twilight of the great Mediterranean civilizations: "There is a way on high, conspicuous in the clear heavens, called the Milky Way, brilliant with its own brightness. By it the gods go to the dwelling of the great Thunderer and his royal abode."

So little understanding did the ancients have of the galaxy, but theirs was an innocent ignorance. They had been willing to learn, to explore, using what primitive tools of investigation they had. Modern man seemed to have lost his sense of awe and wonder. Gilberto da Lisboa, for example, would not see the beauty in this city. Ignoring the bright colors and the smiles of the people, he would call the tall building that dominated the center of the city a heathen temple and would focus only on the conspicuous displays of wealth, of gold, of jewels, for all the people seemed to wear such ornaments, and the builders of the structures that were, obviously, of religious or governmental function had made liberal use of gold and silver. It was truly a planet of unimaginable wealth and thus subject to the greed of Earthmen.

The *Estrêla do Brasil* had come a distance equal to just over a third of the diameter of the galaxy, not to seek kinship with these people who were obviously cut from the same cloth as humankind, but to rob them of their gold and jewels. That sadness colored Astrud Cabral's appreciation of the beauty of the interior of the great building into which she was escorted politely by the tall native, but she quickly regained her interest in her surroundings when she saw that the interior walls were covered in places by what was obviously a written language, a form of pictograph that she knew would be very difficult to learn, for many of the pictographs would be based on objects or forms alien to her Earth knowledge. She had, however, already picked up several words of the musical, soft language, and she was confident that she would be exchanging information with the natives very soon.

The rulers of the city sat on gleaming white thrones on a raised dais. They listened as the tall native who had led the delegation to the ship made his report, although the black eyes were seldom on his face but remained, with open curiosity, on Astrud. When the tall one had finished and had answered all questions, he turned to Astrud, pointing to her mouth and her head as he spoke. He was telling the rulers that she wanted to learn their language, and the man who sat at the center, in a throne slightly more ornate than the others, nodded, spoke, and with a wave of his hand dismissed them.

The home of the tall native was on the second story of a bright yellow blocklike building not far from the center of the city. It was spacious, airy, and well lit by open windows. He was obviously proud of it, for he escorted

her from the main entry room, where there were couches
and chairs covered in the hides of animals, to a kitchen
area where cooking was done on the hearth of a great stone
fireplace, and to a room where weapons of war shared
places of honor with leather body armor and odd-looking
objects of precious metal studded with jewels. She quickly
got the idea that this was the warrior's trophy room, and
she made *oo*ing sounds of appreciation when he showed
her certain objects until he lifted a skull to her face,
laughed, and pointed to a break in the bone with obvious
pride. She understood that the skull was that of an especially illustrious enemy, and she nodded and smiled.

The last room contained a sunken bath filled with
perfumed water, a large, low bed with soft animal-skin
coverings, chairs, a closet in which hung other colorful
costumes such as the one worn by the warrior. He pointed
to the tub and quickly shed his clothing, standing before
her nude and totally unself-conscious. He spoke and made
motions to indicate that she should undress. She hesitated
for a moment, then began to remove her uniform. She was
well formed, much slimmer than most of the women she
had seen on the streets except for the very young, and she
saw the warrior's black eyes—she had noted that all of the
people had the same color eyes and the same thick, black
hair—examine her from head to toe, then she allowed him
to take her hand and lead her down stone steps into the
huge tub. The water was tepid and pleasant. He sat on a
benchlike protrusion and motioned her to sit beside him.
When he picked up a piece of soap and began to lather
her back and shoulders, she felt a warmth begin to spread
through her body, and she made no protest as he washed
her thoroughly, missing no spot of her body. He then
handed the soap, which had a rather pleasant smell, to
her, and she began to lather his back, feeling the hard
strength of him, and a bit later, with a flush on her dark
face and with her heart racing, she washed a portion of his
body that told her that this ritual would end not in the
tub, but on that bed covered with those ever-so-soft skins.

He lifted her from the water, her one-hundred-twenty

pounds light in his arms, and then he dried her with a rough, linenlike cloth and placed her on the bed.

She felt as if she had been displaced in time, lost in those vast reaches of space, and questioned her sanity as she waited breathlessly while he toweled himself off and then came to her with such a sweet tenderness, and then with such manly determination, that she ceased to be Earthwoman with alien, and was just woman, woman eternal, woman fulfilled.

For three days and three nights they hardly left the apartment. Graceful young girls brought food, and although she ate with just a bit of fear at first, the food did not kill her. She soon came to look forward to mealtime to see what spicy, odd concoction would be the main dish.

And she learned. She absorbed word after word, sometimes driving Lythe, for that was his name, into a show of irritation by her insistence, but soon she was able to communicate on a level of basic words, and she tried to impart to him the importance of what they were doing. She did not resist, however, when he, smiling, teasing, lifted her and placed her on that bed with its coverings as soft as any llama wool she had ever felt on Earth.

Lythe could not comprehend interstellar distances. He referred to her and her kind as "from the upper darkness."

"Some say you are gods," he told her.

"Not gods," she said. "People. People just like you."

"With weapons of fire and great noise."

"Yes, weapons you must avoid."

He drew himself up proudly. "I am not afraid."

On the morning of the fourth day she went with him to the government house, and soon a small delegation, including one of the white-robed elders of the city, was under way toward the *Estrêla do Brasil*. When they neared it, the men made motions to undress, as was the custom during truce meetings with an enemy, to show that one did not carry a concealed weapon.

"That will not be necessary," Astrud told them, and she had to repeat it twice before the elder understood.

She did not try to prevent them from approaching the

ship walking backward. She used her radio to talk with Captain da Lisboa and convinced him to meet the delegation outside the ship. He came with sidearms and a squad of Brazilian marines. She felt quick anger, but there was nothing she could do.

"The elders of the Caan, the People of the World, hail you, man from the outer darkness, in peace and goodwill," she interpreted.

And then, "The leader of the people from the outer darkness greets the elders of the People of the World."

"Have you convinced them that it will be best to cooperate with us?" da Lisboa asked her.

"They will cooperate to the limit of their customs and pride," she answered. "They are a strong people, Captain, and they have conquered all the different tribes of this continent. They have a distinctly beautiful culture—"

"They worship heathen idols and gods," da Lisboa hissed.

Astrud grimaced, for she knew that da Lisboa was not particularly pious and definitely not a practicing Catholic. It was as if he too had been taken back in time and was using the excuse of the conquistadores and the Catholic friars from Spain to eradicate entire cultures.

"Tell them," da Lisboa said, "that we will plant our colony among them and that we will build our new city on the sea to the north of their city."

Astrud conveyed the information, and the elder drew himself up and spoke as harshly as she had heard any of the natives speak.

"He says that the shore is the natural place of the Caan. He says that if you want to live on the world, there are islands and other lands."

"We have surveyed the planet from scout ships," da Lisboa said. "There is limited land and much ocean. None of the small land masses would be suitable. Tell him we will settle here, and we wish to live in peace."

Again the elder spoke harshly, shaking his head.

"He says that the gods themselves would rise and strike down the Caan if they broke the sacred covenant. By that he means that this land was given to the Caan by their gods, and no non-Caan other than a slave can live on it."

"Tell them we will trade objects of great value for gold," da Lisboa said.

This brought a nod of agreement from the elder, but he stipulated that the trading would have to be done from one of the other land masses, not from the lands of the Caan.

Da Lisboa's face went red. "I have had enough of this," he sputtered. "Tell them that, like it or not, we will build, and we will plant, and we will defend the lands we have chosen with our weapons of fire and noise."

"So be it," said the elder, turning to give his back to da Lisboa as he stalked away. Da Lisboa turned angrily and went into the ship.

"So there will be war," Lythe said. "But I do not wish to war against my *angine*." There was no real Portuguese equivalent for the word. The closest translation Astrud could come up with was "playlove." There were permanent family groups among the Caan, but young warriors typically remained unattached until they were well into maturity, spreading their favors—and that was the way they looked at it—among unattached young women, playloves.

"Speak with your elders, Lythe," Astrud begged. "Tell them that the weapons of the men from the outer darkness are too powerful for them. Tell them that to go to war would mean slaughter of many Caan."

Lythe shrugged eloquently. "It is to a warrior's glory to die fighting for his homeland. You will come with me so that I will not fight against you."

"I must speak with my leader," she said. "Then I will come to you. Promise me, Lythe, that you will try to convince the elders to delay any action until I have come to talk with you again."

"I will try," he said.

She had difficulty obtaining an appointment with da Lisboa. He was busy. The *Estrêla do Brasil* was off-loading her offensive capabilities, armored crawlers armed with lasers, cannon, and rapid-fire projectile weapons. When she was finally admitted to the bridge, the captain was watching a column forming to march to the sea, with enough firepower to decimate the continent.

"Captain, I beg you to be patient," Astrud pleaded. "They are an admirable people, a people with whom we can live in peace, with whom we can cooperate. The stores of gold and its abundance in nature can be obtained in peaceful trade. Wouldn't that be preferable to destroying a civilization as Cortez and Pizarro did in Mexico and Peru?"

"There is no civilization of value on this planet," da Lisboa said. "We will bring them the light of the true God."

"Hasn't there been enough slaughter in God's name?" she asked. "Must we repeat the terrible things in the history of the Earth here, on this planet?"

"I have a responsibility," da Lisboa said. "First, I am to establish a colony. That I will do."

"And that is your final word?"

"That is my final word," he said.

"Permission, Captain, to go once more to the Caan, to make an effort to dissuade them from attacking."

He frowned. "I suppose there is no important work to be done at the moment by a bleeding-heart anthropologist."

"Thank you," she said.

She found Lythe in his apartment, nude on his bed, surrounded by equally nude and nubile young women. When he saw her, he waved the Caan women away. "Your face is sad," he said.

"I am saddened to think of how many of your people must die if you attack the column that is now moving toward the sea."

"We will allow them to find their place, and then, when they are confident, we will attack," he said.

"They will be ready," she warned. "And they will kill you all from great distances. They will rain great explosions and fire on your heads from the air itself. You will all die."

"I think we will take a few of the men from the outer darkness with us, then," he said with a wide smile, opening his arms to her and motioning her to the bed. She shook her head.

"Is there nothing I can say to keep you from the attack?" she asked miserably.

"It begins as soon as I am purified by love," he said. "I was in that process when you came. Now you must be the instrument of my purification."

She went to him. He would be dead soon. She clung to him in great sadness and, as he loved her, tried to envision, from the reconstruction of the archaeologists, the cities of the Inca and the Aztec before and after the cannon of the Spanish conquistadores, before the pious European soldiers and priests had first looted and then burned the colorful, great temples. She wept as if her heart would break.

The Caan marched out, five thousand strong, the forces of Lythe's city reinforced by the swift arrival of many warriors from other cities north and south on the coast and from villages inland. The women of the city followed the marching army, singing hymns of praise for the bravery of their men, and Astrud went with them to find a vantage point on a wooded hill. She saw the scout ships from the *Estrêla do Brasil* attack the closely packed army with lasers and bombs that exploded in the air and spread deadly hail of shrapnel. She saw them die by the hundreds, by the thousands. She saw the pitiful remnants of the proud army, led by a tall man in a plumed helmet, rush the circle of fire and death on the site chosen by da Lisboa to plant his colony, and then she saw a very few survivors stagger back toward the city.

So it would be throughout the continent. The Caan, undefeated, so brave, so foolish, so confident, would attack and pit bronze hand weapons against the modern arsenal that could have conquered a small nation on Earth.

So it had always been on Earth. Even as she was leaving her home for outer space, the men from the so-called civilized areas of Brazil were penetrating ever deeper into the last remaining wilderness areas, where they converted or conquered the half-starving remnants of the wild Indian tribes they encountered. When the first Europeans had come, they killed or enslaved the natives. They put people who had thrived in the wilderness, in the open air, into gold or silver mines where they died. So it would be here, for the greed of da Lisboa and his people would not be satisfied with the gold and jewels to be looted from the Caan. They would demand more and more, and the women who had laughed and sung in the city would be their slaves.

She numbly walked back to a stricken city. Wails of mourning filled the air. People whispered as she walked in her Space Service whites down the main avenue toward the government building.

"Kill her!" a woman cried.

"Sear her skin with the pain of a thousand embers!" another yelled.

But she walked on and mounted the steps of the building and spoke quietly and calmly to the guards at the main entrance.

The elders were in session, clearly worried. They looked at her, their black eyes burning with hatred. The first elder rose and pointed a shaking finger at her.

"Have you come to gloat over our losses?" he demanded.

"I have come to mourn with you," she replied. "And I have come to tell you the story of a great people, much like the Caan, who once lived on Earth, my world."

"This is not the time for talk," the first elder said.

"But you must listen," Astrud pleaded. "Your warriors are brave and strong, but they will all die unless you listen to me."

"Speak then," the first elder said, seating himself wearily.

"The great people who once lived on my Earth built their cities on two islands in a very large lake," she began, "and they built well. They built beautiful temples, and they lived in abundance, and they ruled all the peoples from their cities to the shores of the far sea. And then one day men came on winged ships across the great waters. They came with towering, monstrous animals that screamed and trampled the people, and with terrible weapons of fire and great noise. Some said the newcomers were gods."

"So it is said of the men from the outer darkness," an elder noted. "Many believe it, for their power is terrible."

"The great people unknowingly fought in a way that gave the advantage to the terrible weapons of the invaders," Astrud continued. "They died bravely. The invaders took their gold and their jewels, enslaved those who had not died, destroyed the great cities, and tore down the temples that the people had raised to their gods."

"Are all men from the outer darkness such barbarians?" the first elder asked.

"So it will be here on the World," Astrud said. "So it will be if you send your young warriors into the face of our weapons."

"It is not in the nature of the Caan to surrender," the first elder said vehemently.

"No, you must fight, and many will die, but if you will listen to me, there is a chance that you will be able to drive the men from the outer darkness away."

"Why would you, one of them, help us?" the first elder asked.

"Because I was playlove with your war leader, Lythe. Because I deplore what my people will do on this world. Because it is time to prevent a repetition of the terrible things that have happened on my own Earth."

"We will listen," the first elder decided.

SEVEN

Evangeline Burr found Paul Warden in one of his favorite places—the picnic grounds overlooking Stanton Bay. Omega's sun was low and orange in the west, and Paul was watching the play of colors in the sunset, waiting to see if there would be, as there was occasionally, a burst of emerald green just as the sun disappeared into the Western Ocean.

"Hi, Vange," he said. "Nice evening."

"You haven't been into the library to see me in the last few days," she said.

"Well, we're pretty busy getting the expedition to the Great Misty River ready," he replied. "I was going to come in before we left."

"I should hope so," she said, seating herself on the edge of a picnic table.

Paul approved of her outfit: shorts and a blouse that exposed her midriff. There had been a lot of changes in almost everyone since the *Spirit of America* had landed on Omega, but Evangeline had changed more than most. Once she would have expired with shame before appearing in public in such a brief costume, and no longer did she diet until she was nothing more than skin and bones.

"I wish I could go with you," she said.

He laughed. "I'd like your company, but I don't think it would be too impressive throwing library cards at something hostile out there."

103

She slid off the table and stood looking up into his face. "Don't you do anything silly," she said, wagging a finger at him. "I want you back in one piece." Her own words surprised her, made her flush. Warden felt a warm glow. He had been thinking a lot about Evangeline lately. Now she stood before him, her short hair done in a smart, sassy style, her body tanned, full limbed, and there was something in her serious eyes that burned through the barrier that had been in place in his mind for a long time, ever since he had first seen Sage Bryson aboard ship. His eyes went wide, and he couldn't breathe for a moment.

"Damn, I've been such a fool," he muttered, the words barely audible.

Evangeline's smile came quickly. "Have you?"

"I don't see how you can put up with such a damned fool," he said.

"Well, I try harder," she said, still smiling.

He lifted his hands, started to put them on her arms, let them fall. He knew doubt. He had been turned down so many times by Sage, it seemed foolish to think that it would not happen with Evangeline, too.

How could he ever have thought that Sage's rather fragile beauty was greater than that of this woman who looked up into his face?

"Vange—" He could say no more. He could not move.

"I'll worry about you, but I know you won't let anything happen to you," she said.

"No."

"Well," she said, "it's getting late. Are you coming back now?"

"No," he answered, wanting to be alone to think about the revelation that had just burned into his thick skull. "Yes," he said quickly, not wanting to let her walk away.

"Well, which is it?" she teased, cocking a hip in a way that made him blink. Was that staid, shy Evangeline flirting, actually flirting with him?

"We're both staying here for a few minutes," he said, reaching for her. She helped. She took a half step forward and raised her arms, and then she was pressed to him and her lips were on his.

"You were never a fool, Paul," she whispered, her breath sweet against his mouth.

The makeup of the expedition to the Great Misty River had been discussed thoroughly by Paul Warden and Duncan Rodrick. Warden picked Renato Cruz as his second in command, because Cruz had had some infantry training at the Space Service Academy. Renato was at loose ends anyhow, since his best buddy, Jacob West, was off on a pleasure cruise with his Polish wife.

There were plenty of volunteers, so there was no problem in lining up people to man and operate the weapons on the crawlers. The rest of the scout force would be in the air or standing by. The defense of Hamilton City would be left largely in the capable hands of two androids, the admiral and Mopro. Duncan Rodrick, although he would have preferred to go, would see them to their base camp and then return to Hamilton.

It was necessary for Sage Bryson to go, since she was the colony's number-one authority on electrical fields, and to Rodrick's surprise and concern, Mandy Miller insisted on going.

"Captain, they'll need a doctor," Mandy had said. "And I will not order any of my people to do something I wouldn't do myself."

That did not make much sense, since all of the Life Sciences staff had volunteered, but Rodrick had decided, after a few moments' consideration, to allow Mandy her wishes. He was, he thought, always thinking defensively where she was concerned. He had kissed Mandy only once, but that unspoken love that still glowed between them, in spite of everything, still colored his thinking about her. If he refused to let her go, would someone remember the gossip that had, most probably, been started by Mandy's husband before he died? But if he let her go and she was hurt, could he ever forgive himself?

It was, Rodrick often thought, a juvenile state of mind for a man to be in—to have a wife like Jackie, to care for her deeply, and still to be burning the torch for Mandy.

"I can use a laser cannon," she had said. "I won't be just deadweight."

This, too, worried Rodrick. She had seen two hundred people slaughtered by the Whorsk, and although she was eminently wise in most things, her hatred for the insectlike people was unreasonable. Rodrick felt sure that if she had her say about it, every Whorsk on Omega would be wiped out. If, as it was suspected, the inhabitants of that mysterious zone along the river were a priestly caste of Whorsk, Mandy could just precipitate a massacre.

He decided, however, that she was too stable to do anything irresponsible. Furthermore, she was the best doctor on the planet, and she wanted to go. His permission was granted.

The operation began early one morning. The scout fleet was used to lift crawlers over the Western Ocean to a point north of the permanent fog bank on the river. This took two days—since the scouts could not make much speed with the bulky crawlers slung underneath—and then another day to ferry the personnel to the rendezvous point. When all was in place, Rodrick, with Clay Girard in the right seat, flew to the western continent, catching up with a setting sun, to arrive at the temporary camp on the river with the sun still hours high.

It was hot in the desert, with temperatures reaching one-hundred-ten degrees at midday. But the air was so pure, so clean, the landscape so different, the river so wide and beautiful that there was an air of picnic in the camp. And as evening came and the temperature dropped swiftly to comfortable levels, the prepared, self-heating rations were ignored in favor of cooking over open fires.

No one seemed to be too worried about what the next day might bring when the crawlers entered the bank of fog that was visible to the south. This concerned Rodrick, but his fears were eased when he talked with Paul Warden and Renato Cruz. Although they were both seemingly relaxed, seated on the sand around the campfire, they were not unaware that they were leading a force of fifty extremely valuable people into the unknown. There would be no overconfidence once the crawlers started moving south.

Rodrick did not seek out Mandy Miller. He was making the rounds of the groups at the campfires, speaking easily to everyone, smiling, nodding at their comments, when he saw Mandy sitting cross-legged in the sand, her hair tucked up to expose that delicate line of neck, one of the things he found so beautiful about her. In Mandy's group were Sage Bryson and two electronics technicians from the *Spirit*'s crew—men who could also double, with their service training, as space marines. He was standing, listening to Sage's report on measurements of the electrical field that was within the fog bank, when a man called from a crawler parked nearby that he had just recorded new readings on the field. Sage and the two technicians left the fire.

"Why does coffee heated over an open fire taste so much better?" Mandy asked.

Omega's two moons were out. One hung huge and swollen on the eastern horizon, the other was zenith high. The low murmur of voices from the others was drowned out by the nearby coughing, growling call of one of the river lions. Mandy shivered. "We saw a pride of them today," she said. "They're huge. It's incredible that Theresita could have killed one with a primitive spear. She was lucky to survive."

"She's quite a woman," Rodrick agreed. He sat down on a log that someone had dragged near the fire. "Speaking of Theresita, anything new on her baby?"

Mandy shook her head. "The last tests I ran showed normal development." She looked down the river where the fog bank gleamed in the bright moonlight. "I think we're going to find the baby's father in there."

"Not Whorsk?"

"I don't think it's quite time for an immaculate conception on this planet," Mandy said with a wry smile. "There was a father. And although we've seen evidence of parallel evolution here, to think that there's a humanoid so similar to us, down to the DNA level, that crossbreeding is possible scares the hell out of me in one way and opens up all kinds of speculation in another way."

"Such as?"

"Well, we began back in the twentieth century trying

to make contact with alien people," she said. "We spent billions of dollars searching for communications from space. We included a message to any alien people on our first puny little space probe that escaped the solar system. We couldn't live in peace with our own kind on Earth, but we didn't want to think that we were alone in this great emptiness that is the universe. But what if we find that there are *men* behind that fog bank, Dunc? What are we going to believe then? It would all be very simple if we found men who worship as we do. But what if we find people like us who worship snakes or chickens or something equally bizarre? Will we be able to get along with them?"

"Well, I've always tried to refrain from worrying about something that cannot be changed," Rodrick said. "Let's wait until you folks see whatever there is to see behind the fog." Then, after a silence, "You seem to be doing fine."

"It's been quite an adjustment since Rocky's death, being a single woman again."

"I'll bet."

"It has its good points." She frowned, as if even that admission was criticism of Rocky. She felt a bit guilty because, try as she might, she had not been able to mourn him. She had mourned, in sort of an impersonal way, the death of all those who had died with Rocky, but she had never been able to bring herself to cry for Rocky alone.

"I have my work," she said. "I'm pleased that you're happy, Captain." She could not bring herself to speak his first name again.

He smiled. "Thank you." And he told himself to get up, to walk away. Just being with her brought back memories of how pleasant it had been to steal just a few minutes with her during the trip out, usually in the observatory. It was a pleasure, it was easy, just to be with her. And he could not stop the thought that if he had waited for just a little while before asking Jackie Garvey to marry him, he could have, after a suitable period of waiting following Rocky's death, been with Mandy, the one woman in his life whose chemistry seemed to match his in every way.

"Funny how things happen, isn't it?" she mused, after a long pause. "If it had been you I had met a long time ago—"

"Don't, Mandy," he said. "I've thought like that, too. It doesn't serve any purpose."

"I'm sorry," she said. "Put it down to the emotional instability of a woman who has gone through some mental trauma."

"No," he said gently. "It's not just that. When I'm close to you, my entire being—my body, my mind, my heart—cries out for you. I begin to concoct silly schemes to be with you. I'm ready to toss everything overboard—responsibility, duty, honor—to have you, even for a few minutes."

She smiled, her eyes glowing. "I know, I know. But we won't scheme. We won't cheat. We can't."

"Will it ever stop, this feeling?" he asked.

She shrugged. "I've been checking over the available men, thinking that if I got married again—"

A pain of renewed loss hit him. "Damn," he said. Then, "I want you to be happy. I want the best for you."

"Yes," she agreed. "Well, here we are. We should be thinking about tomorrow."

"I want you to stay at the rear. I want you to be very, very careful. I've given Paul orders to withdraw in a hurry if he meets any dangerous situation."

"We'll be careful," she promised.

He rose, looked at her one last time, and walked away. He found Clay Girard singing a soft roundelay with a group of the younger members of the expedition and said, "Hate to take you away, Clay, but it's time for us to go home."

Sage Bryson found nothing of note in the new set of measurements of the electrical field in the fog. She pored over the readings for a half hour, and then she went into her small tent and looked over them again and decided that she should tell the expedition commander that nothing had changed. She had seen Paul Warden sitting with Cruz and some others earlier, but when she went out of the tent, he was not there at that particular campfire. She found him talking to one of the sentries who had been posted around the perimeter of the camp, and they walked together back toward the dying fires in the bright moonlight. She made her report, which was quite brief since there was nothing new, and then they walked in silence for a few steps.

"It's a beautiful river," Paul said, gazing out onto the water, made silver by the light of the two moons.

"I've always been a sucker for desolate areas," Sage said. "I was thinking about buying a cottage in the New Mexico desert before I was picked for the *Spirit of America*."

"You've always been a loner, huh?" Paul asked. He was not immune to Sage's beauty, but after his understanding with Evangeline, he no longer ached to hold her in his arms. He was content, at that moment, to talk with Sage as a friend and an associate, and to look forward to getting back to Evangeline when the job downriver had been done.

"I've always had a bit of difficulty relating to people," she admitted. "It may sound silly, but I'm actually glad I had that breakdown. It's nice just to be able to talk with people—with a man, without experiencing that awful pressure, without feeling that the man is thinking of nothing but—"

"You're okay," Paul assured her. "You're gonna be fine."

"I wasted so many years," she said.

"Well, you've got a lot of years ahead of you."

They paused near the riverbank. From out in the stream came a mighty splash. "One of those things with teeth that Theresita told us about," Paul commented.

"Paul, what if we find something with teeth behind the fog?"

"Well, I'm fatalistic about it," he replied. "If we run into anything we can't handle with lasers, rockets, or guns that fire a thousand rounds a minute, then we've had the course anyhow, haven't we?"

"Paul, that's terrible," she said, laughing.

"Yeah, I know," he admitted, grinning. "I'm a little

nervous about it. I don't like going in blind to face some-one who has the capacity to create an electrical field that shields out our detection instruments and shrouds hundreds of miles of river with fog. I've even thought that we ought to leave well enough alone. Whatever is behind that fog seems content to stay there. Maybe we should just let the sleeping dog lie."

"I think not knowing would be worse—to be always on our guard, to go to sleep at night wondering if something will come at us out of the fog before we awake."

"Yeah, I feel a little that way myself," Paul confessed. "Duncan's right in sending us in there." He turned to face her. She was clearly visible in the moonlight, and she seemed more beautiful than ever. "You're not going to give me a hard time like you did that time we went after the miner, are you?"

She laughed. "I can obey orders."

"Good. Don't give me any of that male-chauvinist stuff then. I want men up front. Men who are fast on the trigger and strong. I'm putting you and Mandy in the rear crawler."

"I will need to be in the instrument crawler," she pointed out.

"That's the one at the rear."

"You'll be sending men into the unknown without proper instrumentation," she protested.

"See? You're already giving me a hard time," he said. But he knew that what she said made sense. He growled a bit, then said, "All right. We'll have one crawler out front about fifty yards, then you and I will be in the instrument vehicle. Suit you?"

"That makes sense," she said.

He picked up a rock and threw it as far into the river as he could. There was a splash, followed by a larger splash. "The damned things must hunt at night," he said. He threw another rock, closer in this time, and they saw a huge, toothed head hit the spot where the rock splashed. Sage involuntarily drew close to him, and he put a protective arm around her waist. She stiffened, then relaxed. He felt the slim firmness of her waist, the warmth of her. He told himself to remove his arm, but he did not. He felt confused.

He felt even more confused when she turned, pressed to the circle of his arm, to face him, her breasts pressed to his chest. "If you want to kiss me—" she whispered.

There had been a time when kissing her was all he had thought about. He saw Evangeline's face, but he could not stop himself. He licked his lips and lowered his head to her upturned face and found her lips. They were warm, moist. She shuddered just a bit, and then her arms went around his neck, and she pressed herself close.

I'll be damned, he was thinking, in sheer surprise, for although that kiss was pleasant, there was no fire—none of the thrill he had felt when he kissed Evangeline.

Feeling the change in his embrace, in his lips, she pulled away and smiled up at him. "Thank you," she murmured. "I really do think I'm cured."

"Good," he said, a bit sorry for her because the kiss had meant nothing to him.

"And, my friend, I think you're cured, too," she said.

He grinned. "You're a helluva girl."

"And you're a helluva man," she continued, "and my congratulations to you and Evangeline. You're my best friends, and I love you both. You deserve each other."

"Yeah, I think so," Paul said.

Renato Cruz was at the wheel of the lead crawler. The vehicle's small arsenal had been beefed up for the expedition. The weapons manned by the four space marines who rode with Renato could take out a mainline battle tank with six-inch armor, raze the most heavily fortified blockhouse, send smart rockets around corners, rain fire from flamethrowers, sear with lasers, blast with explosive shot, and cover every inch of an area a hundred yards square with bullets.

Since it had already been demonstrated that radio communication was blacked out in the fog, flexible elastic wires had been strung from the lead vehicle all the way back to the rearward crawlers. Warden was advancing in a single column, to reduce losses if they encountered serious opposition. They tested the communication by wire, and then the column moved slowly southward along the banks of the river. As they came within a few hundred yards of the eerily vertical fog bank, Warden looked up quickly when a sonic boom reverberated down the valley to see two scouts braking to hover over them.

"Morning, guys," Paul sent by radio.

"You're looking good," Jack Purdy responded, from the lead scout ship. "Me and my little buddy are going to be right up here, with you all the way."

His little buddy was Clay Girard, flying his first solo mission into potential danger. Clay was in his element and very proud that he had, at last, gained full membership in the scouts.

"*Apache One*," Renato Cruz called up from the crawler to Clay, who was in Jacob West's scout. "We're going in."

"Keep talking on the radio," Jack Purdy said from *Dinahmite*. "We want to know when communications cut off."

Communication by radio was blacked out even before the rear of the crawler disappeared into the fog. It was as if a switch had been thrown in the middle of one of Renato's words.

"—can't see a thing," Renato was saying from the lead crawler. He was heard in the second crawler. "We're moving ahead at three miles per hour. We've come two hundred feet from the outer edge."

"Okay, Renato," Warden said. "Stop right there and wait until we get a look with Sage's instruments."

Warden eased the instrument crawler ahead and saw the front of it push into the fog without seeming to disturb it. Then it was as if he had dived the crawler into a sea of milk. He stopped. "Okay, we're in it," he said.

Beside him Sage was busy with her instruments. "The same readings we got from the scout ships," she said.

"Nothing more?" Paul asked.

"All I can say is what I've said before, that it's definitely an electromagnetic field."

"You feel anything, Renato?" Warden asked.

"Maybe a little tingling sensation," Cruz said.

"Okay, Renato, ease ahead," Warden ordered.

There were some minutes of tension then, as the lead crawler slowly moved deeper and deeper into the fog. Renato could not see the ground immediately in front of him. His instruments were useless. More than once the crawler bumped into huge boulders and had to detour around them. Renato was nervously alert. He did not want to drive off a high cliff.

"So far, so good," he sent back along the wire.

"We're right behind you," Warden assured the Mescalero.

"No change in intensity of the field," Sage reported.

One by one the crawlers penetrated the fog, and there was constant chatter as they kept each other informed of their status and location.

From above, where Purdy and Clay circled, the crawlers disappeared completely, and they lost all communication. Purdy was keeping Duncan Rodrick informed.

The lead crawler had traveled no more than fifty yards inside the fog when Paul Warden heard Renato yell, "Hey, how about that?"

"What? What?" Warden yelled, his heart pounding.

"Keep coming, Paul," Renato said calmly. "You've got a surprise coming to you in exactly twenty yards. Steer left to miss a boulder, and you've got it made."

"How do you know?" Warden asked.

"Just keep on coming," Renato repeated, and just as he spoke, Warden's crawler burst out of the milky darkness into sunlight so bright that he blinked before the automatic instruments in the crawler's windshield darkened the glass to protect against the glare.

One by one the crawlers came out into the open, and now there was no sign of fog, not behind them, around them, or above them. Overhead was Omega's cloudless, purplish sky. Behind them they could see all the way up the river to their campsite and beyond. On either side were arid, sheer cliffs. Ahead of them was the river and green fields of growing crops extending to a curve in the river far to the south.

"Look," Sage said, pointing upward. They could even

see the two scout ships circling high over them, but their attempts to communicate with the ships brought only silence.

"I *thought* I was nervous before we started in," Sage said. "Now I'm really nervous. I'm trying to come up with some answers, and I'm stumped."

"What answers?" Paul asked.

"It's difficult enough to explain a field that blocks electronic impulses and all light. Try explaining one that blocks such things as that and lets through sunlight with all its different ranges of radiation, *and* lets you look through it from one side."

"I see what you mean," Paul said. "Renato, move out about five hundred yards and let's see what's beyond that bend in the river."

"There's an extensive system of cultivation ahead of us," Renato reported, using the radio now. "This field to our right is a grain crop. Looks like barley."

"Well, let's stay on the river's edge," Warden said. "We don't want to tear up the crops. Stay alert, buddy."

"I'm so alert I'm almost hyper," Renato answered. "See that gadget on the riverbank?"

"I see it," Warden said.

"Know what it is?"

"Looks like a man-powered method of lifting water from the river," Paul said.

"That's what it looks like," Renato confirmed. "Okay, we're approaching the bend in the river." He had been pushing the crawler along quite rapidly, all detection instruments on scan. Behind him the other crawlers were matching his speed, even closing up their ranks until they were running almost bumper to bumper.

"Life signals!" Renato called, as his crawler nosed around the bend and saw the valley extending ahead for more miles.

"Hold up," Warden ordered, increasing his speed to bring his crawler alongside the now stationary lead vehicle.

"Whorsk," Renato said, his optical instruments focused on a distant group of moving figures.

Whorsk they were, looking somewhat like the stickmen drawn by very young children. And as the caravan moved slowly south, they saw in the distance, up against the rocky cliffs and out of the irrigated green zone along the river, a village of reed-and-mud huts. The Whorsk were working the fields, some of them manning the water lifters along the riverbank, some doing various tasks of cultivation with primitive hoes.

"Keep on the alert for airships," Warden warned the entire group. But no Whorsk lighter-than-air ships appeared.

When a small group of the Whorsk first noticed the approaching crawlers, there was considerable agitation, and a few of them ran toward the village, but then, when the crawlers came near, the Whorsk bowed low and watched passively as the crawlers went past.

"Tell me about *that* reaction," Warden said, on an open mike.

"They are unfamiliar with crawlers," Mandy Miller said, "but familiar with those who ride in them."

"How can that be?" Warden demanded.

"Paul, my bet is," Mandy said, "that pretty soon we're going to see someone who looks very much like us."

Now there were boats on the river, boats with drab, dirty sails and oars. Some of them were riding the current southward, using their sails to assist, laden with the products of the green fields. Others were beating their way northward, either under sail or with sail assisted by oars. After a while none of the working Whorsk ran; they merely bowed low if the crawlers came near them and then went back to their work.

"Talk about intensive use of agricultural land," Sage said. "They're farming every inch of land that can be irrigated with river water."

The valley, at that point, was perhaps three miles wide, with the river taking up about one third of it. The two-mile-deep strips on either side were beautifully verdant.

The expedition ate on the go. They were able to move swiftly along a roadlike path on the riverbank—a space that had been cleared, as had the fields, of any protruding stones. In places the stones had been used to form a protective levee along the river. In others they were piled, without any apparent form, under the sun-drenched cliffs that framed the valley. The river made several more sharp bends, skirting around hills and small mountains, and then the desert above the cliffs flattened and the river ran very straight toward the south. The going was easy from that point, and aside from the variety of crops in the green belt, there was no change.

It was late when the river began to make a wide sweep to the west. A line of low, rocky, arid hills appeared. Gradually the valley narrowed, and the green belt was, in places, only a hundred yards wide on either side of the gradually narrowing river. The river's current was running faster, but still the boats plied it, rowers having to work hard as the boats made their way upstream. And then the valley was constricted by the arid hills to a point where there were no crops along its banks, only the roadlike ledge. Ahead, the cliffs became perpendicular.

"We'll stop here," Warden said. He did not want to enter the narrow gorge with darkness coming on. "We're going to circle the wagons, folks, just like they did in the old West. Renato, you oughta know all about that."

"My people were always outside the circle," Renato said, "but I can manage."

Soon the crawlers were parked in a circle, armored prows pointed outward, weapons covering a full arc around the chosen campsite.

"Look," Sage said, pointing downriver. In the narrow gorge Whorsk were on the bank of the river, leaning into heavy ropes that were pulling a riverboat upstream against the swift current.

Warden slept well. He awoke before dawn and watched the sun burst up over the eastern cliff while the others had their breakfasts and prepared for the day. They got under way just after sunrise, and Renato's crawler led the way into the narrow gorge. The river was less than a quarter of a mile wide, and the vast volume of water it carried was moving south at a swift pace.

"Paul, there are three boats moving up the gorge," Renato said. "There's not room for both the crawler and the Whorsk who are on the bank pulling the boats upstream."

"All right," Paul said. "We don't want to force them into the river and cause them to lose their boats. Back out of there, and we'll wait until they're clear."

"We might have to wait a long time," Renato replied. "I see two more coming. Looks as if early morning is their busy time."

Paul thought it over for a moment or two. He was eager to see what was farther down the river. "We'll go amphibious. Take to the river, Renato, and we'll be right behind you."

The power of the crawlers was more than adequate to resist the swift current. If there were rapids ahead, the power of the crawlers would allow them to move upstream against the current, so there was no danger in carrying out Paul's decision. When all were waterborne, they began to let the current carry them into the gorge. There were several Whorsk boats being towed up the river by gangs of the stickmen on the footpath on the bank, and they paid little attention to the crawlers.

The cliffs on either side of the gorge were high, quite smooth, and of a beautiful white stone very much like marble. The gorge extended ahead of them for a half mile or more before it made a sweeping turn.

It was very pleasant on the water. As a safety measure, Warden opened the top of the crawler and ordered the others to follow suit. Should a crawler strike an underwater rock and overturn, no one would be trapped inside a sinking vehicle. The sun was hot, the southerly breeze cool, and the water came now and then in a sweet, cool spray to dampen their faces. As the leading crawlers approached the bend, the current swept them toward the western face of the cliffs, and each driver compensated with the hydrogen jets. Then the first two crawlers swept around the bend and saw an even more constricted gorge ahead of them, but what caused Sage to cry out in surprise were not the gleaming, white cliffs, but something a quarter of a mile ahead down the long, straight gorge.

Titans stood on either side of the river. Over two hundred feet in height, their visored faces looked up the gorge toward the drifting crawlers. In their mighty arms were unidentifiable weapons.

"Hold up," Warden ordered even as he threw power to the jets and stopped the downstream motion of his own crawler.

"And there were giants on the Earth in those days," Mandy Miller said, without realizing that she had depressed her communicator switch.

"These giants are carved of stone," Renato Cruz said, having played his life-detection instruments over the titans. "I'm easing on down."

The stone giants were carved from the cliffs' gleaming white stone, with supporting connections left at their backs to keep them attached to the cliff. They were painted—their skin in flesh tone, their costumes in bright colors. They wore a sort of kilt, painted in stripes of red and black, and their massive chests were bare. Their right arms extended outward and held something shaped like a thick baton. And their heads were covered by gracefully designed helmets painted gold. Golden visors hid their faces.

"The Whorsk said that a race of giants built the city in the rocky highlands," Sage said in an awed voice.

"Have you ever seen anything more beautiful?" Mandy breathed.

"I've seen something very much like those statues," Sage replied, "when I visited the Egyptian museum on Earth."

"Definitely humanoid," Mandy said.

"All right," Warden said. "Let's go."

Just past the two giant statues there was an army of titans in bas-relief, carved into either side of the gorge. An army frozen in stone, an army that carried only one weapon, which was shaped like a thick baton. And then there were writings, and more marching titans frozen in the white stone, and another set of two-hundred-foot titans facing north, as if warning those who drifted down the river to beware exiting from the gorge.

The crawlers, moving swiftly with the current, engines idling, shot out of the constricted gorge into a broad-ening river where the current immediately slowed. At first there was too much to see. Behind them the white stone hills, and ahead of them green areas, a landing field on which sat a dozen of the Whorsk lighter-than-air craft. Armed, insectlike sky warriors milled around the ships. And amid the Whorsk there proudly walked a living, scaled-down replica of the giant statues, a bronzed male, torso exposed to the sun, wearing only a gleaming, white kilt that came to midthigh and that gracefully shaped helmet.

Sage focused the crawler's optics on the bronzed man, for he could be called nothing else, and gasped as she saw the regularity and beauty of his face, and the perfect proportions of his body. He seemed to be looking at them, but he showed no agitation.

"Take a look," she said to Warden, averting her eyes from the screen. She felt oddly weak.

"Good God," Warden said, not looking at the man at all, but looking ahead to a widening of the valley.

On either side of the river, extending for perhaps a full two miles, all the way to the cliffs, was a fairyland city—a painted city, a bustling, busy city in painted stone with huge wharfs along the river, with towering buildings and streets filled with colorfully clad, bronzed people. And above the city, sitting on the brink of the towering cliff and looking rather small in the distance, was a familiar architectural form, a pyramid encased in the white stone of the gorge—the stone obviously highly polished, for it fully reflected the gleaming light of the sun.

"Paul, I get one helluva powerful reading when I point the instruments toward the pyramid," Sage said. "I think we've found the source of that electrical field."

EIGHT

From the communications center aboard the *Spirit of America* the watch officer broadcast periodic bulletins on the progress of the expedition to the Great Misty River. Wherever they were working, members of the colony kept in touch, for Rodrick had alerted everyone. He had used best-and-worst-scenario planning. At best, Paul Warden's group would meet with no danger, no opposition. At worst, it would be necessary to mobilize the forces of the colony. He had issued orders to curtail activity away from the immediate vicinity of Hamilton City and Stanton Bay. So it was that only the petroleum-producing team and two groups of people from Stoner McRae's mineral-search team were in the field.

Stoner sometimes liked working alone, but when he wanted company, he often took along his wife, Betsy, and their daughter, Cindy, when school schedules permitted. He had both with him as he pushed a crawler into the rocky highlands northeast of Hamilton. There, about two hundred miles due east of Lake Dinah, a search team, using the small, wheeled machine that the engineers had adapted from a pipeline cleaner to be an ore detector, had located a small deposit of molybdenum sulfide ore deep in a miner's tunnel. The instruments on the pipeline crawler were not sophisticated enough to tell if there was rhenium mixed with the molybdenum, but since that rare metal was most often found in molybdenum deposits, Stoner was eager to check it out.

Stoner had not told Betsy or Cindy, but he had been working on something new. In the crawler's cargo compartment was an odd-looking, bullet-shaped machine just a little longer than Stoner's height. It had spring-mounted wheels on all sides and was powered by a small hydrogen engine.

Stoner had found Omega to be his greatest challenge— and his greatest frustration. Even on Earth—where valuable metallic ores had been mined for thousands of years and easily reachable supplies of most ores had been severely depleted—there was a richness of metals that contrasted directly with the distribution of ores in Omega's light crust. A geologist and mining engineer accustomed to Earth's bounty found Omega's composition to be puzzling and disappointing. One of the most common elements in nature, iron, was harder to find on Omega than gold or platinum had been on Earth, and the heavier metals were almost nonexistent.

To date, the only source of heavy metals, with gold being most common—relatively—had been the miners. They drove their tunnels deep into the light crust of the planet and apparently encountered the volcanic upthrust of material from Omega's molten, mostly silicon core on rare occasions.

Stoner was not content just to sit back and wait for the miners to bring up enough ore in exchange for the lubricant they needed for their boring teeth. He had determined to do something about it, and the fact that it might be dangerous was not going to deter him.

He had intended to test out his new machine without Betsy's knowledge. He had not wanted to cause her undue worry. But there was no school that week, and Betsy was restless. She had come to love being outdoors in Eden's ideal climate, and she had been insistent when she heard that Stoner had a field trip planned.

Cindy had debated whether to go or to stay and keep in close touch with developments along the great river on the western continent. She was not really worried about

Clay; after all, he was not going to be a part of the ground expedition but would be flying safely high above it all. Nevertheless she had at first thought it best to stay in the colony so she could keep her ears glued to the radio. When Stoner told her that Rodrick had arranged to send out bulletins to all, however, she decided to accompany her parents.

The trip took two days. Late on the second day Stoner homed in on the location beacon left by the exploration team, and they made camp in a small valley nestled among the rocky hills. There had been no recent word from the Great Misty River; but Clay had temporarily returned to Hamilton City after a long tour of flying over the river.

The next morning there was still no word from the crawlers that had disappeared into the fog, and the McRaes could tell by the tone of the duty officer's voice that things were a bit tense back aboard the *Spirit of America* and in Hamilton. But Stoner had his own work to do, and quite frankly, he was beginning to doubt that what he had planned was the best course of action.

"What on Earth is that?" Betsy asked, when he heaved his machine out of the crawler's cargo space.

"You mean 'what on Omega,'" Stoner teased.

"What in hell, then, is that?" Betsy asked.

"Well, I guess you could call it a power sled or a manned pipeline crawler," Stoner replied.

"Oh, no you don't," Betsy warned. "You're not about to go down in one of those tunnels in that thing."

"I knew I should have left you at home," Stoner said, grinning. "That is exactly what I am about to do. It's perfectly safe."

"Stoner!" Betsy wailed.

"Look, we've been sending the small crawlers down the tunnels for months. The miners have accepted them. If miners encounter one, they back off and go into a side tunnel. They're cooperating with us. They'll do the same with this."

Betsy argued a bit more, but she knew her man, knew that once he had set his mind on a course of action, he was not to be deflected from it.

"Your father is a crazy man, you know," she told Cindy, as Stoner rolled the sled toward the open shaft of a miner's tunnel.

"He'll be all right," Cindy said, although she didn't like the idea of her father going down a miner's tunnel, either.

"Stay on the communicator," Stoner said.

"I will," Cindy assured him, running to move the crawler as close to the tunnel as possible.

"Here I go," Stoner said. He had placed the sled on the slope of the circular depression around the tunnel. It took him some time to insert himself, for Stoner—who had been a defensive tackle for the San Diego Chargers—wore the sled rather than rode in it, and the space for his large body was quite cramped. He lay on his stomach inside the sled, and when, at his directions, Betsy closed the entrance hatch and he had clamped it down from the inside, there was room for only the movement of his hands.

The sled moved, under power. The bullet-shaped nose tipped into the entrance to the tunnel, and then the sled disappeared, falling rapidly down the slope until the tunnel leveled. Almost immediately there was total darkness. The sled was equipped with powerful lights front and rear. Stoner braked the sled to a stop, tried reverse power, and pushed the sled backward until he was back at surface level. Satisfied then, he said on the radio, "It works fine."

"Okay, Dad," Cindy said. "Have a nice trip."

On relatively shallow levels, the miner tunnels were well ventilated. The creatures were air-breathers. But it had been found that at lower levels, the air was stale and low in oxygen, so Stoner had his own supply of oxygen aboard. To conserve it, he used outside air as long as possible, while the tunnel ran for several hundred yards on the level at a depth of around thirty feet. He had a crude diagram of the tunnel system attached to the lining of the sled just over the controls. He marked his travel route so he could keep track of the branching tunnels, and with the sled working perfectly, he moved swiftly to the point where the tunnel took a sudden downward turn and plunged at an angle of about forty-five degrees.

He halted there for a moment. His radio communications with Cindy were getting weak. "Cindy, you're breaking up. How do you read me?"

"Faintly," Cindy said.

"Look, I'll be out of range in a minute or two. Don't worry. Everything going fine."

"When can I expect to hear from you again?"

"Give me, oh, forty-five minutes," Stoner said.

"And then what?" Cindy asked, not wanting to put negative thoughts into Stoner's mind, but a little worried.

"Don't worry," Stoner said. "I'll be back within range in forty-five minutes."

On the surface Betsy sat beside Cindy in the crawler, her face pale. "It has just occurred to me that he's doing a solo number here," she said. "I'll bet he hasn't even notified the base about what he's doing."

"Mother, he wouldn't take a foolish risk," Cindy said.

"Of course he would. He's taken Omega's lack of heavy metals as a personal challenge," Betsy replied.

"Don't worry. He'll be back soon."

Stoner had spent a lot of hours far beneath the surface of the Earth. He had crawled along shafts in the gold mines of South Africa at a depth of eleven thousand feet. Being underground was not his favorite pastime, but he had never felt claustrophobic—at least not until, cramped inside a small machine, he began to descend a forty-five degree slope that arrowed straight into the depths of the planet Omega. He began to have difficulty in breathing and switched on the oxygen. Still he did not seem to be able to fill his lungs. He coughed, then tried to wipe away the perspiration stinging his eyes, but due to his very cramped position, he could not reach his face. He panted. And then he halted the sled and had a talk with himself.

"This was your idea," he said aloud. "And it's necessary. It's no big deal. You're only four hundred feet down now. You don't have nearly as far to go as you went in South Africa."

But in all his experiences in mines, there had been people with him and he had been moving under his own power. Now he had to depend on the machine to lift him from the depths ahead of him back to the surface.

"There's nothing to go wrong," he said. "It's a simple hydrogen engine. Hydrogen engines don't fail."

He was breathing a bit easier now. He slowed the rate still more, for it would be necessary to conserve his oxygen.

At five hundred feet the tunnel leveled off. This was no surprise, for he had the information from the unmanned crawler to tell him exactly what to expect. What he did not expect was to encounter a nest. The tunnel widened where there was a large side room, and there, squirming and soft, were a half-dozen young, about three-feet long, looking like ill-formed versions of adult miners. He stopped the sled and activated its cameras. The young miners, either hearing him or seeing him, opened their maws and began to make a hissing sound.

"Sorry," he said. "I don't have any food for you."

He thought it might be a good idea to get the hell out of the vicinity of the nest. Miners did not bother the unmanned crawlers, but if a mama found him messing around with her kiddies, she might be highly unpredictable. He applied power and left the begging youngsters behind, and then the tunnel plunged again, and he was moving fast, faster, eager to get down to the five-thousand-foot level, examine that ore deposit close up, and then send the sled moving upward as fast as it would move.

Now the tunnel went into a tight spiral. He felt as if he were riding a roller coaster. The walls of the tunnel were very interesting, for he was seeing the very guts of the planet and getting an excellent record of rock strata with the cameras. He would be able to run it all through the computer and construct a pretty good model of the planet's crust at that particular point.

Three thousand feet. He was using too much of his oxygen. He forced himself to relax, to breathe less deeply and less frequently. Four thousand feet. The tunnel seemed to spiral on endlessly. The temperature had risen considerably. There had not been room in the sled for climate-conditioning machinery, and he was soaked with perspiration.

He began to wonder if this trip had really been necessary. He had the pictures from the unmanned crawler, and they indicated only a small vein of ore, not really worth sinking a shaft almost one mile below the surface. But there had been something about the way the vein was shaped that had intrigued him. It had the look of a tip, and if he was right, the main deposit would extend outward from that tip into something worthwhile. It would take some intricate instruments and the interpretive skills of a mining engineer to determine whether the deposit was just an isolated pocket or the beginning of a huge deposit.

He slowed as he approached the five-thousand-foot level. He was entering an area of fractured strata. The walls of the tunnel showed some irregularity, as if loose rock had fallen while the miner was digging the tunnel, but the walls had been stabilized by that silicon layer that lined all the miners' tunnels.

He had long since lost contact with Cindy. The radio waves simply would not penetrate a mile of solid rock and could not bend around the turns and twists of the tunnel. He was alone, more alone than he had ever been in his life. When he reached the vicinity of the ore deposit, he was just under one mile straight down from the surface.

He saw a change in the tunnel walls and entered a stratum that made him forget his discomfort: ore-bearing rock. And there was the molybdenum sulfide. He halted the sled. It took him a few minutes to activate all his instruments, and when he sent signals penetrating into the rock, he heard a sharp sound and the silicon glaze on the tunnel wall cracked—the crack spreading for a distance of ten feet or more. Stoner stopped all activity. A rock fall here, even if it did not crush him, could block the tunnel, and he would have two choices—stay where he was and die or push the sled deeper to see how deep the tunnel went, and if there was another exit from it. Since he had not passed a branching tunnel since shortly after finding the miner's nest, he doubted that there would be alternate tunnels at this depth.

But the reading of the instruments was encouraging. He very badly wanted a sample of the ore. He had rigged a small drill and sample taker into the sled. He carefully positioned it and cautiously extended the drill from the sled bottom. He activated the drill gradually, and it slowly cut a half-inch hole in the lining of the tunnel and began to bite into the ore rocks. He heard another crack, and the lining of the tunnel wall crumbled just in front of him, sending a shower of broken stones to the tunnel floor. He had not stopped the drill, and nothing else happened as it carved out a solid core of ore rock and withdrew inside the sled. He breathed again, took one last look around, and checked the instrument readings again.

"Gotcha," he said. But he had only a sample of some pretty good molybdenum ore. He would not know until he got back to the colony whether or not molybdenum ore on Omega carried minute amounts of rhenium like the ores of Earth.

He would have to back the sled all the way up to the first branching tunnel. That meant traveling half-blind, although he did have a tiny screen on the instrument panel, which showed him the view from the rear camera. But he was going up, and that made him feel a lot better. He checked his oxygen supply. It was ample for the trip back to the levels that were so cunningly ventilated by the miners' shafts.

He reached the first branch tunnel without incident and nosed into it. The miners, thick, heavy, and long, had to have places to turn around, since they, like the sled, fitted quite snugly into the uniform tunnels. There was a turnaround at the branch shaft, and within a minute he was heading nose up toward the surface again, the hydrogen engine whining under the strain, wheels slipping a bit on the smooth walls.

"We've got it made," he said joyously, as he reached

the surface levels, only a few hundred feet down. He would zip right past the nest area this time, and soon he would be able to stretch his cramped muscles and breathe the clean, fresh air of the surface.

Now he was nearing the nest. He slowed, not wanting to startle the miner young, and there it was, the alcove cut off the main tunnel, large enough for a miner to enter and, perhaps, to curl up around the depression in the stone floor that contained the young. The lights of the sled reflected almost blindingly off the polished walls of the tunnel. He could see the dark area of the alcove opening, and then, suddenly reflecting back into his eyes, was the glare of a miner's red, angry eyes. The tunnel was filled with the roaring, hissing challenge of an angry beast that weighed more than an African elephant. His sled's lights revealed the miner's open maw and those teeth that could bite a man in two.

Mama, it seemed, had come home. And she did not like the idea of something alien in the vicinity of her young.

Stoner braked the sled to a halt. He considered his choices. There were branching tunnels behind him, but they had not been mapped. If he retreated and tried to find an alternative route to the surface, he would have to do so quickly, for his oxygen supply was almost exhausted. Obviously there was enough oxygen for the miners at this level, but there was not enough for him. If he tried to breathe the air of the tunnel, he would gradually lose consciousness. The miners put out not only carbon dioxide but some pretty stinky gases.

"Listen, Mama," Stoner said, although the miner could not hear him and, if it had, certainly could not have understood. "We're friends. I'm not going to harm your babies."

He blinked the lights, eased the sled forward, hoping that the miner would give way and crawl into the nest alcove, letting him pass in peace. He had no weapons on the sled. He had figured that if he had to use a weapon on a miner, he would be dead anyhow, since the blast of the weapon would probably cause the tunnel to collapse.

The female miner did not give way. Instead, she opened her mouth and showed him her teeth. Those teeth could crush stone. They could crush the nose of the sled, too. And if she tore up the sled and got to him, she could drive dozens of long teeth the size of his wrist at their base through his body.

Lieutenant Jackie Garvey Rodrick had the duty in the communications room of the *Spirit of America*. She was getting regular reports from the *Dinahmite* and Jack Purdy. The day was lengthening, and still there had been no word from the crawlers inside the fog bank. Purdy reported no change in instrument readings or the solidity of the perpetual cloud that hid the lower river from view.

An uncommunicative, concerned Duncan Rodrick had just left the room when Jackie heard a call to base from a voice she recognized as that of Cindy McRae.

"Hi, Cindy," Jackie said brightly. "Where are you?" Since there was no radio traffic other than that of the colony on Omega, air talk had become very informal.

"Is that Lieutenant Rodrick?" Cindy asked.

"'Tis I," Jackie said. "What's happening?"

"Jackie, we're up north, not too far from Lake Dinah. My father is down a miner's tunnel."

"Would you care to repeat that?" Jackie asked, although the transmission had been perfectly clear. "Down a miner's tunnel?"

"Yes. And he's overdue."

"Cindy, hold on. I want the captain to hear this," Jackie said, even as she activated Rodrick's call button. Soon Rodrick was standing at her shoulder.

"It's been an hour," Cindy was saying, after having explained the situation and answered some questions from a slightly angry captain. "And he said he'd be back in forty-five minutes."

"Cindy, I take it you are not in communication with Stoner," Rodrick said, taking the mike.

"No. We lost communication at a very shallow level," Cindy said.

"How deep was he going?" Rodrick asked.

"The five-thousand-foot level," Cindy replied, her voice a bit shaky.

"Damn," Rodrick said, having closed the mike. "With forty-five minutes of oxygen." He shook his head. Jackie took the mike back.

"Cindy, I hate to say this, but there's not a thing we can do."

"You can send the mining machines," Cindy shot back, an edge of fear making her voice sharp.

"Cindy, honey," Jackie soothed, "you know how long it would take to sink a shaft even a hundred feet."

Rodrick took the mike. "Look, Cindy, just hang on. I'll run up there. Flip on your beacon so I can find you."

"Thank you," Cindy said.

"Keep me posted," Rodrick said, not taking time to kiss Jackie as he left the bridge. Soon he was driving a scout at maximum power upward and toward the northeast.

The female miner that blocked Stoner's only known exit to the surface seemed to be content with a standoff. She made no attempt to attack, but neither would she move aside into the nest alcove or back up. Stoner was now rebreathing stale air, and his chest was heaving with the effort to get enough oxygen.

"Move, Mama," he whispered hoarsely. "Be a good girl."

Mama, as he eased the sled forward, showed him her fearsome teeth again. He decided to give her five more minutes. If she had not gone into the alcove in that time, he would move directly toward her, playing a desperate game of chicken. It would have one of two outcomes: He would see her move aside, or he would drive right into those stone-crushing teeth.

"The captain will be here in about a half hour," Cindy told her mother. Neither of them was aware of the golden afternoon sun, the pleasant breeze, the beauty of summer's blooming flowers. The antics of a herd of silver-horned antelope, grazing and frolicking nearby, carefully avoiding the lighter areas of grass that marked miner traps, held no charm for them.

"We've got to do something," Betsy said.

"What?" Cindy asked, on the verge of tears.

"I don't know," Betsy said. But she took the mike, pressed the send key, and said, "Stoner. Stoner, you answer me!"

Cindy was considering wild options. There was the crawler's winch. It had a light cable on it that was capable of holding thousands of pounds. She could lower herself into the tunnel—but the cable had only two hundred feet of length. If Stoner had been that near the surface, he would have been in radio contact.

In desperation, she jumped down from the seat of the crawler and paced, then opened the cargo hatch and found one of the unmanned pipeline crawlers. She had seen them used before. They were simple to operate. She hauled the crawler out, hooked its terminal into the crawler's electronics, and tested. The cameras on the crawler were working well.

It was quite heavy, so she had to push and tug on it to get it to the entrance of the tunnel and into position.

Because of the failure of radio communications as the underground depth of a transmitter increased, Grace Monroe had worked with Stoner to provide a small "brain" for the crawlers, so that they were smart enough to guide themselves once out of radio control—to map, to photograph, and to return to the surface. Cindy sent the crawler down the shaft, and for a few minutes she saw only the polished walls of the tunnel. Then static began to distort the picture, and then there was nothing. There was nothing else she could do.

The receiver aboard Stoner's power sled began to pick up the probing frequencies from the crawler, and he tried to clear his brain. He was getting fuzzy from breathing the stale air of the sled. "Wha's that?" he asked himself. "'Nother sled? Nope. Crawler. Pipeline crawler."

He squinted his eyes to try to see better and saw only the dead-flesh colored miner, with her fierce, red eyes. "Ah, c'mon, Mama," he begged.

The miner, too, had detected the crawler, feeling its vibrations. Now her young were being threatened from front and rear, and she was confused. She could not turn in the tunnel proper, and the thing that was coming at her from behind was getting quite near. She hissed her anger and moved quickly into the nest alcove, curving her body in a C shape around the nest.

Stoner's hands did not seem to want to obey his orders. He was fumbling with the radio. The control mechanism on the pipeline crawler was a simple one and could be manipulated from the sled if he could find the right switches. Finally, just as he saw the gleam of the crawler's light, he found the combinations and slowed the crawler's speed, halted it near the nest. The female miner stuck her head out of the alcove and hissed an openmouthed warning, but she had encountered the crawlers before. She had watched one pass by the nest recently, and although her rudimentary intelligence had no time sense, she registered the crawler as something intrusive but harmless, something connected with the surface beings who provided lubrication in exchange for metals that were, to her, inedible.

Stoner's touch on the control stick was tentative and uncertain, for he was getting more and more dazed by oxygen deprivation. The crawler jerked toward the nest, then halted with its pointed snout quite near the miner. Stoner fumbled with the controls, and his fingers slipped. He tried again. From the snout of the crawler there began to pour a lubricant, now made of petroleum, which seemed to please the miners most. He had installed a container of the lubricant on the pipeline crawlers to be used as a peace offering if a miner should dispute the crawler's passage. Until now, it had never been necessary to use it.

The miner extended her head, and a rough rasp of a tongue began to lap up the lubricant. Stoner's dazed brain registered the fact that she seemed to have a pouch in the bottom of her mouth for storage, and then he was beginning to hope. He eased the crawler forward, and the miner allowed it out of the tunnel floor into the nest area. She was still intent on lapping up the lubricant. Stoner now eased his sled forward slowly, slowly, not wanting to startle her. He was directly opposite the nest alcove, and the miner jerked up her head to open her fierce mouth and hiss at him, but the anger seemed to be gone.

"Atta way, Mama," Stoner said, fighting the urge to close his eyes and sleep. He was past. He gunned the sled, and it began to shoot upward at full speed. Then he knew only blackness.

Cindy and Betsy had no warning. The sled, under full power, shot out of the tunnel like a cork popping out of a bottle. The sled almost made it to the top of the circular depression, then fell back, wheels finding no purchase in the loose dirt. It fell sideways across the tunnel opening, the wheels continuing to turn at top speed. Cindy leaped down the side of the depression. She fell against a spinning wheel, and the rubber cogs made a large welt of bruises on her thigh before she could move. Then she was fumbling at the hatch openers, seeing through the glass that her father was either dead or unconscious.

When she had the hatch open she reached in past his head and his hands to cut off the engine of the sled, then touched his face. It was warm, drenched with sweat, but he was not breathing.

"Mother! Get down here!" she shrieked.

Betsy came sliding down the dirt slope. Together they tugged and pulled but could not get Stoner out of the sled. Cindy, seeing that it was impossible to drag him out of the cramped, cocoonlike space, twisted his head as far to the right as she could and thrust her head down beside his to breathe into his mouth. He tasted of sweat, and she couldn't fit her mouth precisely over his, but she tried; she kept on forcing her breath into his mouth until she saw, at very close range, one of his eyelids flicker and open, and then he was gasping huge lungfuls of air and looking at them as if he did not see them. In a few seconds, however, he forced a grin.

"I guess I made it," he said.

"Of all the dumb tricks!" Betsy scolded.

None of them had noticed that Rodrick's scout had landed. Rodrick was just suddenly there, looking down, and his face was stormy. "Stoner, of all the dumb tricks," he said.

"Have you been writing his lines?" Stoner asked Betsy. He began to extricate himself from the sled. When he was out he said, "Captain, wanta give me a hand with this thing?"

"Leave it," Rodrick told him. "You won't be using it again."

"Well, I might be willing to leave the sled," Stoner said, "but I damned sure won't leave a sample of the best molybdenum ore I've seen on this planet."

Rodrick came down, and the four of them hoisted the sled out of the hole. Stoner removed the sample he had taken five thousand feet down. He felt fine. It had been a little challenging there for a few minutes, but if the sample showed rhenium, it would have been worth it.

"Smart move, women," he said, "sending down the crawler. An old mama miner had me cornered, wouldn't let me past her nest. She had some babies. They're about as ugly as an adult miner, but sorta cute in their own way."

"All right, Stoner," Rodrick said. "It *was* a dumb trick, but if you've got a minable deposit of ore that contains rhenium, well, that's the name of the game, isn't it?"

"It looks good, Dunc," Stoner said, examining the sample.

"Are you all right now?" Rodrick asked.

"Sure," Stoner said.

"You'd better head on home, then," Rodrick said.

"What have you heard?" Stoner asked.

Rodrick pushed back his hair. "Nothing. Nothing since they went into the fog."

"What about the scouts?" Cindy asked, for she knew that Clay was flying again. Her heart sank as Rodrick looked at her, concern in his eyes.

"Cindy, just before I landed I was given the word that contact had been lost with *Apache One*."

"Clay?"

Rodrick nodded grimly. "He was flying Jacob West's ship. He reported a problem and then—"

"Well, I know he's all right," Cindy said firmly. "He has to be all right."

NINE

When the *Spirit of America* lifted from the construction site, rockets bellowing, there had been dozens of cameras recording the event. This time, for this bare-bones ship, the *Free Enterprise*, there were none. The Desert Haven construction crews were gathered at a safe distance as the ship sent up a cloud of smoke and fire from the vast, circular pit in which she had been built. In a private bunker a small group of people, the financial backers, held their breath. Old Bill Farlock crossed his fingers and kept them crossed until the flare of rocket flames had diminished to a mere bright speck in the sky.

Maryann Ward was weeping openly. Brand Roebling took out his handkerchief and wiped his eyes. Karl Zeitz, who had sent no sons or daughters on the trip, wiped his nose. "They'll be back," he said gruffly.

"I hope we're here to greet them," Farlock replied.

"Well, gentlemen," Maryann Ward said, "there go several billion dollars."

"I got work to do," Zeitz told the others, hefting himself from a chair.

"Just a minute, Karl. I want to talk to you," Brand Roebling said. Zeitz turned impatiently. "I've got a Shaw Drive engine at Transworld. I've talked with the subcontractors. We can build a four-man ship capable of interstellar travel for two billion."

"What for?" Zeitz asked gruffly. "So the four of us can take off in it just before the bombs start falling?"

"To use as a courier ship between here and the Cygni planets," Roebling said.

"You just looking for contracts for Transworld?" Zeitz asked. "I've put enough money into space."

"Karl, if there is to be a future, it's out there," Maryann said. "Don't be so hardheaded."

"Well, hell, I guess you're right," Zeitz agreed. "Can't depend on the government to look ahead. Put me in for a quarter."

Maryann kissed old Zeitz on the cheek. "If you weren't so damned cantankerous, I'd marry you."

Zeitz grinned. "Is that how you made your money, Maryann, flirting with old men?"

"Beats working," Maryann said.

Duncan Rodrick, solid-minded as he was, had no idea that his deep concern about the expedition to the Great Misty River was setting the stage for a terrible misunderstanding with his wife that could have been straightened out by a few seconds of explanation. It was not his nature to be overly talkative. In times of crisis he tended to become even less open, and although Jackie could see his tenseness, he was stingy with his thoughts. Of course he was worried; he had fifty people out there on the western continent behind the fog. He was a man who took his responsibilities seriously, and until things were stable enough on Omega to have a formal election, he was responsible for the entire colony.

During the tense time following the disappearance of the crawlers into the fog, he frequently questioned his decision to send them. He personally knew every man and woman on the crawlers, and their loss would be another catastrophe for the colony and a terrible personal loss to him.

Had Mandy Miller not been on that expedition, Jackie would not have let her imagination run wild. But she had once suspected Rodrick of being in love with Mandy, and the fact that Jackie herself had had an affair with Mandy's late husband, Rocky Miller, made her mind fertile ground for suspicions. She interpreted all of Rodrick's concern to his worry about one person—Mandy Miller. If she had asked—or if he had been the sort to speak openly about his worries—the farce would have ended then and there. But the hurt she felt, compounded by her own guilt over sleeping with Rocky just before Duncan had surprised and delighted her by asking her to marry him, made her want to hurt Rodrick back.

She could not justify any overt attack on her husband. In fact, Jackie had no idea what she would do to return the hurt he gave her by, she felt, still being in love with Mandy, but she knew she would do something. She began to get an idea when she ran into Dr. James Wilson, a young, hard-working, happily married man, and the colony's expert on animal behavior. Wilson had been fascinated with the Omegan dragon, Baby, ever since she was brought to Hamilton by Jacob West and the admiral.

First Wilson asked the latest news about the expedition and then, "I don't suppose this would be a good time to talk to the captain about a new project."

"Not at the moment," Jackie said, thinking, *Because he's so worried about Mandy he can think of nothing else.*

"I just went for a ride this morning on Baby," Wilson told her. "She's a fantastic animal. I've never seen an animal take so to humans. She's more fond of humans than our age-old favorite pet, the dog. And she's a very useful animal. She could run all day long at a speed approaching thirty miles an hour, carrying two adults on her back."

"Yes, well," Jackie said.

"What I'd like to do," Wilson said enthusiastically, "is somehow to obtain a male dragon so that we can have a breeding pair. It could be very useful to the colony in the future."

Since getting a male dragon would involve someone going to the southern jungles, Jackie began to get her idea. "I think that's a worthy project, James," she said. "Let's talk about it once the expeditionaries have returned."

To find an obviously humanoid being in the valley of the Great Misty River generated more questions than answers. When the expedition saw the first of the men of the valley, overseeing the work of the Whorsk in the fields, there was, in Paul Warden's mind, one answer: The fellow was so human that Theresita's pregnancy was no longer a mystery. The father of the child was somewhere in the valley.

The tall, bronzed male took no direct notice of the crawlers. Warden ordered slow movement toward the distant city. He saw a few more of the tall, handsome men, one of them fiercely lashing a cringing Whorsk.

"Nice guys," Paul growled to Sage.

"It ties in with what Theresita said about the Whorsk sending shipments of their larvae to the valley," she said. "She knew the larvae would end up as slaves to a superior group of some sort." As she spoke, she was unable to take her eyes from the few valley men out in the fields, for she had never seen such handsome men.

Warden wanted to continue directly to the city, but he was a cautious man. He had fifty people, including himself, as his responsibility. It was very odd that their presence had not created any excitement, only passing looks from the valley men in the fields.

"I think we'd better try to have a little talk with one of these dudes," he said. He ordered the crawlers to halt and draw up in defensive formation. Then he guided his own crawler to a point near a small platform built among the green crops. One of the bronzed men stood on the platform. He watched them without movement as Sage and Warden dismounted from the crawler and began to walk toward the platform along a path.

A group of Whorsk slaves working near the platform looked up, saw the newcomers, and stood idle for a few seconds. The bronzed being on the platform cracked a wicked, long whip over their heads and spoke in a stern, loud voice in the Whorsk language. The Whorsk went back to work at a frantic pace.

Warden halted a few feet away from the platform. The valley man turned to look down, his face mostly hidden by his golden visor. Up close, he looked slightly more than human. He was almost too perfect in his bodily proportions. He was just over six feet tall. His torso, bare to the sun, was not overly muscled like a weight lifter, but obviously powerful. His legs were long and perfectly shaped.

Paul, like most members of the colony, had picked up a few phrases of the Whorsk language. "We come as friends," he said.

The man lifted his visor, removed the helmet. His hair was dark, tightly curled, and cut close to his head. He had a strong, masculine nose. His face was rounded, and his large, wide-set eyes gave a hint of an Oriental tilt under arched, perfectly shaped eyebrows. His lips were full, sensuous.

"We come from afar," Warden said. "We come as friends."

"Your childish attempts to master a language not suited to your vocal apparatus do not impress me," the man answered harshly, arrogantly, and in English. Then, before Warden could express his surprise, "You will continue downriver. Land at the wharf between the two golden towers. You have been expected."

"Just who is it that's expecting us?" Warden asked.

"Go," the man said, leaping lightly down from the platform, turning his back and walking away.

"Well, I guess we go," Warden said.

Suddenly the valley man turned and walked swiftly back to face Sage. His eyes, she saw, were a translucent green, like good jade. They seemed to burn as he looked deeply into her eyes. "I have changed my mind," he said. "I will go with you."

Not waiting for acknowledgment, he took Sage's arm and guided her toward the crawler. "You may call me Yanee," he announced, and once again his odd green eyes pierced her very being.

Warden did not like the way the valley man was looking at Sage. He did not like anything about the entire situation. The man was entirely too confident. He carried only his whip, no sign of a weapon, but he spoke *English*, and he had said they were expected. That told Warden that the people of the valley had capabilities he could not yet explain.

"I will not take my entire group downriver," he decided as Yanee helped Sage into the crawler.

"As you wish," Yanee said.

Paul flipped on his transmitter. "Well, gang," he said, "our new friend here has invited us to visit his city. We'll take two crawlers. This one, and the one Dr. Miller is in. The rest of you circle the wagons and stand by." He glanced at Yanee, but Yanee was ignoring him, concentrating on Sage. "These guys speak English with a trace of a British accent, so if things go a little screwy, don't talk in the open. And be prepared to execute maneuver Sugar-Fox." S.F. That meant "Scram, fast." In that event, the crawlers would try to break out of the valley and into the open desert, where they would have air cover from the scouts and could be picked up. "You're the honcho while I'm gone, Renato."

Mandy's crawler pulled up, and the two vehicles sped down the smooth roadway on the riverbank. They had gone half a mile when Sage gasped and pointed. On the bank of the river was a row of stakes onto which five Whorsk had been impaled—the sharp stake driven up into their bodies from the crotch. Three of the Whorsk were squirming in agony. The other two seemed to be dead. A toothed scavenger bird was tearing at the exposed entrails of one of the living.

Mandy hated the Whorsk for what they had done to the colonists who had tried to leave Hamilton under Rocky's leadership, but such cruelty shocked her. "Paul," she called on the radio.

"Yes, Mandy," Paul said.

"I'm not so sure we should go into the city."

"They are nice guys," Paul said, "aren't they?"

"Maudlin pity for insects?" Yanee asked, laughing. "They are nothing more than beasts of labor."

"Yeah," Paul muttered disgustedly. "Mandy, since we're here to find out what's going on, I guess we'll go ahead."

The road ended just beyond the impaled Whorsk, and Yanee indicated that the crawlers should go into the river. It was only a short distance by water to a large wharf between two tall, golden obelisks. The crawlers were able to get up onto the wharf via a slanted ramp, and there, waiting in tall, stern dignity, were four more valley people, two men and two women.

"Obelisks, a pyramid," Mandy said on the radio. "Paul, anything familiar about all that? And the shape of the helmets?"

"I've been reluctant to admit it," Paul answered.

"A long river through desert, fertile fields in an enclosed valley?" Mandy continued.

"If a Whorsk Moses appears and says 'let my people go,' then we will have something to think about," Paul said.

The leader of the delegation on the wharf was a bit taller than Yanee, and his hair had turned a shade of burnished silver. The two men were dressed in kilts like Yanee, but their short skirts were of a gleaming white, finely woven cloth. The women wore long, shimmering garments that ended just above jeweled sandals. The bodices exposed enough cleavage to catch the eyes of the men in Paul's group.

The leader took one step forward and, with both hands held stiffly at his side, eyed Warden with what could only be called a sneer. His nose, like Yanee's, was long and straight, and his wide-set eyes were slightly hooded at the inner corners, the effect making it seem that the eyes were wider at the outer corners. His helmet was white, laced with gold, and had a golden star mounted at the front. The second male was older, his body showing signs of sagging skin and wrinkles. His skin was tight over his prominent cheekbones, and his lips had narrowed with age. His eyes were mere slits.

The taller of the two women was the more spectacularly beautiful, with large, jade-green eyes, a nose of classic beauty, and a strong but delicate chin. She stood with her head high, a proud posture. Her hair was hidden under a close-fitting helmet, which extended in wings outward over her cheeks. The second woman, shorter, had a more Oriental face and shoulder-length hair, raven black, thick, and heavy. Her full lips turned naturally downward in a cold expression of disdain.

"I am Suses," the taller man said.

"I am Commander Pau—"

"Your names don't matter," Suses cut in arrogantly. "Hear me. You are intruders. Through the Whorsk we have made it plain that you are not welcome here, but apparently your intelligence is lacking. Since you have intruded, we must apprise you of the nature of things on this planet, which you have so ignorantly called Omega."

Paul looked quickly at Mandy Miller, wondering how this Suses knew so much.

"This planet has had a name for sixty centuries, and that name is not Omega."

The three men who had been riding in the back of Warden's crawler and the six men from Mandy's vehicle had formed behind Paul, Mandy, and Sage. They had all noted that Yanee did not carry a weapon, and that the two men on the wharf had nothing more than an elaborately decorated sword in a sheath at their waists.

"You're thinking," Suses said, "that your puny weapons can protect you."

Warden felt a chill, and his hand began to move slowly toward his laser.

Suses raised his gaze up, far above, where two scout ships came slowly downriver. He drew his sword.

Paul's hand was on the butt of his laser.

Suses drew his sword, which had a typical blade and a sharp point, and suddenly there was the smell of ozone in the air, and the trailing scout dropped swiftly out of formation and began to tumble. A scout without power had the gliding characteristics of an egg.

Clay Girard had rested in Hamilton City for a couple of days but was now back with Jack Purdy on standby above the cloud of fog. Jack, in the lead in *Dinahmite,* was lazing along, making wide circles over the river. Clay, in *Apache One,* had his radio on, listening for any order from Jack or any word from below. He had brought Jumper with him, and the little black dog was sleeping peacefully in the other seat. They were making a long, straight run down the river when Clay was suddenly jerked forward in his harness. All power had stopped in an instant, and the ship slowed immediately, then began to fall.

"Jack, I've lost power," Clay said into the voice-activated mike at his throat.

That much was heard by Jack and the duty officer back in Hamilton aboard the *Spirit of America*.

Apache One dropped her nose, began to spin on her axis, and then tumbled. Clay hit the stabilizer jets used to keep the ship in position in space, but absolutely nothing happened. He had been flying at thirty thousand feet. He had only seconds. The ship was falling like a rock, and with the same stability. He was buffeted about, his weight being thrown against his harness, his head snapping back and forth.

"Rockets," he said, having to force the word out between his teeth against the buffeting and the force of gravity. He missed the rocket controls, then forced his hand to them. If he could fire at least one rocket, the drive would stabilize the ship and send it shooting off in the direction in which the nose happened to be pointed at the time of rocket firing.

Nothing.

Wing extension, he thought, and fought to reach those controls. He was falling faster and faster, and there was a good chance that even if he could extend the wings they would be ripped away, but perhaps they would hold and give him some gliding ability, enough to bring the ship out of its tumbling, spinning fall.

His instruments were not functioning. He could only guess that he had fallen through the fifteen thousand foot level as the precious seconds ticked off. There was no pilot-ejection system because one does not eject from a ship moving in multiples of the speed of sound or from a ship in the vacuum of space. He felt full movement in the wing-extension control and waited. Nothing happened. He was falling, accelerating under the force of Omega's gravity. He was beginning to be very dizzy and saw red and black spots in front of his eyes from the buffeting his head was taking. He did not think for one second about dying, only about possible ways to stabilize the ship.

Even as he was fighting the powerful forces of gravity, even as he used all of his concentration in an effort to save himself and the ship, a part of his mind reached out in sympathy to Jumper. The little dog was being buffeted about, and over the roar of wind and the clanging and clacking of the tortured ship, Clay heard one frantic little "yip" as Jumper was thrown out of the harness and banged into the console to disappear from Clay's peripheral vision.

The forward motion of the ship had carried it beyond the fog and the river. As the ship rolled and spun, he could see the brown, lifeless desert whirling past his windscreen. He was going to smash into that sandy, rocky waste, and it was going to happen within seconds.

On the same river but far to the north, the honeymooners had not been working very hard. It was too pleasant to lie on the deck of the boat and soak up the sun, to sit in the shade of the canopy with a tall, cool drink, to make love either in the steamy, damp, tropical air, with sweat to lubricate their movements, or in the comfort of the air-conditioned cabin after a cool shower.

Jacob had managed to photograph a few jumps of the river monsters with huge teeth as they chased frightened tunalike fish leaping into the air. And he had collected enough mud samples to fill all of Mandy Miller's specimen bottles. He himself had no desire to go ashore, where there were things with teeth, but Theresita, remembering the sweetness of the jungle fruits and the nourishing nuts, insisted. Their diet was thus supplemented by the very things that had kept Theresita alive during her much slower drift down the river.

"You know, you savage American," Theresita said fondly as they lay comfortably nude in the sun, "I didn't think I could learn to love you more."

"I have cast an ancient Mescalero charm on you," Jacob said.

"Don't get, how do you say, the big head, but I think I have found myself a *man*."

Jacob made a muscle with his right arm.

"No, idiot," she said. "Most men have muscles." She raised an arm and flipped a certain dangling portion of his anatomy almost painfully with her forefinger. "And all men have *that*."

"It's my brain," Jacob said, raising himself on one elbow and trailing a finger around one firm, large breast, feeling it slide on Theresita's perspiration.

"There is more to a man than muscles. He has to have something here." She punched a finger in the area of his heart.

"Let's stay out here for another month or so," Jacob suggested.

"Why not?" she said, shrugging.

Drifting and dreaming and loving, they killed another couple of days, and then Jacob put power to the boat and flew down the river. He had been listening to the radio chatter and knew that an expedition had started toward the fog over the southern portion of the river. Theresita seemed able to ignore the radio and made no mention of events back in the colony.

"I think we should call in and have them pick us up," he said after they had stood several days and nights alternating watches, driving the boat under full power downriver.

"There is still vacation time left," she said. "You want to get back to join the expedition, eh? Well, I won't let you. I will sabotage the boat first."

When they came out of the jungle and into the plains, Jacob called in and said that they would be at the agreed-upon point of rendezvous the next day. That was on the plains just above the giant waterfall. They reached the point early in the day. According to broadcast reports, the expedition had just gone into the fog. Jacob was restless. He liked Clay Girard, but he figured that *he* needed to be flying *Apache One*, not a sixteen-year-old kid.

Theresita wanted to go ashore. He tied the boat well and accompanied his wife while she gathered biological specimens for the scientists. Jacob sat on a sun-warmed rock, stretched out his long legs, and watched her with great pleasure. If she had found a man, he had found a real woman. It was a union, he thought wryly, not made for convention—an Apache and a Pole—but it was all the union he ever wanted.

He noticed that Theresita was squatting, looking at something on the ground.

"Something interesting?" he called.

"Something odd," she called back.

He got up slowly and walked over to look over her shoulder. Theresita was studying a small patch of needle-pointed, pulpy plants—somewhat like cacti, but alien. There was an odd, enticing fragrance in the air, and, thinking that it was coming from the plants, she broke off a stem and lifted it to her nose. The aroma was sweetly tart and powerful. She turned and looked up at him. Her eyes looked slightly glazed, and she had a dumb smile on her face. Then suddenly she seemed to be boneless, crumpling to the ground and lying motionless.

Jacob squatted beside her. She was breathing slowly, deeply. Her eyes were closed, and when he lifted a lid he saw only white. He shook her, yelling at her. She seemed to be in a stupor so deep that nothing could rouse her. She still clutched the plant in her hand, and he knocked it away, thinking that she had been poisoned. He slapped her face lightly. No response. He ran to the boat and gave an emergency call.

"Jacob," the *Spirit*'s duty officer, Emi Zuki, said, "there's a ship on the way. Estimated time of arrival, just over forty minutes Hamilton time."

He ran back to her. She was lying there as if she were sleeping, a smile on her lips. He gingerly picked up the plant she had been holding and sniffed it. Its odor was not unpleasant, and nothing happened to him. Maybe she had just fainted. Maybe it was something to do with her pregnancy. He put her head on his lap and sat there, praying, first to God, and then to a family of Apache spirits. When he heard the sonic boom that told of an approaching scout, he put her head down gently and stood up, shading his eyes until he saw the scout dropping like a stone to slow, hover, and then land nearby. He lifted Theresita in his arms—a big woman, heavy—and he ran as fast as he could and accepted the help of the pilot to get her into the vehicle.

Dr. Raymond Bryant was on duty in the *Spirit of*

America's sick bay. This was fortunate because Bryant was the colony's expert in toxicology. He took a quick look at Theresita and turned to Jacob. "What did she eat and drink just before this happened?"

"The usual. Distilled water from the river. Ship's stores, some vodka, and the same jungle fruits and nuts she ate before, same as we eat now."

"And nothing else?"

"Not a thing that I know of," Jacob said. "Do you think she's been poisoned?"

"I'm going to run some blood tests," Bryant said. "But she gives all appearances of being quite heavily drugged."

"She was gathering specimens for the botanists," Jacob said.

"Did you bring them?"

"No. I didn't think—"

"Send a ship and get them as quickly as you can," Bryant said.

Jacob did better than send a ship. He took one himself, found the specimen bags where Theresita had left them, remembered the odd plant she had had in her hand, and added samples of it to the others, in a separate bag.

In anticipation of Jacob's return and after having run some quick blood samples, Dr. Bryant had called Dr. Kwait, who was working in the fields near town. Kwait took the bags from Jacob to discard previously identified plants, plants that had been found to be harmless to humans, and ended up with four unidentified specimens—the pulpy, pointed one among them. He narrowed things down by identifying three of the plants as to family, then picked up the pulpy one in a pair of tongs. He sniffed.

"Let's run a couple of tests on this one," he said.

The scientific teams rallied to the new emergency. Grace Monroe was running independent analyses of Theresita's blood and of the juices of the plant. She and the biochemist arrived at the same conclusion at about the same time.

"This is one helluva substance," Grace said to Max,

who was leaning against her worktable watching. "It bonds to the synapses in the brain."

"Sounds grim," Max said. His fields were physics and rocketry, and anything electrical or mechanical.

"It makes the most powerful opiate or hallucinogen seem tame," she said.

"You mean Theresita's just on a drug high?"

"Or low," Grace said.

Max did have a good memory. "Hey, she said she showed all the symptoms of drug withdrawal when she first woke up among the Whorsk."

"Indeed," Grace said. "Now we've got to find something to neutralize this stuff without doing damage." She went to the biochemistry lab, Max tagging along. He was attentively silent as Grace discussed methods with her fellow scientists, then decided to go have a drink when he continued to be ignored. When he came back they were still at it, and Theresita was still sleeping peacefully. Her brain waves showed a pattern that caused Dr. Bryant to check and recheck.

"What's the problem?" Jacob asked anxiously as he watched Bryant work.

"Well, son," the fifty-year-old doctor said, "I don't want to state this positively, but from these brain patterns and from analysis of the hormones in her system, I'd say that she is a woman in the throes of extreme sexual excitement."

Thanks to the work done back on Earth on the chemical products produced by the human brain, the characteristics of the drug were soon analyzed, and an artificial endorphin quickly synthesized.

"You're going to shoot her up with an untested drug?" Jacob asked when Grace explained what they had planned.

"Jacob, how much do you know about brain chemistry?" Grace asked.

"Not much."

"Well, put simply, the chemical in the drug is bonded, literally bonded, to certain synapses in her brain. This prevents the passage of the signals from neuron to neuron. Fortunately, the normal unconscious functions have not been affected—breathing, heart rate, all the things that the brain does without conscious effort on our part—but it's serious nevertheless. We are one hundred percent certain that there's memory loss in this condition. If she stays like this long enough, she will no longer be Theresita. She'll forget who she is and everything she's learned since she was a baby."

Jacob's bronze face was impassive, but he was yelling inside, *No! No!*

"There's really no great risk with this treatment," Grace assured him. "We're not even sure that it'll do what we want it to do, which is dissolve the bonding chemical. But it won't affect any other part of the brain."

"Do it," Jacob said miserably.

He sat beside her, her lax hand in his, as they injected a surprisingly minute amount of the synthetic chemical into the carotid artery leading to her brain. The effect was almost instantaneous. Her eyelids flickered, and she began to writhe in a way that made Jacob's face flush with heat. She was moving as if in the act of love. And then her eyes opened, and she saw Jacob's face.

"Darling," she whispered. "Oh, my darling. Sooooo good."

Then she saw Grace, and her mouth opened and she looked around, startled. "Hey," she said, "I thought we were going to go for a boat ride. What am I doing in the hospital?"

"Just take it easy," Jacob said, squeezing her hand. "Everything's all right."

"Jacob?" There was puzzlement in her eyes now. "Did we go to the river?"

"Yes," he replied.

"Theresita," Grace said, "we think we've found the drug that was used on you when you were hurt. In fact, you found it, in that plant you picked."

"I did?" She squinted. "Jacob, did we go to the city? Did you see it? The pyramids—"

"Pyramids?" Jacob asked.

"You've had a small memory loss," Grace said. "It's the effect of the drug."

"But I *remember*," she insisted. "I remember lying there in a bed, like a hospital bed, and *they* were there, putting something like mud on me, pulling my wounds together, and I felt nothing. I remember—" She halted in confusion. She squeezed Jacob's hand. "I remember *him*. The baby's father."

"Max, I think you'd better call the captain," Jacob said. "Now you just take it easy, honey, until Dunc gets here. Try to remember while you rest."

Rodrick arrived on the run. There was still no word from Warden. He stood beside Theresita's bed and listened first to Grace.

"It's a very odd drug," Grace reported. "She was able to withdraw from her body's and brain's craving for it once they stopped administering it to her, but it has the effect of blocking the movement of thought through the brain, and once it adheres to a synapse, it stays permanently unless treated. We thought at first that it would destroy memory, but now it seems that it merely blocks memory, progressively, the longer it is administered. Theresita was never clean of the dosage she received while she was being healed of her wounds, so she had memory blockage of recent events. But the compound we gave her not only broke loose the new bondings, made when she did nothing more than sniff that odd plant; it apparently is freeing memories that have been blocked since she left the river."

"What can you tell us, Theresita?" Rodrick asked.

"They are cruel and completely self-oriented. They enslave the Whorsk. They are complete hedonists, and they know where you are, how many there are of you, and your weapons capabilities. They are so beautiful physically, each of them perfect, and yet so inhuman in their thinking."

"And their weapons?" Rodrick asked.

"I don't know. I spent my time in a suite of rooms. I could move about but always in a daze. For a long time I was unable to move my arm, where I was hurt, and then Yanee came to me and—" She paused and squeezed Jacob's hand. "That must have been when he started giving me the drug. I remember only—only a haze of sensuality, of endless lovemaking, only now I wouldn't call it that, although it seemed so to me at the time. I would call it now mindless fornicating."

"The electrical field?" Rodrick asked.

"Nothing. He never talked to me about anything but himself—how wonderful he was, how lucky I was to be his. I know only this: They are evil, Captain. Please be careful of them. They were not worried at all that you have spaceships and weapons—only that you were stealing the metals that were rightfully theirs."

"How did you communicate with them?" Grace asked.

Theresita frowned for a moment. "Oh, yes. At first I couldn't understand anything they said. Then one of them, a woman, came to my hospital room and made it clear to me that she wanted me to talk, to give her the names of various objects in my language." She shook her head. "It didn't make much of an impression on me at the time, but I think I understand now. I quite naturally started talking in Russian, but she kept indicating no, no. I don't know why I switched to English, but when I did, she nodded in the affirmative. It seems logical, now, that they'd been listening in on your radio talk and wanted to know more about that language, because, looking back on it, she couldn't possibly have picked up English that quickly. They'd been analyzing it before I came to them."

"What about their language?" Grace asked.

"I really don't remember much about it. It was full of hard sounds, that's all I know."

"Think hard, Theresita," Rodrick said. "Tell me anything you can think of that might give us a clue to their technological and scientific knowledge."

"Well," she said, "aside from jewelry and ornaments, there was very little metal, as I remember. The coverings of my bed were smooth and fine, so they must have good skills in making textiles. *Hmmm.* Oh, the lights. Definitely electrical. And it was cool in my room and later in Yanee's place, so they had some method of air-conditioning."

"Plastics?" Rodrick asked.

"No, I don't think so. The eating utensils were metal, perhaps silver-plated. The bowls were finely made, not just pottery. Oh, there was hot and cold running water, a huge bath carved from some kind of smooth stone, and the toilet flushed with a pull cord."

"Anything else you can think of?" Rodrick asked. "Anything you saw that resembled a weapon? A chance remark you overheard?"

"I never heard any music," Theresita said. "There was no medium for entertainment. No holoscreens."

She mused for a few moments. "And they never smiled. I can remember that distinctly. I never saw one of them smile."

"Okay, Theresita," Rodrick said, leaning over to pat her shoulder. "I guess you'd better get some rest." He was on his way to the door.

"There's one more thing, Captain," Theresita said. "You can see the sky. From the window of the place where Yanee kept me, I could see the river, growing crops, and I could see the sun and the sky."

Rodrick went to the bridge. Ito Zuki, the astronavigator, was on communications duty.

"Have you been able to reestablish contact with *Apache One* yet, Ito?" Rodrick asked.

"I was just about to page you, Dunc," he said. "It's more than a communications problem. The scout's gone down."

Rodrick felt all blood drain from his face.

"No word from Paul?"

"None, sir," Ito said.

"Ito, sound the red alert. I want all qualified combat troops ready. Have the scouts ready to move the force." He rubbed his chin. "Jack Purdy was with Clay, right?"

"Yes, sir. He's over the scene now."

"Tell Jack to stay put. Any sign that Clay's alive?"

"One moment," Ito said, punching buttons. "*Dinahmite*, the *Spirit:* We request a report on the condition of the downed scout ship."

"I'm just going down low now, Ito," Jack Purdy sent. "I'll let you know in a minute or two, but he went in hot and fast."

Rodrick swallowed hard. Clay. Sixteen years old. One

of the young ones who were the future of the colony. "Damn," he said.

Rodrick turned away so that Ito could not see his face. In the midst of crisis he had no time to mourn, but he had trouble controlling his emotions. Losing any man was bad, but losing one of the young ones, ah. Sixteen years old. Clay. For one moment there flashed into his mind an image of the way Clay had looked that day years ago, when he was brought to the bridge, a twelve-year-old stowaway, how he was ready to fight anyone to protect his little dog. Rodrick swallowed hard, ran a hand quickly through his hair, and emptied his mind of concern for Clay, reserving sorrow for another time.

Ito was on the communicator, relaying Rodrick's orders. Rodrick was trying to put it all together. Theresita had said she could see the sun. That was a bit scary. It was one thing to create a field that manifested itself as a fog, but it was something else to be able to control that field so minutely that you could see out of it but not in. He was forming a plan, a desperate plan, and he was not sure he would implement it. He was already missing fifty people and a sixteen-year-old boy who had been like a son to him.

But Mandy is out there, he thought, and then quickly added the other names. He would not let his emotions rule his decisions. It just might be possible to break through the fog, get below it, get inside the protective envelope. There the weapons of the scouts would represent a considerable force.

In addition to being worried, he was plainly and simply angry. He had left a world where greed and idiocy had threatened total destruction. He was sick of war, but it had already begun on a new planet, a planet so large, so bountiful—except for the lack of heavy metals—that it could support a population about four times that of Earth without poverty. It did not always take two sides to start a war. Often in Earth's history, peaceful people had been exterminated by aggressors, but the people on the Great Misty River had made no overt move against the colony.

Had he been wrong in sending an armed expedition to violate their self-chosen privacy?

In this mood of doubt and indecision he looked up as Grace Monroe came onto the bridge. "Duncan," she said, "Theresita remembered something else. While she was still in their hospital, perhaps partially sedated, she was questioned very closely about her planet of origin. She was able to point out our sun to them on what she remembers as being quite a good star atlas."

"What did they have to say to that?" Rodrick asked.

"They laughed, Duncan," Grace said, an odd look on her face. "And one of them said, 'Oh, one of *those*.'"

Rodrick was shaking his head. "I don't think I'm ready to accept that."

Grace continued, "One of the men who had laughed said, 'Well, they were good breeders, even then.'"

Perhaps it was the last remark that made up Rodrick's mind. "Ito," he said, "we'll give Paul another four hours. If we haven't heard from him by then, we'll go in with all the force we can muster."

Paul Warden saw the tall man called Suses raise his sword, smelled something like ozone, then watched in horror as *Apache One* slowed suddenly and began to tumble out of control. He was, of course, astounded by a weapon that could stop a hydrogen engine, but he was a man who had long training in handling emergencies. His hand weapon came out of its holster, and he was pointing it at Suses.

"Listen," he said evenly, "if that ship crashes, you won't outlive the pilot by a full second."

Suses, that cold look of command on his face, lowered his sword and slid it back into its sheath.

"You'd better do something fast," Paul said, watching the *Apache One* tumble off toward the west. He heard a woman laugh. Out of the corner of his eye he saw that the darker female had raised a delicate wand. Alarm sent the impulse to his finger to pull the trigger, and he was also directing his hand to spray the laser beam over all four of the valley people, but his finger would not move. Mandy Miller collapsed. One by one, as Warden fought a creeping paralysis, the others crumpled to the stone wharf. Paul had a floating feeling, as if he were being wafted to and fro in the air by vagrant currents. And then he knew nothing.

Clay had tried everything he had been taught. He had gone through training exercises in which the power to the hydrogen engine had been cut off deliberately. He knew the drill. He knew how to use the engine, the rockets, and the stabilizing jets to bring a ship under control, but with all sources of power—even batteries—inoperative, nothing worked. He had only a few seconds left before *Apache One* smashed into the desert. He had an idea—it was a maneuver he had never tried, because all specifications, all logic, said that it would not work. The mechanism that made it possible was not intended for use in the air. The scout was equipped with a manually operated crank, which could fold or unfold the stubby wings of the craft. It was intended for use by ground crews.

Clay clawed open the covering that concealed the hand crank, jerked the collapsible handle into position, and, fighting g-forces and the battering of his head and body by the spinning, tumbling fall, began to crank as fast as he could. The wings began to fold outward from their nooks in the body of the scout. The whirling, spinning desert was coming closer, closer. He heard a snapping, groaning sound of metal and thought that the wings were going to be ripped off, but he felt a change in the ship's wild tumbling, and then the wings were fully extended. He fought the controls, which, without power, caused his arms to strain. The ship ceased tumbling and went into an ordinary spin, nose downward. He knew how to get out of that, but the ground was there—just in front of him—sandy, smooth, but solid, so solid that he would be nothing more than a jellied blob, hitting it at this speed. He dragged on the controls, making grunting sounds of effort, and the ship stabilized. The nose began to come up, up while the ground was reaching for him.

Jack Purdy, unable to raise Clay on the radio, had followed the wildly tumbling *Apache One* all the way down. "Good boy," he said, when he saw the wings begin to extend slowly. But he had little hope. The wings were designed for conservation of fuel, useful in long, slow photographic flights and for landing without rockets. At the speed the ship was falling, they would surely be ripped out by the roots from the body of the ship, but to Jack's surprise, they held. The ship stopped tumbling, came out of the spin just the way Jack had taught Clay. The nose was coming up. There was a chance if he could get the nose up higher, because he was going down into what seemed to be an old lake bed, with miles of sand, almost as smooth as a runway.

He held his breath. He saw the ship touch, then there was nothing but a giant cloud of dry, powdery sand. He muttered an oath. It was all over.

The nose came up, up, slowly, slowly. Clay could almost see the individual grains of sand, he was so near the ground. The wind of passage was creating a dust cloud behind him. He held her up as long as he could. Without instruments he could only estimate his speed, perhaps something over four hundred miles per hour. He heard a hissing, grating sound, felt a drag, and braced himself. Dust rose to cloud the windscreen, and then he was being buffeted in a different way, as if he were riding over round corrugations. There was now a screaming of distressed metal. He clung to the controls, keeping the nose oriented. He was down, and the ship's momentum was giving him a four hundred mile an hour ride—a wild ride. If the ship slewed, she would tumble, roll, and that would be it. She would wind up as a crumpled ball of metal with some battered flesh inside.

Was she beginning to slow? Yes! Yes! The vibrations were lessening. A quick glance to the rear showed him only the dust cloud extending out behind him. And then the ship hit a slight rise and he was airborne for long seconds, riding smoothly, then slamming down with a crash that threatened to cause him to black out, but still he clung to the controls, trying to keep the ship sliding nose first.

When he lost her, he thought he would be dead in a

second or two. She went spinning across the smooth sand like a spun bottle on a tabletop, and his head was thrown against the cockpit side with a force that caused him to see nothing but black for a moment, then settling dust and sunlight. He was alive. The ship had come to rest. He leaned back and gave his head a few seconds to clear. At first he could not get the canopy open because there was no power. He jerked the cover off the manual canopy crank and had to stop twice to rest, to try to clear his head. Then the canopy was open. He fell back twice as he tried to climb out, but finally made it and tumbled to the sand.

Apache One was finished. The tough alloys of her hull had been battered and worn through by her wild ride over the pebbly sand. Hydraulic and lubrication fluids were seeping into the sand. He heard a hissing sound and realized that the hydrogen tanks had been ruptured. Fear hit him for the first time. He had survived a total power loss, and he did not want to be killed by a hydrogen explosion now that he was safely on the ground. He turned to run, his head still fuzzy, then he remembered.

"Jumper!" he shouted, turning to scramble up the side of the scout.

At first Clay had tried to rig a harness to hold Jumper in the seat when the little dog flew with him, but Jumper did not like that. He got bumped around a little when Clay did acrobatics, but he managed to stay in the seat fairly well by curling up tightly in the curves designed to accommodate a man's buttock. But now he was not in the seat, and Clay was remembering the fierce battering he had taken, even in his harness, in the tumbling ship.

"Hey, Jumper," he called, leaning into the cockpit, his stomach against the side of the ship. There was the sound of the escaping hydrogen. Probably, since all electrical power was off, there would not be any spark to ignite the fuel. "Jumper, where are you?"

There were only a couple of places large enough to conceal Jumper. Clay hung over the edge of the cockpit and ran his hand behind the seats and felt only the equipment normally stored there. Then he had to push himself down farther to reach under the seat. He felt Jumper's warmth and dragged him out by one leg. The little dog was limp and lifeless as Clay lifted him and, with some difficulty, began to push himself up out of the cockpit. He was more worried now about Jumper than about the possibility of an explosion. He figured that if the leaking fuel had not ignited by now it was not going to; but then, as he pushed with one hand and tried to lift himself backward out of the cockpit, a movement on the instrument panel caught his eye. The fuel gauge was registering a serious fuel leak, and more of the instruments were now giving readings.

Electrical power had been restored. The ship was seriously damaged. An exposed wire, a sudden short circuit as one of the automatic systems tried to function— almost anything could ignite the leaking fuel.

He rolled off the scout, carefully protecting the limp body of Jumper in one arm, and scrambled to his feet. His head was clear now, and he knew that he was in deadly peril. He ran as he had never run before, inspired by sheer panic, and in his haste he stumbled and fell, jumped up, and ran as hard as he could. Behind him a fuel-monitoring circuit, damaged, persistently sent its signals to an audible warning system, and a jet of pressurized hydrogen shot out into a tangle of damaged wiring. A live wire jerked and trembled in the force of the jet and then made contact with another wire, and there was a spark.

A great flash of light was followed by a shock wave that lifted Clay and threw him ten feet forward over the top of a small dune. He lay there, stunned, as the roar of the explosion diminished, then disappeared.

"Hey, Jumper," he whispered, remembering the dog in his arms, lifting him, feeling him, finding, to his relief, that Jumper was now breathing. And there was another sound as the *Dinahmite* came in for a hot-rockets landing a couple of hundred feet away. Clay struggled dizzily to his feet and started walking toward the *Dinahmite* even as Jack Purdy leaped out and started running toward him.

"Jumper's hurt," Clay said, as Purdy reached him.

"Kid, that was a piece of flying," Jack said. "Are you all right?"

"We've got to get Jumper to the colony quick so Dr. Wilson can take a look at him," Clay said.

"I mean *that* was flying," Jack repeated.

"Hurry, Jack," Clay insisted. "Jumper—"

Purdy laughed. Here the boy had almost been killed, had saved himself with a display of courage and cool thinking that would have done credit to the most veteran pilot, and all he could think of was the little dog.

"Okay, kid," Purdy said. "Let's go."

"Wait," Clay said, because Jumper had moved in his arms. There was a questioning whine from the dog, and then he was lifting his head and trying to get down from Clay's arms. Clay knelt and placed him on the sand. Jumper got to his feet, fell once, and then wobbled around in a circle, whining.

"He's going to be all right," Purdy said. "I think he just had his bell rung."

Jumper barked once, in total puzzlement, and then lifted one leg and tried to leave his doggie mark on Jack's boot. Jack yelled and leaped away, and Jumper looked up, saw Clay, and barked.

"Let's go," Jack said. "I need to call in and tell them you're all right."

"Tell them Jumper's all right, too," Clay added, as the dog started running toward the *Dinahmite*.

Sage Bryson awoke to a feeling of well-being. She stretched her arms, yawned, and opened her eyes to see a setting of barbaric splendor. She was lying in the center of a huge bed. The delicate lavender sheets under her had the feel of silk. She was dressed only in a filmy, clinging gown. It was the most soothingly comfortable material she had ever felt against her skin, and it was so transparent that the dark circles of her areolae stood out in contrast to the golden skin tone that glowed through the material. On the walls were huge hangings of delicate beauty, erotic pictures woven into that silklike material. The bed, couches, and chairs were of highly polished wood, inlaid with colored stones and jewels.

She got off the bed, and her bare feet sank into a floor

covering of soft purple. As she walked, the silken gown caressed her, making her aware of her body. She was, at first, shocked by the erotic art of the wall hangings, but then she began to be more analytical. It was so well done that its sheer realistic beauty seemed to take away the shock value.

She heard a sound and turned. The man called Yanee was there, a golden tray in his hands. "Ah, you are awake," he said. He put the tray on a graceful inlaid table and lifted two goblets, handing one to her. "This is the wine of the valley," he said.

"It's very good," she replied, after drinking.

"Sit," he said. "As I have told you, I am Yanee. We must get acquainted."

"Where are my friends?" she asked, remembering the others for the first time.

"They are well," he said. "Soon they will be leaving the valley."

"I must go to them," she said.

"In time," he whispered, reaching out for her hand. His touch caused her to shiver involuntarily. To cover her confusion she drank. The wine had a delicious taste and seemed to demand that it be drunk swiftly. Her eyes went wide when Yanee stood and, with a careless movement of his hand, dropped his kilt to the floor. Her eyes widened, and she felt a desire she had never known before. She rose, put down the glass, and made no protest when Yanee lifted her easily and carried her to the huge bed.

Paul Warden awoke in less splendid surroundings. He was looking for a way out of a small, mostly barren room when the door was unlocked and he was told by a valley man standing in the doorway to follow him. He entered a large, elaborately decorated chamber. Artworks had been carved and painted into the stone walls. At the head of the chamber, Suses sat on an elaborate, massive, jeweled throne. Paul saw that Mandy and the others were there, with the exception of Sage.

"Come forward," Suses ordered. "We have wasted enough time with you."

Paul felt for his laser. It was gone. He walked to stand beside Mandy. "Where's Sage?" he whispered.

"Silence!" Suses thundered.

"I don't know," Mandy said in a normal voice, glaring at Suses. "Ask him."

"Where is the other member of our group?" Paul asked.

"We have decided to let you live, since you are harmless," Suses said, ignoring the question. "You may have the land you call Eden if you abide by certain stipulations. First, you will never again attempt to enter this valley, nor will you ever set foot on or fly over this continent. Second, you will cease stealing metals from the miners, for those metals belong to us. The Whorsk will resume their regular trips to the land you call Eden to trade for metals with the miners."

"Is that all?" Paul asked sarcastically.

Suses made an imperative gesture, and several bronzed valley men surrounded the group. "Take them," Suses said. He waved a baton at Paul. "You will leave the way you came, by the river."

Paul started to protest the absence of Sage, but two men seized his arms and began to hustle him toward the door. He put up just enough resistance to learn that, although the valley men were strong, they were not supermen. He felt he could take two of them. He waited until the two had relaxed again, and then he brought his arms forward with as much force as he could and threw the two men into a wall. One of them struck his head and went down; the other yelled something in his own language and rushed at Paul. Warden ducked a wild swing and kneed the breath out of the man, being careful not to kick too hard. He turned. Several of the baton and hand weapons were aimed at him. He spoke quickly, yelling at Suses. "I'm not leaving without the other member of our group!"

A woman in a green, tightly fitted costume leveled a wand at him.

"Hold," Suses ordered, and the woman relaxed.

"Where is she?" Paul demanded.

"The woman who calls herself Sage has chosen to stay, to learn about us and our customs," Suses said. "She will be returned to you at a later date."

"I want to hear that from Sage," Paul insisted.

"I will be happy to kill him now, Suses," the dark woman who had been in the greeting delegation said.

"No, no, they might be useful to us in the future," Suses said.

"They make poor slaves," a man said. "They don't have the durability of the Whorsk."

"Summon my son," Suses ordered. "Tell him to bring the woman."

Paul waited, alert, ready to try to take at least one of them with him, for almost five minutes. Then Yanee came into the room with Sage, dressed in a thin, revealing costume, on his arm.

"Are you all right, Sage?" Paul asked.

"I'm fine," Sage said. "I have been invited to stay on here for a while. I think it will be beneficial."

"We'll have to check that with Rodrick," Paul said. "Come with us to the crawler and we'll radio him."

"That won't be necessary," Sage replied. "I have been chosen to be something like an ambassador to the people of this valley. I'll be able to tell them about us, that we want peace, and I'll learn about them. When I'm ready, I'll report to the captain."

Mandy Miller had seen almost immediately that there was something subtly wrong with Sage's eyes. She could feel that the patience of these arrogant people was wearing thin, and she felt that it was vitally important to get back to the colony to tell Rodrick what they all faced.

"Let's go, Paul," she urged. "She knows what she's doing."

"Well . . ." Paul said indecisively.

"It's all right, Paul," Sage said. "Please go, and please do what Suses has ordered." *Yes, go,* she was thinking, *go and let me get back to the heaven I have found.*

"All right, we'll go," Paul said. "But let me tell you this, Suses. We are few on this planet, and we value every life. Maybe you know all about our weapons capabilities, maybe not. I wonder if your field would stop a ballistic missile armed with a nuclear warhead. If anything happens to Sage, we all might find out."

"Go!" Suses roared. "Before I put you on the stakes alongside the Whorsk rebels."

Warden's crawler was the rear guard on the trip up the river. They had to spend a night, then they were in the fog once more, and quickly out of it, and there were all of the colony's scouts massed overhead.

"Paul," Duncan Rodrick said on his scout's radio, "we're glad to see you."

"I'm glad we made it out before you started the attack," Warden answered, realizing that the massed forces could have meant only that.

"What kind of people are they?" Rodrick asked.

"Pick us up, Captain," Warden said. "From now on we'll have to do all our talking nose to nose, and not on the air."

Back at Hamilton, after the initial debriefing session, Mandy Miller hurried to the library. She asked Evangeline to give her certain reference works and then bent over a viewer in concentration for long minutes. There was an image in her memory, an image of a man mixed with something else, a work of art, a bust. It took only a little while as she scanned rapidly to find the picture she vaguely remembered. The object in question was from a period far back in Earth's antiquity. When she found it, she gasped. The ancient bust had been damaged, the nose knocked off, but it was very well done, realistic, the work of a true craftsman who had lived on Earth around three thousand years ago. The resemblance was uncanny. Suses, the leader of the people of the valley, looked almost exactly like the portrait in stone of Sesostris III, a pharaoh of ancient Egypt.

Paul Warden spent the first twelve hours after the return to Hamilton in conference with Rodrick and several scientists from different disciplines. He added his observations to those already given by Theresita. Neither he nor any of the scientists could explain how Suses had stopped the hydrogen engine of Clay's scout ship in midair, but it was, everyone agreed, an awesome weapon.

Alone with Rodrick in the captain's quarters, having gone without sleep for over twenty-four hours, Warden relaxed with a glass of bourbon from the ship's distillery.

"Dunc," he said, "they look like something out of a period piece. The women are gorgeous, and the men are real studs. They build beautifully, their artwork is fantastic, and they've got the same regard for life that one of those pretty Omegan pussycats has for a silver-horned antelope he's stalking. I had the feeling that they were laughing at us, toying with us. The only time I seemed to get their attention was when I said if they did anything to Sage we'd nuke them."

"I would not want to be the man to release radioactivity into Omega's atmosphere," Duncan said. "Nor do I want to be remembered as the man who brought nuclear war to the stars and destroyed a civilization."

"But if it's necessary? They can stop the combustion in a hydrogen engine, stop all electrical functions at a great distance. They impale their slaves alive on stakes, and they say our women are good breeders."

"Let's just pray that it won't become necessary," Rodrick said. "For now, we'll keep our distance. We'll wait and hear what Sage has to say when she returns."

"What about the metals from the miners?"

"Well," Rodrick said, "I have my mission, Paul, and to complete it, I have to have metals. I guess we'll just have to take a chance. We'll keep searching for metals, and we'll keep on trading with the miners." He drank, then sighed deeply. "And I'll have Max check out those damned hydrogen warheads that the people back home insisted on putting aboard."

TEN

With a song-prayer in his heart to the gods of the Caan, Lythe, most honored director of war, son of Lotel the Elder, and heir to the seat of the most honored, sent his warriors against the massed weapons of the men from the outer darkness. When the first thunderous explosions came on wings from huge, melon-shaped things in the air, he knew all would earn honor through death on that day. Blasts more powerful and more terrible than striking lightning tore huge holes in the Caan's well-ordered attack formation. And then the Brazilians' laser and projectile weapons began to take their toll on the charging warriors.

Lythe was in his place, at the center of the attacking formation, the better to coordinate it. At first he had the protection of numerous ranks of men in front of him. No tribe had ever broken a Caan charging square, but the weapons of the men from the upper darkness did it in minutes, and then there was no one living between Lythe and the defensive line set up by the enemy. He called out his orders in a huge, battle-trained voice and charged, now in the lead.

He leaped over a small drift of sand and, in midair, felt the force of thunder strike him. The force of the exploding bomb, dropped by a Brazilian scout, sent him flying backward over the small dune, to land, limp and seemingly lifeless, behind its frail protection while his well-trained men streamed on to their honorable deaths.

He awoke to a jostling. He felt the warm stickiness of his own blood. Lythe realized he was being carried on a warrior's shoulder.

"Hold," he hissed, the effort of saying the one word making his entire body ache. The warrior halted and lowered him carefully to the ground. "Leave me," Lythe ordered.

The warrior looked down. Lythe, through eyes that seemed to see through a film, recognized him. A good man, a section leader.

"You know that honor dictates that only one shall return to tell of a defeat," Lythe gasped.

"Director," the warrior said, "it is also honor to blend one's battle-stirred blood with his director. Do you forget?"

"I do not forget," Lythe said. He tried to feel, to see his body. He was wounded in perhaps a half-dozen places, and the blood was oozing freely, but he had movement of his limbs, even if his left leg pained him severely.

"Then I will take the honor of saving my director to offset the shame of being the unfortunate one who tells of the first Caan defeat in our history," the warrior said, lifting Lythe.

The movement was torture. Lythe chewed on his lower lip to keep from moaning in pain, and soon he had relief in the form of unconsciousness. When next he saw light, the light shone on the face of his father, Lotel the Elder, the most honored.

"I thank the gods that you live," Lotel said.

"I curse them that I am not dead with my men," Lythe answered.

"Unsay those words, for we have need of you," his father said.

"What service can I do that would wash away my shame?"

"The woman from the outer darkness, the one who was your playlove, tells us strange stories," Lotel said. "You know her best. You will assess her words and see if they have the ring of truth."

"I will live, then, until I have done this service,"

Lythe replied. He moved his legs experimentally and felt a great shooting pain.

"Your wounds are severe but not fatal," Lotel assured him. "Rest now, for you will need your strength. A Caan cannot talk with his enemy from a bed."

Obediently, Lythe slept.

Astrud Cabral was a prisoner. There could be no other explanation. She was a prisoner in relative luxury, in Lythe's apartment; but when she tried to leave, she was turned back firmly but politely by young, virile guards. There were plenty of foods and beverages. There were a few examples of Caan writing, pictographs in huge, leather-bound volumes, and she spent her time trying to relate what she knew of the spoken Caan language to the pictographs, but with little success. She simply did not know enough about the Caan world—the creatures in it, the people's habits, artifacts, or thinking—to decipher the writings. However, the study occupied her time during the five days when she saw only the guards and a young woman who brought her food.

On the sixth day she was summoned from sleep by the guards. She had to dress with the two young warriors looking on interestedly, and then she was escorted from the apartment to the government building with the triangular columns. She entered the same large chamber where she had spoken to the Caan rulers, and when she saw Lythe seated on the dais alongside the white-haired man who seemed to be the prime ruler, she halted in her tracks, gasped, and then ran forward. A guard made an attempt to intercept her, but Lythe waved the guard away. Astrud stood below Lythe.

"You're alive!" she cried happily.

"I am alive."

"Oh!" She could find no words.

"An entire Caan army, all my men, all my friends, are dead," Lythe said sadly. "I have commanded the first defeat in the memory of living men."

"But it isn't your fault," Astrud said. "You have no chance against their weapons."

"It is about these weapons we will speak," Lythe said, "and about the stories you told the elders." He smiled at her. "I'm alive, but there are those here who do not know you as I know you, those who wonder why you, from the outer darkness yourself, would take sides against your own people."

Astrud put aside her personal feelings for Lythe, feelings she was not quite ready to analyze. "I do what I do because this city—and the others, which must be like it—is too beautiful to be looted and destroyed."

There was a hissing from the elders and from the small audience of military men. Lotel glowered and raised one hand. "Men of Caan, you do well to bristle at the attack on our honor, but hold your peace. Have we not seen defeat? Listen to the woman."

"You have not even seen the most terrible of our weapons," Astrud continued. "It is a thing that explodes with the power of the far sun itself and destroys all for a distance of many miles."

First there was an incredulous hiss, then total silence.

"And yet my father says that you advise war against these men from the outer darkness," Lythe said.

"I do, but I do not advise charging into the power of their weapons," Astrud answered.

"But how else can one fight?" Lotel asked.

"At night. In small units. Even with one man creeping into the camp of your enemy to take just one life, even if he must exchange his own life for it."

"You ask that we fight like cowards?" Lythe asked angrily.

"I ask that you put aside your pride," she said, "and fight as if the continued lives of your city, your wives, your children, and your world depend on it, for they do."

"I cannot understand this," Lotel said. "If it is only gold that the men from the outer darkness want, why, there is plenty. We have only to tell our slaves to dig it out of the mines. And there is room for all on this world. There are islands—"

"Would you move *your* nation to one of the islands?" Astrud asked.

"Of course not," Lotel snapped. "This is the home-land of the Caan."

"My leader, Captain Gilberto da Lisboa, has claimed this section of the coast as the home for *his* colony. He has the weapons of thunder and fire. You have only two choices, to flee—"

There was a wild hissing.

"—or to learn a new way to make war. A way I can teach you."

"There is another choice," another elder suggested. "We will mass all our warriors, from all of our cities, and we will overwhelm them by sheer numbers, even if we have to kill the last of them by crawling over piles of our dead."

"I have seen the results of their weapons," Lythe said, shaking his head. "Tell me, Astrud Cabral, of the peoples of the lake back on your world."

She repeated the story of the conquest of the Aztecs by Cortez, and then of the fall of the Inca Empire, and how all was lost, how the people were taken into slavery, and how entire cultures were erased forever. Lythe listened with his chin in his hand, his finely chiseled face rigid, his dark eyes flashing.

"You see," she said, "it came about because brave warriors faced weapons of fire and thunder and would not learn their lessons. You can repeat their mistake, or you can take hope. By daring and persistence, you can drive the invaders from your world."

"The woman speaks the truth," Lythe said.

"Would you, Most Honored Director of War, abandon your honor and skulk through the night to murder?" asked an elder.

"My mate has not yet been chosen. My children are yet unborn. I want my name to live. I don't want my children to be subjects of the men from the outer darkness." Lythe rose. "Come, Astrud Cabral, we will talk of your plans in private." He bowed to his father, then to the others. "And as we talk, the honorable elders will make their decision."

Lythe walked stiffly, his lips set firmly against the

pain that was still with him. The eyes of the people in the streets were hostile when Astrud passed by. "You must rid yourself of the marks of the men from the upper darkness," he said. "Fortunately, you look like a—" The word he used translated into Portuguese as "human being."

She nodded. It would simplify things if she were to stay with the Caan. She shuddered inwardly as the meaning of her thoughts sank in. *Stay*. She was not thinking of a visit, a brief diplomatic mission. No, if she stayed it would be, perhaps, the most irrevocable and final decision she had ever made in her life. She would be the only *human* among the Caan. She would be, if her plan worked, a permanent exile, and farther from home than any exile in history. For moments, as she walked slowly beside Lythe, she wavered. How easy it would be to return to the ship, to tell the captain that her efforts to keep the Caan from attacking had obviously failed, and that there was nothing else she could do. Although she had no intimates aboard ship, she did have people she had come to like—friends. Among the colonists there were some very worthwhile people. But it was the thought of her father that weighed strongest on her mind, making the decision so difficult. The *Estrêla do Brasil* would return to Earth in less than a year. She could see her home again, share her sorrow with her father, and—

Her father. What would he say? She could almost hear his voice. *"Astrud, Astrud, they have carried the Earth's sickness into space."* But perhaps he would say, *"You were right in not becoming a traitor."*

Traitor? To whom? To the dictator whose stated policy was to bring the last of Brazil's Indians into the twenty-first century or exterminate them? To the men who used modern weapons to slaughter Bronze Age warriors?

And, in that moment, as Lythe began to ease his way painfully up the stairs to his apartment, there came to her a clarity of thought that seemed to intensify the vibrant colors of the city.

"If you must apply labels, accept the label of traitor to conquest and cruelty, but reject being a traitor to the idea of humanity."

Astrud had, of course, been exposed to Catholic teach-ings. There was, after all, a Brazilian pope sitting in the Vatican, surrounded by Communist Italy. She had never been able to accept fully the Catholic teachings, although she did not reject the abstract notion of a Supreme Being. Had she been a practicing Catholic, she might have said that God had spoken to her as she watched Lythe strug-gle, his leg stiff, up the stairs.

She told herself that she had intended all along to do her best to aid the Caan in driving the Brazilians—her people—from this world. Had anyone asked, she would have said that no message from God was needed to influ-ence her to do the right thing. She was only doing what any decent human being would do, siding with the hope-less underdog, trying to keep murder, pestilence, and slavery from an admirable people.

By the time they had reached the door to Lythe's apartment, she knew there was no turning back. She was totally committed.

"Take off your clothes and lie down," she ordered, taking Lythe's arm and steering him toward the bedroom. "Let me look at your wounds."

He put up no protest. The shrapnel gashes were healing well, a sign of his robust good health. On a bed-side table were two pottery jars. "The red one contains the ointment to prevent the anger of the god of war," he told her. She sniffed it. It had a strong, antiseptic smell. She smoothed it over the scabbed wounds, and he winced as she touched the largest wound on his leg.

"In the presence of a friend and a playlove," he said through clenched teeth, "I am permitted this." And so saying, he lifted his head and bellowed out his pain and his frustrations in one long, ear-splitting howl. Then he grinned and, sweat popping out of his forehead, fell asleep.

Astrud slept in an adjoining room. Lythe slept undis-turbed that night. Before dawn, Astrud awoke to the sound of voices, and, dressing quickly, went into Lythe's bed-room to find him seated in a chair surrounded by strong young warriors.

"These will be our core people," he explained. "I

have talked with them. They will obey you in my absence. Tell them what you would have them do."

"I have seen deadly looking serpents in the market-place," Astrud began.

"*Pyangs*," a young warrior said in disgust.

"Those you saw had been defanged," Lythe said, "for not even the professional snake handlers could be that near a *pyang*."

"They are deadly?"

"From twenty feet away they spit a venom that is absorbed by the skin and causes death within five breaths," Lythe said.

"How, then, are they taken?"

"With great care," Lythe said, with a bellow of laughter. Then, "By the Sect of Pyang, whose members consider it an immediate admission to paradise to die of *pyang* venom."

"Have the members of the sect capture as many *pyangs* as they can," Astrud said, "and enclose them in something so that they can be transported safely and released without harm to the one carrying them."

"That can be done," Lythe said, "for there is a large, marshy wilderness to the south where only the *pyang* worshipers go. The evil ones breed well there. But what do you plan to do?"

She told him. And members of the Brazilian expedition were to find out quickly.

The deadly reptiles were heat seekers. When they were released in the early morning hours at a dozen points on the perimeter of the Brazilian camp, they started crawling immediately toward the glowing fires kept burning by the sentries and those fighting men who had camped outside the *Estrêla do Brasil*. Thirty-three men died as the *pyangs* spat their deadly venom with great accuracy; as their main venom supply drained, they used the small amount stored in their yellowed fangs to dispatch four more when the officer of the guard came out of the ship at daybreak to supervise the changing of the guard. Meanwhile, some of the *pyangs* had replenished their supply of expellable venom and killed seven more Brazilians during the frantic efforts to clear the camp of snakes.

"Forty-four dead?" Gilberto da Lisboa stormed. "Forty-four? By snakes?"

The next night, after five more men died from the spewed venom, da Lisboa brought the others onto the ship and, using flamethrowers, seared the ground for a hundred yards in all directions from the *Estrêla do Brasil*'s weapons ports, thus ruining a very nice campsite.

That day a scout team in an armored crawler killed two hundred Caan before the four men in the crawler were finally overwhelmed by warriors who charged, seemingly careless of certain death, into the muzzles of the crawler's weapons. And da Lisboa himself was on the ground when, without warning, a hail of spiked balls from the Caan's throwing chains thudded into a group of scientists who had obtained permission to leave the *Estrêla do Brasil* for a walk in the fresh air inside the defense perimeter. That the four Caan who had slung the spiked balls were killed immediately did not lessen da Lisboa's rage at losing four women and two men.

The passing days saw Lythe become more and more agile. Now his wounds scarcely ached, except when he overdid his exercises. He longed to be alongside his growing number of night fighters. Had it been his choice and his alone, he would have joined the death throwers inside the Brazilian perimeter to take a few of them with him into death. He listened to the reports of his warriors with impatience and respect.

Astrud was with him, as always, when a young warrior came running into his apartment. "Director," the warrior said, panting, "the enemy is astir like a hive of stingers. He is off-loading many vehicles and many men."

"The time has come," Astrud said.

"You are sure this da Lisboa will attack the city?" Lythe asked.

"I am as sure of that as I am sure that there is a sun in the sky. He will blame the deaths of his people on the people of this city, since it is the closest center of population to the ship. He will think that by destroying this city, he will solve his problems."

"In our blood wars against sworn enemies, we do not destroy the temples of the gods," Lythe said sadly. "Yet, I believe you, Astrud Cabral. Yesterday a man was taken by the men from the outer darkness. From concealment another of my men watched as the prisoner was tortured with slashes of a knife and by the application of the evil-smelling smoke stick with fire at its tip, used by your leader. Animals who will do that to a helpless prisoner, instead of giving him peace in slavery or a quick death, will commit any evil." He rose. "I will go and give the word to the elders."

Within the hour Astrud saw the first of the evacuation of the city. Soon the streets were packed with quiet, orderly men, women, and children, and domestic animals and carts. They streamed through the southern gates of the city and out onto the flats. From a tower she watched, and before nightfall the line of people fleeing the doomed city stretched to the bay, down the coast, and then inland and out of sight, into the oceanside woodlands.

The first armored crawlers, buttoned up tightly, smashed down the gates of the city and quickly penetrated totally abandoned streets to the central square, the square of the temples. Nothing stirred in the city, save a few domestic pets left behind in the evacuation. When it became evident that the city had been given up without a fight, da Lisboa himself led the way to the temples and supervised the looting of the golden statuary inside. Thinking themselves to be safe, soldiers began to seek their own loot, and by twos and threes they found death from *pyangs* hidden inside jeweled boxes, or from a stealthy arrow fired from ambush, or from a knife applied silently to the throat. It was dark before Gilberto da Lisboa discovered that his force was not alone in the city, that Caan warriors were on rooftops, in hidden niches, in every shadow. The night of terror began.

In panic, a Brazilian marine, seeing his friend fall at his side with a death ball in his throat, opened fire, his laser cannon searing and blasting at the beautifully painted stone walls of the buildings surrounding the square. Others joined him, the combined fire devastating the buildings lining the square and, not too incidentally, killing dozens of fellow Brazilians who, having gone in search of loot, had found terror and were trying to fight their way back to the crawlers in the square.

"What are they firing at?" da Lisboa demanded of his military commander.

"At shadows," the general said, lifting his communicator. "Cease fire. Cease fire."

Gradually it became silent.

"Give the order to leave the city, using the same route by which we entered," da Lisboa said. "We will take the crawlers outside the walls, and from there we will use all our firepower to reduce this place of evil to crumbled pebbles."

The rear seat of the command crawler was piled high with gold. Da Lisboa, not then knowing the extent of his losses among those who had gone looting, was content. There was more gold, but he would not risk losing another man in the darkness. There would be other cities, more gold.

The command crawler began to move. On the other side of the square, a crawler burst into flames with a roar as a Caan warrior gave his life to get near enough to toss a ceramic jug of lamp oil with a wick burning in its neck into the open hatch. And from a darkened street leading from the square, there came a short scream of agony that terminated in a gurgle—a huge building stone had smashed into the windscreen of a crawler moving toward the exit street, landing in the driver's lap to break both his legs. The crawler went out of control and smashed into a brick wall.

Jugs of flaming oil came crashing down onto crawlers from the rooftops. "Open fire!" da Lisboa screamed as the command crawler narrowly missed a building stone.

"At what?" the military commander yelled. Then, "All units, use lasers and cannon on the rooftops and the windows of all tall buildings."

Two crawlers concentrated all their firepower on a

building from which they had seen the blazing jugs of oil being thrown. They kept firing as they raced toward the next corner, and just as they were even with the building and their fire was being played thunderously over the upper story, a decorative pediment laden with heavy stone statuary came crashing down. Tons of weight crushed the two crawlers and the men inside them, and blocked the street. The next crawlers in line, their drivers yelling at the vehicles behind them to turn around, became the targets for jugs of flaming oil and tumbling building stones. Men leaped from their stalled vehicles and found that their hand lasers and pistols were of no use against shadows who struck quickly and disappeared.

Da Lisboa's command crawler had just escaped being engulfed by the falling pediment. It was now in the clear, traveling alone, speeding toward the north gate.

"Look out!" the military commander screamed as the vehicle skidded around a corner. The gate was in sight, but blocked by a ten-foot-high barricade of stone. The vehicle crashed into the barrier with a force that threw its occupants violently forward in their harnesses. Stones began to thud down, and the stink of burning oil came through the vehicle's ventilation system.

"Back up!" da Lisboa yelled.

The driver raced the engine and ground gears, but the vehicle lurched back against newly dropped stones and could move no farther. The gunners were firing a storm of lasers and projectiles. A building stone that weighed at least two hundred pounds shattered the armored glass of a turret and silenced the laser. And now the crawler spun its tracks on stone in a puddle of blazing oil.

"We've got to get out!" da Lisboa screamed as flames filled the viewports and windows. He kicked and clawed his way over a struggling crewman to the top hatch and flung it open. Flame singed his hair. He screamed in pain and leaped as far as he could leap, landing heavily on a flat stone that stood above the sea of burning oil, wrenching his ankle painfully, but clear of the fire. Then he leaped into the arms of two Caan and screamed once more.

*   *   *

The communications officer on board the *Estrêla do Brasil* had been wishing that he was with the expeditionary force to have his chance at some of the loot. When the reports began to come in that the force was under attack, he began wishing that he was there to kill the savages. Then, as the vehicles of the force became silent, he became very content to be just where he was, behind the impregnable hull of the ship and inside the protection of her arsenal of weapons.

While the fighting was still in progress he awakened the ship's first officer. The man who was second in command listened to the reports with growing alarm. He could not understand, or believe, that modern war crawlers were being destroyed one by one by Bronze Age people. Gradually the situation began to be clear to him.

"He has taken the entire force through narrow streets to the central square, where the temples and the gold are," he growled to the communications officer. He did not overtly call the dictator's nephew, the captain of the ship, a fool, but he was thinking it. As it became clear that the entire force of three hundred fighting men and sixty vehicles was being slowly exterminated, he considered his options: Da Lisboa had taken all of the combat-trained soldiers with him; he himself could mount a force of only forty crawlers, manned by civilians and scientists.

"Sir," the communications officer said, "we must do something."

"Send untrained people in where Brazil's best are being killed?"

It was at that point that a distress call came from da Lisboa himself. "We are under attack by overwhelming forces," the general said, his voice high and strained. "We are trapped. Send a relief column immediately."

"Sound the alarm," the first officer said with resignation.

But by the time the untrained people had manned the crawlers and the first of them had exited the *Estrêla do Brasil*, there was no more radio traffic from the expeditionary force. And from the city there arose the glow of fires, and a faint scent of burning oil was carried on a light breeze.

"Post sentries," the first officer ordered. "Relief force, stand by."

At dawn he sent up a scout. The city seemed to be deserted. The weapons of the crawlers had done great damage around the central square. But one by one the pilot in the scout counted burned and smashed crawlers. Of all the vehicles that had gone into the city, only one was unaccounted for.

Aboard *Estrêla do Brasil*, the first officer called a meeting of the government-appointed department leaders. He told them in a soft, sad voice of the events of the night.

"Shameful!" a man shouted. "We must send out the scouts and bomb these savages back into the Stone Age."

"What will we bomb, a deserted city?"

"There are other cities. These savages must pay."

"I'd like to point out," the first officer said, "that our demographers estimate that there are ten million of these people on this continent, not counting the subjected tribes and slaves. Can we bomb them all?"

"What would you suggest?" asked a quiet, sober scientist.

"We came to this world over a thousand strong. We have lost almost two-fifths of our number, including almost every soldier trained in combat techniques. We have lost over half of our ground transportation. While it is true that our weapons are superior and we can kill millions of these animals, I don't think we can kill them all. In the beginning one of our number, Dr. Astrud Cabral, advised that we work with these people for peace. Perhaps we should have listened."

"That is looking to the past," someone said. "There is nothing we can do about the past."

"I will be open to advice," the first officer said, "but it is my recommendation that we lift ship and leave this place. Our probes located two other likely planets, and we have plenty of rhenium and rocket fuel. I say let's find a planet that is uninhabited."

"You want to run," a woman said scornfully.

"Doctor," the first officer replied calmly, "I hereby

appoint you military commander, since our general is dead. Now *you* may organize our forces and attack if you wish."

The woman glowered, but fell silent.

"Should we not search the city for survivors?" another asked.

"There was no sign of life from the air," the first officer said.

"I vote that we go," another woman said, and there was a loud chorus of agreement.

"Good," the first officer said. "It will take a few hours for the engineering staff to prepare us for lift-off."

The first officer, now captain of the *Estrêla do Brasil*, was on the bridge when the duty man on communications called him. "There's an outside call," he reported. "From one of our people."

"Damn," the first officer said. That meant delay of the lift-off. He took the mike. "Captain Antonio Villa-Lobos here," he said.

"Captain, this is Dr. Astrud Cabral," a female voice said, as it was amplified when the communications officer put it on the bridge speakers. "I speak for the honorable elders of the Caan."

"Who in hell are the Caan?" Villa-Lobos asked.

"The people of this continent," the communications officer said.

"How does a Brazilian speak for our enemies?" Villa-Lobos asked into the radio.

"I speak as one who is unwilling to see an innocent nation destroyed," Astrud said. "Here are the terms of the elders of the Caan: If you will begin immediately to ready the *Estrêla do Brasil* for lift-off, the Caan will return to you eleven men who survived the night."

"Terms?" Villa-Lobos snarled. "They dare offer terms?"

"We know, Captain," Astrud went on, "that you can do heavy damage with your weapons and the weapons of the ship. We know that you can kill millions of Caan. But, say the Caan—and, sir, you can believe this—you will never know a day of peace on this planet. One by one you will be killed, even as you kill thousands. You cannot afford the rate of attrition. You may count your casualties to date to test this statement. You must leave this planet. Speaking as a Brazilian, Captain, I beg you to do so and to resist any impulse to do damage as you go, for it would be simple murder and would gain you nothing."

"You, traitor," Villa-Lobos snarled. "Just you wait."

He cut off the radio. "I want that bitch dead," he said. "A traitor to her own people. And I want the thermo-nuclear weapons readied. We will lay waste to this planet when we are in orbit."

He activated the transmitter. "Traitor," he said, "I have ordered the hydrogen bombs to be readied."

"You can do that," Astrud said. "You have the power to kill millions. But have you the right? Have you the evil in your heart to slaughter so many who have done nothing but defend their homeland?"

Villa-Lobos snarled. His every impulse was to do just that, but he thought, *Someday we can come back here. This is a rich planet. There is much gold.*

He spoke to Astrud. "I will make a deal with you, traitor. I will trade the life of this planet for you. If you will come to the ship alone and surrender yourself for trial by your former peers, I will leave this planet and I will not use the bombs."

"No," Lythe said, when Astrud told him of the terms.

"I have to do it," she said. "Otherwise he might make good his threat to use the thermonuclear bombs. If that happens, we have lost, Lythe."

"Then I will go and die with you," he said.

"You can't. They'd kill both of us on sight if you were with me." She took his hand. "Let me do this for you and for your people. We've done you a terrible wrong. My life will not compensate for all those who have died and for the damage to your city, but it will keep you from worse destruction. You have the right to die honorably in battle. You cannot take that right from me."

"It is so," Lythe agreed sadly.

They had parked a salvaged crawler with its radio equipment intact in the shelter of a hill inland from the *Estrêla do Brasil*. Astrud started the engine.

"Captain," she radioed, "I am coming toward the ship in a crawler. You will notice that its weapons have been put out of action. I'll stop it a half mile from you and walk in alone."

"Train every weapon on that crawler," Villa-Lobos ordered. "At the first sign of hostile action, obliterate it."

But as the crawler came into view he was struck by its battered condition. All weapons ports were bent, and the barrels of the cannon were warped beyond use. The crawler halted, and a figure in native dress got out and began to walk toward the ship.

"Does anyone recognize her?" Villa-Lobos asked.

"Yes. That is Dr. Cabral," the communications officer confirmed.

"We will meet her at the forward hatch," the captain said. He was standing in the hatch when Astrud came into the shadow of the ship, walking proudly, her head high. He looked into the face of this woman who had betrayed her country and knew hatred, for she was dark, a *pardo*. It was all clear to him then. The Indians of the interior had never been truly Brazilian.

"You said that eleven of my men were being held captive," he said. "Where are they?"

"They are near," Astrud said. "I wanted to talk with you face to face and have your word as a Brazilian officer that you will not use the weapons of murder against this planet."

Villa-Lobos snarled. "You speak of honor?"

"Of what worth is the life of eleven Brazilians?" she asked.

"I will not use weapons as we leave," the captain said.

Astrud turned and gave a signal. From behind the line of brush in the distance men began to emerge, some of them being supported by their comrades. It took long minutes for them to walk the distance. Villa-Lobos called for the medical staff to treat the wounded. He stomped out to meet the men, his anger flooding over him.

A young officer saluted. His head was crudely bandaged, and there was caked blood on his uniform. "Sir," he said, "we should not have gone into those narrow streets of the city."

"Did the savages mistreat you?" Villa-Lobos asked.

"No, sir. After our capture, we were treated with dignity and honor."

"Get aboard, Lieutenant," Villa-Lobos said. "Your wounds will be cared for."

When the men had been taken in hand by the medical staff, he turned to face Astrud. "Bind her, hand and foot," he said.

Men who had lost comrades and friends did not question the captain's orders. Astrud's wrists were bound, then her feet.

"Your trial for the act of treason is now in session," Villa-Lobos said. "The verdict is that you are guilty of treason and the deaths of many of your own people. Since you love the savages and this planet so much, your ashes will remain here."

At Villa-Lobos's direction, Astrud was carried and tossed roughly to the charred ground directly under the outboard rockets.

"We will be starting rocket firing in ten minutes," Villa-Lobos called to her. "You will have that long to think about the extent of your crime."

She was alone. The hatch clanged shut. She could hear the muffled mutter of auxiliary engines from within the ship. She could not see her watch, and the time seemed to drag on into an eternity. She knew the rocket firing sequence, knew that the rockets near the center of the *Estrêla do Brasil's* mass would belch fire first, and then, in phased rows, the engines would roar into life. When the outboard rockets fired, she would already be dead, charred by the wash of fire from inboard nozzles. Then there would be nothing left of her but ashes, which would be spread widely by the force of the fiery gases thrusting out from the rockets. She closed her eyes and was resigned. She would have chosen to live, of course, but she had already lost so much—her home and her father—that the loss of her life did not seem unbearable. She heard a sharp report and, far away, at the center of the ship, a set of rockets ignited and a rush of heated, acrid air washed over her. She prayed that it would be over quickly, that she would not know pain.

There was another boom of sound, and the intensity of the heat was greater. She was having difficulty breathing, and the exhaust fumes of the rockets seared her lungs. She felt unconsciousness coming and blessed it, and then she was dreaming that she was being lifted, that she was being saved, even as more rockets fired.

Lythe had watched from the moment that Astrud walked to the ship. He saw the wounded Brazilians enter the hatch, saw the uniformed men toss Astrud roughly to the ground. He heard the muted rumblings from within the ship and guessed that the huge craft was making ready to lift itself into the upper darkness. Were they leaving Astrud behind? He left his cover and began to crawl, utilizing every undulation in the sand to cover his movements, toward the ship. When the first of the inboard rockets belched fire and smoke, he felt his heart bump, for it was clear now that the flying thing of fire would kill her. He leaped to his feet and ran. Smoke and fire billowed out through the channels on the underside of the ship. He was soon running blindly toward the spot where Astrud lay, well under the overhang of the great vessel.

He could not see. Heat seared him. His lungs ached with fire from the acrid smoke. If he missed her, ran past her, she would die, and yet he ran and, at full stride, stumbled over her, and sprawled onto the sand. He scurried back on his hands and knees, scooped her into his arms, and ran on in the same direction, toward the sea, two hundred yards away. The force of the expelled gases pushed him, scorched his back painfully, but still he ran, and behind him the roar grew until it seemed that his ears could stand no more. He yelled to relieve the pain of the sheer noise, and just as he thought he would fall, give in, and die there in that acrid, unbreathable air and the insufferable heat, he felt his feet splashing in water, and then he hit the remnant of a wave and sprawled, dropping Astrud. He gathered her up and struggled for deeper water, waves now washing over his head. The fire of the full rocket thrust of the *Estrêla do Brasil* was sizzling the film of water on the beach as the waves reached smooth sand and died. He put his hand over Astrud's face and closed off her mouth and nose and, taking a deep breath, pulled them both underwater. When Astrud's lungs began to spasm, he surfaced into heat and hell, gasped for air, his nose close to the surface of the water, saw Astrud gasping, and then he closed off her nose and went back under. It seemed to be an eternity, and he was becoming dizzy from oxygen deprivation, before, surfacing for perhaps the tenth time, he found relatively clear air, tainted by only wisps of rocket smoke, and then he had to breathe into Astrud's mouth, for her lungs no longer worked. He dragged her to the shallows and lay atop her, weak, his lungs burning, and breathed his life into her until—when he had begun to give up hope—she began to breathe again.

He lay on his back, the cool wash of the dying waves on him, salt causing his blistered back to burn. She opened her eyes. The skin of her cheeks and forehead was red with the heat of her burns.

"Lythe?" she whispered, not sure what she was seeing, knowing that she should be dead.

"Now you are mine," he said. "For I have claimed your life from the fires of the flying house. Now I will care for you."

III

THE GREAT MISTY RIVER

ELEVEN

The military defense android called the admiral had
abandoned his medal-bedecked uniform for the simple
work garb of an enlisted space-service man. He made a
striking figure. He was always neat, his fatigues always
flawlessly pressed. Grace Monroe, his creator, never ceased
to be amazed by his maturing process. She had programmed the rank of admiral into his synthetic brain as a
tongue-in-cheek protest against the military mentality, and
as she had watched the admiral grow up, she had often felt
a bit guilty about it, for he had, early on, developed
qualities that were not consistent with the fact that the
nearest thing to a living biological material in his makeup
were the amino acids in his thousands of individual memory chambers.

From the beginning his functions as a fighting machine had been mature, but he had been like a baby in his
interrelations with others. Grace thought it both sad and
somewhat cynically amusing that it had been an unhappy
love affair that seemed to complete the admiral's maturing
process.

To see the android in action, a stranger would not
have been able to distinguish him from other men, except
for the fact that he was more sturdily formed and more
handsome than most men. He had followed with great
interest the reports from the land expedition to the Great
Misty River and from the relief force that had fortunately

189

not had to attack. During the absence of most of the combat-qualified men he and the towering, hulking defense robot, Mopro, patrolled the colony's perimeters.

Since he needed no sleep, the admiral had plenty of time to pursue his studies. He could merge with the ship's computer, and there had been a time when Grace had been concerned that he would overload his memory capacity. This proved to be a false fear; it seemed that the admiral's unique brain was capable of storing an infinite amount of information.

When the expedition had returned to base, the admiral had sat in on all the debriefing sessions, silent, quietly dignified, and then he retired to his private quarters—he had chosen not to move off the ship—and plugged himself into the ship's computer and spent twenty-four hours in thought and research. It was only then that he sought out his maker and his best friend.

"Grace," he said, "do you believe in magic?"

Grace had learned never to treat a question from the admiral lightly. "There are certainly things in the universe that we can't explain, unless we do accept some element of the supernatural."

"I ask that question because I can find no physical explanation for the field over the Great Misty River."

Grace was still unsure about just how much capacity for original thought the admiral had. She had spent a lot of time thinking about that, and she had graphed, charted, and computerized many of the admiral's thought patterns. There were times when she believed that he was capable of original thought, but then she would compare his work with known material from several disciplines of science and see that it was probably just the admiral's mechanical logic at work, relating data to his storage banks to come up with what, to some, might have seemed original conclusions.

"Dr. Bryson has been doing some interesting work," the admiral said. He seemed perfectly comfortable mentioning the name of the woman whose mental instability had led to an embarrassing public display of his unrequited love for her.

"Have you access to it?" Grace asked.

"Yes. She had to use the capacity of the main computer. She has made an interesting case for reducing Weyl's fourth differential-order field equations to equations of the second order, but I find some weakness in her including electromagnetism in Einstein's incorporation of gravitational fields into the structure of four-dimensional space time, but—"

"You're talking about something that's out of my field," Grace said, laughing. "Have pity on me."

Another element of the admiral's maturity fell into place. He had always considered Grace to be the wisest and best informed person he had ever encountered, and to find out that she was not conversant with efforts to arrive at a unified field theory that would bring atomic theory and electromagnetism under the rule of geometry gave him a new understanding of his own abilities.

"Well, in short," the admiral said, "I think the valley people have the technological ability to control electrons and possibly the fundamental charged particles that make up the electron."

"A good trick," Grace said. "I can see why you're thinking of supernatural powers."

"I'd like to be able to have just thirty seconds inside their computer," the admiral said. "If they have a computer."

"You doubt that they do?"

"They said that they'd been on Omega for sixty centuries," he said. "Yet they live in what is basically a feudal society. They must be the ones who make helium for the Whorsk airships. They have electrical power. But they have no ground or air vehicles, at least not that we've seen, and although they live in rich and luxurious surroundings, they do not seem to have all the hundreds of little machines and gadgets that are such an integral part of a technological society."

"You're saying that if they had arrived at a unified field theory, that would explain their technology as we know it?" Grace asked.

He nodded. "Broadcast power. The weapon used to stop the engine of Clay's ship was relatively small, a sword or wand. I doubt that a power source could be built into so small an object. There were no visible wires or transmission lines, so I assume that the power for the weapons, the lights, and the cooling is broadcast from a central source."

"That would limit them," Grace said. "And if it comes to hostility, it would make our task easier. Destroy the central power source, and they would be disarmed."

"For the same reasons I've stated," the admiral said, "I doubt that the source of their power is nuclear. I'd guess that they utilize solar power, which would account for their settlement of the Great Misty River valley, where the sun almost always shines."

"I think you should talk this over with Duncan Rodrick," Grace said.

"Yes," he agreed. "I've been waiting for him to find some free time. He's been a man with a very heavy load on his shoulders."

"Perhaps things will settle down now," Grace said.

"I have also been thinking about a way to allow Mopro and me to participate in any future action along the river," the admiral said. "I believe that we can protect Mopro with a shielding of lead. He's powerful enough to carry it, and we can scavenge enough lead from the *Spirit of America* to do the job."

"Good," Grace said. "Go ahead with that. Give me computer graphics on what would be needed, and then we'll be able to move swiftly if the captain thinks Mopro will be needed. What about you? It would be a bit more difficult to shield you, since you'd be vulnerable to a strong field in just about every area of your body."

"I haven't solved that problem yet," he said.

He went back to his quarters, and for more long hours he was motionless, only his brain at work. He had become a part of the main computer. Once he was tantalizingly near a breakthrough, but when he ran the equations, so complicated that it took a huge portion of the computer's capacity, it proved to be a false trail.

He made an appointment with Duncan Rodrick and spent an hour talking to the captain about his theories and discussing possible tactics for defense in case the valley people proved to have an offensive capacity, and for attack on the valley if it became necessary. It was during this time that Jackie called and asked to see Rodrick.

"Tell her I'll see her at dinner," Rodrick told the officer on communications duty. This meeting was too important to be disturbed.

With the safe return of the expedition, Rodrick had issued permission for the colony's work to continue. Scouts returned to their main project, mapping all of Omega's land and sea features and making detailed searches over all land masses, with the exception of the western continent that was the home of the valley people. Various routine missions of investigation went out from Hamilton City.

Amando Kwait and Dena Madden, having done the preliminary work on genetically engineered insect-resistant produce, were given the go-ahead by the scientific committee to move their experiments into controlled plots of Omegan soil. Dena's contempt for all Third World peoples had been severely tested by her work with Kwait. She found him to be a fascinating man, a man who knew his field, a considerate man, a hard taskmaster, but fair. And when he strode into the agricultural lab, his face showing a huge grin, and announced that they had been given the go-ahead, she leaped up, threw her arms around him, and gave him a congratulatory kiss.

Stoner McRae was moving a deep-mining rig and a crew to the site of the molybdenum deposit he had checked out at the five thousand foot level. It had indeed contained rhenium, as Stoner had suspected. Clay Girard, a bit bruised and battered from his crash landing in *Apache One*, was trying to ease the aches in his body by soaking up sun on the beach at Stanton Bay and being spoiled and tended by Cindy. Jumper had had his swim, which consisted of a romp through the shallows and a quick dash into the water after a stick thrown by Cindy, and was now frantically trying to dig up a burrowing, crablike amphibian that nested in the beach sands.

Cindy was a bit worried about the dragon Baby,

because Dr. James Wilson, the animal-behavior expert, had received permission from Rodrick to try to find a mate for the friendly dragon, and Baby was going to be airlifted to the South soon.

"I know it's a good idea," Cindy said to Clay, "but she'll be scared."

"She'll be fine," he assured her.

"I wish they'd let me go with her. She'd feel better about being hoisted into the air with me there."

"Well," Clay said, "your dad said no, the captain said no, and I say no, so that's that."

"Big deal," Cindy muttered. "Men."

"If you're so worried about her, I'll go along," Clay offered.

Cindy replied, her face beaming, "Oh, would you? Please do. Maybe you could open a hatch and talk to her during the lift-off, so she'll know that everything's all right."

"I'll do better than that," Clay offered expansively. "I'll ride right on her back."

"But you're still hurt," Cindy said.

Clay laughed. "Make up your mind. Who are you the most worried about, me or Baby?"

"You're impossible," Cindy replied, but she was smiling, leaning toward him as he lay on his back, his skin protected from Omega's harmful rays by a sunscreen lotion. Her lips touched his, and he put his arms around her and drew her to him. The ever-glowing fires of youth flared up, and he pushed her away.

"You're always doing that," she protested.

"That's because I don't want your father to scalp me," he said. "Let's go find Dr. Wilson." He climbed to his feet with a groan as his sore muscles complained.

Wilson had asked permission for a volunteer to go with him into the jungles in search of a male dragon for Baby. Rodrick had said simply, "Well, just pick someone." Wilson had thought it over, but before he had decided who he would ask, the captain's wife, Jackie, volunteered.

"I had in mind a man," Wilson had said, rather surprised by her eagerness to go. "Or maybe the admiral, just in case Baby and I get into trouble."

"I have the same combat qualifications as the most experienced man in the colony," Jackie had replied. "And I want to go."

Jackie herself had not fully analyzed her reasons for insisting on going to the jungles. She knew that she was restless, that something kept nagging at her. In retrospect she would realize that she had fallen victim to human nature, reacting to her feelings of neglect and being taken for granted. After all, she was a capable career officer of the United States Space Service and knew her job well. Yet, as the wife of Captain Duncan Rodrick, her own capabilities had become secondary to Duncan's responsibilities and authority. Before they were married she had been treated as an officer. Now she felt like nothing more than an extension of her husband, and he did not even realize what was happening.

So when she quickly made up her mind to join the jungle expedition without notifying the commanding officer, her husband, she was not being disobedient as an officer, she was just filing a strong protest as a wife, as billions of wives had done, in one way or another, before her.

Jackie had not spent as much time with the dragon as had others, so Wilson thought it would be a good idea for her to make friends with Baby. That was easy enough, since Jackie was easy to love and Baby loved everyone. Jackie found it to be quite exhilarating to ride Baby at her steady, ground-eating pace.

"Well, here's the plan," Wilson said. "My studies of Baby indicate that she's reached her full growth. She's like an eighteen-year-old girl now, nubile. Cindy McRae, who spends more time with her than anyone, gives me regular reports, and it's my opinion, from Baby's behavior, that the dragon is ready to mate. Now, the ideal way to do this would be to find a nest and capture a young male and wait for him to grow up, but it would be quicker for Baby to attract a male dragon of her own age, lure him to a point where we could tranquilize him, and bring him back with us. We'll keep both options open. Baby's keen sense of smell will lead us to one or the other, a nest or a male."

Cindy and Clay found Wilson and Jackie in the scout park, where Jacob West and Renato Cruz were helping them rig a sling that would cradle Baby comfortably.

"Dr. Wilson," Cindy said, "we've been talking, and we think Baby will make the trip better if Clay goes with her to keep her calm."

"That's a good point," Wilson said. "We'll be glad to have you, Clay."

"I'll ride on Baby's back while she's in the sling," Clay offered. "I'll be able to talk to her."

"Isn't that dangerous?" Wilson asked.

"I'll wear a rocket pack. If I fall off, I'll just lower myself to the ground and someone can pick me up," Clay answered.

"What do you think?" Wilson asked Jacob.

"Good idea," Jacob said. "I'd hate for her to panic and hurt herself."

Baby was nervous when Cindy led her into the sling and the scout ship's winch tightened it, but Clay, dressed in space armor and with a rocket pack, climbed onto Baby's back and talked soothingly to her as the sling was lifted until Baby's feet were off the ground. Since it was going to be a long, slow trip, a couple of stops had been planned along the way to give Baby a rest from being carried in the sling. It would be necessary to spend one night in the field, so Cindy got permission from her mother to go along if she promised not to go near a jungle.

Renato Cruz, in *Apache Two*, and Jacob, in a borrowed ship, would fly the airlift. As they prepared to leave, Jacob activated his radio and said to Clay, "I think I'll dump you off in that big lake where the big underwater animals are."

"Why would you want to do a thing like that?" Clay asked.

"Well, you smashed up *Apache One*, didn't you?"

"I brought her down in one piece," Clay retorted. "At least I didn't let her clobber in and be fragmented."

"Yeah, well, maybe I won't dump you," Jacob growled.

He would miss *Apache One*. Although all the scout ships had come off the same production line, each ship had its individual characteristics, and it would take him a long time to become one with another ship the way he had been with *Apache One*.

They had a nice night, camped out in the southern woodlands where a variety of wild fruit grew and where areas of trees were interspersed with grasslands. Then, on the second day of travel, they watched the land change as the beginnings of the vast, tropical jungle thickened, leaving only occasional clearings. They would reach the mesh landing surface atop the canopy in the deepest area of jungle late in the day, and after talking it over, it was decided that it would be best to camp another night. Then they would be at the mesh landing surface early the next day with many hours of daylight available to rig a way to lower Baby to the jungle floor and make an attempt to find a male dragon.

It was hot and steamy at the campsite in a small clearing that just barely gave the two ships a landing place. The men alternated standing guard, for they were in the land of the huge battering-ram creatures, the dragons, and other giant reptiles with teeth. They had landed in the early evening, and from the time Baby had been released from the sling she was restless, pacing the clearing, poking off into the surrounding trees so that she had to be called back constantly by Cindy, the one she obeyed best.

"I think she knows she's near home," Clay commented as they prepared for bed. Baby continued to pace restlessly, causing considerable confusion in the small clearing.

"Baby, lie down," Cindy ordered, and with a whining sigh, the beautifully scaled animal thumped her two tons of legs and body down near Cindy's bedroll.

Jacob, taking the first watch, was *very* alert. There were things out there that had not even been seen yet, much less named or identified. He had heard Theresita's descriptions of animals that would have made a six-ton African elephant look small, one of them so fierce that it

could kill and devour one of the battering-ram creatures—
and the rams were armored, and about four times the size
of a rhino.

So here he was, back in the jungle, while Theresita
was at home because Mandy Miller had wanted to run
some more tests on the baby. What in the name of his
Apache ancestors was he doing back in the jungle? He still
remembered how Baby's mama had sunk a set of impressive teeth in a tender portion of his anatomy as he was
being pulled up on the winch from the jungle floor.

When Renato Cruz relieved him at midnight, he
sighed and made his way to the fire that he had kept
burning to discourage the jungle animals. He was sleepy,
but the idea of closing his eyes when things like those
seen by Theresita were out there did not appeal to him.
He leaned back against his bedroll and listened to the
sounds of the jungle. From a distance he heard a terrible
scream of pain. Some jungle creature had just become a
meal for something with teeth. He shuddered. The others
were sleeping soundly, James Wilson making a small whistling sound. Jacob kept his laser ready and had his hand
on the butt of his pistol, a weapon that shot explosive
rounds and made a lot of noise. Sometimes noise was just
as effective against wild animals as something deadly. After a while his hand went lax and fell from the weapon,
and he slept.

Renato paced around the edge of the clearing, a laser
rifle at the ready, safety off. The fire was beginning to die
down, so he walked to it and threw on some deadwood.
Baby lifted her long neck, and the firelight reflected from
her eyes. "Easy, girl," he whispered. "It'll be morning
soon."

He was at the farthest distance from the campfire
when he heard Baby snort and then begin to make an odd
but rather sweet sound in her throat. He saw someone
move, then realized that it was Jackie Rodrick.

Renato did not know exactly what was going on between the captain and his wife, but he knew that something had happened, because he had answered the call
when the ships were about six hours away from Hamilton,

moving slowly because of the burden slung under Jacob's ship. The captain's voice had been formal, crisp. "Please put my wife on the communicator, Commander Cruz," Rodrick had said. Usually the captain would have been informal. Jackie, riding in Cruz's ship, had reached for the mike.

"This is Lieutenant Rodrick," she had said, her voice as stiff and formal as the captain's.

"I've been looking for a roster for the two-ship expedition to the jungle," Rodrick had requested. "I have not found it."

"I'm sorry, Captain," Jackie had said. "I filled in a roster, but I guess I forgot to file it."

"Please give me a list of the personnel," Rodrick had requested.

"List as follows," Jackie had said, and then she had listed the names of everyone aboard the ships without giving her own name.

"And?" Rodrick had asked.

"And Lieutenant Jackie Rodrick," she had answered.

"Thank you, that will be all," Rodrick had responded coldly.

"What was that all about?" Renato had asked after the contact had been broken.

"Oh, I just goofed," Jackie had replied, smiling. "I didn't enter the personnel list in the computer."

It was not like Jackie to forget regulations. She was as much a stickler for the rules as her husband. Renato began to wonder why, and he came to the conclusion that Jackie had not wanted the captain to know in advance the name of at least one of the members of the jungle expedition. And after thinking it over, he concluded that that name could only be hers.

But it was not up to him to concern himself about the personal affairs of the captain and his wife. He was just doing a job. He had a sling on his ship, too, in case they found a male dragon. He would fly the *Apache Two* to the mesh landing surface, would do his part, would fly the captured dragon home. He decided that he would not want to be in the captain's position, being married to a beautiful woman who happened to be a strong-willed and very capable space-service officer.

When Baby started to make those musical, pleasant sounds in her throat, and Jackie, wakened by the noise and by Baby's stirrings, sat up, Renato started walking back from the far end of the little clearing. Jackie moved to Baby's side. Lying down, with her eight-foot legs folded under her, Baby's back was as high as Jackie's waist. She patted Baby on the back and whispered soothingly.

From the jungle there came a call that Renato had never heard before, a musical trumpeting that rang through the air brazenly and caused a commotion among some night birds in the treetops. Baby lunged, bringing her feet under her, her long, slim body knocking Jackie's feet out from under her so that she fell on her stomach across Baby's back. She started to yell as Baby's long neck whipped around, her teeth gleaming in the dim firelight, for she thought that Baby was going to bite her. Instead, the dragon closed her mouth on Jackie's right leg and, without causing pain, threw Jackie's leg over her back. Then she lunged to her feet, Jackie clinging to the finlike projections, and, before Jackie could throw herself off, was running at full gallop for the trees.

Renato yelled at Baby to stop. He could hear Jackie telling her to "Whoa, Baby," and then she was gone, melting into the surrounding darkness. He ran to the spot where she had entered the trees. He could see the marks of her passage, the underbrush thrust aside, and he could hear her moving, already from a distance. He turned and yelled to Jacob. Jacob came awake with both hand weapons ready and, after taking a moment to orient himself, ran to where Renato was gazing off into the darkness.

"What the hell happened?" Jacob demanded.

"Baby just took off," Renato answered.

"Well, there's nothing we can do about it," Jacob said. He wasn't about to go into that jungle at night.

"Jackie's on her back," Renato added.

"Oh, damn," Jacob moaned.

"We going after her?" Renato asked.

"That dragon is moving at about thirty miles an hour," Jacob said.

"We'd better report."

"Yeah, I guess we'd better," Jacob said, blowing out a deep sigh. "It'll be light in about five hours, and we can conduct a search from the air with the life detectors."

Jacob himself got Rodrick on the radio and made the report.

"I don't quite understand why she rode Baby into the jungle," Rodrick said.

"We don't know either," Jacob replied. "I'm sorry, Captain." He felt inadequate and was asking himself what he could have done to prevent it. He could not really blame himself, but he was, after all, the senior man on the small expedition. And he knew how Rodrick must have been feeling, because he knew how he would feel if he were told, from a great distance, that his wife had ridden off alone into that jungle on the back of an animal.

On that morning Duncan Rodrick had other concerns. During the night the duty officer aboard the *Spirit of America* had wakened him, as per orders, to say that the ship's long-range detection instruments had spotted a small fleet of Whorsk airships off the coast toward the west. For the rest of the night the fleet had been using the winds to tack toward the coast just north of Hamilton.

At dawn Rodrick lifted off in a scout to investigate. The rest of the scouts were standing by. The admiral and Mopro were on alert to guard Hamilton City. Mopro's weapons could down any airship before it could get into position to drop the crude explosive devices used by the Whorsk. Jack Purdy was on Rodrick's left wing as they shot northward. The Whorsk fleet had come to a halt just offshore, and only one ship was proceeding over the land.

They had no difficulty locating the airship; it was heading southeastward toward the city, but still a couple of hundred miles away when Rodrick first saw it, low, ungainly looking. "All right, Jack," he said, "let's go down and take a look."

Rodrick's ship led the way. He slowed to almost

hovering speed and eased up alongside the ship. There were half a dozen of the insectlike Whorsk in the crude gondola. Rodrick turned on his hailer and played a tape made by Grace. Her voice, speaking in the Whorsk language, warned the ship to turn away from the city. The Whorsk in the gondola showed no signs of understanding, and the airship continued toward Hamilton. Rodrick played the tape again. Still the ship went on. He eased closer and opened the ports covering the ship's weapons and fired a laser beam across the ship's bows. The Whorsk were visibly agitated, but they calmed when a tall, bronzed, handsome man stood, thus allowing himself to be seen by Rodrick. One of the valley men was with the Whorsk.

Rodrick was about to speak in English, using the outside hailer, when his radio came to life, and an arrogant, clipped voice said, "You continue to take our metals from the miners. We will give you just this one last warning."

Rodrick saw the man's arm lift, and he juiced power into the scout's engine, because the man was extending a rodlike weapon toward him. The hydrogen engine hissed, and he was thrust back into his couch by the g-forces of acceleration, but then there was an eerie silence as the engine cut off and the ship stopped accelerating. As the ship started to tumble, he stabbed for the stabilization jets. To his relief, they were operational. He tried to start the hydrogen engine. No luck. He had not been flying high, and things were happening fast. He punched controls and the hydraulics extended the wings so that he had some gliding room, enough to take the ship out of the foothills of the Renfro Mountains to land smoothly on a grassy plain. He went in gliding; then, as the ship stalled, he inverted her and fired the rockets to make a rocket landing and burn a patch of grass in a circle around the ship. He opened his canopy, heard the roar of rockets firing, and saw Jack land the *Dinahmite* not a hundred yards away. He grabbed the mike. Max Rosen was on the bridge of the *Spirit of America.*

"Max, prepare for attack. They're using the field weapons, with a valley man aboard the airships. Use long-distance homing rockets and knock them out of the air before they get close."

But the attack did not come. The single airship that had penetrated the land mass turned and rejoined the others offshore, and then the entire fleet disappeared to the west. The hydrogen engines of the two downed scouts started without problem, and Rodrick was soon on the bridge of the *Spirit of America* with Max, Paul Warden, and the admiral.

There had already been some discussion. "If they're using broadcast power," Max said to the admiral, "they can curve it around the contours of the planet."

"The captain said the weapon was rather large and tubular," the admiral commented. "I think it more likely contains a source to store power."

"Whatever," Max said. "They can reach us right here in Eden, and I don't like that."

"But they have to come on the Whorsk airships," Rodrick remarked. "We can spot them far enough away to prevent a repetition of this morning's events."

"Have you considered stopping the gathering of metals?" Warden asked.

"The collection of rhenium is not negotiable," Rodrick said firmly.

"Then I guess we'd better start getting ready for another visit," Max remarked.

"Admiral," Rodrick said, "how's your work coming?"

The admiral shrugged. "It's very interesting, but I have nothing to report. I request permission to examine Dr. Bryson's personal notes in her quarters."

"Granted," Rodrick said. "And that brings up another subject, gentlemen. Paul was told that Sage Bryson would be returned to us. If they had intended to do so, the trip they've just made would have been an excellent time for it. As you know, Dr. Miller suspected from the looks of Sage's eyes that she was under the influence of drugs, perhaps the same drugs used on Theresita. I for one don't like having a member of our colony being held by those people, but I'm not sure now is the time to try to do anything about it. Does anyone have a suggestion?"

Paul Warden felt a pain in his stomach. He was no longer in love with Sage, but to think that she, who had been the victim of childhood abuse, should be in the hands of people who used drugs to induce sexual compliance was enough to make him very angry. He kept remembering his idea of sending a hydrogen warhead dropping down directly on the beautiful city, but he knew that was impractical for several reasons—not the least of which was the fact that Sage would die, too, if it were done.

"Dunc," Max Rosen said, "I think the only thing we can do is wait." Max had seemed to mellow after his marriage to Grace and after having been named second in command. "We've got the whole scientific community working on the problem of those weapons, but we're trying to rush through work that several generations of scientists on Earth could not accomplish. Much as I'd like to go in now after Sage, I think we'd better wait until we know a bit more about what we're up against. Meanwhile, I suggest we just get ready for any attack and, as you say, knock down any Whorsk airships while they're still a couple of hundred miles from us. If we knew the range of those damned weapons they have, we could be a little more relaxed and maybe not go off half-cocked and kill Whorsk that intend us no harm, but we can't take a chance. I'd hate to think what that weapon might do to the ship's computer or to the nuclear generating plant."

TWELVE

Four scout ships circled low over the northern portions of Columbia's equatorial jungle. One of them was flown by Duncan Rodrick, with Clay riding shotgun position and operating the life-detection instruments. The primary purpose of the search mission was to locate Rodrick's missing wife, but valuable information was also being gathered.

Although the density of the jungles was relative and the northern portions were as wild as anything along the Amazon, it soon became apparent that conditions for large animal life were more favorable with increasing distance from the equator, where the steaming heat and incessant rains produced growth so verdant that apparently only the battering-ram creatures could move about with any ease.

In the area of fifteen degrees north latitude, trees grew to a towering height, and the canopy of the jungle was solid, but there seemed to be less dense undergrowth. There were also more relatively dry areas. At the equator hundreds of thousands of acres were jungle wetlands, with the bases of the trees always bathed in torpid water.

With each new life-sign signal, Clay was feeding information into the ship's computer from the terminal aboard the scout, and when all readings from the scouts were correlated, a pattern became evident: There were three large and distinguishable life signals for land animals and a horde of smaller signals. The intensity of the signals told scientists the approximate size and weight of the animal, and only one was not tentatively identified. The battering-ram creature and the enormous predator that Theresita had seen in battle with a ram were distinguishable, and the third large animal seemed to be of a size with the ram's predator.

The puzzling thing was that there were, as yet, no life signals recorded to correspond with Baby's size and bulk. She would have registered about half the weight of a smaller battering ram, and her long neck and tail would have elongated the signal. It seemed as if she had disappeared from the face of Omega, and that her kind was very rare.

It was Cindy McRae, flying with Jacob West, who first observed that, as one of the large life forms moved in the jungle below, there were times when the signal simply ceased. She had been tracking one of the great beasts while Jacob circled slowly, wings extended for aid in gliding.

"Hey," Cindy said, "something just went wrong with the instruments."

Jacob looked at the life-sign indicator and, in that age-old tradition of the operator of a machine, leaned over and tapped on the glass over the instrument repeatedly with his forefinger.

"We'll have to go back to base and have it fixed," he said, reaching for the radio switch.

"No, wait," Cindy said. "I've got the signal back."

"Next time I'll kick it and it'll start working sooner," Jacob said.

Below them, the giant reptile Cindy had been tracking turned one-hundred-eighty degrees and began to backtrack. Again the signal disappeared and began again in less than a minute.

"Jacob," Cindy said, "look at that band of slightly darker green directly under us."

Jacob turned the scout so he could see better. There was a band of darker green in the canopy. It meandered like a winding river, its color definitely darker than the surrounding jungle.

"I've lost the signal again," Cindy told him. "Every time the animal goes into that dark-green area, I lose the signal."

Jacob passed that information along to the other scouts, and it was soon established that the winding areas of darker green laced the entire area, and when a large animal went under that dark green, the signals stopped.

Duncan Rodrick discussed the phenomenon with Max Rosen, who was on the bridge of the *Spirit of America*, and Max discussed it with Grace, who considered the natural blocking of the ultrashort frequencies of the life detector very interesting. Grace requested samples of the dark-green foliage. Jacob went down, hovered, and let the scout's hull sink a bit into the thick canopy, and Cindy opened a hatch and plucked samples of the large, shiny, dark-green leaves.

It was time for Jacob to return to base, but he detoured slightly to the south, to the area where the landing mesh was still perched atop the canopy. "Yep," he said, "we put the landing grid down on an area of that dark green. Right over there was where we found the nest where we got Baby." He got on the radio and said there was a possibility, since the dark-green area near the landing grid supported the varieties of nuts and fruits most favored by omnivorous Baby, that the dragons lived mainly in those darker areas and were thus screened from detection by the natural shielding of the leaves.

None of this made Duncan Rodrick feel any better. He was still puzzled by Jackie's actions and had no idea why she had attached herself to the expedition to the jungle without even informing him. And why had she chosen to ride Baby off into the jungle?

Jackie's wild ride had begun so quickly, she had been too surprised and shocked to leap off Baby's back. When Baby turned and tucked Jackie's leg over her back, all Jackie could do was hang on. In seconds Baby's long legs had taken her deep into the stygian darkness of the night jungle. As the undergrowth thickened, Baby once again twisted her long, flexible neck back and gently pushed Jackie down until she was lying with her face and torso pressed against Baby's back, holding on for dear life to one of Baby's dorsal fins. The fins on Baby's neck fended off lashing branches as the dragon began to move swiftly.

Jackie had very quickly passed a point of no return. She was not about to jump off Baby's back into that blackness. She was already disoriented. In the total darkness she had no sense of direction and would have been hopelessly lost a hundred yards from the clearing.

Now and then Baby paused and gave a particularly musical call, a call Jackie had not heard from her before. Once there came that answering bugle of sound, sweet and yet brazen, and Baby crooned in her throat and pressed on swiftly.

After two days of steady movement with just brief stops so Jackie could relieve herself, drink from a stream, or just stretch her legs, Jackie knew that they were a great distance from the clearing. "I hope you know what you're doing," she told Baby, "because I sure don't."

Baby knew exactly what she was doing. Only her finely developed sense of smell could have followed the delicately scented trail through the darkness. She had been taken from the jungle while quite young, but her instincts led her, taught her quickly how to find the best way through the dense, tangled undergrowth, and warned her once that there was something dangerous nearby, so that she left the trail and circled far out before coming back onto her path to pick up the scent.

Again there came that bugling call, and she answered with a musical warble. The call was repeated, and Jackie could tell that its source was now very close. Through the light that filtered down through the dense canopy, she could see the huge boles of trees, a shimmering of golden fruit on a low-growing tree, and now Baby's neck and head. And as Baby slowed and pushed her way into a clearing where the underbrush had been uprooted and piled in a dense mass around a circle, she saw the object of the dragon's search.

"Well, well," she said approvingly. "Baby, he's a handsome one. In this land there be dragons."

Baby halted, and the ruff around her neck inflated to show brilliant yellow, blocking Jackie's view of the other dragon. The bugle call of the male came, softer now. Baby turned, twisted her neck in what actually seemed to be coy flirtation.

Then the male dragon saw, or smelled, Jackie. His neck extended to its greatest height, and he roared in menace. He took a few prancing steps toward Baby and lowered his head in a position that could only be a threat. Baby's ruff deflated, her neck went down, her fins stood up to their greatest height, and there came from her long throat a howling growl even more menacing than that being made by the other dragon.

"Hey, kiddies, let's not fight," Jackie said, truly frightened.

The sound of her voice halted the male in his tracks. He raised his head, his bright eyes curious, and his neck twisted as if questioning. Baby's growl subsided, and she moved sideways toward the dead brush, which acted as a barrier around the clearing. Jackie's leg was pressed against that barrier.

"Easy, Baby," she said slowly.

Baby twisted her long neck and pushed her warm, moist muzzle against Jackie's side, making whining noises. "Want me to get off? Is that it?" Jackie asked.

She climbed up the barrier, found a solid limb, and hoisted herself into a tree laden with the golden ripe fruit that was Baby's favorite. It was full light now, and Jackie could see the beauty of the scales on both dragons.

The male was about a foot taller in the back than Baby. His scales were darker, more brilliant. He was indeed a handsome one. But he seemed uneasy. Baby was back in her coy pose, ruff extended in yellow glory, but the male was watching Jackie.

"Don't mind me, kids," she said. The male lifted his long neck and growled at her, and Baby moved swiftly to put the bulk of her body between the male and the tree in which Jackie was perched. The male backed off all the way to the other side of the clearing and turned his back. Baby, crooning musically, extended her ruff still further and began to prance. She worked her way to the center of the clearing and hopped on stiff legs, bouncing into the air to the accompaniment of short, soft cries. Then she began to turn, dancing now, lifting one leg at a time. It was, Jackie thought, very graceful.

"He's playing hard to get, Baby," she whispered.

Baby, as if reacting to that, stopped prancing and walked, head high, to the barrier directly under Jackie. The male twisted his long neck and watched as Baby lowered her ruff and turned her back. Then his ruff went up, a brilliant red, and he bugled. Baby was silent. The male moved, stiff-legged, to the center of the clearing, where Baby's prancing had further packed the detritus, and hopped. He hopped on four stiff legs, and when his feet landed all at once, the sound was like the beat of a giant drum.

When it became apparent that Baby's courtship was going to be a long and drawn-out ritual, Jackie plucked a soft, ripe fruit and began to eat. The two dragons were at opposite sides of the clearing, inactive. Baby looked up and gave her begging call. Jackie plucked a fruit and tossed it down, and Baby caught it, chewed, with juice dripping, and called again. She caught in her mouth the second fruit and then turned, pranced toward the male, extended her neck to within inches of his head, and made a soft, purring sound. The male took the fruit from her mouth and ate.

"I'll be damned," Jackie said. "You're going to have to support this lazy beggar?"

It became breakfast time, then, with Baby coming back for more fruit and giving every other one to the male. The male had edged closer to the barrier under Jackie, who plucked a fruit and held it, although Baby's neck was thrust up and she was begging.

"No, Baby, he's going to have to take this one from me," she said. "Come here, my friend." She exposed the fruit to the male with tossing motions, saw his eyes following the movement of the fruit, then tossed it. He caught it in midair and chewed, his brilliant eyes on Jackie. She tossed another, which he caught and gave to Baby.

"All right," Jackie said. "Now that's more like it. No male chauvinism in the dragon world, buddy."

It took about two dozen fruit each to satisfy the hunger of the two young lovers. Then it was back to the courtship. It was hours before they were dancing together, side by side in the center of the clearing, hopping up and down like animated pogo sticks.

Jackie said, "Baby, let's get on with it so we can get out of here."

But Baby seemed to be in no hurry. The character of the courtship had changed. Now the male was showing his crimson ruff constantly, and Baby had become aloof. "Baby, this is no time to be coy," Jackie complained, for her perch in the tree was becoming decidedly uncomfortable, and the day was passing.

By late afternoon the two dragons were side by side, calmer, their long necks twining and caressing. Jackie had been wishing for cameras to record the graceful, beautiful, sometimes comical mating dance of the dragons, but most of all she wished that Baby would finish the job, send her boyfriend packing, and return to the camp. She had heard scout ships passing overhead several times during the day, and she knew that the others must be concerned about her—not to mention Duncan. Nevertheless, she thought with grim satisfaction that it served him right if he was worried.

She knew that night was going to come swiftly to the jungle. Twilight would be brief. She dreaded to think that she would have to spend the night on the tree limb, but then she remembered how Theresita had woven a platform from branches to make a bed. She began to break off limbs after finding a broad, flat V of limbs branching out horizontally from the main truck. After slowly building a platform of branches and cushioning it with leaves, she was more comfortable. Below her the two young lovers were oblivious of her, lost in their own fulfillment of nature's second most powerful instinct.

Jackie gathered more fruit. She was thirsty, so she

found overripe fruit, squeezed the pulp into a hard rind, drank the juice, and threw away the pulp. That helped but did not totally satisfy her thirst. Darkness came in one rush, and the day noises of the jungle were replaced by the sounds of nocturnal creatures—the rustle of leaves above her as some animal prowled the treetops, a heavy crashing sound from the distance, the odd cries of a night flyer. In the clearing below, all was quiet, and she could not even make out the shape of Baby and her friend.

Jackie slept. She awoke to a rhythmic, musical, rather plaintive whining and recognized the timbre of Baby's voice. More silence. Then, well past midnight, she heard almost human sighs, small, musical sounds, and movement, regular, rhythmic. Then silence. But she was awakened again, early in the morning, by Baby's musical hummings. At dawn she saw that both dragons were lying down, side by side.

"I hope to hell you enjoyed it," she said, for she was stiff of limb, again in need of relieving herself, thirsty, sweaty, and quite disgusted with how long the courtship and mating rituals had lasted.

Baby rose, stretched, nuzzled her mate into wakefulness, and called to him until he too arose. She came to stand under Jackie and begged. "All right," Jackie said. "All right, lazy. Seems to me you could pick your own fruit." But she fed them a dozen fruit each, touched by their way of sharing with each other.

When she had had her fill, Baby came to stand with her side up against the brush barrier and called impatiently up to Jackie.

"Oh, so you're ready to go now, you shameless, hussy," Jackie said. "You've had your romp, and now you want to go home."

She climbed down, and while Baby stood very still, Jackie climbed onto her back. Then Baby turned, snorted to the male, who had been watching suspiciously, and went out through the almost concealed opening in the barrier. The male came behind, but once into the jungle, he took the lead and turned toward the east, or at least it seemed to be the east to Jackie, judging by the light of the sun, which was mostly concealed from her by the jungle's canopy. They had traveled almost the whole day before Baby complained and nipped the male on the tail, pushed into the lead, and turned north. This contest of will went on for some time before Baby's impatience convinced the male to follow her lead.

"Baby, I'm not sure," Jackie said, "but I think the camp just might be to the north of us, you know?"

Baby continued toward the north, moving steadily, now and then letting the male come alongside for a bit of neck-rubbing. The male no longer paid any attention to Jackie.

The following day Baby led the way across an open area where the undergrowth was unshadowed by trees. This cheered Jackie, for if Baby continued toward the north, they would reach an area of diminishing trees with wide areas of a tough, tall grass, and they would be clearly visible from the air. Unfortunately, she once heard a sonic boom from the south, which told her that the search was being conducted there, miles from her position.

When it was late, Baby seemed to be looking for something in particular. She ultimately found a fruit tree with broad, spreading limbs and stopped beside it. She stayed there, looking back at Jackie, until Jackie climbed into the tree. "So we're gonna spend the night here?" Jackie asked.

There was enough fruit on the lower limbs for the two dragons to pick themselves, but Jackie played with them anyhow, tossing fruit down to them each in turn. They seemed to enjoy the game, and the male really got into the spirit of it, begging just as Baby begged.

"I think we're going to be friends, you handsome devil," Jackie said, tossing a fruit. "So you're going to need a name, aren't you?" She mused about it. "Let's see, you're fancier than a peacock, and twice as beautiful. If you were a girl, I'd just call you Beauty. How about Adonis? Nope. Too pretentious. Let's see. You're Baby's lover. Baby and—Baby and her love, her beau. Beau. Hey, Beau." She threw him a fruit and then would not throw him another until, by calling his name, she could make him look up at her.

The sounds of mating came again that night from below the sleeping platform Jackie had constructed, and the travel toward the north began next morning, after another contest of wills between Baby and Beau. Finally, Baby set out by herself, not looking back.

"Are you just going to leave him? Was this just a one-night stand for you?" Jackie asked. "Or a three-night stand, as the case might be?"

The male was lost to view in the jungle, but soon Jackie heard a mighty crashing behind them and turned in alarm to see Beau coming at top speed, using his eight-foot legs to leap some underbrush, using his weight to crush others. "Kid," she said to Baby, "I think you've got him hooked."

She got a bit nervous when they came upon a broad river with waters stained dark by vegetation, but she soon discovered that Baby was a fine swimmer. The two dragons plunged in and moved through the water almost as fast as they could move at a trot. Nothing with teeth bothered them. Baby set the pace, moving ever northward.

After two days of flying search patterns over the jungle near the clearing from which Baby and Jackie had disappeared, Rodrick was seriously worried. One new type of life signal had been added to the colony's knowledge, and it was a provoking one. Renato Cruz had picked it up to the south. From the strength and shape of the signal, the creature weighed over four tons, was a hundred feet long, and tubular.

"The king of all snakes," Mandy Miller said back in Hamilton when she analyzed the recorded signal. "I would estimate that it has a body with about a four-foot diameter and could swallow a human without any strain." She got in touch with Renato by radio and asked him to monitor the signal to try to learn more. Renato, not fond of snakes, went down low, picked up the signal, and told Mandy that the creature moved through the jungle with undulations at a speed of about ten miles per hour.

"I just hope that Jackie and Baby don't run into anything like that," Renato said.

As the sun sank low on the third full day of the search, Duncan Rodrick sent out an all-units signal, waited for everyone to gather on the channel, and said, "When the light fails, we will abandon the search."

"Oh, no," Cindy moaned. She was flying with Jacob again. By acting as observer and instrument technician, she was freeing a more highly trained man or woman for other work. "We can't just quit and leave Baby and Jackie alone down there." She had visions of one of those huge snakes that Renato had located.

"Well, he's the boss," Jacob said. "I'm sure we'll keep sending ships down on a regular basis. Lieutenant Rodrick is smart enough to find a place where she can be seen." *If she's alive,* he was thinking, for he knew what sort of monsters prowled that jungle, not even counting the big snake of Renato's.

"Maybe she'll light a signal fire," Cindy said.

"If she'd been wearing her laser, she could," Jacob said. "But she had on only her uniform pants and shirt— what she was sleeping in. And in that jungle there's no possibility of finding flint or of making fire by the friction method. No, she'll have to find a big clearing and do something like spell out a distress code in dead branches, something that will stand out against the green. Those monkeylike things that live in the treetops give off a life signal so nearly like that of a person Jackie's size that we'd have to be right on top of her to pick her out by the signal."

"She's alive," Cindy said fervently. "I know she is. She's had service survival training, hasn't she?"

"Sure. Everyone who graduates from the Space Service Academy spends some time in the jungle, or they did before the South and Central American countries got too hostile. Before we left the Earth, the only place jungle training was available was in the kudzu thickets in the deep South or in Florida, and that wouldn't be the same as where I trained, in Panama. I'd guess Jackie got in on the real stuff. She can take care of herself. After all, Theresita survived for months in the jungle."

"We'll have to check the clearing where we camped every day for a while," Cindy said. "Will you do it, Jacob? I'll ride with you."

"Sure thing. I'll put in a request when we get back to base."

He spoke to Rodrick in the scout park that evening, when all the scouts had returned. Rodrick expressed his appreciation for Jacob's concern. "We can't tie up a ship that's needed elsewhere, Jacob," he said, "but any time one is available, I'd appreciate it if you'd do just that."

If the threat of the valley people from the Great Misty River had not been hanging over the colony, the lovely, long, pleasant hot summer days would have been a total joy. The inland oil fields were producing well. A plastic pipeline had been completed. Plastics, based on petroleum, were the colony's lifeblood. The plastic-fabricating machines, brought out from Earth, were infinitely adaptable. The pipeline itself was fabricated by one of the great machines. Oil was pumped into the machine on one end, and out of the other came the still-hot pipe, seamless, and endless as long as the supply of oil held out.

The streets of Hamilton had been paved in a special tough plastic. Here and there colonists were adding on rooms or amenities such as sun decks and swimming pools to their homes, for anyone had the right to use a fabricator that was not operating on a priority project.

Allen Jones and his marine biologists were finding ever new and sometimes deliciously edible forms of sea life. Amando Kwait's crops were lush and plentiful, and the experimental plants he was helping Dena Madden to develop were beginning to form fruit. All indications were that the engineering of sepraskin, that outside layer to protect the fruits and vegetables from insects, was a success.

Stoner McRae was camping in the field, where the mining machine was sinking a shaft toward the five-thousand-foot level, and the deposit of molybdenum ore held promise as a source for rhenium.

Grace Monroe had been asked to work with the dark-green foliage from the jungle that had the capacity to block out energy of certain wavelengths. She was finding it to be an interesting project, but Max was irritated because she was burning the midnight oil in her lab when he wanted her home at his side. But his irritation showed only in his pained look, and not at all when he was near Grace. It was impossible for him to be short or irritable with her—he had known the extent of her dedication to her work when he had proposed to her, and any expectation or hope on his part that she might change just because they had married would be unrealistic.

"It takes only a thin layer to block the wavelength used by the life detectors," she told Max when he came into the lab at the end of the workday to see if she was ready to go home. "I have something I'd like you to take a look at."

He bent to peer into an electron microscope and saw a very regular pattern of molecules.

"They are aligned so perfectly," Grace marveled. "And in nature!"

Max's imagination was kindled. He grunted and played with the controls of the powerful microscope.

"What are you doing?" Grace asked.

"Just thinking."

"You'll get it out of focus."

"So?"

"So nothing. I can get it back in focus," Grace admitted.

"You put this on the atom scanner yet?"

"No. I've got that scheduled. I'm just trying to determine some of the basic properties first."

"Oughta put it on the scanner," Max suggested. He had a hunch, but he did not want to voice it.

"Your wish is my command," Grace said, going to work to put a minute leaf section in place. While she worked, Max called the technician on duty at the fusion-fueled generating plant and warned him to be prepared for a heavy drain of power to Grace's lab. The scanner was a power-hungry piece of equipment.

"You test this stuff for magnetic properties?" Max asked, as Grace readied the machine.

"I expect you'd find the usual," Grace said.

"That's not like you, to make an assumption," Max teased, a slight hint of scolding in his voice.

Grace paused, looked at him. "No, it isn't, is it? On Earth, we'd expect to see the usual, the influence of the magnetic poles. But we're not on Earth, are we?"

"Not lately," Max replied.

"You run that while I clean the lens on the scanner," Grace said.

Max had not done such picky, lab-type experimental work since he had been in school, and for a while he was all thumbs. Finally, however, he had the leaf section positioned in a machine that would measure the alignment of electrons. He grunted.

"Something?" Grace asked. She was just about ready to turn on the atom scanner.

"Take a look," Max said.

"What's that?" Grace asked, as she examined the projection of the magnetic imager. "Is the machine malfunctioning?"

"Nope," Max said.

"But it's showing a field, and it's certainly not a magnetic field."

"Got that scanner ready?" Max asked.

The images on the screen of the scanner deepened the mystery. They expected to see the normal controlled chaos of particle movement. Instead, what they saw was a regularity of direction that was against all the known laws of atomic theory. The spin of electrons in the hydrogen atoms was uniformly in the direction of the long axis of the leaf from which the leaf segment had been taken.

"You want to explain that?" Max asked, his face showing that he was deep in thought.

"Not yet," Grace said, "because without further investigation I'd have to say that nothing like that can happen short of intervention by a supernatural power."

It had been four days since the all-out search for Jackie and Baby had been canceled, and for four consecutive days Cindy and Jacob had circled over the clearing where Jackie and Baby had disappeared, and then had flown slowly homeward. On the third day, in the same area where Renato Cruz had picked up the huge snake's signals, Cindy saw them. "Eeoo. Yuck," she said, shuddering.

"Say that again for me," Jacob said. He circled, and this signal seemed to be from a slightly smaller specimen, no more than seventy-five feet long.

"Somehow," Jacob said, "I don't think that man will ever want to build permanent settlements down here."

"*This* member of the race won't," Cindy said, crinkling her nose at the thought of Baby, or Jackie, facing such a monster.

On the fourth day, after flying over the clearing with the usual results—nothing—Jacob took a slightly different route home in order to cover still another strip of the jungle to the north of the clearing.

"That's supersnake again," Cindy said, as they neared the northern fringe of solid jungle and were beginning to see the grassy clearings among the solidity of green. "No, it's not the same one. This one is bigger." This one, she found when she ran the signal through the computer, was as big as Renato's. And it was moving at high speed, arrow-straight, toward a large clearing to the north of their position.

Although she was very much interested in the various forms of wildlife in the jungle and was constantly seeing new bird or animal forms, Jackie had had enough. She sweated even at night, and her uniform was always damp. She was developing an uncomfortable rash on her body where flesh rubbed against flesh. Even though the northward journey had started from a point relatively near the northern abatement of the jungle, Omega's distances were four times the relative distances on Earth, and even when Baby could approach her steady, smooth, only slightly rocking pace of about thirty miles per hour, it still took days to reach that area where, in spots, the jungle began to thin and an entire day would pass without rain.

The two dragons enjoyed being able to move freely in the open, their long legs lifting them well above the high grass. Beau would dash ahead, turn, rush full tilt at Baby, and then turn aside at the last minute, calling out in obvious pleasure. Baby was setting a rambling course now, as if looking for something in particular. What she found was a small stream next to a large clearing with acres of grass studded with isolated trees. She seemed content, and Jackie was too, for the clearing was a good place for them to be spotted from the scout ships.

There were fruit and nut trees growing around the clearing, and the water from the stream, although discolored by vegetable matter, tasted sweet. While Baby and Beau had a nice swim, Jackie removed her clothing and had a bath, standing only in knee-deep water, because now and then she had heard some impressive splashings from up or downstream. She rinsed out her uniform and hung it in the sun to dry. It was dry within an hour.

"So we're going to stay here for a while?" Jackie said to Baby.

They played "let's feed the dragons," although there was enough fruit on lower limbs so that Baby and Beau could have fed themselves. Jackie made a nice comfortable nest for the night, and then she turned her thoughts to creating some sort of sign for the scouts, just in case they flew over without having their life-detection instruments on. She had no way to make a fire. She had tried the friction method during her survival training and had never been able to make it work. There were plenty of dead limbs on the jungle floor to make a sign visible from the air, but the grass in the clearing was higher than her waist. She tried to tramp down the grass in an area at the center. It was slow, hot work, and as soon as she had bent the grass and jumped on it, it would spring up behind her.

Baby and Beau, watching her with obvious curiosity, helped. Their weight was so great that when their relatively small hooves pressed the grass down, it stayed down. And when one of them rolled playfully, a large area of grass was depressed. "That's the idea," Jackie said, as Baby joyfully pranced toward her. Jackie began to jump up and down, stiff-legged. Baby cocked her head. "Come on, lazybones," Jackie encouraged, jumping. Baby stiffened her legs and hopped. "Good girl," Jackie said, still hopping. Baby hopped. Beau nuzzled her and began hopping.

"Now you two keep your minds on what you're doing," Jackie said.

With two multiton animals hopping as if on springs and moving together, a circle of trampled grass was being cut. It was as if they were creating a soft nest like the circle of cleared and trampled ground in the heart of the jungle where they had done their courtship dance. By the time it was growing dark and Jackie retreated to her own berth in the fruit trees, there was a flattened circle of about fifty feet in diameter in the center of the clearing.

She heard an odd, new sound during the night. It was not a loud sound, and she was surprised that it had awakened her. There was a rattling, clicking noise, as if multitudes of small pebbles were being stirred. It diminished into the distance, and she went back to sleep.

In the morning she began to carry dead limbs from the jungle, choosing those from a particular kind of tree that bleached out white after they had fallen. She tried to get Baby interested in helping her, but Baby scorned carrying sticks in her mouth and instead either tagged along or capered in the clearing with Beau. It took Jackie all day to carry enough sticks to make a twenty-foot letter H in the area of trampled grass, and she was tired enough to be glad to climb up to her nest in the tree.

She started the next day by tossing fruit down to the dragons. Baby came up to the tree after eating, and Jackie climbed aboard for a ride across the clearing to the stream. After a drink, and after refreshing herself without undressing, she whistled to Baby, swimming in the stream with Beau, and the dragons came out. Baby lay down so that Jackie could climb on, and then they started at a leisurely pace back toward the center of the clearing.

A rumbling boom came down from the sky, a scout passing somewhere nearby at supersonic speeds. "It won't be long," Jackie said. "We'll be going home."

Beau was walking beside Baby, quite near. "What about you, big boy? Are you coming home with us?"

Beau had gotten to the point where he looked at Jackie when she spoke. He turned his head and opened his mouth and bugled at her.

"Yeah, I like you, too," Jackie said, grinning.

Baby stopped abruptly.

"What's happening?" Jackie asked.

Baby gave her call, and Beau stopped, turned, and walked to stand beside her. Baby twisted her neck and nudged Jackie gently. "What?" Jackie asked. "You want me to get off?" Baby moved closer to Beau until Jackie had to lift her left leg to keep it from being caught between the brightly scaled bodies. Baby nudged. "I think I get it," Jackie said. "You want him to carry the load for a while? I'm not so sure about that, Baby." But since Baby continued to nudge her with her muzzle, Jackie reached over and patted Beau on the back. He remained calm, so she put her hand on him and said, "Now you be a good boy, Beau." Then she put one leg over, and Beau turned his head around and bugled softly.

"All right?" she asked. Baby gave Jackie a nudge that actually lifted her weight, so she had to shift over to Beau's back to keep from being pushed all the way off.

"Nice Beau," Jackie said, as he twisted his long neck around to look her in the eyes. "Now if you don't like this," she continued, "I'll be happy to get off."

But Beau made a soft sound and began walking. Baby capered in circles around him, darting in now and then to touch his muzzle with hers.

They lay in the trampled circle for a while in the morning sun. Jackie scanned the empty sky, hoping to see a scout coming for her. She dozed and awoke to the sound of pebbles being stirred. It was coming from the trees nearest the circle. Baby and Beau were standing, very still, necks extended as high as possible, eyes trained on the trees.

"What is it?" Jackie asked.

A low, rumbling growl came from deep within Baby's long neck, a sound that made Jackie shiver. "Look, Baby, if whatever it is scares you, let's get the hell out of here."

She stood and looked around. The tall grass was rippling in a light wind. From the nearby trees came a raucous chorus of disturbed birds.

"I think I'll go climb my tree," Jackie said, starting toward her nest. Baby moved quickly to block her path, and made it obvious, by her actions, that she wanted Jackie to stay in the cleared circle. Beau pranced stiff-legged to the edge of the clearing nearest the trees, and now he was voicing that low, eerie, rumbling growl.

Something moved in the shadows of the trees. Jackie heard that distant sound of pebbles clicking together. And then one of humankind's universal nightmares thrust its head out from the trees into the glaring sunlight—a gray, wedge-shaped head fully six feet across. A slender tongue the size of a man's arm flickered out, felt, and tasted the air. Eyes one foot in diameter looked like black glass.

Jackie screamed.

The head of the king of all snakes jerked at the sound, and foot by foot, yard by yard, a scaled, gray and pink striped body emerged behind a slightly more slender neck, a body that grew until it was six feet in diameter.

The snake slithered into the clearing, scales clicking, a waterfall of sound. The huge body curved, thrusting aside the grass that was not tall enough to hide the snake's bulk. The curving, slithering back was exposed like that of a surfacing whale.

"Baby, I'm heading for the tree," Jackie said, her heart pounding in fear. She started to run, but Baby quickly put her body between Jackie and the edge of the clearing, reached out, seized a loose fold of Jackie's blouse, and tugged.

"Baby, dammit, that thing might not be big enough to eat you, but it can swallow me whole," Jackie cried, but the dragon pushed her to the far edge of the clearing, growled that strange, menacing growl, and then turned to face the snake.

The huge reptile sounded like a tin can partially full of pebbles being rolled steadily. Beau's red ruff had been extended to its greatest limits, and his long tail was lashing back and forth threateningly in short arcs. Baby ran to stand beside him, extending her own ruff. The snake lifted its massive head, fixed those two huge, black-glass eyes on the dragons, and gave a hiss like high-pressure steam escaping. Beau roared and began to sway from side to side on his long legs. The head of the snake moved slowly, steadily, coming ever closer. The long tongue flickered. Baby was swaying, too, and it was obvious that both dragons were tense, muscles quivering.

Suddenly, the huge head lunged. It came toward Beau like a wrecking ball, and Beau bounced, leaping high and to one side. The head thudded to the ground, overlapping the trampled area of grass.

It all happened so suddenly that Jackie had trouble following the swift movements. First the giant snake struck, its mouth open to show terrible, back-curved teeth, and then in a blur of motion Beau was out of the way and the snake's head made a solid thud of sound on the ground. Baby was in the air, her legs stiff and sharp hooves pointed, coming down with her weight on top of the snake's flat head. The head jerked, throwing Baby off-balance. She crashed to the ground on her side, rolled, and was back on her feet even as the head was withdrawing to slash toward the spot where she had fallen. This time it was Beau who landed with his tons of weight on the snake's head. When the head withdrew again, blood was running down to film one of the glassy eyes.

Baby, seeming to be unshaken by her fall, bounced off to one side, and the snake's head followed her motion, made one feint, then struck. But Baby went straight up in the air, landed with all four feet on the snake's head, bounced off, and sprang away even as Beau landed on the head right behind her. The snake's huge body was writhing and coiling, but the head was moving feebly. One after the other the dragons threw all their weight onto the snake's head, their sharp hooves cutting and penetrating, and then, with a bugled cry of triumph, Beau stood still. Baby jumped up and down on the snake's head, blood splattering, for a few more times before she was satisfied. She came into the clearing, ruff deflating, and called to Jackie.

"Baby, you are not only beautiful, you are valiant," Jackie said, her stomach churning.

Baby called to Beau, who was sniffing the snake's head as if to be certain it was dead. Then the two dragons came to Jackie. Baby folded her legs under her, and Jackie climbed quickly aboard, thinking that maybe they knew there was another of those things of sheer horror out there, but the dragons merely wanted a bath. They galloped to the stream and washed off their bloody feet gingerly before plunging into the water while Jackie watched from the bank.

Cindy spotted Jackie's white H against the green background. Straight lines are rare in nature, and the two parallel uprights with the horizontal crossbar of the letter H are easy to see from the air. She was so excited she could not speak. She punched Jacob on the shoulder and pointed, and Jacob immediately peeled off and sent the scout screaming down toward the clearing.

"Oh, no," Cindy cried, as she saw the gray and pink corpse of the huge snake, its head lying just outside the trampled area.

"I see it," Jacob said. "Open the weapons ports, Cindy."

Cindy punched the right buttons. She drew a bead with a laser cannon on the snake's head as the scout continued to lose altitude rapidly. Then she punched magnification into the optics and focused on the snake's head to see that it was cut and battered, with blood everywhere.

"Jacob, I think it's dead."

"I don't want to have to face whatever it was that could kill it," Jacob said. "Do you see anything?"

"No."

"I get big life signals from the treeline along that stream," Jacob said. "Be ready with that laser."

"Jackie was here—," Cindy said sadly.

"Yes," Jacob replied. "I'm going to hover. Use all scanners."

Jackie did not hear the hydrogen engine of the scout over the splashings of the two dragons. When Baby came out of the water and shook, making a shower, Jackie yelped at her and ran. Baby chased her playfully and overtook her, seizing her by the back of her blouse. Beau pranced up to get in on the fun and nuzzled Jackie.

"The two large life indications are moving this way," Cindy said.

"See anything else down there?"

"Nothing. The body of that monster is still warm. Shows light red on the heat indicator."

"I think we're just about to see what killed it," Jacob said, holding the scout perfectly still on its hovering jets, turning the nose slowly to point toward the line of trees along the stream.

"Hey!" Jackie yelled, so loudly that Beau shied.

"Hey!" Cindy yelled, as two dragons and Jackie came loping out of the trees.

Beau jerked to a stop. "It's all right," Jackie assured him, patting his side. "Take it easy." The scout hovering fifty feet off the ground was the prettiest sight she had seen in years. She waved and yelled. Beau was nervous. Baby came alongside, and Jackie said, "Let's go see who has come after us, Baby." She climbed on Baby's back.

Beau lagged behind. The scout landed in the trampled area, and Cindy stuck her head out and yelled a greeting. Baby trotted up, and Jackie got off. Jacob and Cindy were now standing outside.

Jackie was relieved to see that Duncan was not aboard the scout. She knew that she had some explaining to do. After days in the jungle, and after thinking that she might become a meal for the king of all snakes, she was not nearly as angry about his apparent concern for Mandy Miller as she had been.

"She's found a mate," Cindy said dreamily, "and he's beautiful."

"It was love at first hop," Jackie informed them.

"Have you ridden him?" Cindy asked.

"Baby tamed him rather quickly. Look, I can't say how glad I am to see you two."

"Looks as if you had some excitement here," Jacob remarked, nodding toward the snake.

"I'll tell you all about it later," Jackie said, cringing. "Right now let's have you two make friends with Beau and see if we can gain his trust so that he'll let us airlift him home."

It took a while, but Baby seemed to understand what her friends were trying to do. She stayed close by Beau and encouraged him. He took to Cindy quickly and Jacob a bit more slowly, but it was hours before they could get him to come near the ship. Meanwhile, the word had been spread that Jackie was safe and that if things worked out, there would be a breeding pair of dragons in the colony.

Jack Purdy and Clay flew down carrying both of the slings, and soon Clay was riding Beau as if they had been friends all their lives. Beau was having his first taste of human's food and liking it. He was a sucker for candy and soon was begging shamelessly for it. Using bribes of candy, Clay got him to stand still to have the sling put under his belly. He remained calm until Jack lifted ship and put a strain on the sling, then he got a bit panicky.

"It's going to take a while," Clay said. "We'll have to spend the night here."

Jackie considered having one of the scouts fly her back to Hamilton. Now that her little adventure was over, however, she was having a bit of a challenge in justifying her behavior. Looking back, trying to remember her state of mind when she had gone off to the jungle without so much as telling Duncan her intentions or, above all, getting the permission of her commanding officer, she was feeling, she realized wryly, much as a small child feels when she knows that she has done something wrong and that punishment, even if only in the form of a disappointed look or a voiced reprimand, is inevitable. She decided to put off the reunion with Duncan until everyone, including the dragons, had gone back to Hamilton.

Spending another night in the open was all right with Baby and Beau, as long as there was a tidbit of candy now and then. And the next day the training began again. By midafternoon Beau was allowing them to lift his feet off the ground, as long as Cindy or Clay was on his back.

Since it was too late to travel far that day, the homeward trip was delayed one more night. Then the two ships lifted off side by side, with Clay and Cindy riding on the backs of the dragons, both of them in suits with rocket packs.

The entire colony turned out to welcome the new addition. Beau, seeing all of them, got a little nervous, but Clay kept talking to him and giving him bits of candy, and Baby soothed him with her soft muzzle, and he soon began to show off a bit, prancing and extending his handsome red ruff.

"Clay, you and Cindy stay with them until Beau feels at home," James Wilson said.

Nothing would have suited Cindy better. She rode Baby, and Clay rode Beau, and Jumper ran alongside Baby to the clear creek where the dragons had a bath and Beau got acquainted with the small dog.

"I think it's so cute," Cindy said, as she lay next to Clay on the smooth, soft moss of the creek bank. "Look at them. I think they're really in love."

The two dragons were resting side by side on the other bank of the creek, Baby's head lying on Beau's side.

"It must be something in the air," Clay said, leaning up on one elbow to kiss her.

Within a few days Beau had been taught his lessons— not to eat the crops, not to walk on gardens. And he had learned how to coax tidbits out of the colonists, vying with Baby to summon the lady or gentleman of the house to a friendly window by bugling softly.

Duncan Rodrick had been present when the two scouts with the dragons suspended in slings underneath had been lowered slowly, carefully. He appeared to be quite calm on the surface, and indeed he was thinking mostly about how nice it was that there was now a breeding pair of dragons. He was also admiring the skill of the pilots as they lowered the ships until Baby's and Beau's feet touched the ground at almost the same instant, slack came into the slings, and Clay and Cindy were climbing down to assure the two colorful animals that everything was all right. He stood with his hands clasped behind his back until the harnesses were removed from the dragons and the two ships lifted a few feet, slid sideways in the air, and landed side by side.

Jackie had been able to do some repair work on her appearance, but her uniform was the worse for wear. When Rodrick saw her climb down from the scout, he first felt a sense of gladness, but it was tinged with just enough guilt to make him feel angry. Not once but several times, even as he told himself that he did not really *want* that, the what-if questions had haunted him during Jackie's absence. What if she were dead? And the answer to that, coming from deep within him, was—*Mandy, Mandy, Mandy*.

Yet he had not wished Jackie dead. Instead he had felt anger and loss and frustration and pain. And he was glad to see her back—so glad that the sight of her sent a surge of elation, a visceral longing to be near her, through him. He strode forward and met her. She had her head lowered, and she looked up at him from beneath her long, dark auburn lashes with a repentant half smile on her face.

"That was a foolish thing to do, Lieutenant Rodrick," he said, and it came out much more harshly than he had intended.

So it is coming, she thought, her heart sinking. Not, "Hey, babe, I'm glad to see you, happy that you're safe"; just recriminations. She lowered her gaze and did not see him reach for her. She only felt his hands on her arms and the strength in his arms as he pulled her to him and crushed her, almost painfully, to him.

"Idiot," he whispered. "You had me climbing the walls."

She looked up. Was that actually wetness in his eyes?

"If you ever—" he said, and then he could not finish because his lips were on hers. Someone nearby was whistling as he clung to her. *So, dammit,* he was thinking, *maybe a man* can *love two women*. Or maybe, he thought, he was not yet fully grown up—holding that childish crush on Mandy Miller—but whatever it was that was going on inside his head, this woman meant the world to him, any world, be it Earth or Omega.

As for Jackie, gone were all the doubts. It no longer

mattered what had happened between Duncan and Mandy. She was where she belonged, in her husband's arms, and she was glad now that she had gone to the jungle as she had, since *this* was the result, for his reactions did more than a million words to convince her of her status in his eyes.

THIRTEEN

Mandy Miller was in summer uniform when she knocked on the door of the Rodrick home just after dark. The uniform was not official; it had just been adopted by most of the colony's women because of Eden's dry, hot days and because the colony still depended on the limited capacity of the *Spirit of America*'s automated tailor shop. Fashion had not been given a high priority, although Amando Kwait had already produced a crop of the long staple cotton that was the best fiber suited for making cloth, and there was no shortage of material.

It was a matter of taking the time to design clothing, and then to program the equipment in the tailor shop to produce the selected patterns. To meet the needs dictated by Omega's summer weather, the tailor shop was producing shorts in three colors and a simple cotton camp shirt to match.

Mandy was expected, since she had called, after having missed Rodrick during the workday. The door was opened by Jackie, who was dressed like Mandy but in a different color.

"Hi, Mandy, come on in. We've just finished dinner," Jackie said.

If there had been any strain put on the Rodrick marriage before or by Jackie's unauthorized journey to the southern jungles, it was not evident to outsiders.

Duncan Rodrick was in the living room of the spacious house. The smart plastics of the walls had been turned to be opaque, and there was a soft glow of light emanating from the walls and ceiling.

"Captain, I'm sorry to have to disturb you at home," Mandy said.

"No problem," Rodrick replied. "Coffee? Or we have wine from Amando's vineyard. It's not bad, if you haven't tried it."

Mandy laughed. "There are those who say that it's Amando's finest achievement to date, even considering what he's doing with insect control through genetic engineering and those wonder plants of his that are going to produce all year long."

Jackie poured a glass for herself and for Mandy. Looking at Mandy strictly from a woman's viewpoint, it was easy to see why Rodrick would have been attracted to her. She was a bit older than Jackie but younger than Rodrick. She was in the full bloom of womanhood—mature, very well-rounded, not an ounce of overweight, no blemishes on her long legs. Jackie still tended to be rather girlishly slim, although she was by no means a girl.

All right, she told herself. *Knock it off.* She had told herself repeatedly that she had been wrong in thinking that Rodrick was concerned only, or mainly, with the safety of Mandy Miller while the expedition to the Great Misty River was out of contact. She had promised herself no more silliness. Rodrick had married *her.* He had chosen *her.* And yet she could not help but remember that when Rodrick had married her, Mandy's husband had been alive.

"Captain," Mandy said, "I want to talk about Sage Bryson. I am very worried about her."

Rodrick shook his head. "That's a subject that eats at me all the time."

"She chose to stay," Jackie reminded him.

"Under the influence of a drug?" Mandy asked. "We were given no choice. They had those weapons trained on us. True, she *said* she wanted to stay, but I'd stake my professional reputation that she was already drugged. If it was the same drug they used on Theresita, it's a mean one. We can only guess at the long-term effects, but we're sure that it could lead to serious brain damage and, at the very least, a loss of memory. Judging from our work with Theresita, the drug's short-term effect is that of a powerful aphrodisiac."

"It can be made from that plant that Theresita found along the river?" Rodrick asked.

"Yes," Mandy confirmed. "And it takes only a minute amount to be highly effective."

"I don't think we'll have any problem with our current population," Rodrick said, adding one more worry to his already large collection, "but I don't like the idea of having a drug easily available that heightens the sex urge. Jackie, remind me to talk with Amando, to find out the distribution of that plant. We don't want future generations of druggies, and a drug like that might be too great a temptation for anyone to resist."

He wearily ran his hand through his hair. "Well, Mandy," he said, "we're all worried about Sage. If you're asking whether I have any plans to go after her, I don't. I have thought about it. Just looking at it from a practical viewpoint, we could use her knowledge in the work being done with that vegetation from the south that blocks out certain electromagnetic waves. But I'm just not in a position to risk more lives. Those people on the river have left us alone since that one incursion of the Whorsk airship. It seems to me that they would have to have a limited offensive capacity if they need to depend on lighter-than-air craft to reach us here in Eden. We can spot the Whorsk ships a couple of hundred miles away and knock them out of the air before they can bring their impressive weapon within range. We can protect ourselves without the loss of a single life, Mandy, but could we send in a battle group to get Sage without loss?"

"They told Paul that they would return her," Jackie commented.

"I understand your position, Captain," Mandy said. "But I'm looking at this as a doctor. Somehow Sage got through the psychiatric screening on Earth without her deep-seated neuroses being discovered. She knew beforehand that part of her duty in the colony would be marriage and childbearing. But the old wounds erupted, and she came close to being the first permanent mental patient on Omega. If the valley people are using that drug to give her the same treatment that they gave Theresita while she was with them, it might not be good for her to come back. When the drug wears off and she realizes what she's done, I don't know what will happen to her emotionally."

"I'm sorry," Rodrick said, "but all we can do is wait and stay alert. Since those people are so jealous of the metals we get in trade from the miners, I think that sooner or later they'll have to come to us, because we're going to keep on accumulating metals. The next move will be up to them, and we'll be ready for them."

Initial exploration had shown the great marshes on the southern coast of the Eden peninsula to be the site of the richest oil-bearing deposits yet discovered. Plenty of oil to fill current needs was being produced by the wells in the rocky highlands, but the oil geologists were looking to the future and were drilling a test well on a hummock on the northern fringe of the marsh.

The drilling crew consisted of three men under the leadership of Elton Dark, the man whose discoveries had allowed the squeezing of oil from deposits thought to be unrecoverable on Earth. Elton's men called him the tall Texan because he was only five-feet-six-inches tall and spoke with a back-country Texas drawl. Short but stockily built, Elton Dark, at forty-five, was a match for any man in his crew. He had compensated for his shortness by long study and practice of a half-dozen ancient methods of hand-to-hand combat, and the strength of his small frame was amazing. He was married to a woman who stood four inches taller than he, and their two children showed signs of taking after the mother.

Elton was having a ball on Omega. After years of searching already pumped-out fields for just a few barrels of usable petroleum, he was in an oil geologist's heaven. He had a whole planet whose oil resources had never been tapped—a planet four times the size of Earth—and everywhere he went, he found the right underground formations for oil.

"If'n they was a pipeline to Earth," he often said, "we could drown 'em in oil."

There was not much work for a man to do once the drill rig was in place, pulled there by one of the large crawlers. A camp had been set up on dry ground five miles to the north of the drilling site, and each morning the four men made a leisurely drive to the site to see how far the rig had penetrated during the night, service the machine, and collect samples of insect and animal life for the scientists in Hamilton City who were always pleading with field crews to bring them new species.

Elton's one weakness was fishing, but not just any kind of fishing. He was of that ancient and pure breed of angler who felt that the only sport was fly-fishing. Since sports equipment had not been a high priority as a part of the *Spirit of America*'s cargo, Elton had had to make his own equipment in the shop he had built onto the back of his house in Hamilton. There he used both salvaged and native materials to tie what his friends said were some of the damnedest-looking flies they had ever seen.

"Wa-al," Elton would say, "ain't they some pretty odd fishes here? An odd fish needs an odd fly, boys."

Elton's one concession to modern techniques in fishing was the use of plastic in making his fly rod and line. He fashioned his line-storage reel from scrap on a metal lathe, taking infinite care with each small part.

The network of waterways in the marsh had attracted Elton's interest from the first time he had flown over them, and he had been waiting for an opportunity to cast his flies upon the waters to see what dwelt thereunder. With the drill rig working well and not much to do but wait until the drill penetrated the rock mass far under the surface, Elton inflated a small boat, told his three men to keep on keepin' on, and embarked from the hummock with the same high hopes entertained by fishermen for thousands of years.

The marshlands seemed to be safe enough. The shallow waters did not appear to support any large forms of

life, such as had been seen in the southern lakes. There
was an interesting variety of amphibians, some froglike,
but nothing with fangs or teeth had been detected. Nevertheless, Elton went armed, although he soon removed his
arms belt and tucked it into a waterproof compartment at
the front of the small boat. Small insects came to examine
him occasionally but without biting, and curious waterfowl
followed him, swooped to take a look, saw that he was too
big to eat, and flew on. It was, as Elton had said previously to his men, "a gawjus day."

"Now come on, you little honeys," Elton coaxed after
he had laid a variety of flies enticingly atop the water in
the waterways around and near the hummock. "You ain't
gonna disappoint ol' Elton, are you?"

He paddled the boat back past the hummock, heading deeper into the marsh. The three men of the crew,
bare to the waist, were lazing in the sun.

"Hey, Elton," one of them yelled, "you promised
fresh fish for lunch."

"Jest hol' your horses," Elton yelled back. "I ain't
learned the language of these marsh fish yet."

He paddled around a hummock and was out of sight
of the drill rig. He made careful note of the route he took
so that he would be able to find his way back without
having to use his radio—and probably earning a horse
laugh from the men for having gotten lost. As he came
into a winding, narrow waterway, the motion of the boat
told him that a slow current was moving. He drifted and
began to lay what he thought was his prettiest fly up along
the grass. Something hit like a tornado.

"Whooooeee!" Elton yelled as he gave the fish line. "Oh,
yeah!" he said, as he began to work the fish, feeling that he
would have to be careful or lose it. It took him a full ten
minutes to get the fish to his net, and when he dipped it
out, it was a frantic, gleaming beauty, slim and streamlined.

"Boy, you are indeed a fighter," Elton said as he
slipped the hook out of the fish's mouth and lowered it
gently into the water, where it gave one mighty flip and
was gone. "Go tell your buddies ol' Elton is here, and he
wants to play."

He played until late in the day, hooking fish with regularity and drifting on the current in that winding waterway. He did not save any fish because that variety had not been tested for edibility, but he had himself a ball. When he figured he had had enough action, he stowed his fishing gear and began to paddle back against the current toward a particular shape of hummock, which would guide him in the right direction. He was humming happily, fulfilled, full of admiration for the fighting ability of that breed of fish, when a hand jerked the paddle away, and with a splash two monsters from the dark lagoon—or at least that was what flashed through his mind—shot up and took turns trying to stab him to death with sharp knives.

Following his flash of fear at the suddenness of it, he lashed out with his left hand, and his fighting callus on the edge of his palm crushed the throat of a Whorsk—for in a split second he had recognized the two attackers for what they were, and then he was thrusting his right arm up to ward off a downward stab of the other Whorsk's knife and bringing his left in under. He heard the breast carapace of the Whorsk crunch, and the thing fell back and flopped feebly in the water.

"Wa-al," he said, diving for his laser pistol in the compartment.

The water had calmed. The two Whorsk had sunk. Elton used his hands to paddle over and retrieve the floating oar, and then he headed for the drill rig, paddling as fast as he could, because he had used his belt radio and could not get a rise out of the men at the rig. He missed his way only once in the maze of the waterways, and then he saw the top of the rig and heard Whorsk voices. He eased up to the end of the hummock and peered around.

"Oh, you bug-faced bastards," he moaned, because he saw blood and his three dead pals being hacked apart by about a dozen Whorsk. He took out his laser and began to blast. The Whorsk fell quickly, only one of them being able to run and jump into the water to disappear.

He made it to the hummock, kicked aside a few dead Whorsk, and stood, weeping, looking down on the mutilated bodies. They had all been real good ol' boys. He heard a sound behind him. He whirled, and three Whorsk came dashing out of the water, knives ready. He lifted his laser but then changed his mind—he needed to express himself. He had just lost three friends, and it had made him hoppin' mad. He put the laser in the holster, snapped the flap, and met the leading Whorsk with a kick to the stomach that sent the stickman flying. He dodged under a knife blade, came up with a finger jab under a Whorsk chin, and heard the snapping sound of the outer skeleton. He took his time with the next one, feeling just a bit ashamed of having such a great physical advantage over the Whorsk. He killed the last one with a combination of flying kicks, then looked around. All was quiet.

He went to the crawler and activated the beacon, then called, "*Spirit*, this is Drill Team Three. Do you read?"

"We read you, Three," Ito Zuki said. "What's happening, Elton?"

"Wa-al, things I don't like one bit," Elton said. Then, as water erupted all around and a passel of Whorsk came swarming up onto the hummock from the dark waters, he said, "'Scuse me for a minute, Ito. I got somethin' I havta take care of."

He used the crawler's laser, sweeping in a circle—the deadly beam crackling and sizzling as it contacted the charging Whorsk.

"Elton," the radio was saying, "are you in trouble? Do you need help?"

It was over in a minute. It had been, of course, a slaughter. The Whorsk had not even been carrying bows, only knives. Elton figured that was because it would be difficult to swim underwater with bows, arrows, and spears.

"No," he told Ito, "I don't need any help right this minute, but I guess you'd better send down someone with three body bags."

"Elton," Ito said, his voice rising, "what's going on?"

"Wa-al," Elton said, "I got me three dead friends down here, Ito. Seems them Whorsk thangs swim underwater pretty good, like an ol' snappin' turtle or somethin'. They got the boys unawares."

"Stand by," Ito said. "We'll send help immediately."

"Ya'll might send a ship south of here," Elton suggested. "They's got to be one of them airships around somewhere."

There was. A Whorsk airship had landed on a large hummock two miles to the south of the drill rig. Jack Purdy shot it down as it tried to rise, and later, three Whorsk were picked up alive.

While he waited, Elton covered the mutilated bodies of his friends with canvas from the crawler, and he had had his cry for them by the time Duncan Rodrick landed a scout beside the drill rig, which was still drilling, and looked at the piles of dead Whorsk.

That same day a minerals team was attacked on the south shore of Lake Dinah, with one man wounded seriously by a Whorsk arrow.

Elton rode back to Hamilton with Rodrick, leaving an armed crew with the drill rig. He had a gash on his left arm. Mandy Miller offered Elton a local anesthetic.

"Wa-al, Mandy," Elton said, "I don't think I'll need it."

"I have to clean that gash," she said. "It's going to hurt."

"Not as bad as my buddies was hurt," he said.

He gritted his teeth, and sweat broke out on his forehead as she cleaned the wound. "Now wait," he said, as she ladled a dark substance from a jar and started to apply it to the wound. "First you half kill me cleanin' that li'l ol' cut, and now you're gonna put mud in it?"

Mandy laughed. "I know how you feel, Elton. I spent a lot of years learning how to be totally antiseptic and studying various wonder drugs and learning to stitch up wounds. But this mud from Theresita's River does a better job of killing Omegan germs than anything we've got, and it'll heal that cut without much of a scar—which there would be if I stitched it."

"I'll be doggoned," Elton said.

*　　*　　*

There were some unanswered questions. The most important question was this: How did the two Whorsk airships penetrate Eden's land area without detection? Jack Purdy first flew a crew of technicians to the wreck near Lake Dinah to investigate. The airship was heavily damaged, and Purdy stood by while the techs cleared away the heavy folds of the gasbag from atop the gondola, then began to sift through the wreckage underneath. The Whorsk occupants of the gondola had jumped out and glided to the ground on their leathery glider wings, and had been captured. Jack was halfway expecting to find the body of one of the very human people from the Great Misty River in the wreckage.

The gondola yielded a variety of Whorsk weapons, some water bags, and containers of food. There was nothing to give a clue as to how the ship had entered Eden's airspace while avoiding detection. Jack was about to call it quits and head for the wreck to the south, on a hummock in the marshes, when a technician said, "Jack, there's been a little fire here."

Jack walked over and looked. The boards of the gondola's bottom had been scorched, and a hole about six inches in diameter had been burned through.

The technician was looking down through the hole. "Let's move the planks," he decided. Another technician helped him, and they cleared away the planking of the gondola.

"Looks like fused metal," the technician remarked as he examined a blackened, small mass lying on the ground. He touched it tentatively. "It's cool now."

The same blob of fused metal was found in the other wreck in the south. Lab tests showed the two melted masses of metal to be an alloy of aluminum. This discovery added one more element of concern: If the valley people had the capacity to make aluminum, their technology was quite advanced. Then one of the melted blobs was cut carefully, and what the technicians saw caused them to call Duncan Rodrick to the lab.

"Captain," one of them said, "take a look at this cross section. See the patterns of different colors? This larger, dark area here still shows a weak electrical field. I'd say that it was a small power supply—a battery or a solar accumulator. And there are the remains of circuitry. It was a complicated little gadget."

"And its function?" Rodrick asked.

"Well, I can take a wild guess based on what we know about the valley people," the technician said. "The ship down south possibly came in over the water and the marshes, flying with the gondola so low that it was dragging the grass, and our detectors might have missed it. But the one up by Lake Dinah had to cross hundreds of miles of land, and in addition to the detectors aboard the *Spirit*, we had scout ships in the air at all times. Even if that one hugged the ground, we'd have picked it up. I think this little gadget is a portable field generator, which makes the same kind of field that is hanging over the river."

"Such a field would have blocked our detection instruments," Rodrick verified.

"I don't see any other explanation," the technician said.

Rodrick once again was forced to order limitations on all field teams. He had a round-the-clock relay of scouts flying Eden's perimeters. The two attacks had changed his attitude about leaving the valley people alone. He called Max Rosen, Paul Warden, and the admiral to his quarters.

"We've lost three more men," he said. "That is intolerable. They have forced us to take action. The question is, what action will we take?"

"There's a historic precedent for this," Warden said. "Back in the nineties the Russians and some of their stooges were using terrorism as a weapon of conquest. There was no way to defend a civilian population against terrorists willing to die while making a violent political statement. Some attempts had been made previously to hit the bases where terrorists were trained, and that seemed to work fairly well as a deterrent. In the eighties, before the Republicrats took over, a Conservative president whose name escapes me at the moment risked a direct confrontation with the Russian air and naval forces by wiping out the military capability of three of the Middle Eastern nations who trained and financed terrorists."

"You're saying we should hit them where they live, in the valley?" Rodrick asked.

Paul nodded, his eyes locked with Rodrick's.

"If they've got portable field generators that allow them to sneak airships past our detection system, we're bound to lose more people. The Whorsk have a totally alien set of values about life," Warden said. "They don't seem to mind getting killed. Elton Dark told me that the Whorsk kept running into the direct field of fire of the laser cannon until the last of them was dead."

"How's Grace doing with the interrogation of the captives?" Rodrick asked Max.

"They're perfectly willing to talk," Max said, "but all they say is that they were sent to punish us for stealing their metals. When she asks them about the instruments that were melted down, they just say that it was magic from the Eepera."

"Eepera?" Warden echoed.

"That seems to be their name for the people of the valley," Max explained. "I think they're telling the truth. I don't think they knew what they were carrying."

"Grace is taking one of the melted instruments apart almost molecule by molecule," the admiral said. "I should be there to help her."

"Any results so far?" Warden asked.

"As a matter of fact," the admiral said, "we have been able to determine that there is a similarity of electron motion between some of the lighter elements in the melted instrument and that natural vegetation from the jungle."

"Meaning?" Rodrick asked.

"Meaning that the valley people—the Eepera, if you will—have found a way to alter basic atomic functioning," the admiral said.

"Admiral," Warden asked, "do you and Grace envision any offensive application of this technique?"

"We've already discussed that," the admiral said. He spread his hands. "Knowing no more than we know now, it's impossible to say." He turned to Rodrick. "I suggest, Captain, that you give us two or three more days."

Rodrick nodded. "Just keep me posted. In the meantime I think we'd better send these Eepera a message. We'll use air-to-ground missiles and aim for that area north of the city, to explode in the fields. I don't think their electrical field can cancel the law of gravity. And we'll use mechanical contact fuses so that there'll be nothing electrical about the warhead."

Two scouts lifted off later that day, armed with a half-dozen simple air-to-ground missiles. The warheads were high-explosive charges, nonnuclear. The assignment had been given to *Apache One*—Jacob West had appropriated a new scout, and that name was painted onto her bow—and *Apache Two*.

Jacob had been instructed to stay well above the fog, to aim his missiles just within the protective barrier of fog on the northern end. The two scouts slowly flew upriver side by side, and when they were almost past the fog bank, Jacob gave the signal to fire. Four missiles lanced out from the scouts and, under rocket power, dove into the mist. The two scouts hovered above the predicted point of impact, all instruments functioning.

Jacob was watching his digital timer. "Five, four, three, two, one." Nothing happened. It seemed unlikely that the electrical field could muffle the large explosive power of the warheads.

"Contacts!" Renato yelled. "Four. To the north."

Jacob jerked his eyes away from the digital timer. The four contacts on the air-detection instruments were low and moving away from the scouts. "Follow and cover me," Jacob ordered, diving the scout under power. He went down, riding the northern wall of the fog and chasing the four contacts. Under magnification he recognized the sharp, deadly outlines of his own missiles just as they impacted into dry desert without exploding.

Jacob hovered low, picked out the least damaged missile, and with Renato flying cover, landed.

"Keep in mind that there's enough explosive in that warhead to damage even an Apache superman," Renato warned his buddy as Jacob got out of the scout and walked cautiously toward the missile.

"I'm not going to touch it," Jacob reassured Renato, using his belt radio. He squinted at one battered missile from twenty feet away, then from ten, and then he was kneeling beside it.

"It split open on impact," he reported to Renato, who was overhead. "I can see the charge. It's deformed, of course, but it looks just like what it's supposed to be, ten pounds of expand. The impact fuse took quite a beating. It's scorched, too. I'd say something caused a lot of heat in the head."

"Let's go home and get someone who knows more about explosives," Renato said.

"It's still hot," Jacob said, after putting his hand lightly on the exposed impact mechanism.

"Come on," Renato urged.

"You talked me into it," Jacob agreed.

Back in Hamilton, Rodrick listened to the radio chatter. Max Rosen was on the bridge of the ship with him.

"Good trick," Max said. "First they deflect a hundred pounds of missile moving in free fall at around a thousand miles an hour, and then they disable an impact fuse without setting off the charge."

"Too good a trick," Rodrick remarked. He opened the transmitter switch. "Jacob, from just above ground level I want you to fire everything you've got. See if you can stir up that fog by exploding charges at its edge. Send your remaining missiles at maximum acceleration directly into it."

The two scouts used cannon and laser. The explosive rounds pelted the desert floor, raising great clouds of dust and satisfying noises. Rounds, exploded at the very edge of the fog, tore holes in the mist. Laser beams charred sand and rock, swirled the fog at the edge, and seemed to disappear into the cloud when fired directly into it. The two remaining rockets sped straight on into the fog, hugging the ground. No explosions were recorded from within the fog bank.

*   *   *

Rodrick's face was grim. The captain's mess was full, each chair taken. Some department heads had to stand.

"We'll make this brief," Rodrick began. "Once again we've had to reassess the technological capacity of the valley people, the Eepera. As of now, we've tried every weapon we have—with the exception of nuclear warheads—against their defenses, and they've blocked everything. I'm told by our physicists that if we tried to use a thermonuclear warhead, their field would fuse the components, and it wouldn't explode. We don't know, however, what effect a thermonuclear explosion would have if it were detonated outside their field, near enough to it to let the blast affect the field. I don't want to do that. I'd like suggestions."

There were many questions but few suggestions.

"Are we any nearer to understanding just how this field is generated?" Rodrick asked, looking at Grace Monroe.

"Not really," she said. "We have an experiment under way now that we think is going to duplicate the alignment of electron motion that occurs naturally in those jungle leaves. If we can do that, we can build a sort of shield ourselves, around our own electronic equipment. We can't say, of course, whether that would negate or in any way affect the field generated by the Eepera."

"Captain," Paul Warden said, "this may be an oversimplification, but if we sent in all our forces, I think our weapons would operate once we were through the fog."

"We can't be sure of that," the admiral said. "I am very impressed by what they did with our missiles."

"Something that generates enough heat in a very short time to melt impact fuses could do serious damage to the human body," Rodrick added.

"We need more time," Grace said.

"I hope they'll give it to us," Rodrick remarked. "All right. Aside from standing by with thermonuclear warheads and being on the alert here in Eden for attacks from the Whorsk, it seems there's nothing to do but wait. Grace, and all the rest of you who are working on this problem, I'd like you to drop all other activities. If you have projects under way that are critical, see the admiral.

He'll reassign them to those who are not involved in the field research. We need one of two things: a way to get nonnuclear weaponry through their shields, or a way to counter that field and its various effects. Any questions?"

"Yeah," Stoner McRae said. "Why don't we just cut off their water?"

A few people laughed.

Stoner rose, and his scowl silenced the laughter. He walked to the head of the table and stood by Rodrick. "Juke," he called, and the entertainment robot rolled into the dining room.

"Jokes?" asked someone.

"Have you heard about the girl with the thirty-forty-sixty figure?" Juke said. "Went to masquerade parties as a pear."

"Shut up, Juke," Stoner said, and the robot jerked to mechanical attention beside him. "Show 'em the map."

Juke sent electronic signals that slid the cover off a large screen on the wall at the head of the table and also gave orders to the library computer. A map appeared on the screen.

"This shows an area about a hundred miles below the great falls," Stoner said.

"If you're talking about building a dam there, Stoner, the river is ten miles wide," someone said.

"Elevations of the western cliffs, Juke," Stoner said, and the map graphics rotated on the screen to show a profile of the cliffs. "The cliffs are fairly low here," Stoner said. "In this particular spot, just two hundred feet."

He tapped Juke on the metal head. "Rotation, Juke."

The map rotated, as if the viewpoint was from an airborne vehicle lifting up over the cliffs to look straight down.

"Note the elevation contour," Stoner said. "Particularly this dry canyon, which cuts into the riverside plateau from the west. And notice that there is a gradual drop in elevation just past the riverside plateau."

"You're thinking of diverting the river," Rodrick said.

"I sure am," Stoner replied, tapping Juke on the head again and motioning him away. "If we deprive them of their water, it will bring them to their knees without a single shot being fired or an American life sacrificed. And we can do it without having to penetrate the fog bank."

"How long would it take?" Rodrick asked.

"Off the top of my head, without doing any on-site surveys, I'd estimate six weeks, two months."

"All right, Stoner," Rodrick said. "Do your surveys and get me a feasibility study as quickly as you can. Jack, see that he has transportation and anything else he needs." He smiled. "Thank you all for coming."

Clay Girard stood on the riverbank and looked across the grass and undergrowth toward the western cliffs. He had volunteered to work with Stoner on the surveying. The cliffs looked very high to him. The river behind him was wide, very wide, and probings had told them that it was almost one hundred feet deep at its center. It was, Clay thought, a very big river.

Stoner had explained his preliminary plan to Clay during the flight out. "We'll start from the west," he had said, tracing his finger along the contour lines of a map. "We'll have one helluva lot of earth to move, but we can airlift the big earth movers in and attach bulldozer blades to all the crawlers. When we get to the solid rock of the plateau, we'll have about a quarter of a mile of blasting to do, up to the edge of the cliffs. Then, at the river, we'll make a channel leading to the cliffs. Then we blast through the last of the stone in the cliffs and use the broken stones to build a coffer dam at an angle pointed upstream into the river. After that all we have to do is blast the retaining wall near the river, and the river helps us."

Clay had seen what Stoner meant. The spot Stoner had picked for the new channel was on the inside bend of a long curve in the river. When the new channel was blasted open, it would offer a straight line of flow to the vast amounts of water, water that now flowed straight into the Eepera's cities and fields.

Soon Clay and Stoner, with Jack Purdy hovering overhead in a scout for protection, were finished measuring the earth to be moved in the valley. Clay lifted his scout and landed on top of the cliffs. There they were in the full glare of the hot sun, but Stoner and his survey team moved swiftly. By the end of the day they knew exactly how many tons of material would have to be moved, dug, blasted, and shifted.

Soon the heavy earth movers were airlifted to the western construction camp, and there was an excitement in the air. Men and women were working willingly, and as the days passed and huge amounts of earth were being moved and the western end of the channel began to deepen as the land rose higher, the project sorted itself out into two shifts, working fourteen hours each, around the clock.

The camp and working sites were guarded night and day by a team of men under the orders of the colony's sergeant at arms, Adam Hook. That force included the admiral and Mopro. The depleted population of Hamilton felt a bit insecure at first, with so many people and both their defense robots away, but they had the weapons of the *Spirit of America* and a twenty-eight-hour alert system. Only the scientists working on the challenge of unraveling the Eepera's electrical field defenses were excused from their turn at guard duty.

Security was also beefed up at the construction site on the river when, as the cut encountered solid rock, it first became necessary to blast. The blastings came with regularity—as quickly as the earth movers and crawlers could clear away the pulverized rock. A sense of immediacy and an atmosphere of tension prevailed, for if Eepera had any sort of detection capability at all, they would hear the blastings, although the edge of the fog bank was over three hundred miles downriver.

FOURTEEN

As her burns were treated, Astrud Cabral had spent almost all her recovery time in making her decision. She had been reluctant to tamper with the Caan's Bronze Age culture, but she feared that her Brazilian countrymen would be back someday. There was, in any Latin people, a strong strain of vengeance. If they came again, they would come with soldiers instead of scientist-colonists. She guessed that she would have from five to ten years to prepare the Caan.

Now, as she watched, the earth heaved. There was a blast of air, followed by the sound of an explosion. Earth and stone rose in a dusty cloud, and for what seemed like a long time there was a heavy hail of clods and stone, and then there was only the dust.

Astrud walked from behind the protection of a huge boulder and stood, hands on hips, until Lythe, her tall, handsome warrior, joined her. Astrud's face was scarred by burns, but the smooth areas of skin did not detract much from her attractiveness.

"Men who have such destructive power are crazy to fight each other," Lythe said.

Astrud put her hand on her mate's arm. "I agree with you. But we cannot depend upon my countrymen having a change of heart, and there is much work to do so we can protect ourselves."

The black-powder plant near the city, which was being

slowly constructed, was crude. It utilized a large deposit of potassium nitrate found near the marshes. The saltpeter was mixed by hand with sulfur and charcoal carbon. Slaves used a mortar and pestle to pulverize the ingredients. The resulting mixture was moistened with alcohol and blended into a paste, which then hardened and was ground into irregularly shaped grains, so that fire could pass throughout a charge and cause quick burning.

Lythe's planet, Astrud learned, was rich in resources. She had been astounded when she visited some of the nearby mines where slaves dug gold and silver. She had seen enough gold in just two mines to glut every gold market on Earth. And other metal ores were just as plentiful. Iron was there for the digging. Crude furnaces were smelting iron in three different locations, and the warriors of the Caan were awed by the still-crude iron and steel weapons that were coming off the forges.

Astrud's efforts were changing Caan society. Since her weapons factories required much labor, slaves were pulled out of the fields and from domestic service. Already there was much grumbling among the Caan women, who, for the first time in their lives, were faced with doing domestic chores themselves. The loud and sometimes tearful complaints amused Astrud. She knew that the Caan could not even begin to imagine the changes she had in mind for their society.

It was a real challenge for a twenty-first-century woman—without reference material, with only her own knowledge and her memory—to think of altering a Bronze Age society into something that would have a chance against modern weapons and ruthless men who put God on their side whether He wanted to be there or not. Astrud's sustaining hope was that once she had taught the Caan all she could remember about science and theory, there would arise Caan thinkers and scholars to take over. It was ironic and sad to her that the first modern things to be made by the Caan were gunpowder and weapons. Her goal was to manufacture reliable cannon within three years, and that alone necessitated the development of an entire technology. She knew that the black powder being produced in some quantity was crude, but she did not have the formula for more advanced gunpowder and had no idea how later developments altered the old and simple black-powder formula.

She envisioned the cannon firing an explosive shell. She was working with one of the slaves, who had shown talent in working iron, to build a muzzle-loading rifle. She had one shop making plowshares, for food production had to continue. With an iron plow and animal power, a few slaves could do the work previously done by many under the direction of the elders. Astrud began to take the slaves for her own projects.

Lythe had become very interested in the crossbow. He had worked with her and the slaves, and from her basic design produced a weapon that utilized a mechanical crank. With gears tediously filed out of a circular piece of steel to put enough tension on the weapon, it shot a metal bolt with enough force to penetrate the Brazilian body armor. Lythe had one shop doing nothing but turning out crossbows and bolts.

Astrud knew that by the time a Caan got close enough to use the crossbow, he would have been exposed to a deadly hail of projectiles and laser beams, but she knew too that many Caan would have to die if the Brazilians came back with military reinforcements. There were times when she guiltily and selfishly wished that the rulers of the three major nations of Earth had precipitated the final war there. In that event, there would never be an invasion of Brazilians, and she could breathe easily and learn how to be a better mate to Lythe and mother to the child she now carried in her womb.

Sometimes it was difficult to make Lythe and the elders understand. "If the weapons of fire and light of the men from the upper darkness are so superior," Lythe asked, "why are we wasting our time with crossbows and black powder? Why don't we just make lasers and missiles?"

Astrud could only shrug and try to explain that she did not have the knowledge and that the Caan did not have the tools or the manmade materials needed. She realized quickly that there were many things she did not know.

What makes a dry-cell battery work? What machines are needed to extrude wire to wind turbines to make electricity? What steps would one take to manufacture a single safety pin? What is the firing mechanism of a hand grenade? What steps did metalworking go through to enable men to develop the skills, knowledge, and tools to build the first steam engine? Where does one start to build a metal lathe to enable a man to turn intricate pieces needed to construct other useful machines?

She would have to stick to basics. But is a cannon barrel cast? How do you get the hole in a musket barrel?

The basics. Black powder. Greek fire. Oil oozed up in several places in the marshes, and when it was mixed with black powder, it became a sticky, hot-burning tar that would cling to a Brazilian tank or crawler and make things decidedly uncomfortable for those inside.

Well, cannon were probably cast. Molten steel poured into a mold, but of what material was the mold made? And what do you use to polish the inside of the barrel, and how much black powder do you use for the charge?

She found that master builders—the designers and builders of the temples, the public buildings, and the monuments—had a basic understanding of mathematics. She spent hours with them, teaching them what she knew of algebra and geometry. To her pleasure two of the men were very excited by the concepts and became her first two mathematicians, leaving their building work to spend their days and their nights mastering the new concepts and then moving on past Astrud's limited knowledge.

The first cannon belched smoke, and a solid round shot dribbled out the end of the barrel—Astrud had been too conservative in the use of powder. Soon there were wheel-mounted fieldpieces, but they still had to be fired with a lighted match, and the first attempts at developing explosive round shot had resulted in the death of two slaves when the shot exploded in the barrel. But the Caan would not let Astrud despair. She was encouraged to continue, in spite of the failures, with the transformation of the society.

*   *   *

On Omega, Becky Dark, wife of the tall Texan, Elton Dark, tucked her silken blond hair under her hard hat and mounted up. At five-ten, slim, physically fit from tennis, swimming, and her diving as a member of Allen Jones's Marine Sciences staff, Becky looked good in her work blues. She had learned to operate heavy equipment during the lean days, just after she had shocked her family and a good portion of Fort Worth society by marrying a ragtag graduate student from Texas A&M.

Becky loved the desert. She did not really like the sea. She worked with Allen Jones because each member of the colony had a duty to contribute, but she did not like the feeling of being waterlogged after a day's work and was a little nervous all the time when she was diving. There in the desert, where the Americans were at work to divert the Eepera's water supply, a little boom town had sprung up, with tents, outdoor cooking and campfires, and people tensely excited about doing a challenging job. She was a happy, laughing dynamo of energy, always one of the first out of the sleeping bag, always one of the first to climb aboard a giant earth mover just after sunup when the day shift began.

Elton liked working with his wife. It brought back to him the sweet years before their first child was born, when they did not have a penny to their names and he was having to earn a living doing just about anything he could find to do, instead of working at his chosen profession—finding oil deposits.

"Git 'em up, move 'em out," Elton yelled across to Becky, as they each climbed the ladder into the cab of an earth mover. Becky grinned at him and stuck out her tongue playfully. The big hydrogen engines purred into life. Soon the dust was flying as the machines tackled what was known among the volunteers on the project as Stoner's Folly.

The two earth movers bounced and roared into the cut side by side, engines racing. Becky was gaining a slight lead, and with a grin Elton eased off a bit and let her swing under the loader first.

As he sat waiting, Elton looked around. It was one

hell of an impressive project. You had to go a long way back into history to find anything to come close to matching it. The Culebra Cut in the Panama Canal, later renamed the Gaillard Cut, probably matched it in degree of difficulty, since those old dudes had had to move millions of cubic yards of mud, dirt, and rock with shovels and steam engines, but the Gaillard would be dwarfed by Stoner's Folly. The Folly was going to have to accommodate the total water flow of a river ten miles wide and a hundred feet deep, a river that drained thousands of square miles of rain forest. When the final barrier was blasted away, one hell of a lot of water was going to come roaring down the Folly cut with a force that would be more than spectacular.

Elton had to go even further back, into prehistory, to find anything comparable to the flood that would wash through the cut. It would be, in relative miniature, a scene reminiscent of the tail end of the last Ice Age on Earth, when the ice dam holding back the glacier melt in Canada broke, and the flood of all floods gouged out the Columbia Gorge.

There were other comparisons to be drawn, too. Those who had been involved in the building of the *Spirit of America* knew once again that feeling of urgent excitement, the commitment that comes during a crash project. In view of the mighty effort taking place, it was possible to forget that this massive movement of megatons of rock and dirt was not for the permanent advantage of the race, but was an act of war.

Great blasts shattered the desert air with regularity. After each blast, even before the dust had completely settled, the earth movers and crawlers rushed into the cut for another load, and in selected spoil areas, mountains of earth and splintered rock began to rise.

And not a day went by when someone did not ask, over a campfire, a meal, or just in conversation with fellow workers while waiting for their turn at the loaders, "I wonder if *they* know what's going on up here?" *They*, of course, were the valley people, the Eepera. At such times it was reassuring to catch a glimpse of the multiweaponed defense robot, Mopro, on one of his tours, or to see the admiral standing tall, and to look up and see the regular patrol of the scout ships.

On an early morning, before the heat of the sun made being outdoors uncomfortable, Sage Bryson strolled alongside the river in a park flowered with the most beautiful of Omega's flora. Water had just been sluiced through the irrigation trenches, and there was a good smell of wet earth and growing things. In a grassed area ahead of her, Eepera children were gathered.

Sage wore a blue, filmy, clinging, loosely draped garment that hid little. She had taken to walking in the park daily, much to Yanee's puzzlement.

"Come back to bed," he had told her that first day when she awoke shortly after sunrise and slipped away from his arms. "It's indecently early."

Yanee usually slept until midmorning. He spent some hours in breaking his fast, bathing, and preening—sometimes taking an hour to decide which kilt he would wear that day. Occasionally he had duty in the fields, overseeing the Whorsk slaves. On such days he would make a brief appearance in the fields just after midmorning, come back to his apartment for a midday rest, and then spend two to three hours in the fields in the afternoon.

Evenings began with small gatherings, with pleasant idle chatter over wine and food. It was fashionable for one to speak English, but only a few had taken the mental effort really to learn the language, so the conversations were mostly conducted in the language of the Eepera. No one seemed to be especially interested in teaching the language to Sage.

She had lost all sense of time. She lived in a glow of well-being and waited impatiently for the nights, when the social groupings broke up and Yanee, usually quite mellow with wine, carried her to his huge bed.

Of late, however, Sage had been moody. She glowed with health, but something nagged at her. She tried to use the walks in the park for thinking, to determine just what it was that was troubling her, but it was difficult to concentrate. Flowers perfumed the air. She could feel the individual muscles in her body as she walked. It made her feel as if she were a sleek young lioness.

What was there to trouble her in this paradise?

Nothing.

They could get along without her at the colony. No one there would miss her. Evangeline was sweet, but she had her own things going.

Sage laughed. If Evangeline thought that Paul Warden, with his bulging muscles and sappy smile, was handsome, she could have him. A surge of need went through her as she thought of the perfect body of Yanee.

Of course, she missed her work. But when she really thought about it, what good was her work? She had spent years going over and over the calculations and theories of men long dead. What had *she* ever contributed? What did it all matter? There was only one thing that mattered. She started to turn, to start back, but she realized that Yanee would still be sleeping and that today was his day for traveling by river to the north to check on the fields in the far end of the valley.

She turned her attention to the children, each of them perfect. Two of them glanced at her briefly and returned to their game. It was a slow, sedate game, with little movement. The faces of the children were beautiful.

But what was wrong?

A few birds sang. Something made a thud down by the river wharfs. Otherwise the city was so quiet, so calm. As she passed an intersection, she looked to the east and saw that there were only a few people walking on the streets. On the cliff at the edge of that neighborhood she saw the gleaming white pyramid and was reminded that she had never gotten around to asking anyone about it.

Or about the source of the lighting in Yanee's house.

But how could one be moody on such a day? She started to hum, and a thought came to her. She turned and looked back at the children. The little melody she was humming was gay and lilting. But the children did not smile. No one smiled. There was no music.

Ah, so that was it. She liked music. Was she just

missing music? She would have to ask Yanee why there was no music and why no one smiled. He did not seem to mind her smiling at him. At one large gathering, however, a woman had asked her, "Why do you so contort your face when you speak? Are you in pain?"

Oh, well. They *were* an alien people. And they knew how to live! Whorsk slaves did the work and prepared the meals, although they were seldom seen. She would have to learn the language, so that she could take her place in that most favored pastime—conversation. She would ask Yanee for more simple books, because those in his home were too advanced for her rudimentary knowledge of the language. She would ask him for some that were made for children instead of the ones he favored—all on erotic subjects.

It was such a lovely day. She would have a leisurely lunch and, perhaps, spend an hour in the circular pool behind Yanee's house, get just a bit of sun later when it was not so hot, bathe in scented water, and have her usual glass of afternoon wine. Yanee would be back early and perhaps they would bathe together before going out for the social evening. The food would be delicious, as usual. And she would make a greater effort to understand the language when they were not speaking in English. Then they would go home and— The thought seemed to melt her, driving all evidence of her moodiness away.

The Life Sciences building sprawled on a broad terrace on the south side of Stanton Bay. Plans for the building had been drawn back on Earth, and construction had been computer-directed, with two of the huge plastics machines working full-time for almost a year. As the various stages of construction were completed, equipment had been moved from the labs aboard the *Spirit of America*. The ship would have only emergency and first-aid capability for the trip back to Earth, but that would be enough because the trip, once fuel was available, would be made in a matter of mere days.

The patient rooms in the Life Sciences building were little used. Everyone chosen for the colony had been in glowing health, and Omega was a healthy planet. The labs were always busy, however, for Dr. Mandy Miller's section was the largest single group in the colony, with responsibilities not only in human medicine but in all areas having to do with plant or animal life. Amando Kwait was nominally attached to the Life Sciences section, since his work had to do with plant life, but he had, in his agricultural section, almost total autonomy.

Even with so many Americans involved with Stoner's Folly on the western continent, the Life Sciences complex bustled. The final section to be completed housed Mandy's offices. There she had her own small but well-equipped laboratory, an operating room, patient treatment rooms, and a small suite of care and recuperation rooms. Her administrative duties left her little time for research or practice, but she had taken it on herself to be Theresita Pulaski-West's personal physician.

Theresita was a big woman, and her pregnancy made her look bigger. The pregnancy was nearing term, and Mandy had scheduled weekly visits for Theresita. For her latest visit Theresita was wearing a gaily flowered dress and sandals. She walked into Mandy's office, her posture perfect, causing her stomach to protrude impressively.

"I think you built the hospital so far from town to be sure I get my exercise," Theresita said, lowering herself into a chair.

"You look good," Mandy said, and indeed, she did. Her skin was flawless, glowing. Her eyes were clear and bright, and she had held her weight gain exactly to Mandy's recommendation. "How's junior?"

"I think he is going to be a soccer star," Theresita said, smiling. "I also think he is going to weigh fifty pounds."

Mandy laughed.

"How else could I be so front heavy?" Theresita asked, spreading her hands.

"Well, assume the position," Mandy said, rising and leading the way into the examination room.

A fetus had no secrets from modern medicine. Without so much as penetrating Theresita's skin or subjecting mother or baby to potentially damaging rays, Mandy's instruments had confirmed, quite early, that the baby was a boy, and as the fetus grew, Mandy knew that it was perfectly normal, with all usual appurtenances in the proper positions and numbers, that the baby's brain was developing nicely—even a bit more rapidly than normal.

"He's getting just a little restless," Mandy said, as she looked at a perfect image of the baby in its fetal position.

"He is not the only one," Theresita replied.

"Ah, he likes the sound of his mother's voice," Mandy said.

"He can hear?"

"Oh, sure."

"All right then, junior, listen to your mother: Stop kicking me in the kidney."

"Well, Mama," Mandy said, turning off the machines, "everything is looking good. In about thirty days that little fellow is going to want his first breath of air, and there'll be no stopping him."

Theresita heaved herself up and slipped back into her clothing.

"Got time for a juice break?" Mandy asked.

"My commanding officer and my doctor have relieved me of all duties, so I have nothing but time."

They talked about the project on the western continent, about how empty the colony seemed with so many people gone. Theresita told Mandy that she was so bored that she had actually called Juke to her house to tell her jokes. Mandy laughed.

"I must be keeping you from your work. . . ." Theresita said.

Mandy sighed. "I almost wish someone would relieve me of all duties for a week or so." She stood and escorted Theresita to the door, for she did have much to do. She closed the door, turned, and loneliness hit her in a wave so powerful that she almost called Theresita back. But then she felt an unreasonable and instant resentment toward Theresita. She stopped in midstride, cocked her head, and thought about that totally unexpected reaction.

Rocky had not wanted children, and he acted like

such a baby himself sometimes, Mandy had not pressed the issue.

"Ah," she said, "so that's it." She wanted a baby, too, and was resentful that Theresita, who was her same age, would have one and she herself would not. Worse, she did not even have a man in her life, so there was no baby on the horizon.

She poured another mug of juice. She had a dozen things to do, but she sat with both elbows on her desk, mug clutched in both hands, and stared moodily at the wall. At least a hundred women in the colony were in various stages of pregnancy. They were doing their duty to increase Omega's human population. She was reminded that Duncan had suggested that it might be a good idea for her to make a new attachment.

Duncan.

The pain of loss that never seemed to grow less keen whitened her knuckles on the mug she held in front of her face. And it was utterly senseless, completely without logic. There had been no chance that she would have Duncan. She had been a married woman, and then when Rocky was killed, Duncan was married. For her to have Duncan Rodrick was not, it seemed, her destiny. And yet it was joy just to see him. Now and then, when she felt especially lonely, she indulged in girlish fantasies. She would be alone with him on one of the islands of the southern seas. They would walk hand in hand with the warm, dying wavelets washing over their bare feet. The fantasies then became sexual, for she was a mature, healthy, normal woman.

She knew that she was, and had been, in a depressed emotional state. Had she seen such symptoms of melancholia in a patient, she would have recommended treatment by the psychiatric section. But when things seemed to close in on her, and she began to picture Duncan at home with his wife, she turned to her religious belief for solace. She prayed on her knees. This she did after Theresita's visit, and she arose with a feeling of relief. God, the Bible told her, would never put upon her a trial she was not capable of facing.

Then, as she began to plow through a stack of paperwork, she used a portion of her mind to picture all of the unattached men of the colony. Although her marriage to Rocky had been far from perfect, she felt that she was not meant to live alone. She tried to imagine life with this one and that one and found the choice to be severely limited. Most of the unmarried men were too young for her. None of them really interested her.

The loneliness threatened to come back. She left the paperwork and walked through a covered mall to the lab where Grace Monroe had set up her equipment. Grace was taking a break. Cat was curled in her lap. Cat was a VR-1 creation of Grace's, with a brain equal to the admiral's or the repair robot's, Makeitdo. Cat was made of a highly adaptable synthetic, which could be stretched, molded, or compressed to any shape. When Mandy opened the door, Cat cocked its ears, leaped from Grace's lap, and raced to rub its back against Mandy's legs. She bent and picked Cat up.

"Cat, you are becoming very beautiful," she said, rubbing the sleek, natural-feeling fur of the robot. Cat had started experimenting with growing hair back on the ship, and it had taken it this long to perfect the technique. Cat had decided that its preferred shape was that of a rather small Abyssinian cat, and the brown-flecked fur was near perfection now.

"Grace, are you working a bit too hard?" Mandy asked, seeing the dark circles under her colleague's eyes.

"It's an interesting problem," Grace said.

"Any progress?"

"I think if I had a day with the particle accelerator back at Transworld, I'd have the answers I need."

"Well, speaking as your doctor," Mandy said, "remember that we're only human."

Grace smiled. "Thank you. Max has been giving me the same advice, but I think we're getting close, Mandy. I believe that the field put up over the river has something to do with altered particle motion inside the hydrogen atom. And I feel as if we're in a race against time. I know that Duncan hasn't expressed any such thoughts and is not the kind to put pressure on us, but when they complete that cut out there in the desert and divert the river, there's going to be a crisis. I'd like to have a way to negate that field and even to use something like it as a defensive shield for our own people before the final confrontation with the Eepera."

"Is there anything I can do?" Mandy asked.

"Give Max a mild tranquilizer," Grace said, with a smile. "And if you can get him to take it, you're a better woman than I."

Max Rosen was taking his new responsibilities very seriously; he was that kind of man. With Rodrick back and forth to the project on the western continent, Max was in charge at Hamilton base. Max had not been alone with Grace, except in sleep, for more than thirty minutes at a time in weeks.

"I'll see what I can do," Mandy said.

Mandy knew that she should be working, but she could not face being alone in the office. She walked around the curve of the bay to the city proper. Baby and Beau, the two dragons, also a bit lonely with most of their friends gone, met her and vied with each other in offering a ride. Mandy mounted Beau, and they went sweeping off in that smooth lope, with Baby calling a halt to do some polite begging at the window of Betsy McRae. Betsy gave them two cupcakes each.

"I've been coaxed into going for a ride," Mandy told Betsy. "Want to come along?"

"I'd like to," Betsy said, "but I'm running a computer program for Stoner. The shaft up by Lake Dinah has reached that deposit of molybdenum ore, and the team is sending readings in. It's looking very good. I think the ship will be on its way home within a few months."

"That's wonderful," Mandy said, wondering if she should return to Earth permanently. "Well, my trusty steed is getting restless." Beau was shifting on his feet and looking around at Mandy, eager to be off.

"All right, go," Mandy said.

She let the dragons go where they would, and they went to one of their favorite places, Jumper's Run, where

Mandy gave way to temptation, stripped to the buff, and joined them in rollicking in the water. But soon her sense of responsibility forced her to dress and coax Baby out of the water for a ride home. She had set out from the Life Sciences building on the excuse of finding Max, and when they were back in Hamilton she used her belt radio to find that Max was on the waterfront talking to the marine expert, Allen Jones. She guided Baby to the small dock where Allen tied up his boats.

Max's face was twisted in a look of pain, a look that Mandy recognized as his thinking expression. She waited for Baby to kneel, then she got off. "Am I interrupting?"

"Not at all," Jones said.

"Hi, Mandy," Max growled. He, too, had dark circles under his eyes. "Allen was just discussing taking a couple of underwater craft up the Great Misty River from its mouth."

"I haven't had a chance to talk it over with Rodrick yet," Allen said, "but I think it can be done. I doubt seriously that their field would affect the instruments of underwater boats. We need to know more about those bas—excuse me, those people, and I think this is a good way to do it."

"Well, Allen," Max said, "you go ahead and get ready, and I'll clear it with Rodrick as soon as he gets back. I'm sure he'll give you a go-ahead if you can do it without risk."

"Great," Allen said. "We'll need two scouts to airlift the boats."

Max nodded. "Walk me back to the ship, Mandy?"

"Sure," Mandy said.

They walked for a way in silence, then Max cleared his throat and said, "If you can get her to take it, you're a better person than I, but I think Grace needs a mild sedative or something. She's been putting in about eighteen hours a day in the lab."

Mandy laughed. "She told me the same about you."

Max snorted. They had walked to a point out of sight of the dock. Picnic tables had been set up under a stand of umbrella trees.

"I have it with me," Mandy said.

"Now, Mandy—"

"Now, Max," she mimicked, "you just come right over here and sit on this bench."

"I haven't got time for this," Max said.

Mandy took his arm, led him to the picnic table, pushed him down, pulled a flask from her pocket, and detached two collapsing cups into which she poured a rich, brown fluid.

"What's this?" Max growled.

"The distillery's latest brandy," Mandy stated, sipping. "And it isn't bad."

Max drank. "Not bad at all."

"Now, are doctors so bad?"

"That's my kind of doctoring," Max said, extending his cup again.

"Grace is all right," Mandy said. "I was just by to see her. She's strong and healthy. No one ever died from lack of sleep."

"And there's nothing wrong with me," Max stated, "except that I'd like to be out there where the action is." He smacked his lips in appreciation. "Not bad at all, and the best little tranquilizer yet."

He left Mandy seated at the picnic table, the flask still open in front of her. She poured another cup, sipped, and felt tears come to her eyes. Duncan—he was there, in her mind, in her body, and she could not get rid of him . . . was not even sure she wanted to.

The gathering in the house of Yanee's best friend that night was larger than usual. Sage had come to know all of Yanee's friends by name, but she did not, by any means, know everyone in the city. She knew that she was moving in the highest society, for Yanee was the son of the ruler, Suses, and would someday be elevated to the throne.

There was talk of a projected journey to a larger city in the delta, where, it was said, the shellfish were so succulent that they need only be cooked unseasoned to be utterly delicious. A game of posing was played, in which men and women struck erotic poses and held them, motionless, for perhaps three minutes. Yanee insisted that Sage play. She struck her pose, and there was polite applause.

She was pleased by how much of the conversation she could follow. For example, she understood perfectly when a handsome younger man approached Yanee and said, "Are you not tired of her yet?"

Yanee lifted a hand languorously. "You will be the first to know."

Then Sage did not understand a couple of words when the young man said, "But the ——— has not ——— yet."

"I am displeased by that," Yanee confessed.

"Why are you displeased?" she asked when the young man had gone.

"It is nothing," he said. "Just talk."

"If I displease you, I want to know. Then I will correct what I am doing wrong."

"We'll give it a few more weeks," Yanee said, and then someone called out that the ———, another word that Sage did not understand, was beginning. One by one and two by two, people began to drift out of the main room. It had happened before, and Yanee had never suggested that they join whatever action was going on in other rooms.

"We're left almost alone," she told him. "Why don't we join the others?"

"There'll be time for that," Yanee said. "Now we will go home."

That, after all, was why she lived, why she felt that the days would never pass. She took his arm and smiled up at him happily.

"I do wish," he said coldly, "you'd stop making those horrible faces at me."

Clay Girard flew *Blue Rover* at five thousand feet over the big cut. All his sensors were on, all his weapons armed. Behind him flew the two *Apaches, Apache Two* flying slow and heavy with the entire mounting of the *Spirit of America*'s largest and most powerful laser cannon slung underneath. The laser cannon would be used in the building of the dam. Clay and Jacob West directed Renato as he lowered the cannon and set it on a crawler that had been modified for that purpose.

Earth movers and crawlers were working on both sides of the river cliffs now. The big cut was only one hundred yards from the riverside edge of the cliffs, and the gap was narrowing with each blast. In the valley, a trench three miles wide near the river, narrowing slightly as it reached the cliffs, had been dug rather easily, since there was only the age-old accumulation of river silt to move.

Once the huge laser cannon housing was down, Clay zoomed up and made a quick circuit of the site, going down river almost to the fog bank. Rodrick had told all scouts to be especially alert during the next few days.

Clay was impressed by the amount of work that had been done in so short a time. On the desert, mountains of spoil had altered the landscape. The cliffs were being chewed away by blasting, and tons of stone had been dumped and piled in a huge, two-hundred-foot-wide line from the cliffs to the river's edge. That was the beginning of the dam that would guide the waters of Theresita's River into the new cut.

Satisfied that everything was clear, Clay loafed over the site, watching the activity below. They were losing no time. The big laser cannon had been positioned, and even as he watched its deadly beam shot out to play in a continuous, sizzling, smoking fury over the levee. So great was the heat, it was difficult to see anything but a red glow through the smoke and steam, but when the cannon stopped firing, a fifty-foot section of the piled rocks had been fused into solidity.

Allen Jones had flown to the site with Jacob West. He had joined a small group including Duncan Rodrick to watch the first firing of the laser. Now, standing with Stoner and the captain, Allen asked, "How long do you estimate before you open the cut, Stoner?"

"I think we need to have about three or four miles of dam in place in the river itself," Stoner said. "It'll take another month, I'd guess."

That gave Allen plenty of time to put his plan into operation. "Captain, I've been talking with the first officer about going up the river from its mouth in underwater boats."

Rodrick thought for a minute, then nodded for Allen to continue.

"We've seen their fields on the northern end of the populated areas of the valley, and that one city," Allen said. "We have no idea whether there are other cities downstream. We know that the fog bank covers the valley for fifteen hundred miles. We know we might have to fight these people, and we have no idea how many of them there are. By going up the river, I can tell you whether or not their cities extend all the way to the delta and get a pretty good estimate of their population."

"You're assuming that their weapons won't be effective underwater," Rodrick said.

"I've talked it over with a few of the people working on the problem, and they don't see how they could be."

"We didn't see how they could stop a hydrogen engine, either," Rodrick reminded him. He held up a hand to keep Allen from protesting. "Allen, it's a fine idea. I'll approve it on the condition that you take no unnecessary chances. You have no idea of water depth—"

"It'll be deep," Allen said. "With the volume of water that river carries, you'd be able to take an ocean liner as far inland as you wanted. There's a hundred feet of water right here."

"How about navigation?"

"We'll have to feel our way along, but there's no problem. Our instruments can spot an object six inches across at a hundred yards. We'll be able to map the bottom of the river as we go, pick the main channel, stay under until we're through the fog, and then take careful looks without showing anything larger than your fist above the water."

"All right, Allen." Rodrick slapped Jones on the shoulder. "I'm glad you thought of this. I didn't. And now that you have, get on it as soon as possible."

IV

MAGIC FROM
THE EEPERA

FIFTEEN

Airlifting the boats from Eden to the western continent, over thousands of watery miles, was tedious, since speeds had to be kept below the sonic level. Carrying a boat, even a streamlined, thick-hulled underwater boat, did not do much for a scout's aerodynamics.

The fog bank along the coast was over fifty miles wide, and even then it did not cover all of the delta. On either side were marshes, islands, and winding waterways that were uninhabited except for a variety of bird and some animal life. Allen believed that the main channel to the sea would be toward the center of the fog, and it was there that the scouts lowered the two boats into the sea and left them.

At that point the water was relatively shallow, and soundings of the bottom indicated river silt. The two boats headed north. Well after Allen figured that they should be nearing the mouth of the river, their instruments could not pick up land on either side or in front. Allen guessed that they had hit the main channel of the river dead on, and that it was over twenty miles wide at its mouth.

At hourly intervals one boat would rise near the surface and extend a sophisticated optical instrument until its tip was just out of the water. The boats were traveling slowly and cautiously, so it was six hours before Allen surfaced his boat and saw, to the northwest, low-lying land and, as he increased magnification, a splendid city set far

271

back from the river's bank. They had penetrated past the fog. He could see the endless stretch of water behind him and the sky above him, and the eastern bank was a small darkness off on the horizon.

There was no boat traffic in the broad reaches of the river, but when they surfaced an hour later, Allen spotted a small Whorsk sailboat in the distance, near the western bank. The city was more clearly seen now. It rose in glowing stone from the flat plain of the delta. Behind it were low and rocky hills and desert. It took a while for Allen to spot the pyramid. It was on what seemed to be a man-made hill directly in the center of the city, only its tip was higher than some of the other buildings.

Now it was possible to increase speed because the depth of water was more than ample. Their detection instruments showed some pretty big underwater animals, but it was possible to dodge them if they came too close, for those boats were fast and highly maneuverable. Thirty miles up river there was another city. The valley had narrowed, and now both fringes of the desert were visible in the distance from the middle of the river.

When night overtook them, Allen ordered both boats to surface. There, running silently on powerful hydrogen jets, they could reach speeds of fifty miles per hour.

There was a city on one bank or the other roughly every hundred miles. By morning they had sped past seven cities, in addition to the two near the delta, and each had its gleaming white pyramid. At night the pyramids were lit, apparently from within, and shone like huge diamonds. As the valley narrowed and the cliffs were closer, the pyramids were set atop the cliffs.

By day Allen could see the Whorsk working in the fields. He was getting a bit woozy from exhaustion, so he turned the controls over to one of his men and slept for a few hours. When he awoke, he checked with the on-board computer operator, who had been feeding photographs and visual sightings into the computer.

"All of the cities seem to be the same size," the operator reported. "We have estimated the number of buildings from the photographs. We can assume that multi-

CITY IN THE MIST

family housing is the rule, since they are all pretty big and have several entrances, balconies—all the things that go with multifamily dwellings. It's not precise, of course, but I'd guess that the population of each one of the cities is about ten thousand."

Another day and a night of upriver travel revealed the same pattern: cities of the same size, spaced a hundred miles apart—each with its pyramid, each with its miles and miles of fields and Whorsk slaves working them. The Eepera seemed to be a very methodical people.

"I think we can safely guess that there will be about fifteen to twenty cities in the valley," Allen Jones said. "Figuring ten-thousand Eepera per city, that's about a hundred and fifty to two hundred thousand."

Some days later, on the bridge of the *Spirit of America*, he was making his report to Duncan Rodrick and Max Rosen.

"They're not invulnerable," he said. "On the way back, just to test them, we ran on the surface at fifty miles per hour day and night. If we were spotted, they gave no sign of it."

"The estimated numbers seem too small," Max said, running his hand through his tousled hair.

"I've been thinking about that too," Allen said. "But I think we're pretty accurate. I can't see them packing dozens of people into small units in the city. That just wouldn't be their style. I keep remembering how they laughed and said our women made good breeders. Maybe their women don't have children as easily or as readily as ours. Or maybe they just keep the population low by artificial means in order to maintain a set standard of living."

"Allen, you've just implied acceptance of the claims of the Eepera that they have been in contact with Earth people before," Rodrick said.

Allen shrugged. "Ever since men began to suspect that the little lights in the sky were suns like our own and began to speculate that there might be other worlds out there, we've been torn between the fear that we were alone—the only intelligent race in the galaxy—and the fear that we were not alone, that somewhere out there were beings smarter, stronger, and more technologically advanced than we were.

"Periodically, throughout history, some writer would try to make something of a couple of Bible verses in Genesis—one about giants on the Earth, and the other that says something like 'the sons of God found the daughters of men to be fair and took them to wife.' In writings even older than the Bible, the scribes of Sumer recorded, apparently with seriousness, that their priestesses went to the god-house atop the sacred ziggurat and literally mated with a god, thus producing men like Gilgamesh, who were half-god, half-man. There is hardly an ancient body of myth from any race that does not mention the union of human men or women with the gods.

"Now I don't know what to believe. I've seen cities with massive pylons and architecture that would have made the Egyptians of the Golden Age feel right at home, and pyramids about the size of the ancient ones outside Cairo. So we now know that we are definitely not alone. We've seen only one alien planet, and we've met two alien races, both of them just a bit more savage than even the Russians, one of them with some puzzling technology. You tell me."

"I'll tell you this," Max said irritably. "It's too damned crowded out here. One of the reasons I wanted to come on this little outing was to get away from masses of people."

"The pyramid is a fairly basic geometric form," Rodrick suggested.

"Yes," Allen said, "and to this day on Earth there are still men who are arguing whether or not different races came up with the shape independently or if all pyramid builders were influenced by the Sumerian ziggurats."

"But you're buying the idea that these Eepera were in contact with ancient Egypt?" Rodrick asked.

Allen shrugged. "I'll accept an Earthlike antelope, Earthlike cats, a lot of things as either parallel evolution, a natural movement of life, or as divine creation. I find it hard to accept as coincidence an art form that depicts half-naked men in kilts always shown in profile. No, the large carvings and paintings we could see on various buildings are *very* Egyptian."

"That's interesting," Max said, "because it would mean that these fellows have been perfectly static culturally for five or six thousand years. Hell, even in ancient Egypt the art evolved, and at one point went through a definite revolution. If these people have been drawing and painting in the same way for fifty or sixty centuries, they can't be too smart."

"Good point, Max," Rodrick said, although he was wondering, with a bit of amusement, where the old bear of an engineer had learned about Egyptian art. He put his hand on Allen's shoulder. "Good job, Allen. I'm not approving your running on the surface deliberately to attract their attention, but good job."

"I'd like to go out to the project now, if it's all right," Allen said.

"Hang around until this afternoon, and I'll fly you over," Rodrick said.

Elton Dark and his tall blond wife sat side by side in their earth movers waiting for a turn at the loaders. They were now working in the river valley itself. While they waited they watched a scout ship hover, lower, and hang motionless while men on the ground strapped cable around a rectangular slab of stone that measured a full twenty-five-feet long.

"It seems to me that the weight of that slab of stone would rip the fasteners right out of the hull," Becky said, using the earth mover's radio.

"In effect," Elton said, "the hull of the scout is all of a piece, and the way they got it lashed, the strain is distributed over a wide portion of the hull."

The scout lifted slowly, the huge slab of stone following ponderously. The stone would be lowered carefully into the water to join with the dam being slowly extended at an angle going upriver.

"Isn't it funny," Becky remarked, "that one of the greatest engineering projects ever completed is being done over eleven light-years from where these machines were made, and will be seen by only a few of us?"

The same processes were being performed on the far side of the river, so far away that the east bank was just barely visible. Slowly, load by load and stone by stone, a wall was being built in front of that massive flow of water, and already, because of the constriction, the current was moving faster in the center of the river. The western portion of the dam extended four miles now, a smooth, fused-rock highway over which the giant earth movers and crawlers sped to dump loads to be fused into solidity, at least near the surface, by the huge laser from the ship. The eastern section was nearing the two-mile mark. When the gap in the middle of the river was narrowed to three miles, the water raced through, and the backup threatened to flood over the top of the dam. It was the moment for which everyone had been waiting. The object was not to back up the river and form a lake; the object was to coax the river into a straight-line flow, directly into the cut.

Stoner McRae was a little nervous. He stood on the strip of land on the western shore that had been left as a retaining wall and looked down the huge cut to the west, miles and miles—a huge gash cut through the cliffs to lead into the arid sands miles away. If all went well, those sands would soon be awash, and somewhere out there—he had not surveyed to see exactly where—a new lake would form or the river would find its way into another channel and go wandering. He just hoped—and he had done some checking on this—that the stream would not quickly cut a new channel leading into the old one below the dam. If that happened, all the work would have been done for nothing.

Stoner looked at his watch. There were six hours of daylight remaining. Rodrick had come out to see the show. Stoner looked at the river, at the sun, at the cut.

"Trying to put it off, Stoner?" Rodrick asked, with a grin.

Stoner grinned back. "You crawled right into my head." He started walking toward the south, checking the well-placed charges as he went. When he was well past the dam, he paused and pushed the send button on his radio. "All personnel," he said. "We will blast just as soon as we've run a body check. Section leaders, count all your workers and all your equipment. All personnel report their positions to section leaders. We don't want anyone in the cut when we turn on the faucet."

No one was going to be in that cut. When the charges went off, lifting out that last section of earth, there would be one mighty waterfall as the river rushed into the lower elevation. Within ten minutes everyone was accounted for. The heavy equipment had been moved well downstream. Jack Purdy was flying overhead with his cameras, ready to record the event.

Stoner lifted his radio. "Admiral, are you in position?"

The admiral was standing atop the cliff, on the brink of the new cut through solid stone. He had set up some measuring instruments in the bottom of the cut for Allen Jones, who wanted to know the exact force exerted by the wall of water that would soon rush through. To take advantage of the viewpoint, from the brink of the cut, he had also set up holorecorders.

"In position, sir," the admiral confirmed, "and all equipment is ready."

Cat, who had sneaked aboard one of the last scout ships to come over from Hamilton, was crouched at the brink of the cut, tense, looking down with its head hanging over the edge.

"Fire in the hole," Stoner sent. "Ten. Nine."

The riverbank lifted, seemingly intact for a few split seconds, and then pulverized as the force of hundreds of pounds of that easily manufactured but highly potent explosive, began to swell. Following the eardrum-splitting roar of the blast, there came a thunderous rumble, and the waters near the western shore began to swirl; as the dust cleared they could see a wall of water thirty-feet high roaring toward the cliffs and washing the walls of the cut as it boiled onward.

From where the admiral stood, it seemed that the segment of land that held back the river was lifted into the air. Then, even before the debris of the explosion ceased to rise, there appeared a muddy, smooth-topped wave, a mass of water that looked solid. It seemed to grow in height as it rushed into the cut. The admiral had the holorecorders going, their mechanisms set on automatic tracking. Cat, glowing green with excitement, twitched its tail nervously.

The wall of water filled the deep, wide cut and rushed toward the cliffs. The admiral, awed by the force of it, moved closer to the edge and glanced down to see the instruments far below. He checked the receiver strapped to his waist; lights glowed its readiness. There would be only split seconds of recorded information as the wall of water struck the instruments before they were ripped from their position and destroyed by that surging force.

The admiral was absorbed in the sight, indeed almost hypnotized by it, and he glanced down as Cat, alerted to danger by that rushing wall of water, climbed his leg and found more security curled around his neck.

Now the water was sending its shallow, rushing advance ripple to within yards, then feet, of the instruments. The instruments took the advance ripple, disappeared, and then the full force of the wave hit them.

Directly below where the admiral stood with Cat draped around his neck, the water hammered at the wall of the cut, rising swiftly, moving at an impressive speed. Feeling as if he had momentarily lost his balance, the admiral looked down into surging, rushing chaos. His first thought was to try to salvage the holorecorders as the earth moved again under his feet. Solid rock seemed to drop, and he realized that the rushing water had undermined the side of the cut, something that had seemed impossible. As Cat, now a fluorescent orange, sent him a panic message, he leaped, seized the holorecorders, and almost made it to safety. But the edge of the cut fragmented and a twenty-foot-wide section of solid stone dropped ten feet suddenly, leaving the admiral suspended in midair before he jolted down on the stone that was fragmenting, disintegrating under his feet even as it fell.

The admiral did not fear death, for he was not sure in his mind that the lack of existence on his part could be defined as death. Death was a condition of a once-living entity. He was electronic and mechanical. He thought, he felt, but did he *live*? Yet he knew that his existence was to be terminated, for not even his well-constructed body would be able to survive those raging waters. He would be smashed against stone, dragged over the rocky bottom of the cut, tossed, rolled, and dismantled.

He felt regret. There were so many fields that he had not had time to explore, so much knowledge to gain, and now it was ended. He and Cat were falling among the fragmented stone, some boulders the size of small crawlers. Among those jagged stones they would be ground and crushed, even before the water could do its work.

There was nothing he could do. Then suddenly, he felt the law of gravity suspended with a suddenness that jerked his neck and did considerable damage to his plastimetal tendons. He knew in that instant how a man felt—back in the old days when such punishments were still used—when he was hanged by the neck.

He was jerked to a halt. Small stones pounded him. He bounced upward as if he had been suspended by a large rubber band. Cat had elongated itself, looping its upper body around a jutting rock while its lower body was half-wrapped securely around the admiral's neck.

The admiral looked down. They were within fifty feet of the flood, which had reached its highest point and was rushing past in a sea of foam. He looked up. His neck did not operate properly. One artificial tendon had been stretched. It would require some minor repair so he would be able to function, even if his neck would not turn fully to the left. He said, "That was excellent, Cat. Thank you."

Cat sent him a groan of effort. It was time to do something about the situation. He reached up, found a handhold, and eased his weight off Cat.

"It's too bad," he said as Cat relaxed and began to put itself back into form, "that I've never studied rock climbing." They were a hundred feet from the top of the cut, and the walls almost sheer.

"I believe, Cat, if we work together, we can make it," he said. He directed Cat to extend itself once again, to

find a hold in a small, vertical crack in the rock. Cat
stretched, jammed itself into the crevice, and became
anchored, and then the admiral pulled himself up slowly
to find another handhold. It took a half-hour. Then they
stood on solid rock again, and the admiral tried to turn his
neck to the left. Cat leaped from his shoulders and ran
several yards back away from the brink, having had enough
adventure for one day.

Allen Jones was on the eastern section of the dam.
"Stoner, the water level has dropped a foot here and is
going down fast," he said.

Downriver, where the workers were congregated, the
water level was falling on the bank. As the mighty flow of
water swept into the curve where the cut had been made,
the current ran directly into the gash in its bank. Within
five minutes, as the mighty wall of water rushed onward,
filling the cut, overflowing into the dry sands, almost half
of the volume of flow had been diverted. The flood spread
as it exited the cut, and the sands began to drink. Megatons of water would be accepted and held by the sands.
The forward momentum of the flood slowed. The advance
was now a mile-wide film of water, creeping forward,
much of it disappearing into the thirsty sands.

A great cheer went up, and Stoner lifted his hands
over his head like a victorious boxer. But he had only a
moment for celebration. "Clay," he called into his radio
belt. "Tell me what you see."

Clay was flying circles over the advancing flood. "The
main force of the water is still moving just a little south of
west," he told Stoner. "There's that large depression like a
bowl directly in its path."

"Stay with it for a while, Clay," Stoner said. "The real
test is going to come when that depression is filled and the
water overflows and looks for a way out."

But Clay could not stay there that long. The depression was roughly twenty miles across, and by the time the
sky was growing dark, the depression was not half-filled.
The desert was swallowing tremendous amounts of water.

In camp that night tired people were protected by

double security. The great river below the dam was only half its former self. Rock and mud islands showed their heads along the banks, and the high watermark, in places, was a full twenty feet above the present water level. A message was being sent downriver, but it would take a while for it to reach even the first Eepera city, that city where Sage Bryson was staying.

With morning, the river was still almost eighty feet deep at the center. The work continued. Scouts acting as sky cranes laid a foundation of huge slabs of stone on the river bottom; then the earth movers and crawlers laid broken stone atop the slabs. And when the wall of stone showed above the water's surface, the laser cannon fused it, to the accompaniment of much steam and smoke. Weeks later, when the last load was hauled and the last laser-fusing firing cooled, it was possible to drive a crawler across the river and to look down upon a jumbled slope of rock to an almost dry riverbed on the downstream side.

Surprisingly, there were few fish left high and dry. Apparently the fish had followed the retreating water to the south. What *were* left high and dry, it was discovered as Clay flew down the riverbed, were dozens of the huge, long-toothed, torpedo-shaped river monsters. Twenty feet long and five feet thick, they flopped in the mud and shallows, showing those huge, destroying teeth in snaps and lunges. Clay decided then and there that he was never going to go swimming in *that* river.

The cascade of water through the cut was impressive. Confined to the narrow gorge, the river fought its bonds, rushing, leaping, swirling at whitewater speed until it was freed, once more, into the desert. The bowl-shaped depression was filled that day, and a trickle of water began to wander over the sands again. Stoner took to the air with Clay to watch. He held his breath when the advance waters curled toward the south, then breathed again as they veered westerly toward still another natural bowl.

"Looking good, Stoner," Clay said.

"So far," he replied.

Clay swallowed and began to work on his courage. It was something he had been intending to do for weeks now, but with Stoner so busy, he had not had the opportunity. Now he had Stoner alone in the scout, and it seemed to be the perfect time, but he could not find his tongue. When finally he spoke, it came out as a croak. "Stoner?"

"Yeah," Stoner said, leaning over the optics to watch the advance fingers of the flood creeping across the sands.

"Stoner, I—" He gulped. Stoner did not take his eyes off the optics. "Stoner, you know Betsy said that, well, that we—I mean me and Cindy—that we, uh, didn't have to wait until we were too old to get married."

"*Ummm*," Stoner said.

Clay waited to see if Stoner was going to say anything else. "Well, Stoner, what do you think?"

"I think we're looking good," Stoner said. "I think I can see maybe a prehistoric riverbed off to the west. If that's what I think it is, it leads all the way to the ocean in that big indentation to the west of the river's mouth."

"I mean what do you think about what Betsy said?" Clay managed.

Stoner looked up from the optics. "What did she say?"

Clay swallowed again. "That Cindy and I didn't have to wait until we were old to get married."

"Married?" Stoner lowered his face to the eyepiece again.

"Stoner—" Clay said.

Stoner looked at him again. Then he smiled. "I agree with Betsy."

"You do? Wow!" Clay shouted.

"It's a new world, Clay," Stoner said. "We've got the best of medical care. I won't mind a bit being a grandfather before *I'm* old."

Clay blushed and stuck out his hand. Stoner shook it solemnly. "Gee, thanks, Stoner."

"Hey, what's the big deal? We've all known all along you two would get married someday."

"Well, I don't know."

Stoner laughed. "Listen, it is a big deal. The biggest." He put his hand on Clay's shoulder. "I can't think of anyone on Earth or Omega that I'd rather have as a son."

Clay gulped. He could not say anything. Then, flying low, he said, "The water's flowing into that next depression."

"So it is." Stoner lifted his eyes from the viewer. "Well, it'll take a while to make this new lake. We might as well get back to camp."

Duncan Rodrick was setting up defensive positions on both sides of the river just below the dam. He was using the earth-moving equipment to dig in his crawlers so only the snouts of their weapons showed over the earthen mounds. He did not know how effective earth would be against the field weapons of the Eepera, but he figured that a few feet of solidly packed earth would not help the weapons any. He had a constant patrol of scout ships flying downstream, one of them always keeping an eye on the bank of fog to see immediately anything that moved out of it.

Mopro was roving back and forth atop the dam. The admiral was on the east bank, duplicating Rodrick's work there. Rodrick had discussed the situation with the admiral, who had based his opinions on his complete file of military history from the dawn of recorded time.

"Since we have seen no evidence of ground transportation," the admiral said, "it is likely that they will come by air."

They would have to come. It had not rained along the Great Misty River since the *Spirit of America* had landed on Omega, and climatologists said that rain in that valley would be at least a ten-year rarity. They would have to come, because their crops depended on water from the river. Their lives, not only long-term but short-term, probably depended on river water, too, for it was unlikely that they would have dug wells when so much water, water of good quality, was there for the taking. All that was needed to make the river water drinkable were holding basins to settle out the silt. Yes, the Eepera would come, to see what had happened to the river that had been the source of life to them for, if one were to believe them, sixty centuries.

"The first force will probably be small," the admiral

said. "When they see the dam, I believe that they will go to one bank or the other and approach it by land."

"We'll stand ready to consolidate our own forces by moving men to the threatened side," Rodrick said.

"A good plan, Captain," the admiral responded.

"I want the order passed that no one fires until I give the word," Rodrick said.

"Yes, sir," the admiral agreed. "It would be to our advantage and theirs to settle this matter peacefully."

"Given the worst possible scenario," Rodrick said, "when do you estimate they could reach us?"

"If they started upriver when they first noticed the river level falling, ships could be emerging from the fog at any time," the admiral replied.

But as the days passed, it became evident that the Eepera had not started upriver at the first drop in water level. Workers without combat training had been sent back to Hamilton, although Becky Dark had stayed with her husband. Mandy Miller had flown out with a portable burn and wound treatment center, with the medical robot, Doc, setting up shop on the east side of the river. And, to the surprise of everyone but Paul Warden, Evangeline Burr had come, too, bearing arms.

Astrud named her first son Lythe the Younger. Lythe was a good father. He liked to hold the baby, cooing and jabbering in a most unwarriorlike way, and Astrud loved to see him show that he had love and heart. Lythe wanted to have another baby right away, but Astrud had discovered that the women of the Caan had a way of choosing their own time for babies, a way most men did not even know about. It was a clear jelly made from the juices of a marsh plant. The jelly was strong alkaline and odorless, and when used properly, it could not be distinguished from the natural feminine fluids. She, too, wanted another child, perhaps a girl, but she had work to do.

She was building rockets. She had no hopes of making a workable guidance system, but black powder was plentiful, and she had found a variety of giant bamboo that, when dried, made a splendid body for her rockets.

She capped the lengths of the hollow bamboo with sheet metal shaped aerodynamically, filled a chamber with Greek fire and the back end of the bamboo with black powder. She had accidents, of course, with her rockets blowing up on ignition, or fizzling off directionless, but she gradually began to master the art so that she could send up a barrage of rockets that would land roughly in an area one hundred yards square and spread flaming Greek fire over everything.

She also had batteries of simple cannon firing explosive round shot that was about eighty percent reliable. An enlarged company of Lythe's warriors were armed with muskets, and although the weapons were crude, concerted fire from the one hundred musketeers was reasonably effective.

Lythe wanted to test his new company of musketeers by raiding into the territory of an unconquered tribe far to the north, but Astrud protested. It was one of the few times Lythe had seen her become angry.

"You called the Brazilians barbarians because they used superior weapons to slaughter your people," she stormed, "and now you want to take your own superior weapons into slaughter against innocent people."

"We need slaves," Lythe retorted.

"You need to put to work all the lazy bums who have been living on the produce of slave labor," Astrud argued.

"Sometimes," Lythe said coolly and evenly, "you are a very wise woman, sometimes not."

"If you take firearms against men armed with bronze-tipped arrows and bronze swords, I will no longer help you. I will let you face the Brazilians alone."

Calmly, Lythe approached her, and she thought that he was going to embrace her and tell her that he was sorry. Instead, with a smile, he lifted her, threw her across his knees, and applied his hand solidly to her bottom. She screamed, once, and then went rigidly silent. When he released her, she stood, looked at him with blazing eyes, and asked, "Are you quite finished?"

"You are wise, my mate, and we listen to you with respect, but you are a woman. My woman."

She walked to a weapons rack and pulled down a fine sword with a newly fashioned steel blade and a well-wrought hilt. She whirled, swinging the sword with all her strength. Lythe recovered from his surprise just in time to throw himself to the floor and roll away as she drew back the sword again and cut deeply into the chair in which he had been seated.

Lythe leaped, his own sword coming out of its sheath, but he stopped his blow in midair, muscles bulging. She stood with her sword hanging down, panting, tears of rage and frustration running down her cheeks. Lythe threw his sword aside and knelt in front of her, bowing his head.

"If you would kill me, then strike," he said sadly.

"Oh, you son of a bitch," Astrud said, throwing her sword aside, where it hit the wall with a crash. She knelt and lifted his head. "Don't you ever, ever lay hands on me again."

"Not even when you take my manhood and try to clothe yourself in it?"

"Not even then," she said, putting her hands on his cheeks. "I know you are a man, the finest man of the entire world. But I am not a child to be spanked."

"No," he agreed, "you are not. But can I be permitted to inform you when you are stepping beyond the bounds of womanhood without risk of having my head sliced off?"

She laughed. "Yes, damn you, just tell me. I am *not* unreasonable."

"Only at times," he said, taking her in his arms.

The next crisis in their personal relationship came a few days later. "Lythe," she said, "will you please ask for an audience for me with the elders?"

"What reason shall I give them?" he asked.

"I am going to propose methods of training the slaves in the use of arms," she said.

"Arm the slaves? Are you mad?"

"It is time. Only a few remain in domestic service, and only a few in the fields. The rest are becoming craftsmen and skilled workers. The government is supporting them, giving them, in effect, a salary for their work."

"Yes," he said, "and some already feel that they are superior to Caan simply because they can make a gun. However, it is the Caan who can *use* a gun."

"If the enemy returns, the slaves would increase our numbers," she said.

"And if he doesn't return, the slaves will turn the weapons against their masters."

"The solution, then, is to have no masters, only freemen. The slaves are a minority. They will present no threat. Indeed, if you give them something to work for— their freedom, the right to own property, to have homes and to be able to improve them, and to know that their children will be trained, be schooled, and be freemen— you will find that they will make better soldiers than the cavaliers of the cities who play at arms because it is the custom."

"Woman, woman," Lythe said, "how you do trouble me."

But he stood before the council and spoke proudly. "My mate, Astrud Cabral, who came to us from the upper darkness with the secrets of other worlds, will make a suggestion. I ask only that you listen and that you consider this: She speaks as one who has traveled among the stars. She speaks with the knowledge of a people who knew the secrets of metals and fire and the force of the heavenly lightning. She speaks of the future, and I, Lythe, most honored director of war and heir to the most honored, say that you will listen."

When Astrud suggested calmly and with great logic that the slaves be freed and trained in the use of arms, she was hissed from the chamber. It was no big thing, she knew, for she had seen others hissed from the chamber for less, and her status was such that she could have reentered and requested another audience, on another subject.

Lythe remained. "Elders," he said, "today you hiss at the idea. Will you hiss when the enemy comes with thousands of warriors armed with the weapons of fire and thunder and the cream of Caan manhood dies in fighting for this world?"

"My son," said Lotel the Elder, "we value the honor-

able Astrud Cabral. We have hissed away an idea whose
time has not come."

"To expect a slave to fight is without reason," another
elder said.

"They work side by side with Caan warriors at the
forges, in the places where the cannon and the rifles are
made. The slaves are the more skilled, for our men are
new at this thing called work. I say that they have earned
the right to share the bounty of our life," Lythe said. "And
in pointing out that the slave, given something for which
to fight, will make a fierce warrior, I think Astrud Cabral
is right."

"Set the example for us, then," taunted an elder.
"Free your own slaves and have them eat at your table."

"Free them I will," Lythe said hotly. "However, my
table is my own, and only those I invite eat there, be they
slave or Caan."

Only three families of Lythe's slaves still worked the
acres of his fields. The others were becoming skilled craftsmen in the various factories. He called them all together
on a day of rest and spoke to them, with Astrud standing
by his side.

"Many of you saw the attack on our city by the men
from the outer darkness, and some of you lost friends and
relatives. You have suffered, as the Caan have suffered,
but you are in slavery. This I think is not right. Today I
say this to you: Would you earn your freedom?"

There was a silence. A man who had helped to develop the mold to cast the first cannon touched his nose in
respect and said in a quiet, shy voice, "You feed us well,
master. We have a place to sleep and to rear our young.
We do not complain, but we would hear more about
freedom. Would it be freedom to return to the lands of
our birth?"

"Would you want to return?" Lythe asked. "You are
from the south, are you not? There, a generation ago,
Caan warriors destroyed everything. Today it is the land
of the Caan. Your people exist only here, as slaves."

"What freedom, then, master?" the man asked.

"To have your own land. To build your own home

with the strength and skill of your own hands, to have your children in training and in schooling."

"How do we earn this right, master?"

"I ask you first—would you fight for freedom?" Lythe asked.

"Against you, master, no."

"Against outsiders who would destroy all," Lythe clarified.

"I would fight for my life," the spokesman said. "Certainly I would fight for my life *and* freedom."

"All who will pledge their loyalty to the Caan, all who will continue their own work while training in the use of arms and in learning the meaning and responsibilities of freedom, all who are willing to fight for the country that is yours, the only country you have, will now step forward."

After a long, uneasy pause, the slaves began to step forward, one by one.

Lythe turned to Astrud with a grim smile. "Now, my love, since this is your idea, they are your responsibility." He turned and walked away.

"You must realize," Astrud said to the slaves, "that freedom does not mean the freedom from work. Have you seen me work?"

"We have, mistress," the spokesman said.

"And have you seen the honorable director of war work and train for fighting?"

"We have."

"Freemen at times work harder than slaves."

Someone laughed, and the laughter spread. "Perhaps they are not doing us a favor," someone from the rear called, and the laughter got louder. Astrud raised her hand.

"Freemen in the employ of this household do not go about in rags," she said. "Those of you who work at fashioning garments will begin to make the clothing of freemen for all. Freemen who work in the armaments plants should eat well. From this day you will draw, from agricultural stores, the same food that is eaten in the master's house."

There was a cheer.

"All the children under sixteen years of age will report to my records keeper as soon as they are properly clothed, for assignment to training and schooling. And tonight, the winekeeper will distribute one bottle of this year's vintage for each person over sixteen."

There was a greater cheer.

"And anyone who is late for work tomorrow morning will have a percentage of earning deducted from his pay," Astrud said. "I have one more thing to say—all of the Caan will be watching you. The freedom of many depends upon how you conduct yourselves as freemen. If you are slothful, if you are drunken, if you become contentious and contemptuous, the Caan will say, 'these are nothing but slaves.' If you conduct yourself well, this is only a beginning."

And so, as Astrud had kept track of the passing of standard Earth days, weeks, and months by her watch, which was the only thing remaining to her that reminded her of her home, her place of origin, the Caan watched Lythe's great experiment with amused interest.

She knew that it would take at least two years of sublight cruising for the *Estrêla do Brasil* to approach a new planet, settle the colonists, leave the planet, and head back to the Earth. Then another year or two to approach the Earth, organize a military expedition, and return to the planet of the Caan. She believed that she would truly have to have the Caan ready for possible massive invasion within five years.

When a young ex-slave who had worked in one of the black-powder plants discovered that magnesium made the black powder burn cleaner and explode with more power, her dreams seemed real. The seeds of knowledge she had planted among the people of her new planet were bearing spontaneous fruit.

SIXTEEN

The great council of the city of Suses stood on a riverside wharf and watched with impassive faces as a group of Whorsk slaves attacked a stranded monster in the mud of the riverbed. The shrill voices of the Whorsk carried to them. The monster slashed with its head and neatly removed the legs from a Whorsk, but the others kept on stabbing it with makeshift spears.

"Shall I kill them?" asked Yanee. "Too many of them have left their work."

Suses, the ruler of the city, shook his head. "Let them have their fill of meat. It will only make them stronger for their work."

The wide river was a muddy, empty depression. The Whorsk fighting the monster sometimes sank in the muck to their knees. Along the banks the stands of green water plants were bedraggled, and underwater growers made a slimy, green covering of the mud formerly covered by shallows. In the center of the river a channel of running water curled its way southward, flowing sluggishly.

"This cannot, of course, be allowed to continue," Suses said.

"It is recorded in the annals," said an elder, "that the river level fell thirty feet just over a thousand years ago."

"And the waters came back," another continued. "We must have patience."

"Will you be patient when your storage tanks are

empty of water and you have to crawl in the slime to drink from that?" Suses asked, pointing toward the distant channel.

"It is reported that it is the same in the fields to the north," Yanee said.

"That *would* seem logical," Suses said. He sighed and looked up at the blazing sun in the midday sky. Already the exposed mud was beginning to dry and crack near the banks. For weeks now the river level had been falling. Each day Suses arose expecting to see the trickle of water in the channel begin to swell. Each morning he was disappointed.

The overseers in the fields had put all slaves to work carrying water by hand from the retreating channel. The crops were, for the moment, safe. However, it would not be many days before they began to suffer, for it was impossible to carry enough water to irrigate all the fields.

"It is time for us to investigate this phenomenon," Suses said. "Yanee, you will fly upriver, past the protective shield. It is my thought that perhaps some natural accident to the north has blocked the natural flow of the river."

"Father," Yanee protested, "you know how I hate to be confined in close quarters with those filthy animals, and how it sickens me to fly."

"You are my son," Suses said. "I have spoken."

Yanee spent the rest of the day preparing, selecting an outfit from among his collection of costumes. He did take time out to visit friends in the evening, with Sage on his arm. He had reconciled himself to his difficult and distasteful task and now even relished the attention it brought him.

"Do you think you will have to go all the way to the lands of the jungle?" a wide-eyed woman asked.

"I will go as far as it is necessary to go," Yanee said.

The young man who had asked Yanee if he was tired of Sage put his hand on Sage's arm and said, "This one will be left alone, Yanee."

"That can't be helped," Yanee said.

Sage had just begun to understand that Yanee was going away. "How long will you be gone?" she asked him.

Yanee, his chin held heroically high, said, "Who can say?"

"We can't have this one lonely," the young man said, caressing Sage's bare arm. "As your friend, Yanee, I see it as my duty to care for her while you are away."

"Thank you," Yanee said. He looked at Sage. "Since she is obviously defective, not having yet ———." He used a word that Sage had heard once before and had not understood, but she knew that he was being critical, and she was hurt.

"What have I not done?" she asked.

Yanee looked at her coldly. "You have not conceived my child," he said.

In her constant glow of happiness and well-being, the thought had never occurred to her. Now it was vaguely disturbing. She seemed to have a memory associated with the subject. Her brow creased with the intensity of her effort to remember. A girl, a big girl. Ah, Theresita. Theresita had been pregnant.

"*I* wouldn't care whether she conceives or not," the young man said. "I have heard her wild cries of pleasure coming from your room."

"Have you been spying on me?" Yanee asked.

The young man laughed. "One has only to walk past to hear." He made a smirk, the nearest thing to a smile that Sage had ever seen. "You have been very selfish, Yanee, keeping all that wildness for yourself."

Yanee spread his hands. "It is true. I confess. I will no longer be selfish. She has been wanting to join in the ———" There was another word that Sage did not understand. "So be it. She is yours."

Yanee turned and strode away, his back very straight. He was so very handsome in his military gear. Sage looked after him in puzzlement, and then the young man led her by the arm toward another room, and a group of men and women were with them.

"You will remember this night," the young man told Sage. "Your first night of ———" That word again.

Beyond a door, a hallway, then another door was a large chamber. The only furniture was a huge, soft floor covering, as thick and as soft as any bed, and a refreshment center along one wall. People began to throw off their clothing. The young man seized Sage's gown and lowered it to expose her breasts. She gasped and tried to keep him from stripping her.

"Look! She is frightened," the young man called out.

"Give her something to be frightened of," another man said, leaping to stand in front of Sage, nude, his manliness quite evident. He bent and thrust himself up under Sage's gown, and memories of something horrible, frightening, and disgusting threatened to overwhelm her—something so awful that it cut through her drug-induced euphoria to make her a screaming, fighting, clawing bundle of madness. She saw blood spring up on a face where her fingernails had left their mark. Her knee contacted the genitals of the man who had tried to attack her, and he groaned and fell. Her combat training, which had been drummed into her so deeply that it was almost instinct, allowed her to use all her potential, all her strength, and that was enough to do damage, as she used techniques developed over the centuries on Earth. There were a broken arm, loosened teeth, and two men down with pain in the groin so severe that they were out of action. One was gasping for breath, having narrowly escaped having his larynx crushed.

She stood alone, her gown in ruins, hanging by one strap to her shoulders. The women had backed to a far wall and stood looking at her in horror. She turned and ran out the door, fled down empty corridors to find the entrance, and then was on the street. She ran without direction until her lungs were burning. She leaned against a wall, panting, her mind in turmoil. Childhood horrors rushed at her, and she gnawed a knuckle until the pain cleared her head a bit. She looked around. She was not a child. She was a woman. Where was Yanee?

Yanee had given her away. He had given her to men who were going to use her as she had been used when she was a child. Yanee, who had made her so happy.

What was she to do?

Go to him. Tell him how he had hurt her. He had left the party. He would be at home. She started walking rapidly, holding her torn gown together with one hand.

But he had said that he was tired of her. He had *given* her to that other one. A devastating sadness bent her double, and sobs shook her body. She had no place to go. That word, that word she had not known, had meant a half-dozen of them coming at her, forcing her, using her, hurting her.

She found herself on the eastern edge of the city, near the cliffs, and the usual coolness of the desert night made her shiver. The glow of the pyramid bathed her in soft light, while the light of Omega's two moons made the desert shimmer. The desert extended away to the east forever—flat, desolate, studded with darker outcroppings of rock. There was only the huge, glowing pyramid to break the desolation.

At that moment she could remember only the scene in the large chamber—the hands of one man on her, another thrusting himself against her—and Yanee, who had discarded her.

There was the desert. There she would be alone, safe from them. There she would not die.

She started walking, and her direction took her quite near the base of the pyramid. There she walked on a light covering of sand over stone. She started to skirt around a stone retaining wall and saw that it was one side of a walled walkway leading to the pyramid. The structure towered over her, glowing whitely. It seemed to reach for the sky, to threaten to engulf her. The surface was smooth, a perfect triangular plane extending upward and upward to a dizzying height. Awed, she stood with her head tilted back, the desert behind her. She did not see the two dark figures that emerged from the shadows of the walled walkway.

"Earthwoman," a voice said.

She screamed and turned to run, fell, and scrambled on her hands and knees. A hand closed over her arm and pulled her to her feet. The men on either side of her were unlike anyone she had seen in the city—small, thick of chest, broad of shoulder. Their faces in the glow of soft, white light were dark; their eyes, hooded. They wore white, pleated gowns, their heads gleamingly bald.

"Do not struggle, Earthwoman," one of them said in English. "You will come with us."

She no longer had the will to fight. All the fight had gone out of her back in that room where half a dozen men had fallen to her unexpected and skilled defensive fury. She did not even try to cover her nakedness. She let her head drop, leaned on the two men for support, and allowed them to half-carry her up the walled walkway toward the towering, overwhelming pyramid.

Jack Purdy's *Dinahmite* loafed over the desert, angling in toward the drying, cracking, empty bed of the once-great river. He was ten miles north of the edge of the Eepera's shield, making a routine patrol. To the west he could see the new river winding down the prehistoric riverbed past the two great lakes that had been formed in the desert. Already green things were beginning to grow along the new river and around the lakes.

Purdy was bored. The dam had been finished for almost a month now, and the constant state of security alert at the dam site was getting to be a drag, and flying over the same stretch of desert and river had lost its charm.

He checked the ship's chronometer and saw that it was time to report. "River base, *Dinahmite*."

"*Dinahmite*, river base," said Becky Dark, who was taking a turn on communications.

"Tell 'em to set an extra plate for lunch," Jack said. It was almost time for him to be relieved.

"Fresh fish today, Jack," Becky told him. "My Elton condescended to use regular tackle and take a few people with him instead of being the fly-casting purist. The fish in the new lake are really hungry."

"Sounds good to me," Jack said. "By the way, the official report for this hour is same as before."

"Sounds familiar," Becky said, writing down the phrase, same as before, beside the hour on her report sheet.

"*Dinahmite* out," Jack said.

"*Dinahmite, Blue Rover*," a voice said, and Jack recognized Clay Girard.

"Come in, Clay," he said.

"I'm fueled and ready if you want to knock off a half-hour early."

Jack grinned. Clay was the only scout eager enough to add a half-hour onto his tour. Clay had not put in as many hours in a contour chair as Jack and the others had. Jack had seen Clay on his regular tours of duty, flying the proper course to cover the assigned points but flying upside down, spinning the ship on its horizontal axis, practicing long glides. That was all right. That was the way a new pilot learned all of the little quirks of a scout, and if Clay enjoyed it, Jack was more than willing to give him a half-hour from his own duty schedule.

"You can talk me into that real easy, Clay," he said. "I'm cruising two hundred directly over the river at the edge of the fog. Gun 'er down here and pick up at the east bank, point victor able."

"See you in ten minutes," Clay said.

Jack yawned, did a three-sixty scan of the sky, saw only the purplish-blue and the high bank of fog, the desert, and the drying riverbed below. He started to whistle a little tune, and a vision of Dinah, who had died on the first planet to be approached by the *Spirit of America*, flashed into his mind. Her memory was no longer painful. He smiled, remembering how they had once danced to that particular song, and how sweet it had been; then he was musing about how nice it would be to have her here with him in the *Dinahmite*, just to talk and while away the time.

"Well, girl," he said, "it was great while it lasted. But I wish you could have seen this Omega world of ours. You'd have liked it, Dinah." Then he grinned. "You're getting worse, boy."

He changed his voice to falsetto and said, "But it's all right, Jack, unless you start answering yourself."

He had turned north, the stern of the scout toward the fog. He was tooling along, wings out, just a little less than two hundred miles an hour ground speed. Nice and easy. Another day. Maybe the Eepera were never going to come out of the fog. Lunch in twenty minutes. Fresh fish.

"I'd like to explore that desert," he said, as if he were talking to Dinah, because, just maybe, she could hear, somewhere, somehow. "Be fun, wouldn't it? No camels or horses, but maybe Baby and Beau could take the desert, if we had enough water. But best just to take a crawler. Bet you'd like that, too."

He paused, as if waiting for an answer, and with a shot of adrenalin into his gut, he *knew* something was behind him. He jerked his head, looked out the rearview glass, and saw a Whorsk airship emerging slowly from the fog. Even as he pressed his transmit button, another airship poked its nose through.

"*Dinahmite* to base. We've got company. Two coming out of the fog. Clay, get down here fast."

He punched buttons and the scout's wings folded into its hull even as his forward speed increased with a force that pushed him back into the contour couch. He did not want to be within range of those weapons that could stop a ship's power in midflight. He turned and scanned.

"Four of them now, base," he said. "Magnifying scan. Whorsk in the gondolas. No, hold it. There's a man. An Eepera. And another. Looks like two Eepera in each gondola."

"Jack, I'm on your tail, coming down," Clay said.

"Wing me, boy," Jack said. "Weapons ready?"

"Ready," Clay replied.

"We'll stay at least five miles away from them," Jack said. "And remember, Rodrick said don't fire unless fired upon."

"May I suggest, sir," Clay said, "that we extend wings, just in case."

"Good thought," Jack said. With the wings out, if the Eepera weapon reached them, they could glide down to the desert.

Under magnification they could see the faces of the

Whorsk and the Eepera in the gondolas. There seemed to
be some agitated conversation going on between the Eepera,
and one of them was pointing toward the two scouts.

"Clay, keep switching your scanner back and forth
between the two to the east. I'll watch the other two. If
you see one of them point a weapon, yell."

"Roger," Clay said.

The airships continued directly north, staying over
the dry riverbed. Clay and Jack circled them, keeping a
distance of about five miles.

Duncan Rodrick was standing atop the large laser
cannon from the *Spirit of America*. The weapon had been
positioned on the west bank, just below the dam. It had
been several hours since the Whorsk airships had emerged
from the fog, and Rodrick could see four tiny dots in the
sky far to the south. Slowly the dots grew larger. When it
was possible to distinguish the outlines of the ships with
the naked eye, Rodrick sent, "All personnel, hold your
fire. If they try to fly directly over the dam, we'll use the
laser cannon on this side to blast them." He was not
willing to let the airships get directly over the dam to drop
the explosives that the Whorsk had used in battle against
them.

The ships drew nearer. They were close enough now,
Rodrick knew, to see what had been done, to see the dam
and the diverted river now emptying its waters into the
western desert. Sure enough, the ships stopped their forward motion and drifted on a slight breeze toward the
eastern bank.

"Looks as if they are headed for your side of the river,
Admiral," Rodrick said.

"Affirmative, sir," the admiral said.

The ships began to turn, and Rodrick could see the
Whorsk laboring mightily on the pedals that turned the
airscrews mounted at the rear of the gondolas. They began
to descend and landed, one by one, on the eastern bank.

Paul Warden was manning the laser cannon with
Evangeline as his sighter. He was keeping the muzzle of
the weapon aligned on the lead airship.

"Paul," Rodrick said, "there are so few of them that I don't think we'll need to shift men to the other bank. I'm going over. Keep them in your sights."

"You got it," Paul said, grinning over at Evangeline. She had surprised everyone by coming over to take part in a fight, and he was pleased.

Rodrick guided a crawler onto the dam and began to move at top speed toward the far bank.

"They are all out of the gondolas," the admiral reported. "I see the usual Whorsk weapons, and the Eepera are carrying those thick wands."

"If they start toward you, give them some warning fire," Rodrick said. "Don't let them get close with those weapons."

But the Eepera seemed content, for the moment, to stand in front of the airships and look at the dam. Rodrick was getting close enough to see the ships now, having crossed the miles-long dam at a speed of forty miles per hour.

"Captain," came the voice of the admiral, "they are aiming their wands at your crawler."

Rodrick spoke, but even with his first word the power went off in the crawler, and the vehicle began to coast to a stop. His radio and all electronics were out. He was still a half mile from the bank and the admiral's position, but he had given orders. Force was to be met with force. He saw the massive bulk of Mopro kneel. Two explosive shells blasted upward from the robot's knee cannon, and a Whorsk airship disappeared in smoke and fire.

Rodrick pushed the start button, and the hydrogen engine of the crawler came to life. "Do you read me, Admiral?"

"Loud and clear, sir," the admiral said. "Sir, two of the Eepera have separated themselves from the group and are walking toward us."

"I'll be there in a minute," Rodrick said, wheeling the crawler off the dam, onto sand, and then cutting sharply toward the admiral's position. The two Eepera were about a hundred yards away when he joined the admiral behind the dirt embankment. "Are they carrying their weapons?"

"Affirmative," the admiral said.

"Mopro, lay a line of projectiles directly in front of them," Rodrick said, and instantly dust was spurting up in front of the two Eepera as Mopro fired.

"Hailer," Rodrick said, taking the hailer mike from the admiral. "If you come any closer with weapons, we will destroy you and your ships," he said, his voice booming out over the desert.

The Eepera stopped. They consulted. One of them lifted his wand and aimed it.

"Fire for effect, Mopro," Rodrick ordered, and the Eepera who had lifted his weapon spurted blood and was thrown violently backward as a hail of small projectiles hit him.

"Mopro was not slowed by any electrical effect," the admiral reported.

Rodrick nodded. The defense robot was enlarged past his usual size by a heavy layer of lead, a shield against the Eepera weapon. The lead had proved effective. Rodrick picked up the hailer.

"We don't want to have to kill more of you," he said. "Put down your weapons and come forward."

Yanee had felt the winds of death near him. He had seen his companion almost dissolve in a battering of projectiles. He had seen the invincible weapon fail. Confused, he looked back at his other men, who stood before the remaining three airships. Never in history—at least not since the total conquest of the native Whorsk—had an Eepera died in battle. Now his friend was dead, and he was having terms dictated to him.

"He's hesitant," Rodrick said, watching. "If he lifts his weapon, Mopro, don't kill him, just make the dust dance around him."

Yanee made his decision. Perhaps the weapon had malfunctioned. With the weapon set on full charge, nothing living or mechanical could function. He lifted his wand, and the earth smoked all around him, and he heard the thunder of the explosive rounds. He squeezed and played the deadly beam over the creature that was threatening him, but the storm of fire continued, drawing closer. With a sigh of frustration, he lowered his weapon.

"We will give you one more chance," Rodrick said, the hailer sending his voice to echo and reecho off the cliffs. "Put down your weapon and come forward."

Yanee was curious. He was angry, but he was also curious. These Earthlings had done a mighty job in a very short time. And his weapons had no effect on their creature. He decided that it would be interesting to talk with them. He bent and laid his weapon on the sand, stood, and marched handsomely toward the dam.

"Keep an eye on the ones by the ships," Rodrick ordered. He climbed up the dirt embankment and stood waiting for the Eepera. He had heard from those who had visited the valley how handsome these people were, but he was still impressed. This one was a fine specimen. He looked like a movie hero in a period piece. He let the man come to within twenty feet, and then he said, "All right, that's far enough."

"I am Yanee."

"I am Captain Rodrick Duncan."

"You have done a very bad thing."

Rodrick was silent.

"Your work is impressive, but we cannot allow you to stop the flow of our river."

"Nor can we allow you to send your Whorsk to raid us, to endanger our scouts, to kill our people," Rodrick said.

Yanee looked puzzled. "But you are stealing our metal."

Elton and Becky Dark, manning the lasers on a crawler, were listening to the exchange. Elton shook his head and said, "I think that dude's gyros are wobblin'."

Rodrick, too, was a bit amazed by Yanee's look of outraged innocence and his words. "Do you have the authority to talk about an agreement between us?"

"I am Yanee, son of Suses."

Rodrick was getting a bit irritated. "Am I supposed to be impressed?"

"Of course."

"Why?"

"Because I will be ruler of the city."

"Then you do have some authority?"

"I have the authority to tell you to dismantle this dam immediately," Yanee said.

"He's definitely operatin' with mismatched software," Elton said to Becky.

"I think you'd better listen to me," Rodrick said sternly. "The dam stays. How long will it be before your fields begin to dry up? Before you have no drinking water?"

"Things are already quite critical," Yanee said. "That's why you must dismantle this thing now."

"You are the son of the ruler?"

"That is correct."

"I want you to return to him. Do you read English as well as you speak it?"

"There are those who can."

"Good. I have this in writing, and I will send it with you, but I will tell you now. Go to the ruler and tell him that there will be no water in this river until we are assured that there will be no further invasions of our lands on the eastern continent; until the member of our group who is being held in your city is returned to us; and until we are allowed inspection of the entire valley to assure ourselves that you can do us no harm."

"You must be joking," Yanee said. "Besides, it will take days for me to return to the city. I assure you that Suses will say the same as I. Your arrogance is insupportable. We will be forced to destroy you."

Rodrick walked forward and handed Yanee a large envelope. "Our demands are written here," he said. "Now go back to your ruler and tell him we will give him one week. Then we will come in after the woman."

Yanee looked puzzled. "Why do you make so much of one woman?"

"It's our way," Rodrick replied.

"I'll go," Yanee said, "but Suses is going to be very angry."

"I'll chance that," Rodrick said.

"Before I go, may I see the creature who killed my friend?"

"No."

Yanee was shocked. He was not accustomed to being refused any request. He drew himself up sternly. "When we kill you, I will see that you live to face me."

"My pleasure," Rodrick said.

Yanee walked slowly back toward the ships. When he picked up his weapon and turned to stare back, Mopro was at the ready, but he sheathed the wand, toed his dead friend thoughtfully, and walked back to the ship. Soon the airships were lifting, and then they began to make their slow way back down the river.

"Was that dude for real?" Elton Dark asked as Rodrick came back behind the embankment.

"He talked like a spoiled child," Mandy said incredulously.

"A spoiled child with a weapon against which we have little defense," Rodrick said.

"Sir," the admiral said, "permission to take the tapes from Mopro back to Hamilton."

"All right," Rodrick agreed. "Anything you can tell us about them now, Admiral?"

"Only that the instruments we installed on Mopro's shield recorded an electromagnetic force, sir. Perhaps Grace will be able to tell us more once she has a chance to examine the tapes in the lab. Since it's unlikely that we'll experience another attack, I'd like to work with Grace for a day or two."

"Two days," Rodrick said. "And Admiral, tell Grace that we all need to have a shield against that weapon. Whatever it takes, we have to have it."

Oscar Kost was feeling bilious. He did not like the feeling of being strapped down in a contour couch. He had been definitely uncomfortable as he had waited for the millions of minute vibrations and the thunderous rumblings as the multiple rockets of the *Free Enterprise* began, one by one, to pop into combustion.

There had been times in his life and career when Oscar had been accused of being a pessimist. He had never agreed with that tag, for he considered himself to be a positive thinker with wild optimism tempered by a sense of reality. For example, it did not seem to occur to anyone he knew that the ship could blow up. He, knowing a bit about physics, rocketry, and the history of humankind's mechanical ventures, realized that a bug in one of the many rocket engines could cause a rending, tearing, fiery explosion and that such an explosion would spread rapidly, making the ship one huge fireball fragmenting to rain debris down on the desert below.

Oscar did a lot of thinking as the starship rose from its Utah berth. He wondered if it would not have been better for him to have stayed home, but he had been with Dexter Hamilton for a lot of years now, and he guessed that it would not have done for him to have sent Dexter and Jennie off to the stars without the moderating influence of his own optimism tempered by a sense of reality. Dex tended to be a dreamer, and Oscar felt that now and then a realist had to grab a dreamer by his ankles and pull him back before the sun burned his feathers and sent him tumbling down.

Then, too, Oscar was curious. As Dexter's right-hand man, he had talked personally with everyone aboard the ship, and there were some pretty interesting characters. In spite of his apparent misanthropy, at times, Oscar was truly a lover of people. He did love some more than others. Take Leslie Young. He had fallen in love with that woman the first time he had met her, when she was a National Service Corps officer helping to guard the building site when the *Spirit* was taking shape in that hole in the desert. His love for Leslie was not all fatherly, either, although he of course recognized the impossibility of it being otherwise. It was just a joy to see her in action. She took no nonsense but was always polite. She was approaching the adventure with a joyous anticipation. Being with Leslie both on board and after planetfall would compensate for the discomfort and sheer terror that he felt with g-forces pushing him back, making his arms weigh a hundred pounds each.

There were others who would be interesting to watch as well. Dexter, of course, with his Jennie at his side. He had been the first one to recognize Dexter Hamilton's nature, when Dexter was a mere freshman at the University of North Carolina back so many years that he did not like to try to remember the exact date. He had seen the dreamer in Dexter then and had recognized a kindred spirit, for, although he was well-grounded in the sciences, he felt—even if he could not come up with a theory to prove it—that someday, hopefully in his lifetime, some young man would find a way to beat Einstein's constant and enable a spaceship to travel faster than the speed of light. Harry Shaw had done just that, and by a happy accident of fate, Dexter was the President at the time, a far-seeing man who had put Harry's calculations into action.

And there was that astounding bit of fluff, Jean Roebling. It was a puzzle how that girl and the dependable, solid, straight-thinking Derek could be of the same flesh and blood. Thinking about Jean, Oscar tried to laugh but was unsuccessful, since the g-forces tended to make his face into an unalterable grimace. He had laughed at Jean's attempt to bring the equivalent of a department store aboard the ship. Maybe they should have let her. The female frills, the high fashions, all the little feminine doodads might have been great morale boosters once the ship had reached its destination and the approximately one thousand people aboard had to settle down to no-frills living on a new planet.

Enterprise could have carried Jean's department store. She was slightly smaller than the *Spirit*, but she was still one big mother of a ship. The weight savings had come mostly from cutting down on the life-support systems. There were no large green areas to help regenerate oxygen, for example. *Enterprise*, thanks to Harry Shaw's recalculations of the Shaw Drive equations, would not have to spend years cruising at sublight speed to get out of the gravitational force of planetary bodies. There was no swimming pool, because *Enterprise* would not be spending years in space and therefore required less water.

No shortcuts had been taken regarding safety aspects, however. And she was as well-armed as current technology permitted. Like the *Spirit*, she carried everything needed to establish a colony on a virgin planet, and Oscar wanted to be part of that process.

In short, Oscar Kost, staid, irascible, seemingly locked into the academic life, was a dreamer, too, and his wild dream was to know what lay out there beyond the tiny boundaries of the solar system. Now he would see it for himself. And he would have a chance to talk with some people he admired greatly, like Duncan Rodrick.

When the rockets cut off and he was thrown forward against his harness, he breathed a deep sigh of relief. He had a private screen. He could see the curve of the Earth's roundness below him, and there, far off, the moon. He started to unbuckle his harness, but Harry Shaw's voice stopped him.

"All personnel," Shaw said through the ship's communications system, "please remain as you are in your acceleration couches. We have reached orbital altitude, and now we will make some slight adjustments."

Three times rockets fired, each time giving Kost a bit of a jolt.

"All personnel," Shaw added a few minutes later, "our orbit is now stable. You may proceed with your duties."

Oscar's first duty was to yank a bottle of good bourbon out of his locker and have a swig, then to go to the Hamilton cabin to see how Dex and Jennie had fared.

"Wasn't that fantastic?" Jennie asked, her face glowing with excitement as she let Oscar into the cabin.

"Fantastic as hell," Oscar muttered.

"Come on, Oscar," Hamilton said. "Admit you're enjoying something for once."

Oscar made a face and shoved the bottle toward Hamilton. Hamilton grinned and took a drink. Jennie reached for the bottle and tilted it.

"Well, I thought you said it was just fantastic?" he teased, because he had never seen Jennie do anything so unladylike as drink out of a bottle.

"Just because it was fantastic doesn't mean that I wasn't scared," Jennie admitted, laughing.

The ship would remain in orbit for a time, the duration depending on how long it took for the crew to check out all systems. She was, as the *Spirit of America* had been, an untested vehicle.

"Well," Hamilton said, "why don't we take a stroll?" A spin had been induced in the ship's outer wheel, so gravity was almost equal to Earth's. "See how the others came through."

The ship was big enough to make a stroll more than a few minutes' outing. The length of time was extended by stops to chat with excited people who were congregated in the corridors and in the public areas. Oscar had to smile wryly when he saw Jean Roebling, in a mauve creation that seemed to be a cross between a tennis outfit and a short formal gown, gesturing excitedly to a group of young men.

"Looks as if our glamour girl made it all right," Oscar remarked.

"Don't be catty, Oscar," Jennie said. "She reminds me of a beautiful butterfly."

"Who's being catty?" Oscar asked.

"Remember that butterflies are not just beauty in motion," Jennie said. "They do, after all, serve a basic purpose in nature."

Oscar snorted. But there was something to what Jennie was saying. Jean Roebling would, at least, give the young, unmarried men something to think about at night.

Hamilton did not want to presume on his status, but Jennie did a bit of coaxing and the three of them were quickly admitted to the control bridge. Harry Shaw, very busy, shot them a grin and a thumbs-up sign of victory. They watched the bridge crew scurry around as the natural-looking robot in fatigue dress worked with the ship's computer and system after sytem was given the green light. Shaw took a moment and came to stand with them.

"Looks good," he said, his face split in a wide grin. "I'd estimate we'll be able to take the big jump in about forty-eight hours."

"No need to rush it," Oscar said, sneaking a look at a screen showing the good, blue Earth.

"I know how you feel, Oscar," Shaw agreed. "She's pretty from up here. Tough to leave."

"But we'll be back," Jennie said. "And, God willing, we'll be able to do something to make her as pretty from up close as she is from out here."

The countdown to Shaw Drive engagement continued flawlessly. Oscar left the Hamiltons in their cabin and went in search of Leslie Young. He found her in her office. She was at her communicator console, taking reports from the security staff all over the ship. Shaw took a seat after helping himself to a cup of coffee and watched and listened in admiration as Leslie demonstrated her no-nonsense efficiency—not being overbearing, but leaving no doubt who was in charge. Finished, she surprised and pleased Oscar by coming to him, bending, and planting a kiss on his cheek.

"Well, you old bear, we're on our way," she said.

"So it seems."

"I have to make some rounds," Leslie said. "Walk with me?"

"I've just done that," Oscar said. "I'll pass."

Leslie was about to persuade him when the door burst open and Jean Roebling blew in, as fresh as a spring breeze. "Leslie, darling," she cried, "I'm having a small, intimate little celebration party in my quarters. You must come. The wardens of this flying prison did allow me to bring a few tins of Beluga and five bottles of very old wine aboard, and I think now is the time to enjoy them." She smiled blazingly at Oscar. "Please come, Dr. Kost."

"Caviar gives me heartburn," Oscar grumbled.

"I've decided duty can wait," Leslie said. She took Oscar's arm and pulled him to his feet. "Come on, Oscar."

It turned out to be a gathering of old friends and some family in Jean's quarters. Derek Roebling shook Oscar's hand and then held Leslie's hand for more than the time required for a handshake, causing Oscar to look at him with new eyes. It flashed into his mind that Leslie was, after all, unmarried, and that it was understood that breeding children was to be a major portion of every man

and woman's duty on the new world. He reckoned that
Derek might almost be good enough for Leslie.

He left Derek and Leslie talking, stepped over a few
feet, and nodded to Hilary Diaz, who was sitting in Jean's
contour couch looking a bit glum. "Quite a trip," he said.

"Yes," Hilary replied.

Oscar sat on the wide arm of the couch. She moved
over slightly. "You're not having any of Jean's goodies?"
she asked.

"I think I'll wait and sample the wares of your mother's food factories," Oscar said. "They must be good, if you're
a testimonial to them."

"Well, I grew up eating Ward products," Hilary said.
"Examine and judge accordingly."

Oscar laughed. "Good enough for me." He accepted a
glass of wine from Jean. Hilary refused. "I don't see Roberto," he ventured.

"I don't either," Hilary said. "Almost never."

Oscar blushed. He had put his foot into it. But he had
known already that the Diaz marriage was not one made
in heaven.

"You know, Dr. Kost," Hilary said, "if one judged
this venture just from the people in this room, some
erroneous guesses could be made."

"What do you mean?"

"Well, take Derek. He looks like a space jock out of
uniform, and he's a teacher. Your friend, Leslie Young, is
the wholesome type. You'd guess her to be a teacher,
maybe, or a woman devoted to home and children, and
she's capable, tough-minded. Jean. She seems to be absolutely worthless."

"Appearances are deceiving?" Oscar asked.

"I wouldn't be surprised at all to find some good
metal under all that fluff," Hilary said.

Oscar had a good sleep, twelve hours of it, and then
after breakfast he let his old friend Jennie coax him into
accompanying her toward the center parts of the ship,
where there was no gravity. A little bit of that was enough
for him. He banged his knee painfully and retired from

zero-gravity soaring but stayed to watch Jennie experiment until she could soar down a corridor skillfully without banging into a bulkhead.

"It makes me feel quite young," Jennie said breathlessly, as she soared back to bring herself to a halt with hands and feet extended.

"I'm hungry," Oscar said. "Let's find Dex."

Hamilton was with Harry Shaw. The time was growing near for lightstep to be activated. Soon all things familiar would disappear, and then, with no time lapse, the ship would be over eleven light-years from the Earth.

"Oscar," Jennie asked musingly as they had lunch in one of the large dining areas, with people talking excitedly on all sides, "what do you think we will find out there?"

"A new life."

"And what about our friends who went out on the *Spirit of America*?"

Oscar took a bite and chewed thoughtfully. "They made it to the 61 Cygni system. . . ."

"They'll be alive," Jennie said. "I can feel it."

SEVENTEEN

Suses climbed the carved steps in the sheer cliff on the outskirts of his city. The heat of the sun was unpleasant, and his robe was soaked with perspiration before he was halfway to the top of the cliff. Behind him struggled the members of the city council. At the rear was Yanee. All were dressed in ceremonial robes.

When the party finally reached the top of the cliff, the sun reflecting off the sand of the barrenness around them caused them to squint. Suses wiped perspiration from his forehead and turned to glare at his son. He found it difficult to believe that Yanee had been intimidated, that one man had been killed by the Earth people.

"We will be late, Father," Yanee said respectfully.

Suses took some deep breaths and started walking toward the pyramid. By day the towering structure's gleaming white surface caught the sun, resulting in a glare painful to the eyes. He reached the walled walkway and straightened his shoulders, took one look behind him to see that the others were with him, then walked proudly toward the far entrance, which was a tiny, dark opening in the base of the pyramid.

Inside, the floor was cool, polished stone, the walls the same. The long entry shaft was lit by a soft glow that seemed to come from the walls and the ceiling. Then the shaft opened into a huge chamber, and at the center, under the ceiling that was a full forty feet high, was one

312

thronelike chair on a dais. Suses's party of city officials formed a line, and all of them bowed before Suses stepped forward to lead the way toward the dais.

The man who sat in the chair was small, dark, and wizened. His head was totally bald. A stocky, short, round-faced monitor stood to the right and behind the chair. Both were dressed in dark-gray robes with long sleeves.

"Honored Father," Suses said, bowing again.

The seated figure waved a hand to set the delegation at ease, but no one relaxed. The monitor spoke. "The Honored Father desires clarification of the reports made by the Prince Yanee."

Yanee took one step forward and bowed. "It is as I have said, Honored Father. Our weapons had no effect on a large, odd being—I presume it to be mechanical—and the Earthmen were protected behind thick earthen ramparts."

The monitor had other questions regarding the number of Earthmen, the nature of their weapons, the construction of the dam. Finally, seemingly satisfied, he nodded and bowed his head.

The seated man spoke. "You acted quite properly, Prince Yanee."

"Thank you, Honored Father," Yanee said.

"Please withdraw now and await our call in the chamber of the gods," the seated man said.

The delegation bowed, then walked with straight posture to an opening in the western wall of the huge chamber. When they were gone the monitor said, "They have come a long way, Father."

The old man rubbed his wrinkled face with a knotty, twisted hand. "My heart aches for our poor, beautiful children."

"The situation is critical. The crops are dying in the fields. All of the slaves are at work carrying water from the few remaining ponds of standing water in the riverbed. The flow of water has ceased entirely, and soon the sun will evaporate all the water that is left. The sea encroaches on the delta. Already serious damage has been done by saltwater to arable lands."

The old man nodded slowly. "We doubted the ancient records of our ancestors," he said. "We equated their accounts of mechanical men with folklore or myth." He sighed. "We have been wrong, my son. We have been too complacent. We have neglected the science of our ancestors, content behind our shield, certain that our weapons would be sufficient against any threat, save the ultimate one, against which we were, and will always be, helpless. We underestimated the vitality of those whom we made a part of us."

"I know that regret is useless," the monitor said, "but, oh, if our ancestors had been more careful in their selection of a planet, one with metals—"

"Study the records," the old man said, "and you will see that our ancestors had no alternative. The choice planet of our neighboring star had been seeded with the deadly virus. Had the enemy not overlooked this dim, insignificant sun of ours, our people would have perished in space." He sighed again. "No, the blame is ours, ours and our fathers', and our fathers' fathers'. We chose to live in ease and comfort, when we should have made sacrifices, when we should have built and maintained a mobile strike force."

"The time is near," the monitor said.

"Come, then."

They walked to the rear of the large chamber, the younger man slowing his pace to match that of the elder. The touch of a palm caused a solid section of wall to glide aside soundlessly, and they stepped into a brightly lit room with tidy racks of equipment occupying most of the floor space. Other small, swarthy men in the same gray robes tended the equipment.

The old man walked stiffly to a chair before a complicated panel and sat down.

"We are ready, Honored Father," a young worker said as he began to push buttons, putting the Honored Father in communication with the leaders from all twenty valley cities. From speakers mounted in the console before the old man, a voice said, "The Council of Twenty awaits the words of the honored father of the city of Suses."

The old man spoke into the microphone and repeated the information given to him by Yanee. He spoke of the weapons of the Earthmen. "In conclusion," he said, "we must believe they have, in just over three thousand of their years, advanced to a technological level of T-nine. While it is true that they are few, we have no way of knowing whether there will be more of them. Here, as I see it, are the decisions we face: For our first option, we can choose to make peace with them. You have heard the terms that their leader dictated to Prince Yanee. Should we choose to follow that course, we would still have alternate choices. For example, we can tell them that the pyramids are sacred and can be entered only by members of the priesthood. We can try to persuade them that our own city is holy and off-limits to Earth people. Our second option is to appear to agree to their terms, then draw them within range of our power sources and destroy them."

The old man took a deep breath. His face had gone waxen, and he seemed to be weakening. He made a visible effort and spoke again. "In the second choice there is danger. Prince Yanee's disrupter beam had no effect on what appeared to be a mechanical fighting machine armed with potent explosive weapons. I will warn that those weapons are powerful enough to do serious damage, perhaps even to disable our power sources. Now I have spoken. I remind you, however, that it is, most probably, the city of Suses that will feel the first force of the Earth people's weapons if we choose war. We will allow the usual time for discussion and consideration."

There were no clocks visible in the room. The old man leaned back in his chair and closed his eyes. Now and then a question would come from the speakers, in different voices from different cities along the Great Misty River, and they would be answered by the monitor. A woman, dressed in the same gray robe, her thick, dark hair cut in bangs on her forehead, brushed neatly in a short, straight-edged bob, brought liquid refreshment, and the old man seemed to feel better after he drank. He leaned forward and said, "We will now hear the decisions of the Council of Twenty."

A voice came. "I, Sistank, Honored Father of the city of Sistank, say that we must destroy the invaders."

Then, one by one, nineteen other voices stated the same decision in different words.

"So be it," the old man said, nodding to the monitor.

Once again Suses and his city council stood before the raised chair in the huge, barren chamber. The old man nodded at their bows. "The decision is this: You, Prince Yanee, will go once again to the north. You will tell the Earthmen that we agree to their terms."

Yanee's face showed astonishment.

"Tell them that we will welcome them to our city and that we will do as they demand by allowing a complete inspection to determine our weapons capabilities."

"Honored Father!" Yanee protested.

"Silence, my son," the old man said. "I am not finished. You will appear to be quite friendly. You will encourage them to come in full force, so that we can honor all of them with a tour of our city. You will lead them, in their mobile vehicles, along the river road so their vehicles are forced to travel single file. A delegation will be waiting at the outskirts of the city. You will tell the leader of the enemy forces that you must advance first, to assure the city's elders that all is well. When you are clear, we will destroy the enemy with the prime power source."

Yanee's chest rose, and a look of grim satisfaction was on his face. "Forgive me, Honored Father, for doubting your wisdom."

A scout ship saw a single Whorsk airship emerge from the fog bank. Jack Purdy, chief of the scouts, was in the air immediately. The Whorsk in the gondola were peddling furiously. A single Eepera stood in the bow, arms crossed, no weapon in evidence. Jack flew in close, and the Eepera spread his hands, showing Jack that he was not armed. Jack pointed toward the north and nodded.

Duncan Rodrick met the Eepera in front of the earthen ramparts protecting his crawlers.

"I am Yanee, Prince of the city of Suses."

"We meet again," Rodrick said.

"We have decided that war would be undesirable for both our peoples," Yanee said.

"A wise decision," Rodrick replied. "We came to this planet in peace. It is big enough for all. And, by working together, our peoples can gain mutual benefit."

"So it is said by our elders," Yanee agreed. "We invite you, all of you, to our city. There you will be honored. We will open our secrets to you, in exchange for your secrets."

"Our secrets are here for you to see," Rodrick offered.

"If we are to show you our weapons, we will expect the same."

"That sounds reasonable," Rodrick said. He was perfectly willing to explain the workings of a laser cannon and the intricacies of the missiles and projectile weapons because it took a well-developed industrial complex to manufacture them, and the Eepera seemed to be limited to one type of electronic weapon and faced the same shortage of metals that plagued him.

"I will be your guide," Yanee said. "We will not follow the route of the first group you sent into our valley. We will travel the desert and enter the valley by a hidden road just outside our city."

"I warn you that any sign of treachery will be met with force," Rodrick said.

Yanee drew himself up. "You have the word of a prince of Suses."

"We leave in the morning," Rodrick went on. "Now, if you'll allow me to offer you the hospitality of our camp—"

"With pleasure," Yanee said, for he had seen an attractive blond Earthwoman standing atop the earthen embankment, and he was eager to speak with her. He hoped that somehow he could save the Earthwomen from death. To his disappointment, he had no opportunity to speak with the blond woman, or any other Earthwoman. He was shown to a tent, where two guards were stationed. As he refreshed himself, he saw that the two men continued to stand guard outside. He had a meal with the captain and two other men, one of whom was called an admiral and was almost as well-built and almost as handsome as an Eepera. When he was walked back to his tent by the captain, the two guards were still there.

Rodrick called a council of war with the admiral, Paul Warden, and Jack Purdy. They met at the dam and stood on the fused stone, looking out over the moonlit river.

"I'd like your impression of our friend," Rodrick said.

"He's right pretty," Warden said. "I don't know, Dunc. The guy never smiles. If you're asking me if I think he's telling the truth, I don't know. I can't read him at all."

"He's a man with a lot of pride," Jack said. "And he didn't give me the impression that he thought he'd been beaten."

"Admiral?" Rodrick asked.

"Mopro was monitoring Yanee's vital signs and his alpha waves," the admiral said. "He was very calm. If he was lying, he did not react as one of you would if you were lying. But he's a person of royal blood. The autocratic mentality is different. I doubt that he would feel any guilt at all about lying if it served his purpose. If so, then he would not give off any of the telltale signs."

"Paul, we'll need to leave a force here at the dam," Rodrick said. "Enough personnel to man the big cannon, and at least three crawlers."

"Now, Dunc—" Warden protested.

Rodrick grinned. "Hey, we all want to go, but if this is just a ruse to lead us away from the dam into the desert, I want someone here who can defend this place. You're it, Paul."

"We'll need air cover going into the valley," Jack said. "I'd also feel better if we had the answer to that damned beam weapon of theirs."

"When I last talked with Grace," the admiral told them, "she was making progress. Perhaps if we could wait a few more days—"

"No," Rodrick said. "We've got an invitation. I don't want to give them any time to prepare for us. They must be in pretty desperate conditions for lack of water by now.

If this offer of friendship is genuine, I think we should be
humane enough to do what we have to do and get their
river flowing again as soon as possible."

"Captain," Jack said, "I think I should take a scout
through that fog and have a look before we go in."

"I've been thinking about that, Jack," Rodrick said.

"Paul says he didn't see any high elevations along the
river when he was in the city," Jack said. "I believe if I
made a run at top speed across the valley, say at about
fifteen hundred feet, I could get a quick look and have the
cameras running. I'd be through and gone before they
could bring any weapons to bear."

"That's assuming you'd be under the shield at fifteen
hundred feet," Rodrick said. .

"If not, I'll have some good pictures of solid fog."

"Let me think about it, Jack," Rodrick said. "We'll
have time while we're moving south. In the meantime, I
want you to send one of the *Apaches* back to Hamilton to
act as communications officer and have the other stay
here, so we can have one on that end and one on this end
speaking in their own language. The Eepera learned English easily enough, but if you'll remember, they asked
Theresita to speak in English instead of Russian, so they
don't just automatically understand any language. With
the Apaches doing the air-talking, we should be able to
keep in touch with Hamilton base without their understanding everything we say."

Jack Purdy pushed the *Dinahmite* up to Mach 3. He
was flying at fifteen hundred feet over the western desert.
The ground below him was a blur; ahead was the fog. The
impact of the speeding ship blasted a hole in the fog, and
he was flying blind, all instruments dead. And then, with
a suddenness that hurt his eyes, he was in the full glare of
sunlight, and below him were fields, the muddy, cracking
riverbed, and the beautiful city. His instruments were
functioning, his cameras whirring for the few seconds he
was over the valley. He jerked his head to get a look at the
gleaming white pyramid, and then he was in the fog again.
When he burst out into the sun over the empty desert, he

slowed, did a victory roll, and arrowed the *Dinahmite* northward, climbing over the fog.

He heard Jacob West and Renato Cruz talking in Mescalero. Renato, who had drawn the short straw andwas back in the communications room of the *Spirit of America*, sounded as excited as a man could sound in that odd, guttural language.

On the west bank of the river, a few miles below the dam, Jack spotted the caravan of crawlers, twenty-two vehicles. He used his braking rockets, dropped the ship, and landed in the sand a hundred yards ahead of the lead vehicle. When the crawler came abreast, he yelled out to Duncan Rodrick to come aboard. When Rodrick was in, Jack punched up the tape on the scout's viewscreen and slowed it so that there was time to get a close look at the valley and the city. Whorsk were struggling through drying mud, carrying containers of water from a muddy pond at the middle of the miles-wide riverbed. A few Eepera could be seen in the streets of the city. The white pyramid was impressive.

"Very quiet," Rodrick commented. "Run it again."

Rodrick used stop motion when the city was shown so he could examine the images closely. There was no sign of preparation for war. If anything, considering the fact that there was a genuine crisis, the city seemed too calm. He stopped motion again as the pyramid was centered on the screen.

"Did you get any instrument readings on that?" Rodrick asked.

Jack punched buttons. "It reads like stone," he said.

"White marble?" Rodrick asked. "Give me magnification. I can't see any joints."

The image became slightly fuzzy, but the gleam of the white pyramid filled the screen. On highest magnification Rodrick saw a pattern of rectangular cracks. "Damned fine stone fitting," he pointed out.

"There are stoneworks in several of the ancient Earth civilizations that you can't drive a knife blade between," Jack said.

"Okay, Jack," Rodrick said. "Good job. Let's wait here for a little while, until Clay gets here from Hamilton."

"What's going on?"

Rodrick grinned. "Grace has two gadgets for us," he said. "We can't be sure until we test them in action, but she thinks she's built a field generator that will block out the Eepera weapons."

"Hey now," Jack said, his face beaming.

The *Blue Rover* went ballistic from Hamilton, shortening the time of the trip across the Western Ocean as much as possible, came out over the desert with a thunderous sonic boom, flashed down, and did a fancy landing fifty yards from the *Dinahmite*. Rodrick, now standing beside his vehicle, in which Yanee sat with his arms crossed, looking straight ahead, recognized Grace as she, then Clay Girard, dismounted from the scout. Each of them carried a small, square metal box. He walked to meet them.

"The cavalry has arrived in the nick of time, Grace," Rodrick said.

"I just hope this contraption works," Grace remarked. "It's a product of some haste."

"Captain, I could put one of these on my ship," Clay offered, "and fly through the fog to test it."

"Thanks, Clay," Rodrick said, "but I think we'll mount it on the chief scout's ship."

"It just plugs into any auxiliary power source," Grace said. "I didn't take time to rig off and on switches, so it'll be powered when a connection is made."

One of the metal boxes was tied down securely under the left seat of the *Dinahmite*. Rodrick had decided to mount the other in the crawler with the most firepower, the lead vehicle in which he was riding. Yanee watched without interest. The admiral, sitting directly behind Yanee to keep an eye on him, said, "Grace, this is Prince Yanee, of the city of Suses."

Grace, who had been working with an average of four hours sleep per night for weeks, was not in the mood to be sociable. She merely nodded, then turned her attention to Rodrick, who was finding a place for her metal box in the front of the crawler.

Yanee bristled. She was not as young as the one

called Sage, but she was attractive. "I am not accustomed to being ignored," he said.

"I helped care for the people your Whorsk killed not long ago," Grace retorted. "Perhaps it's best that I do ignore you instead of following my inclinations and kicking that supercilious look off your pretty face."

Yanee lunged forward, only to be restrained by two hands that clamped his shoulders like vises. He turned in surprise to the man called the admiral. He had never felt such strength in a man's hands.

"Easy, Grace," Rodrick said. "He's an envoy of peace."

"Peace on him, too," Grace responded. She bent, plugged her gadget into a power source, and nodded when indicator lights glowed. "All right, Dunc," she said. "That should do it." She took Rodrick by the arm and led him out of the hearing range of Yanee. "Dunc, I won't take time to go into the scientific jargon. What we've done is to invalidate totally the laws of probability as far as the motion of electrons inside hydrogen atoms is concerned. The effect is to turn back all forms of electromagnetic waves. We think we've arrived at a basic form of the field generator those people use, but of course they've refined it. We have no idea, for example, how they broadcast energy. We all believe—and I'm praying we're right—that the odd little field these boxes create when electrons are spinning in a uniform plane and direction will stop the beams of their weapons. Don't put it to a test unless you have to, at least not until we can do some more work."

"Grace, you've gone more than the extra mile," Rodrick said. "And it looks as if you could use some sleep."

"About twenty-four hours straight," she admitted. "But I can stay awake until we find out what happens when you go in there. I'd like to go with you."

Rodrick looked up at the purplish sky. "Grace, if anything bad happens in there, Max is next in line to take over command of the colony. I wouldn't want him to have to face that responsibility alone."

"That makes sense," she said. "Be damned careful, Duncan."

Rodrick walked over to the *Dinahmite*. "Jack, we

estimate that the fog is about two hundred yards thick. Give my lead vehicle ten minutes to clear it, and then you come on through."

Ten scouts were in the air, circling the halted caravan. Jacob West, much to his disappointment, was riding on the ground, in the lead vehicle with Rodrick. Rodrick climbed into the front seat and gave the go signal to Jacob. "Tell base we're moving."

It was possible to travel at the top speed of the crawlers on the flat desert. The distance to the fog bank was covered in just over five hours, bringing them to a point marked by a tall, rugged outthrust of stone along the edges of the fog. Yanee pointed Rodrick to a gap between large boulders, and as the crawler went into the fog, Jacob slowed to less than five miles per hour. Yanee's instructions were to drive straight ahead.

There was a lightening of the fog, and then sunlight. Rodrick told Jacob to stop, after the other crawler in line behind them had also emerged from the fog. They were directly across the river from the city, and there was a steep switchback road leading down the face of the cliff. There was no sign of hostile activity. Rodrick could see the ten scouts overhead, taking up positions as ordered. It was hard to believe that he could see them so clearly and they could not see him, and that radio waves could not pass between his vehicle and the scouts.

"I assume that your vehicles can negotiate the mud of the riverbed," Yanee said.

"Yes, they can," Rodrick answered.

"Suses and a delegation of the elders will meet you at the wharf on the near side of the river," Yanee said. "Then they will escort you to the city."

"Go," Rodrick told Jacob, and the crawler dropped off the cliff top onto the narrow, winding road. At the base of the cliffs the road ran directly to the river through a grainfield that was turning brown from lack of water. At the river the road turned to the north at a ninety-degree angle. The wharf was two or three hundred yards upstream. Rodrick could see several robed and kilted Eepera there. "Take it slow," he told Jacob. "We don't want to alarm them. All vehicles," he said, using the radio, "load and cock. Be alert."

"Why do you give such an order?" Yanee asked indignantly. "You can see that my people on the wharf are unarmed. And why have you brought the flyer in?"

Jack Purdy's ship was hovering directly overhead, having cleared the fog.

"We will not fire unless fired upon," Rodrick answered. "Admiral, does Mopro detect any kind of electrical field?"

"None, sir," the admiral said. The admiral was taking as great a risk as any of the humans, because his thoughts, his memories, his personality, his feelings, all were nothing more than electrical impulses stored in his artificial brain and his cloud-chamber computer storage areas. If he were exposed to the strength of the Eepera's field, his body might be capable of functioning again, but all that was the admiral would be gone.

"You will stop here," Yanee said, when Rodrick's vehicle was less than two hundred feet from the end of the wharf extending out into the riverbed.

"Why?" Rodrick asked.

"Unless I am allowed to go forward alone and assure my father that I am not a prisoner, your actions will be taken as betrayal."

"Yanee, I don't think I like that," Rodrick said.

"It is the agreement I made with my father. You must comply, or I will not be responsible for the results of your lack of cooperation."

"Stop," Rodrick said into the radio. The caravan came to a halt. The vehicles had left intervals of about twenty yards between them. "Yanee, we don't have much time. Tell your father immediately that one of my conditions is that he turn off the field so that my scouts up there can see that we're okay. We have thirty minutes from the time we entered the fog bank before they blast through the fog with all missiles firing."

"There is time," Yanee said.

Yanee walked slowly, proudly. He did not look back. On the wharf he saw not Suses, but four others, and he knew that his father was in the city, prepared to make these Earthmen pay dearly for their intrusion.

The prince had not yet reached the end of the wharf when the admiral said, "Force field, sir!" That information had been relayed instantly to him by Mopro, in a crawler at the center of the caravan. An instant later Rodrick heard a yell from the crawler behind him.

"All power dead, Captain."

"Admiral, tell Mopro to stand by," Rodrick told the admiral. "Can you contact him without power?"

"Communications are open," the admiral said, just as a blinding flash of light caused a boom of sound as it lanced down across the wide, dry river at an angle and the last crawler in line erupted in a massive explosion.

"Tell Mopro to fire at will," Rodrick snapped.

"We have power!" Jacob yelled.

"Open fire," Rodrick ordered, even as Mopro's long-range cannon began to pump repeated explosive rounds into the city across the river, the barrage walking along the rooftops, likely locations for the weapons being used against them.

Behind him, as the bits and pieces of the destroyed crawler began to fall, Rodrick saw Americans bailing out of the disabled vehicles and scurrying for cover in the grain-field and along the riverbank. Another blinding flash of light came with the crack of thunder, and it was so bright that Rodrick could not trace it back to its source. He knew that Mopro's ammunition was limited to what the big defense robot could carry, plus the spare magazines in his crawler. Another crawler disappeared in a shattering blaze of fire.

Clay was flying circles over the fog at just under six hundred miles an hour, using speed to make himself a more difficult target, just in case someone down there— someone who could see him although he could see nothing—decided to take a bead on him. One experience in a scout with all power off was enough.

"Hey!" he yelled as the fog beneath him lit up in a

yellow flash of light. "What the heck? Did you fellows see that?"

"I saw something," another pilot radioed.

Thirty seconds later the flash came again. "Something's going on down there," Clay said. "I'm going down."

"Clay—" someone shouted, just before Clay's radio went dead as he dove into the fog. It seemed to take forever for him to get through the fog. He found himself tensing all muscles, as if in preparation for smashing into the ground, and then he was blinking in bright sunlight, and he realized that the city was smoking from the firepower of Mopro and the lead crawler. A flash of light lanced across the sky to blast a crawler miles away across the river.

"Captain!" Clay shouted. "Do you read?"

"Loud and clear," came Rodrick's voice.

"It's the pyramid!" Clay yelled, his voice pitched high in his excitement. "There's a weapon in the very tip of it. I'm going after it."

Rodrick watched the pyramid. In about twenty seconds he was almost blinded as a flash of light came and another crawler exploded. Then, as his vision cleared, he saw *Blue Rover* diving, and a beam of light from the tip of the pyramid shot out toward it but missed as the scout corkscrewed expertly. Far above, the fog turned fiery and swirled.

Clay had the tip of the pyramid on magnification on his optics. As he looked, he saw a four-foot-deep segment of the needle-sharp point of the structure swivel, and, heart pounding, he threw the scout into evasive action, rolling, making a corkscrew in the sky even as he kept his sights aligned on the dark opening in the tip of the pyramid. Another beam of light blinded him, slashing by so close that its charge made his hair stand up and prickled his skin, and he could hear the boom of its passage. He pressed buttons, and four missiles shot out, streaking, leaving their marks of combustion on the sky. Then he brought all lasers and cannon to bear, and just below the rotating tip of the pyramid, a missile impacted to obscure the whole area with smoke, but as he zoomed up to avoid crashing into the pyramid, he saw through the smoke the flash of laser and projectile impact.

Once past, he zoomed straight up into the fog, looking back through the rear optics just before he flew into the fog to see the smoke clearing. He was not sure whether the armed upper point of the pyramid was still intact. He dived, came into the sunlight, corkscrewed defensively, and aimed for the pyramid. It took him a second or two to focus the optics, and then he saw that the upper ten feet of the stone structure was missing. There were no more flashes of light. Across the river, fire was directed at the city from all of the surviving crawlers. He slowed, looked down directly on the top of the pyramid, saw a black cavity, and movement inside. He zoomed and dived straight down, charring the interior of the exposed cavity with his lasers.

The city was taking a thunderous pounding now. Clay banked toward the riverbed and pressed his send button. "Captain, I believe you can cease fire now."

Rodrick had come to the same conclusion. He had seen the air strike on the top of the pyramid, and suddenly, behind him, a few crawlers had opened fire, indicating that they had power back. "Cease fire," he ordered, and there was silence. The other scout ships were coming down, signaling. They could see clearly. There was no more interference with their instruments or their radios.

"Scouts, take up a pattern," Rodrick ordered, and the hovering scouts positioned themselves, weapons at the ready, to cover the entire area.

"All right," Rodrick said, "let's go have a word with *Prince* Yanee."

Yanee stood on the near end of the wharf. His cheeks were wet. He had just seen thousands of rounds of high-explosive projectiles and the slashing beams of the lasers destroying his beautiful city. He was unable to move. The decoys who had been posing as Suses and the elders had fled to the north, but Yanee could not move. He saw the man who had so hurt his city leap down from his vehicle and walk swiftly toward him.

"So much for the word of an Eepera noble," Rodrick

said to the admiral, walking beside him. He let his right
fist come up from his hip, and the blow sent Yanee sprawl-
ing. He lay there, head lifted in stunned pain.

"Get up," Rodrick ordered, and when Yanee did not
move, the admiral yanked him to his feet.

Rodrick led the way across the river. Now and then a
crawler would break through the cracked, drying mud
crust, and the driver would have to use jets to propel the
vehicle to more solid ground. Fires burned in the city.
Smoke towered into the clear sky. As Rodrick's crawler
came up onto the solid bank, he heard a call from a
circling scout ship.

"Captain, a group of about one hundred men and
women just came out of the pyramid. They're moving off
to the south."

"Lay fire in front of them and turn them back,"
Rodrick ordered. "I want to talk with whoever was manning the weapons."

EIGHTEEN

The crawlers entered the city with all personnel on full alert. Fires were smoldering, and fallen stone blocked some byways. No one was in the streets. The scouts had reported that the people who had tried to move to the south from the pyramid had gone back inside the structure in the face of warning fire from the air. Miles down the river, looking like a far bank of cloud, there was a vertical wall of fog. It was evident to Rodrick that the fog shield over the city of Suses had probably been powered from the pyramid, and that there were other, similar, power sources downriver.

Some time had been consumed in getting all the crawlers into position. They entered the city at different points, each assigned to patrol a specific sector in the event of further resistance. The scout ships had searched the area of the valley not now protected by the shielding field. Several Whorsk airships were on the ground at a landing field upriver, but the Whorsk seemed to be indifferent to the events in and around the city.

One crawler had been detached to try to find a way to the top of the cliff where the pyramid was located. The carved stone stairway was discovered, and after checking with Rodrick, ten heavily armed men climbed the stairs.

Clay was flying wing to Jack Purdy, keeping an eye on the pyramid and the desert surrounding it. They saw the men reach the top of the cliff and approach the pyramid.

"Clay, want to go down and take a look?" Jack asked.

"Sure," Clay said.

They landed side by side not far from the entrance ramp and joined with the armed men. Clay and Jack were at the rear as the men moved through the entrance and into the long corridor that was lit by a glow of light that seemed to come from the stones of the walls and ceiling.

"Not very fancy," Jack remarked as they entered a huge chamber, barren except for a straight-lined, massive chair on a raised dais at the center. The men spread out and spotted a doorway. Two of them entered, weapons ready, creeping ahead cautiously.

"Anything in there?" someone whispered loudly after a few seconds. One of the men appeared in the doorway. His face looked odd. He made a "come on" motion to those in the large chamber.

Jack and Clay followed the armed men through the doorway and halted in their tracks. The lighting was dim, orangish, like an Omega sunset, and the light had a bizarre effect on a riot of colorful images that lined the walls—strange, stiff humanoid forms with the heads of birds and animals. The images were carved in stone and painted in bright colors, and between them, the walls were covered with rich tapestry. On the ceiling colorful creatures sprawled, stretched, strode.

The chamber was huge, rectangular, perhaps a hundred feet long. At the far end, before an array of those stiff, strange animal- and bird-headed images—these carved from stone in the round and painted to seem almost lifelike—were men and women dressed in gray robes, all of them kneeling to the images and, as they bowed and then extended their hands high to bow again, they were droning a chant in a language filled with exploded consonants.

Jack Purdy was the senior officer present. The armed men from the crawlers turned to him, for the kneeling, chanting people continued to ignore them.

Jack moved forward. Clay, awed by the impressive, beautiful room, jumped to his side. They halted just behind the last row of kneeling people. The chanting continued.

"Hey!" Jack said loudly.

Almost as one the people stopped their chanting. A wrinkled old man pulled himself laboriously to his feet at the front of the group and turned to face them. "We are ready to die," he said in English.

"I don't think that'll be necessary," Jack said.

Although the others were silent, they continued their vigorous bobbing up and down.

"Who are you?" Jack asked.

"I am Ahmes, Honorable Father, keeper of the source."

"Well, sir," Jack said, "were you the one who gave the orders to use the weapon in the top of this place against our vehicles?"

Ahmes lowered his head, then raised it, chin high. "I was. For it is my responsibility to defend my children against invasion."

"I think my captain is going to want to talk to you," Jack said. "Let me say this. We don't want more fighting. We didn't want it in the first place. What can we expect from you?"

Ahmes stared over Jack's head. "We fight no more here in the city of Suses."

Jack whispered to Clay. "See if you can find the captain. Tell him where we are and ask him to get up here on the double."

Clay went into the large, empty chamber and tried his radio, but there were too many tons of stone around him. He had to go outside.

Jack gathered the colony men around him and said, "Somewhere in this pile of rock there's a power source. Judging from that beam weapon, there should be some pretty fancy hardware. A couple of you stay here. I don't think these people are going to do anything but pray, but keep an eye on them."

By the time Rodrick arrived, the admiral with him, a thorough search of the two chambers had been completed. There seemed to be no exit from the chamber where

Ahmes and his people still knelt, and only the one entrance to the large, empty chamber.

Rodrick, too, was impressed by the room of the images. He was not the only one, of course, who felt as if he
had stepped back thousands of years into the past, into
ancient Egypt. The style of the art was very Egyptian but
with differences. For example, the heads of what must be,
he felt, gods were recognizable, in a few instances, as
being the head of a hawk or a crocodile, but in others the
forms were totally alien.

"The old man up front seems to be the boss," Jack
told him.

Once again Ahmes struggled to his feet.

"I take it this is a place of religious significance,"
Rodrick said, without greeting the old man.

"It is a sacred place," Ahmes confirmed.

"We don't want to have to damage it," Rodrick said,
and at those words there was an outburst of chanting from
the kneeling people. "We must, however, know the where-
abouts of your weapons and your source of power. We
have lost all the lives I intend to lose. Will you show us, or
shall we begin to take this place apart, stone by stone?"

"To reveal the secrets of the gods is forbidden," Ahmes
said, his voice quivering.

"We're going to have to live together on this planet,"
Rodrick reminded the old man. "We have stated repeatedly that we would like to live in peace. The choice is
yours."

"That is in the hands of the gods, and my brothers to
the south," Ahmes said.

"For the time being you are to remain here in this
room," Rodrick said.

"That is our intention, to die here with the gods,"
Ahmes said.

Rodrick left a guard with orders not to disturb the
kneeling, bobbing people, then went back into the main
chamber. "Apparently they live inside the pyramid," he
said. "There has to be a weapons room and a control
room somewhere. Call base, Jack, and tell Max what we're
up against. Tell him we need some way to sound through

solid stone for cavities. And ask him to find someone who
has an interest in Egyptology. Then call Paul Warden and
brief him on the situation, too. Tell him to stand by to
restore the flow of water in the river. If we don't come to
an agreement with these people soon, this whole valley is
going to become a desert. I'm going back in to talk with
that old man."

He asked Ahmes to walk with him to the other end of
the chamber of the gods, where they could not be
overheard.

"Look," he said, "your river is empty. Your valley is
dying. You spoke of your brothers to the south. They, too,
have no water. Do you have a way to communicate with
them?"

"I do," Ahmes said.

"We don't want to destroy you. We want only to be
allowed to live in peace in our section of this planet. Even
to work with you in peace. Put me into communication
with the other cities. We know about them, and where
they are. We have penetrated into the valley from the
mouth of the river by water." Using information from
Allen Jones's report, he listed the cities, their distances
from the mouth of the river, and their distances from each
other. Ahmes was impressed.

"You call yourself the father of your people," Rodrick
continued. "Will you allow them to die? Will you allow
the valley to wither—all vegetation to die in the heat of
the sun—to become like the desert around it?"

"It is you who have stopped the flow of the sacred
river," Ahmes said simply. "It is you who must restore it."

"Understand me. We are few. We came to this planet
a thousand strong, but because of you and your people,
we have lost over two hundred of our number. We can't
lose any more and expect to survive. If you force me to
make a choice, I will choose my own."

"And destroy sixty centuries of civilization," Ahmes
said sadly, shaking his head. "We have done all that we
could do. We did our duty by resisting you. Now it is up
to the gods."

"Are you saying you won't help me to prevent war with the other cities in your valley?"

"The gods will decide," Ahmes said. The old man staggered. Rodrick reached out to support him, but he fell. One sound escaped his throat. Rodrick knelt and felt for a pulse in the old man's throat. As he looked up, a young man, hands clasped before him, was approaching.

"He's dead," Rodrick said.

"It is the will of the gods," the younger man said.

"I'm sorry."

"He was in the fullness of his years."

"Who are you?" Rodrick asked.

"Now I am Ahmes, Honorable Father, keeper of the source."

"That means you're his successor?"

"By the will of the gods."

"Perhaps you will not believe it is the will of the gods to let your people die and the valley to wither," Rodrick suggested.

"I have been praying and asking for guidance."

"And what have the gods told you?" Rodrick asked.

"That we are to be punished for our past neglect of our defenses," the new high priest said. "So be it."

"They all sound like a bunch of lunatics to me," Max Rosen said. He had come from Hamilton City and was now in the main chamber of the pyramid with three men from his engineering staff. They were using an instrument that sent powerful impulses into the stone of the structure. "Dunc, we've wasted enough time on them. The work of the colony has come to a halt. We don't even have enough men to keep on schedule at the rocket-fuel plant. Let's just give them back their river, go back to Eden, and get to work. They can't hurt us."

"Max, they blasted four crawlers from eight miles away with a weapon that makes a laser seem tame."

"I want to know about my own people," Max growled. "I want to know if there's still an Earth. We need to get the ship back in space. We're getting so damned close. We're getting pretty rich ores from that mine of Stoner's.

We'll have enough rhenium in a few months, but if we don't get a move on, we won't have enough rocket fuel ready."

"Allen Jones estimates that there are one hundred fifty thousand to a half-million people in the cities along this river, not to mention the Whorsk slaves."

"Well, you're right, of course," Max said, calming down. "And I am curious. It doesn't make sense. Those pretty boys who live in the fancy houses in the city don't even know enough about technology to turn on a light switch. The lights come on automatically in their houses. And these little brown monkeys who live here—how in hell have they developed a force field, a beam weapon, or a power source that lights a whole city?"

"That's why you're looking for a way out of this chamber, Max," Rodrick said. "The answers are in a secret room somewhere in this pyramid."

"Oh, by the way, I ran a check. Our only man who had any extensive knowledge of Egyptology was killed with the Rocky Miller group. But Evangeline has been doing some reading and research ever since the first expedition here reported Egyptian-style architecture and a pyramid. She's up at the dam."

"Good. I'll send someone up for her," Rodrick said. "Keep on keepin' on, Max."

"Yeah," Max growled, his face contorted as if in pain as he swept a section of the stone wall with his instrument.

Grace had drafted the admiral as a bodyguard. She had made a cursory examination of the two chambers inside the pyramid, and she also believed that there was something interesting hidden away somewhere in that structure, something that generated quite a bit of power. The lights were still glowing inside and outside the pyramid itself except for about twenty feet at the shattered top, and the town was still receiving electricity for its lights and air-conditioning, apparently from the only electrically powered equipment in the city.

Grace had left Max to continue the examination of the

pyramid, with a specific request to send for her immediately if he found the interesting parts—the power room and the weapons room. "I'll see what I can learn in the city," she had told him.

The streets were deserted, except for an occasional Whorsk slave and the heavily armed and armored Americans from the colony. The ornately columned government building had been heavily damaged during the battle, and it was deserted. There seemed to be no places set aside for business—only the handsome, square-lined buildings that housed living areas.

"I think it's time we paid a call on someone," Grace told the admiral after they had explored the city in a small crawler from the riverside to just below the cliff. She picked a building at random. A heavily carved door opened easily, and they found themselves in a garden room, a wide, airy, open area with skylights. The plants were wilted, many of them brown and dead, and there was a smell of decay in the air. Grace chose a corridor leading off the atrium, and then a door, but when she knocked, there was no response.

The admiral tried the door and found it locked.

"We have to start somewhere," Grace said, shrugging.

The admiral drew his laser and, with a seemingly effortless push of his shoulder, shoved the door open with a cracking of wood.

At first Grace thought the beautiful people scattered around the luxuriously furnished room were dead, but there was a familiar smell in the air. Alcohol, in any variety, has a certain underlying aroma. She approached a scantily clad woman, a perfectly formed and absolutely beautiful woman, impressive even with mussed hair and with a bit of saliva escaping her lips.

"I'd say they're quite thoroughly intoxicated," the admiral commented.

"I'd say the same," Grace agreed.

She examined the other rooms. In two bedrooms the beds were occupied, and the condition of the occupants— nude, as beautiful in their nudity as ancient Greek statues— made her shake her head. An examination of several other apartments produced the same results. Then, as the admiral found an unlocked door and threw it open, she saw her first conscious Eepera. He was nude. He stood, swaying from too much alcohol, in the center of a bedroom with sleeping men and women all around him.

"Now you have come to kill us," he said in English.

"Not at all," Grace replied.

He looked at her blearily and took a few unsteady steps toward her. "I have heard that you Earthwomen were attractive."

"Thank you," Grace said.

The man turned and began to pull limp, naked bodies off a rumpled bed. He turned to Grace. "Come," he said, indicating the bed.

"No, thank you," Grace answered.

"But I have been told, and it is written, that you people vied with each other to lie with us." He brandished an aroused object of manhood at her and asked, "Have the puny Earthmen anything like this?"

"Let's get out of here," Grace said to the admiral.

She entered one more apartment in another building. A woman awoke as they stepped into the main room and screamed, tried to scramble away, and fell. The admiral took her arm and helped her to her feet. She had glorious red hair, a face that would have been instant fame back on Earth, and a scarcely concealed body that made Grace feel just a bit old.

"But you can't be an Earthman," the woman said to the admiral, her green eyes wide. "You're so handsome."

"How is it that you all speak English?" Grace asked the woman, who looked at her imperiously before answering.

"It was something to do."

"And why are all of you drunk?"

"Why not?" the woman asked. "Without the protection of the honorable fathers, we are helpless before you." She cocked her head. "Isn't that unbelievable? *We*, helpless before *you*."

"Your men had no weapons?" Grace asked.

"When your airmen destroyed the power source, our weapons were not functional." She put her hand on the admiral's cheek. "If I must be a slave, I will be your slave, and I will please you so that you will treat me kindly."

"Go to bed," Grace told the beautiful woman distastefully, turning and walking rapidly from the room.

"Don't leave me to be taken by another," the woman begged the admiral.

The admiral, unwilling to hurt any creature unnecessarily, said, "If you are to be a slave, I promise that you will be mine. Rest now."

"Children!" Grace sputtered as they walked toward the atrium entrance to the building. "They're nothing but children. Faced with what they think is the end, they drink themselves into a stupor. We've wasted enough time here."

Just before Grace and the admiral entered the empty chamber of the pyramid, Max located a portion of wall with a cavity behind it. The wall seemed to be solid stone. He called the other men over, and they began to look for unusual seams, anything to allow them to get through the wall without demolishing it.

Evangeline happened to walk out from the god chamber as Grace came in. She hurried to meet Grace. "It's fantastic," she said. "There are alien features, but that room could be a temple in the Old Kingdom of Egypt."

"The hieroglyphics?" Grace asked.

"I'm unable to read them," Evangeline said, "but I do recognize a few symbols. The system seems to be the same as Egyptian writings of the Old Kingdom. I think I can translate them with the help of the ship's computer."

"How about the spoken language of the priests?"

"It has the same pattern as ancient Egyptian," Evangeline replied.

"We'll have to get my translation machine over here," Grace said.

"I have had food and water brought to those people in there," Evangeline said. "They seemed grateful."

"But they still won't give much information?"

Evangeline made a face. "Everything I asked about was a secret of the gods."

As part of his trial and error method to get at the cavity behind the wall, Max sent a hot charge into an area that showed readings indicating the presence of bits of metal. Quickly, silently, a section of the wall slid open, and the men behind Max reached for their sidearms, for before them was a room filled with electronic equipment and two startled men in gray robes who whirled as the door opened.

"Hey, Grace!" Max yelled.

The two priests stood stiffly, eyes straight forward. Grace stood beside Max, holding his hand. "Totally alien," she whispered. "Look at the labels on the panels. That's definitely not hieroglyphics. That's printing. A language that uses an alphabet."

"Man, it's going to take a Chinese jigsaw-puzzle expert to figure this stuff out," Max said. "It looks like the laboratory of a mad scientist in a science-fiction movie."

Suddenly a strident, angry voice spoke in a hard, explosive language.

"Ah," Max said. "There's a speaker. We must have broken in on these boys while they were having a conversation with someone." He went to a console and looked at a panel of buttons and switches. "If we could figure out how to work this thing, we might find out who's on the other end."

"It is forbidden for anyone other than a servant of the gods to touch that," said one of the priests.

"Well, suppose you touch it, then," Max told him. "Whom were you talking to?"

"To our brothers to the south," the priest answered.

"I want to say a word or two to your brothers to the south," Max said. "Touch this thing and tell them to listen."

"Only the voices of the servants of the gods—"

Max jerked his laser from his holster and held it by the muzzle. "Listen you," he snarled. "This is sacred stuff, all this equipment, right?"

"Sacred to the gods and our honorable ancestors."

"I'm going to give you exactly thirty seconds to get over here, call the cities to the south, and tell them to put someone on who can speak English. If you don't, I'm going to see just how sacred all this junk is." He made a motion to smash a delicate-looking assembly, and the priests threw up their hands and moaned.

"Well?" Max growled.

"We must have an opinion from the honorable father."

"Ten seconds," Max said, "Nine, eight, seven—"

"Do as he says," one of the priests told the other.

"Speak English," Max ordered the priest, as he sat down at the console.

"My brothers," the priest said, "our innermost sanctuary has been penetrated by the Earthmen. One of their leaders forces me, on threat of destroying the voice of the gods, to allow him to speak with you."

A voice in that harsh language spoke.

"English," Max said.

"Will you hear the Earthman?" the priest asked.

"We will hear," a voice said in English.

"Good," Max said. He leaned over the priest's shoulder, having spotted the mike by the way the priest had been talking. "All right. To whom am I talking?"

"I am Sistank," the voice answered, accenting the last syllable. "I speak for the brothers of the Council of Twenty."

"I am Ro-zen," Max said, also accenting the last syllable. "I speak for a group of Earth people who are sick and tired of your arrogance and aggression. Now you listen to me. Right now you don't have a river, and you are not going to have a river until you come to terms with my captain. He'll be here shortly, so I suggest you gather your council of however many it is and get ready to talk sense, or you're going to have a long, thirsty summer."

NINETEEN

Evangeline, with two young and alert Space Service Marines from the *Spirit of America*'s crew, had followed corridors and openings leading away from the oddly equipped room where Max and Grace and other scientists were beginning to puzzle out the functioning of the communications equipment. One of their initial discoveries had been that most of the banks of equipment were not functioning.

First, Evangeline found the living quarters for the pyramid priests. Although most rooms were small, they were tastefully furnished and decorated with objects of gold and silver and, most interestingly, many items that had a familiar look and the obvious signs of great age. Evangeline was certain that she looked at and held objects crafted on Earth in the time of the early dynasties of Egypt, the age of the pyramid builders.

Next she found books—real books, thousands of them—all leather bound. They were in a vast, long, narrow vault lit by a glow emanating from the walls and ceiling. Before she began to examine them, Evangeline looked for a filing system and found it, a card-file system, the language the same as that which she had seen on labels on the communications equipment. It was evident that the priests had a two-language system. They spoke the language used by the handsome men and women of the city but apparently kept records in another language, which used an alphabet.

She began to plan a way to put a terminal for her own library computer into the priests' library. She was awed by the number of books and eager to begin to dig out the secrets that she was sure would be contained in the thousands of large, leather-bound volumes.

Clay Girard and Jack Purdy, meanwhile, had joined with another search party. From the entrance to the pyramid's living quarters they discovered an elevator shaft and, after some experimentation, were surprised to find that the elevator was working. They rode it upward and stepped out into a room filled with electronic equipment. There was a feeling of power, a smell of ozone in the air. Jack sent Clay back down the elevator to find a couple of scientists, and Clay came back with a nuclear engineer and Grace.

Grace went immediately to a massive bank of instruments on a floor-to-ceiling panel at the back of the room. There was so much static electricity in the air that it made the tiny hairs on her arms stand up. "There's quite a lot of power coming from somewhere," she commented.

The nuclear engineer said, "I think we're going to be very interested in just how that power is generated. My guess is that the sun is the source."

"With the entire surface of the pyramid as solar receptors?" Grace asked.

"Possibly."

Above the power room, Clay found a shambles. The chamber was open to the sun, looking upward through the shattered tip of the pyramid, and the room had been charred by his scout's laser. Grace took a look and agreed with Clay that this destroyed chamber had been the weapons room. But twisted and melted metallic things could be examined, and perhaps they could deduce from the ruin the nature of the beam weapon that had been so effective.

Meanwhile, Max Rosen was experimenting with the one console that was still operative in the communications room. "Dunc," he said, amazed, "have you noticed the wear on the instruments where an operator's hands would touch?"

Although the console was neatly painted, the metal

itself had been worn. Rodrick was reminded of ancient stone steps, worn by centuries of the passage of human feet.

"And it looks as if they've cannibalized all the other equipment to keep this one radio working," Max noted.

"Too bad," Rodrick said, "because some of these other banks look very interesting."

"We need to get Grace and the admiral working on the language," Max said. "These symbols here—" he pointed "—seem to be mathematical symbols. Look at the difference. On this radio that's working, the digits are in groups of three. Over there it goes up to ten digits. If that has something to do with range, that bank over there had broadcast power in multiples of this one. And since they were able to pick up our radio transmissions well enough to learn to speak our language from them, if this one has planetary capability, what the hell was that big one used for?"

"I see what you mean," Rodrick said.

Max was pushing buttons and switches systematically. Suddenly the voice of a scout burst out from the speakers. It was Renato Cruz, finally freed from his job as communicator aboard the *Spirit*. "That's how they eavesdropped," Max said, and made a label in English to attach to that button. He pushed the button he had seen the priest use to talk with his colleagues downriver.

"*Apache Two*, do you read?"

"Loud and clear," Renato said.

"Your position? This is Rosen."

"Yeah? How you doin', Max? I'm just about to go ballistic from Hamilton Base. On the way to the valley."

"See you," Max said, then closed the transmitter. "Good range," he told Rodrick.

"How'd they hear through the shield?"

"Good question," Max said. "I'll keep working on it."

Rodrick left Max bent over the console and went to have a look at the power room and the destroyed weapons room, where he found Grace.

"Apparently the field transmitter was in the upper

section that Clay destroyed," she told him, "or at least part of it."

"Well, I'm damned glad he did it, although it would have been nice to have it intact," Rodrick said. "Any clues as to how it worked?"

"We're ninety-percent sure that the source of power is solar," Grace said, "and if so, it's more efficient than anything we've ever come up with."

"Well, Grace, you're in charge here. I don't want to pressure you, but there are more cities with pyramids down the river. I'd hate to have to take each one of them the way we had to take this one. Keep me posted."

"Sure," she said, then asked, "Any word of Sage?"

"We've questioned people in the city and the priests. No one seems to know what happened to her. Yanee said he left her in the care of one of his friends, but we haven't been able to locate that friend yet."

Elton and Becky Dark were on duty, patrolling the streets of the city from a crawler. When they were relieved, they climbed to the top of the cliff and entered the pyramid. The word had spread that there were odd and wonderful things there, and Elton and Becky spent an hour or so looking at the radio room, the power room, and then the room of the gods. The priests had been persuaded to go to their quarters and to remain there, so the room was empty, save for the dozens of half-relief and free-standing images of beast- and bird-headed gods.

Grace Monroe's team was gradually putting together a computer image of the interior of the pyramid. Data was entered into a terminal on the command crawler, relayed to a circling scout, and then sent back to the main computer on board the *Spirit of America*. Grace had started the engine of the crawler and buttoned up the top so that the air-conditioning could work. She saw the computer image form on the small screen. The construction of the pyramid indicated great skill on the part of the builders, for unlike the massive stone pyramids of ancient Egypt, more effective use had been made of interior space.

There were still teams inside probing the stone walls,

searching for more hidden doors. A series of storerooms
was located in the middle levels, under the power room,
which was far up in the pyramid. And beneath the storerooms, the floor of the main chambers gave echoes of a
large cavity below. Grace entered all the incoming information into the computer and was able to help the teams
inside to find connecting passages as the computer predicted chambers in unprobed areas.

Elton and Becky were pressed into service. Elton
wielded a sounder, and Becky read the dials. "What you're
looking for is a stairway leading down to that large cavity
under the main chambers," Grace explained. "The computer predicts that there will be an entrance either from
the main chamber or the room with all the statues."

Elton and Becky Dark were alone in the room of the
gods. They began on the eastern wall and worked their
way around. The instruments showed thirty feet of solid
stone on the eastern and northern walls, and then they
began to work behind the standing statues on the western
wall. There was a thickness of stone there, about fifty feet,
quite capable of holding a hidden corridor or other rooms.

"Hold it," Becky said, when they had checked the
wall almost to the center of the room. "Sweep back and
forth there."

Elton moved the probe, and Becky checked the readings outlined, finding a space that corresponded in size to
other hidden doorways already located. "That's it," she said.

They began to take finer readings to locate the mechanism that operated the door, and then Elton sent a live
charge into the mechanism, and a solid slab of stone
folded inward to reveal a lighted passage.

"I'll notify the others," Becky told him.

"C'mon, honeybee. Let's take a look ourselves first,"
Elton urged, moving into the opening. The corridor immediately took a right-angle turn, and there were steps
leading downward. After about ten feet, the steps ran into
a solid stone wall. At right angles another flight of steps
went farther downward. Elton led the way. The soft glow
of light continued to come from the walls and ceiling.
They reached another right-angle turn and more steps.

"What do you think?" Becky asked. "Are we about thirty or forty feet below the level of the floor in the main chamber?"

"At least," Elton said.

There was one more flight of steps, and then the steps ended in darkness.

"Does the air smell stale to you?" Elton asked.

"Musty, dry. Yes, a little stale."

Elton reached the bottom of the steps and stood on a landing. The light from the stairwell penetrated only a few feet into the gloom, but he had the feeling that he was standing in the entrance to a large space.

"Honey," he said, "you wanta go back and git us some kind of light?"

"Not without you," she said. "I'm not going to leave you here."

He laughed. "Don't worry, I ain't goin' one step into *that*." That was a darkness so stygian as to seem solid.

"Let's both go," she said.

"Yeah, okay," he agreed. "Jest a minute." He took one step forward, pushing his toe along the stone floor to be sure he had solid footing. Both gasped when a dim glow began to lighten the darkness, increasing gradually, and as it grew, things began to take shape. Directly ahead was a larger than life-sized *thing*, a thing of scales and teeth, and as it emerged from the darkness, its eyes seemed to glow.

"Git back!" Elton shouted, turning to push Becky back onto the landing. Behind him the lights began immediately to dim again. He looked and saw that the thing had not moved.

"It's a stone carvin'," he said shakily. "That's all."

"Elton, let's get a floodlight."

"The lights come on when you step on the floor," he said. "Watch." When he eased back into the darkness, the lights began to glow, and he forced himself to stand there with that *thing* looking down on him with eyes that seemed to glow until there was enough light to see that it was indeed stone, painted to look like some kind of animal he had never seen.

"Elton, look!" Becky gasped, pointing to a wall some fifty feet away to the left.

There, placed side by side, in mummiform cases made of some transparent material, stood a row of priests with bald heads and women with the dark, straight-cut hair. They were all dressed identically in white robes, with accents of beautiful embroidery. Their eyes were closed, but they looked as if they were merely sleeping.

"More of 'em," Elton said, pointing to the other wall. "Maybe this is where they keep their spares."

"Suspended animation?" she asked. "But there's no machinery."

"Let's take a look."

Elton led the way. As they slowly neared the row of transparent containers, they could see that the skin tone of the people inside was lifeless, and when they were quite near, it was obvious that they were not alive.

"Look," Elton said, "the container ain't even airtight." He swung the front of one of the containers outward. It opened easily. He touched the skin of a hand. "Some form of mummification," he said.

"Don't do that," Becky hissed, as he lifted the skirt of the white robe of the woman he had touched. "You dirty old man."

"Mummification," he said, as he pointed to a line of rough stitching that held together an incision from the woman's sternum to her pelvic bone. "Eviscerated, I'll betcha. Then filled with somethin'."

"Elton, let's get out of here. This is their cemetery."

"In a minute," he said.

All of the wall space was lined with the dead. There was an arched opening in the far wall, a dark room beyond it. Elton took Becky's hand and walked among the statues. The lights glowed up as they entered the other chamber, where they found the same transparent containers and their contents of priests, women, and children of various ages.

"Hundreds of them," Becky said nervously.

"These folks look older in this room," Elton said. "The skin is more papery, and the fabric has begun to discolor."

"I want some fresh air," Becky said.

"There's still another room."

"Oh, all right."

More of the same, but now, along the back wall of the third room, the dead began to look less lifelike, the fabrics dingy, the skin browned and fragile.

"I'm going," Becky said.

"There's one more room."

"They'll look like Egyptian mummies, just skeletons with dry skin stretched over them."

"They can't hurt ya."

Becky stuck out her tongue, but she took his hand and followed him. The lights came on, and it was as she had said. In some of the containers the dead had started to fall apart, so that a desiccated, bony arm might be lying at the bottom of the container.

"Yuck," Becky said. She stood in the doorway as Elton made the rounds of the room, trying to keep her eyes on the statues instead of looking at the dead. She missed seeing Elton go into still another room until she felt, suddenly, that she was alone with all those dead people, with several large chambers between her and the stairs, and buried far underground away from the fresh air and the sun.

"Elton!" she cried out, an edge of panic in her voice. The word echoed and reechoed. "Elton, dad-gum you!"

She saw him come out of a doorway. Even at that distance and in the uncertain light she could see that his face was pale and strained.

"Honey, you'd better come see this," he said in a normal voice, and in the quiet of the tomb it sounded loud and harsh and reverberated for some time.

She ran across the room, dodging among the statues. He took both her hands in his. "Jest keep cool, hon."

"What is it?"

"Come to think on it," he said, "maybe you shouldn't see it."

"No, I want to see it."

This room was different. The lights seemed to be brighter. The containers, although shaped the same, were of thicker material, and each had a metal plate with writing on its base.

"Honey, it's a sorta museum, a display room," Elton said as she approached the first container and saw a fierce and bearded warrior, a bronze axe lifted, his eyes bright, almost alive, his costume topped by a plumed helmet.

"He looks alive!" she whispered.

"The container is sealed. They must've used a different process. Take a look at this next one."

A beautiful Egyptian princess, dressed in all her finery, held a mirror and examined her dramatically made-up face.

"Okay, honey," Elton said. "There's a lot more of the same thang, all types of people from what seems to be the same period of Earth's history. We can look at 'em later if ya want to." He took her hand and led her across the room, walking between displays of a pride of lions, a tiger, and very Egyptian-looking dogs and cats.

"Whorsk," Becky said. There were three of them, a male, a female, and a young one.

"Brace yerself," Elton warned as he led her to the next display.

She screamed.

Sage Bryson, dressed in a filmy gown, the nipples of her breasts standing out sharply, a pleasing smile showing her white, even teeth, her eyes sparkling in the light, looked out at them from a sealed container. The container was new, the metal plate at its base gleamed with newness and freshly incised lettering.

The airtight container stood on the raised dais in the main chamber. The room was crowded with Earth people. Duncan Rodrick stood on the dais beside the container from which Sage looked out, smiling. Beside Rodrick was a somewhat nervous priest, Ahmes, Honorable Father, keeper of the source.

"I wanted you all to see this," Rodrick said. "And I've asked the high priest to explain it."

Ahmes swallowed, then thrust his hands behind him and lifted his chin. "We have given great honor to your

Earthwoman. As a great warrior-woman, she was selected to spend eternity among our honored dead. Only a few people in the past sixty centuries of your time have been so honored. She will live forever in beauty and will be of educational value to untold generations."

"What he's saying," Rodrick said bitterly, "is that Sage was stuffed and mounted for display in what they call their Museum of Life."

Someone coughed. The sound was loud in the silence.

"I'm told that she felt no pain," Rodrick said.

"Absolutely not," Ahmes replied. "And the ceremony was performed strictly according to law and ritual. She was allowed to know the honor being done her. She could see—although there was no pain—the initial stages, the removal of the viscera, the drawing of the blood—"

"Oh, my God," a female voice cried out.

"In fact," Ahmes continued, "she was favored by the gods, for, with their help, our healers were able to keep her conscious and aware until the very last—until it was time to remove the heart and brain."

There was a deadly silence in the room, in spite of the crowd gathered there. Ahmes looked around, composed, his head high, quite proud of himself.

"You may go now," Rodrick said.

Ahmes looked doubtful. An armed guard motioned to him. He stepped down from the dais and followed the guard out of the chamber.

A woman was weeping softly.

Rodrick spoke quietly. "Their way of thinking is totally alien to ours."

"They seem to have no more regard for life than the Whorsk," Mandy Miller said.

"Perhaps they taught the Whorsk," Jack Purdy suggested.

"I confess that I'm at a loss as to what to do," Rodrick said.

"I think we'd be justified in exterminating all of them," Mandy said, but then she shook her head. "But that would make us no better than they."

"Captain," Max Rosen said, "I'm not willing to leave them in a position to stuff and mount anyone else."

"What should we do, Max?" Rodrick asked.

"Destroy their power sources."

"And lose how many people doing it?" Rodrick asked.

There was a silence. Rodrick knew that something had to be done, but he was not willing to lose more people.

"Captain, may I speak?" Evangeline asked. Rodrick nodded. "Sage was my friend, and I'm going to miss her. There's no logical reason why she should be dead, but she is. And I know how Mandy felt when she said we should exterminate all of them, but I've seen great beauty in the city and in the artwork in this pyramid. I can't help but feel that there has to be good in a people who can build and make such beautiful things. And in that library I found there are books that I believe will cover a period of thousands of years, books that I think will give us new insight into one of the Earth's most interesting ancient civilizations. We could destroy this entire valley. We could kill many of the people. But since they have such light regard for life, I don't think that's the way to impress them."

"I can't quite believe they would value their own lives as lightly as they value the lives of others," Mandy said.

"We don't have to attack each city individually to kill them all," Max said. "All we have to do is keep the river diverted."

"Killing them by lack of water is the same as killing them with weapons," Evangeline pointed out. "We have to give them back their water."

"Not before we come to a solid understanding with them," Max growled.

"We have to make them free the Whorsk slaves," someone said.

"That might kill them, too," Max said wryly. "They don't know how to work."

Rodrick held up his hand for silence. "By the sampling of comment, I take it that the majority opinion is that we should try to negotiate with the priests in the other cities. Am I right?"

There was a murmur of affirmation.

"Oh, all right," Max said. "Let's give 'em one more chance."

Mandy and Grace joined Rodrick and Max in the communications room. At first Max got no answer when he began to call, but he kept trying, demanding that Sistank, the only name he knew, answer his call.

After a quarter hour, Sistank's voice came on. "I am Sistank."

Max moved aside so that Rodrick could sit down. "Sistank," he said, "this message is for you and the other members of your brotherhood in all of the cities along the river. First of all, you must understand that we value each individual life. Killing a human being is a crime among us. We will not, and I want you to believe this, tolerate even one more death of one of our people at your hands or by the Whorsk under your leadership. Do you understand what I am saying?"

"I hear," the surly voice responded.

"We have not killed the priests in the pyramid of the city of Suses. We were forced to kill many of the people of the city in self-defense, and one or more priests may have been killed when we were forced to destroy your weapons. We do not intend to kill. We hope to avoid further battle with you. We off peace, but it must be on our terms. First, you must turn off your force field so that we can see your installations, to be sure you are not preparing offensive actions against us."

"That is impossible," Sistank said, his voice going unnaturally high. "Do you have the stupidity to believe that the shield was put in place for concealment from *you*?"

"Diplomats they ain't," Max growled.

"For whatever reason the shield was installed, it must be turned off," Rodrick responded evenly. "Otherwise we will have to destroy your weapons and perhaps your power sources, as we destroyed the weapons of the city of Suses."

"The shield will not be turned off, and you will not

find us as unprepared as were our brothers in Suses. The gods will protect us. The weapons of the gods are invulnerable."

"So thought the people of this city," Rodrick said.

"Duncan, may I speak to him?" Mandy asked.

"Can't hurt," Max said.

Mandy sat down, keyed the transmitter. "I am Mandy, high priestess of the great God Jehovah," she began. "Hear me. You have made war on my people, and you have angered my God, who is all powerful. Tonight, when the two moons have set, when the sky is in darkness, the great God Jehovah will demonstrate his power to you. Look up to the sky when the moons have fallen below the horizon." She turned off the transmitter.

"I hear you," Sistank said, and then there was silence.

"I think I anticipate you, Mandy," Grace said. "You want to give them a light show."

"One or more thermonuclear weapons detonated in space," Mandy replied.

"Two should do it," Rodrick said. "That's an excellent idea, Mandy, using their own superstitions against them."

Two hydrogen bombs, mounted on ground-to-space missiles, arced up from the *Spirit of America*. Their trajectories took them to the skies over the western continent, and deep enough into space so that only a minor amount of radiation would affect Omega, that to be captured by the radiation belts that circled the planet, just as the Van Allen belt circled Earth. The sky turned white with a fierce light, and even as that light faded, the sky burned again.

Duncan Rodrick was in the communications room of the pyramid, watching the implosions on a portable screen. Within seconds of the first flash, the radio came to life. Sistank's voice was almost hysterical.

First Sistank screamed in his own language and then, "Fools! You fools, you have killed us all!"

"The force released in space will not affect us," Rodrick said evenly. "But we can release that force directly atop your cities. We once again offer you the opportunity to have peace, to work with us. Otherwise we will have no choice but to destroy you."

Sistank was breathing hard, his voice harsh. "With the morning you will find that the shield is down. It no longer matters. Destroy us if you will, for it is only a matter of time before your stupid use of nuclear weapons will bring destruction upon this entire planet."

There was no more. Duncan tried to raise Sistank but got no answer. Just after dawn he flew the length of the valley and saw the beautiful, golden cities and the rich fields. He flew low over several cities and past the pyramids. There was no hostile action. No answer came from Sistank or any of the other cities when he used the radio back in the pyramid. He called for Ahmes, the high priest.

"Last night we detonated two thermonuclear bombs in space to demonstrate the power of our weapons to the other cities," Rodrick said.

The high priest's face went gray. He fell to his knees and began to pray in his own language.

"Sistank intimated that something would happen, that destruction would come, because of that," Rodrick said. "What did he mean?"

Ahmes looked at him, eyes wide, a look of fear on his face. "Now *they* will come," he said, "for the power of the atom is the only power that can threaten them. They will rain destruction down on the entire planet from far away. Death will come without notice, and there will be no life left on all the world."

"Who are they?" Rodrick asked.

"The Masters," Ahmes said. "Our people, from whom our ancestors escaped so many centuries ago. Now I hope you are satisfied, Earthman, for you have truly killed us all."

TWENTY

"My delicate, fragile little flower of a wife," Jacob West said, "you are breaking my fingers."

Theresita was squeezing Jacob's hand as a contraction ripped across her belly. She was breathing through her teeth, fast and shallow. When it was over she said, "I will trade *this* for the pain of a few broken fingers."

"Once or twice more," Mandy encouraged.

Theresita tensed, then began breathing hard again.

"Ah," Mandy said. "Push hard now."

Jacob heard a wet plopping sound, saw Theresita's face grimace in pain, and felt his hand being squeezed hard. Then there was a flurry of movement, and Mandy was holding something wet, squirmy, and bloody with her hand. The baby's cry made Jacob jump.

"Well, there he is," Mandy said, extending the wet, squirmy, bloody thing toward Jacob's face.

"Hi, kid," Jacob said uncertainly.

"Let me see," Theresita panted.

"Just let me clean him up a bit," Mandy said.

When the baby was beside Theresita, she looked down into a pretty little baby face and smiled. Another doctor was working down between Theresita's legs.

"He's perfect," Theresita said. "Hey, look, he sees me."

"He can't see much right now," Mandy said.

"No?" Theresita moved her finger in front of the baby's eyes, and the eyes followed the movement.

"Well, maybe he sees a blur of movement," Mandy conceded. "You can go on out now, Jacob. We've got to do a bit of tidying up. He was a big one." She reached for the baby.

"Leave me alone," the baby said.

"What?" Mandy yelped.

"I am very hungry," the baby said. His hand motions were jerky and uncoordinated, but he managed to seize the flap of Theresita's hospital gown, and he pulled hard enough to expose her swollen breast.

In order to furnish power for Grace Monroe's translation machine, the admiral had strung a lead from a large crawler into the pyramid's library in the city of Suses. The translation box had been altered to analyze the language of the priests and was being used quite efficiently as a computer terminal by Evangeline. Mopro was outside. Down in the city Whorsk slaves were cleaning up rubble, and already the damaged buildings were being repaired.

It had been less than a month since Paul Warden and Stoner McRae had blown up the dam across the river. Enough of the harvest had been saved with the restoration of water to provide for the needs of the city. The water had come again just in time, and the harvest was under way all along the fertile valley. There had been no direct contact between the Americans and the inhabitants of the cities downstream, but the shield was still down and no further hostile actions had been taken by either Eepera or Whorsk.

Amando Kwait was tired after a long day of overseeing the automatic harvesters in operation in the fields of Eden. The crops had produced well. Grain, corn, and potatoes—all the staples, in fact—were going to be in surplus, and the genetically engineered specialty vegetables and fruits had proven their worth by resisting all attacks by insects. His new ever-bearing fruit and vegetable plants were beginning to produce their first harvestable produce and would continue the year round.

Amando was a bit surprised to find Dena Madden waiting for him in his new house on Stanton Bay. He had moved off the *Spirit of America* because the engineering staff was readying the ship for the voyage home. Three more months of production from Stoner's mine, plus the minute amounts of rhenium from the miners, would see the ship's Shaw Drive fueled. The rocket-fuel plant was in production, working twenty-eight hours a day.

"Why is it you like tomatoes so much?" Dena asked, handing Amando a Bloody Mary made from fresh juice and the ship's vodka.

"They're pretty," Amando said simply. "They taste good."

Dena lifted her glass. "I've never told you this, but I was very much against working with you."

"I sensed that at first," he admitted, surprising her. "I have had the feeling for some time now that you've come to grips with it."

"What are you sensing now?" she asked, looking up at him through her long, black lashes.

"What I am sensing now is too beautiful to be true," he said.

"Have a little faith," she urged, smiling. "Our work is done. I've been released to go back to my section."

"That makes me sad," he said.

She put down her glass and cocked her head. "Hey, you're an intelligent, thinking man, a man of new and original ideas. Why are you so slow to understand how I feel about you?"

Amando swallowed the last of the drink. He seemed to have difficulty forming the words. "Can I hope that you—"

"Try me," she said.

He almost fell over a table getting to her, and she went into his arms. "I have always been a total sucker for big men," she said, as his arms wrapped around her and lifted her from the floor.

*   *   *

Duncan Rodrick was on the radio with Grace. "Dunc," she said, "we're making progress. The priests are not eager to help, but Ahmes did consent to help us with a basic glossary of English-to-Eepera words. Evangeline is keying it into the computer now. I'd say we can begin translation of the books in a day or so."

"How's the morale of the pretty people in the city?"

"It's eat, drink, and be stupid," Grace said. "A continual party, as if the world were about to end, but the Whorsk are going about their business, even without overseers. The repair work is going well. There are some odd birds here, Dunc. There are two different races. I'm sure you noticed the difference in how they look. The ones you call the pretty ones, like Prince Yanee, they call themselves Eepera. Then there's the caste of priests. The priests and their women are small and dark with faces straight off an ancient Egyptian wall painting. The priests *never* call the pretty people of the city Eepera, but instead always refer to them as 'our children.' "

"Have you been able to drag more information out of Ahmes or anyone else about the mysterious Masters, whom they're sure will come and blow up the planet?"

"They're all very closemouthed. They are sure that their gods are going to punish us for fooling around with their sacred records."

"How do you figure it, Grace?" Rodrick had great respect for the woman's intelligence.

"So far it's mostly guesswork," she said, "but I have a feeling that there was an alien race that came to Earth in the time of the early dynasties of Egypt. Maybe its members were running from someone, either their parent race—the Masters—or another race. I know that they fear *them*; they fear the Masters more than they fear the gods. They seem to think that the Masters are all powerful. They're sure that the Masters have detected, or will detect, our nuclear explosions and will come to destroy this world."

"Think they will?"

"I'm not sure. If they're so threatened by nuclear weaponry, why haven't they destroyed Earth?" Grace asked.

"We've been popping off nuclear explosions there since 1945."

"Good point. Well, keep me posted."

"Sure thing." She laughed. "I'm going to approach these books with some misgiving. It's going to be a blow to my pride to find that all those science-fiction writers were right and that one of the earliest civilizations on Earth, possibly all of them, came as the result of alien intervention."

Although the threat was there—the possibility that some superrace of killers would come swooping out of the intergalactic distances sowing destruction—life in the colony went on. Max was spending most of his time at the rocket-fuel plant, where production was flowing nicely. D.C. Broadfoot and his engineering crew were working on the *Spirit of America,* preparing her for the return journey to Earth. Amando and his agricultural people were stocking the green areas aboard the ship with Omegan plants, many of which Amando was sure would help to reclaim the lost areas of cultivation on Earth and increase the production of food dramatically.

Paul Warden made his choice, speaking to his Evangeline as they stood under one of Omega's moons in the cool desert night, the glow of the pyramid lighting Evangeline's face. "I've been pretty dumb, Vange," Paul said. "So I'll ask two questions. First, can you forgive me for being blind?"

Evangeline smiled. "A man who makes snap decisions is not always right."

"Is that a yes?" he asked, encouraged, his crooked grin in place.

"Yes," she said.

"Okay. The second question is this: Do you think you could stand having me around the rest of your life?"

Evangeline's face was serious. "I could handle that."

He did not know what to do then. He wanted to kiss her, but she was being so calm, so matter of fact, that he knew doubt.

"Vange," he said, "I could kick myself for not speaking before—" He paused.

"Before Sage was killed?"

"Yeah."

Now she smiled and moved closer. "Paul, I knew. You didn't have to speak."

"Well, I never want you to think that I'm saying I love you just because Sage—"

"Are you saying it?"

"You bet," he said.

"Say it."

"I love you."

She had to make the first move, putting her arms up, and then, with a huge sigh, he held her.

Clay had spread an air mattress on a mossy bank on the upper reaches of Jumper's Run in the Renfro Mountains. The night was pleasant, with just a hint of fall in the air. Behind him he could see the shadowy movements of Cindy inside the lighted tent. He had had to do some fancy talking to get everyone to agree to allow them to camp out alone in the mountains. It had been Duncan Rodrick who had made it possible.

"Clay can handle himself," he had told Stoner and Betsy. "We'll patrol the coast, and he can keep in touch at regular intervals."

A night bird was calling. There was only one moon, but it was full and bright. The little stream sang to him as it tumbled over its rocky bed. He had seen shadows of monster fish in the pools that afternoon while he was setting up camp.

He heard the sound of a fastener opening and turned to see Cindy silhouetted against the light from inside the tent. He swallowed in a gulp, for she was wearing something tiny and frilly.

"Beautiful night," he croaked as she came toward him and sat down on the mattress.

"I thought I might be a little uneasy, out here all alone," she said. She sprawled beside him, her hair trailing on his chest. "But I'm not. I feel safe with you."

Well, he was only sixteen, and those were heady things she was saying. He grinned. He put his arm around her and felt warmth and softness through the very thin garment. He gulped again.

"Cindy, do you feel a little funny?"

"As if we're doing something we shouldn't be doing?"

"Yeah, like that."

She giggled. "A little."

"Well, listen," he said. "We don't have to—I mean if you don't want—"

She traced a finger over his bare chest. "Isn't it nice that we can stay out here as long as we want to? We can stay up as late as we want to and eat when we're hungry and fish and swim—"

He giggled. "In the nude?"

"If we want to," she said in a small voice.

He buried his fingers in her hair and cupped the back of her head. "Cindy, let's always be friends."

"Oh, yes."

"There's no hurry about that—that other."

She pushed herself up on her elbow. "*Hmmm?*"

"Is there?"

"No," she said.

"But I can kiss you anytime I want to," he said, and there was a feeling of wonder in him at that miracle. "That is, if you want to, I mean."

She pushed against him and found his lips, and although time stood still, the moon did not, and it was higher in the sky when he sighed and pushed her away. "I can't stand much of that."

"I thought that's why we got married, because you couldn't stand much of that."

"Oh, wow," he exhaled, pulling her to him, her soft body partially atop.

"Me, too," she whispered.

After a while he knew that *something* had to happen. "Cindy?"

"*Mmm?*"

"I've never felt like this before. I've never—uh—well, you know."

"I know. Me neither."

"I don't want to do anything to hurt you."

"I guess we'll just have to learn together," she said.

He began to explore her soft, warm, girl mysteries. "Sounds like fun," he whispered hoarsely.

It was.

And skinny-dipping and having water fights in the cold, sparkling stream were fun, as were eating fresh fish cooked over an open fire under the moonlight, and taking long, beautiful days of exploring the surrounding countryside. A week passed, and they had trouble remembering what day it was.

"In about a hundred years we'll think about going back to town," he told her one lovely evening as she clung to him.

"Or maybe two," she said.

But they knew it was time to go home, to settle into the new house that was being built for them, to get on with the work at hand.

"We'll give ourselves three more days," Clay told her.

"I hate to see it end."

"We can come back on every anniversary."

"I'd like that."

"Want to climb that hill off to the north today?"

"Sure."

"Great. I'll get the packs ready."

The hill, however, would have to wait. While he loaded the packs, he had the radio on. The exploration and minerals teams were working, and he could keep track of where they were by their reports. Stoner was up north at the molybdenum mine. *Apache One* was flying a mapping grid east of the tall, snowy mountains of the interior. The colony was busy and life was normal . . . which, on Omega, meant always exciting. He was whistling, listening with only part of his attention to the radio chatter when a strong voice made him freeze.

"*Spirit of America, Spirit of America,* this is the *Free Enterprise.* Come in."

"Cindy! Hey, Cindy!" he yelled, and she came running half-dressed out of the tent to see what was wrong.

It's a ship!" he yelled, grabbing her and dancing her round. "A ship from Earth."

The great ship was a sparkle of light in the cloudless sky as sunlight caught her hull, a tiny daytime star that first glowed red and then began to enlarge as the retrorockets slowed her orbital speed and she came down, down, growing by the minute. After a long, long time there was a sound of muted, distant thunder that grew into a bellowing roar as the ship grew larger and larger and then seemed to cover the sky. Her markings were visible—the red, white, and blue of the stars and stripes prominent.

The entire colony had turned out. Their cheering was drowned out by the thunder of the great ship's rockets as she lowered in a cloud of dust and rocket exhaust to settle into a grassy plain about two miles from the outskirts of the town.

To most it was an overwhelmingly emotional, inspiring event—an unexpected link with the home they had left behind. But to the few who had known the critical state of world affairs on Earth, to those who had, for years, wondered if the bombs had fallen, if there would be anyone alive on Earth when and if the *Spirit of America* returned, it was an event of deeper meaning.

Knowing that the priests in the cities along the Great Misty River would be listening, Duncan Rodrick had told Harry Shaw, captain of the *Free Enterprise*, to keep radio talk to a minimum. Rodrick had a thousand questions burning inside him as he watched the ship settle and heard the thunder of the rockets diminish and cease. One thing he knew, however—nuclear war had not come to Earth as a result of the great battle of South America, the battle that had been going on when the *Spirit of America* lost her communications on the outward trip.

Now the members of the colony were rushing toward the ship. It was an emotional time. Even Stoner McRae's eyes were wet. As if sensing the drama of the moment, Harry Shaw kept the hatches closed until the group of pioneers had reached the ship and were clustered around the main hatch.

They saw a trim, neatly uniformed man stand in the hatch and salute them, and they cheered. And then they saw a familiar face, a face they had seen many times on Earth viewscreens but that just a few of them had seen in person. He was in a familiar pose, his hands clasped over his head in a symbol of victory.

"Dexter," Harry Shaw said, "you will not be the first to set foot on this planet, but you will be the first from this ship."

"Thank you, Harry," Dexter Hamilton replied. "It's an honor I'm not sure I deserve, but thank you."

He met Rodrick at the foot of the ramp. "Mr. President, it is a surprise and an honor to see you," Rodrick said, grinning hugely.

Hamilton made no attempt to control his emotions. He clasped his arms around Rodrick. His eyes were wet. Then he pulled back and sniffed, and looked around and waved.

"Well, Duncan," Hamilton said, "we've brought you some more people and a few things you might be able to use, along with some things, like my aging body, that will be of doubtful use."

"What we want first, Mr. President, is news." He handed Hamilton a hailer, so that everyone would be able to hear.

"I won't make a speech," Hamilton said, "although I've never felt so emotional as I do now. Captain Rodrick said you all want news. Well, she's still there, the Earth. She's wounded and she's hungry and she's troubled, but as of a few days ago—"

Rodrick picked up on that phrase "as of a few days ago" immediately and looked up at Harry Shaw, who winked at him, thinking that Rodrick was surprised. Rodrick was, but at knowing that Shaw had made the same discoveries about the Shaw Drive that Max and Grace had made under stress.

"—the big bombs were still in their cradles. Mexico had fallen to the Brazilians. When we activated the Shaw

Drive, the Republicrat administration was making noises
about going to war, but I don't think they would have.
The Russians were making their usual noises, and in all
honesty, the situation was still nip and tuck. We must get
these two ships back to Earth, bring the people there
hope, and give them the promise of new worlds, with
freedom and plenty."

Hamilton paused and looked around. "This looks like
a good world, my friends, and there are a lot of people
aboard this ship who want to set foot on it, so let's drop
the ceremony so you can get acquainted with those who
are going to be sharing this world with you."

Juke was in his glory. On the main street of Hamilton
were new people everywhere, people who had not yet
been blessed with his jokes. It was one gigantic party.
People were shaking hands, exchanging tales of Earth and
of Omega, dancing and eating. The ship's distillery had
been shifted into high gear.

Omega and Eden were putting their best feet forward
with a golden autumn day.

"I won't say the drinks here are watered," Juke was
telling a family who had come out on the *Free Enterprise*,
"but this stuff is what our police use to sober up drunks."

"I'm hungry for the latest news from the Earth," he
told another victim. "Is it true the Jolly Green Giant is
getting a little brown around the temples?"

Juke was keeping the music going, pouring it out
from a series of speakers up and down the street. Some
young people were dancing. Most of the children of the
Free Enterprise had gathered to watch a show put on by
the family of dragons, organized by Clay and Cindy. They
gave an exhibition of riding, then allowed the newcomers
to meet Baby and Beau and have a short ride.

The children fell in love with Baby's triplets because
they were small, squeakily friendly, and as playful as
kittens. There were two females and one male. The male
baby was mischievous, dodging in and out of the crowd,
sometimes knocking the smaller children off their feet
with his careless tail. He had made one run through the
crowd, snatching a morsel of food from the hands of a little

girl, when Clay yelled at him and gave chase. He caugh
the little male in the open riding arena and grabbed hin
around the neck like a rodeo rider bulldogging a calf. The
little dragon bleated and struggled.

"You've got to behave," Clay said. He put his weigh
on the dragon's neck and threw him to the ground. The
kids yelled and clapped, and as part of the show, h
decided to continue the rodeo act. He jerked off his belt
gathered three of the little dragon's feet in one hand, and
wrapped the belt around them, threw up his hands as if h
had been competing against the clock, and bowed to the
applauding audience. The little male bawled piteously a
he struggled to get free, and Baby came on the run. Baby
was impressive on her eight-foot legs, and Clay, hearing
her protesting his treatment of her offspring, said, "Hey
Baby, take it easy."

But Baby made no threat. She threw herself to the
ground, rolled onto her back, held three legs together and
bleated at Clay as if to say, "Look, if you must play rough
play with me and leave my little one alone."

To the sound of children's laughter, Clay released the
little male, who ran to his mother and looked back at Clay
accusingly.

Not everyone was celebrating. Some very serious peo
ple were gathered in the captain's mess aboard the *Spiri*
of America. Duncan Rodrick had just finished recounting
the series of confrontations with the people of the Grea
Misty River, beginning with the first raid of the Whorsk
the attack that resulted in the death of the dissident grou
led by the former first officer, and was answering ques
tions from Dexter Hamilton, Shaw, and others from the
Free Enterprise, when Jackie came into the room.

"Captain," she said, "Grace and Evangeline are land
ing now and will be here in about ten minutes."

The two women had been notified of the arrival of the
Free Enterprise. One of the archaeologists from the *Free*
Enterprise was an Egyptologist, and he kept asking ex
cited questions until Grace and Evangeline, both dusty
and looking very tired, came into the room and were

escorted to seats by Max and Paul. They were introduced to the newcomers.

"I think you two have some information for us?" Rodrick said.

"We finally got things rolling three days ago," Grace told him. "The translations are still a bit stiff and some technical terms might be in doubt, but we've sampled quite a few dusty tomes—some so old that the paper is crumbling—and *they're* copies of older books. Before Evangeline gives you a summary, let me say that I wasn't quite sure I wanted to know the whole story of aliens in ancient Egypt. Because of my pride, I wanted to continue to believe that we humans pulled ourselves up by our own bootstraps. I went into those books with a pretty belligerent attitude. Those short, dark priests are not very nice, and my pride didn't want to admit that they, perhaps, started the Egyptians on the road to cultural development and what we call civilization."

She paused, and a bright smiled wiped the tiredness from her face. "I think you're going to like what Evangeline has to say."

Evangeline opened a notebook. "This is all very, very sketchy. There are thousands of books in that library, covering six thousand years in minute detail. Some of my information comes from the books, some from their high priest, Ahmes. He began to be a bit more cooperative when he realized that we could actually read his sacred books. I remind you, however, that whatever Ahmes told us is from a highly opinionated source and does not always agree with material in the books—at least in those areas where we've cross-checked. But I think I can give you a brief history of the valley people."

She settled herself in her chair. "The evidence seems to be quite firm that an alien starship landed somewhere in the Nile valley. The Eepera claim that the ship landed on Earth six thousand years ago, but the evidence disputes that. For example, the Eepera books state that the three large pyramids had been completed. That, of course, shaves centuries off the Eepera's six-thousand-year claim." She smiled. "That pleased us, because it meant that the

Sumerians and Egyptians had already reached a very sophisticated form of culture and society. Civilization on
Earth was not planted there by aliens."

"There are pictures in the old books of the original
aliens. I don't think you'd ever get the Eepera to believe
it, but those first visitors to Earth weren't very pretty.
They were scrawny, thin, and weak-looking, and although
definitely humanoid, they were inferior physically to the
ancient Egyptians."

Grace laughed. "That's why the sons of the aliens
found the daughters of man to be fair and took them to
bed," she said.

"There's a lot of work to be done," Evangeline continued, "and I'm so glad that the Egyptologist, Dr. Hiram
Abdul, is with us now, because when the Eepera left the
Earth, they brought with them a good sampling of Egyptian artifacts, and I'm sure that their writings will tell us a
great deal about the Egypt of the time at the end of the
Pyramid Age. But I'm rambling.

"For a long time after the landing, the aliens didn't
mix with the local population. They had landed badly,
doing damage to their starship, and they spent all their
time repairing the ship and sending out exploration parties
to decide whether or not the Earth was a suitable home
for them. They had fled what they called 'grinding bond-
age.' Their description of life on the home planets—which,
incidentally, seem to be located all the way across the disc
of the galaxy from our sector, many, many parsecs away—is
frightening. They describe the direst forms of cruelty and
tyranny. And they speak of an ancient and evil empire
ruling stars and planets scattered over thousands of parsecs. It is this empire that the valley people now fear.
Ahmes, for example, is certain that our nuclear explosions
will be detected, and the evil Masters will come and
destroy a potential threat to them. The Masters' rule is
based on nuclear power, and any other society possessing
it cannot be tolerated."

"Ahmes told us that the empire has instruments placed
throughout the galaxy to detect a nuclear explosion," Grace
said.

"The thing that had enabled the aliens to escape the Masters was an invention—a generator capable of creating a field that would block all forms of electromagnetic waves. They were able to hide from their pursurers on Earth under the protection of the field. They could detect the Masters' search ships and knew that sooner or later one of the searchers would become suspicious about a cloud that stayed permanently in one spot and would come down to investigate. They lived in fear, and it was decided to desert the ship and mingle with the native population. It was felt that their intellectual superiority—their advanced knowledge of science and technology—would make it simple to gain control of the Stone Age people of early Egypt, but they got a surprise. They couldn't use their advanced weapons for armed conquest—use of the weapons would have alerted a search ship—and their attempts to take over Egyptian institutions didn't work. Egyptian society was already old, and very structured and stiff. Knowing how to build an electric motor didn't impress the Egyptians, because their society didn't have the basic industry to supply the necessary raw materials. And instead of taking over, the aliens, finding the daughters of men to be very sexy and desirable, were gradually absorbed, going native."

Evangeline looked at Grace, who took the cue. "The children of the aliens had an intellectual advantage, however, and many sought advancement through the various priesthoods. Gradually, a different type of children began to be born, the pretty ones. Perhaps it was some sort of mutation brought on by the mingling of two sets of alien genes.

"The aliens didn't stay long on Earth. The small, dark aliens realized that if they remained, all traces of their culture and tradition would be absorbed by Egypt. The aliens made so little impact on the well-established Egyptian society, they can't even be detected in recorded Egyptian history. But the Egyptians—"

"With the vitality of Earth people," Grace said proudly, smiling at Evangeline.

"—made a mark on the aliens. Indeed, the true ruling class, the priests, are more like ancient Egyptians than either the original Eepera or the pretty Eepera of the present-day cities. But the small, dark priests decided that if anything of their race and culture was to be salvaged, they had to leave the Earth. By this time—we're guessing that not more than sixty years had passed—the search in the vicinity of the Earth had been called off, and they could lift ship."

"We'd wondered," Grace said, "at the coincidence of finding these people here, out of all the possible planets. The simple fact is that, according to their old star charts, charts with empire markings, 61 Cygni is the nearest star to Earth that had, or has, habitable planets. So it's not really a coincidence that we both came to 61 Cygni from the Earth."

"The Eepera from Earth were almost caught by the empire near the Cygni system. They were getting ready to land on the planet of 61 Cygni A when they were surprised by an empire warship. They managed to escape, but the empire ship seeded the planet at 61 Cygni A with the virus that killed three of our people," Evangeline said. "The Eepera took a desperate gamble. They blew up all their lifeboats and launches, plus some nonvital ship's hardware, and left the wreckage for the Masters' ship to find. That, apparently, convinced the Masters, thus leaving the Eepera from Earth free to settle here on what we call Omega."

Grace took over again. "They had been Egyptianized. They had brought Egyptian gods, customs, women, artifacts—even Egyptian thinking with them. The caste of priests was more Egyptian in thought than Eeperan. The priests settled in the valley of the Great Misty River and protected their first city with their generated fog field. They cannibalized the spaceship for its metals and built field generators and the one weapon for which they still had the technology—the solar beam weapon, which they call a disruption wand. They had been vitalized by interbreeding with the Egyptians, so their population grew rapidly. They built lighter-than-air craft and discovered that there was a native race, the Whorsk, who built cities of stone—cities like that one discovered by Stoner McRae. Gradually, in bloody wars, they conquered the Whorsk and worked out a system that endures today. The Whorsk trade for metals with the miners, then trade those metals to the Eepera for helium for their airships. The Whorsk fell in love with air travel and abandoned their stone cities. Since they have no particular attachment to their young, they don't mind at all trading their surplus larvae to the Eepera to be enslaved."

"The rest is a repetition of history," Evangeline said. "A society based on slavery becomes corrupt. The Eepera divided into two distinct classes, which do not mix. There are the small, dark, quite Egyptianlike priests, and the mutated handsome ones. Both are very prideful. Both devote themselves to lives of pleasure, but of vastly different kinds. Their technological skill has deteriorated."

"There is one thing we must consider," Grace said. "All the electronic equipment in the pyramids was built by the Masters for use aboard the starships. That means it is thousands of years old, and some of it is still operating. The pyramid itself is a solar collector, and the generator has not been opened in centuries, which makes it quite a machine. Some of the technicians actually believe that the power source is a gift of the gods. They will not be able to repair the damage done to the solar beam weapon in the Suses pyramid, because they don't have the raw materials, the skills, or the manufacturing facilities. They're down to the last few of their spare parts for the operating radios. Even if we hadn't blown up the weapons in the Suses pyramid, it would probably have ceased functioning in years, decades, who knows, for lack of spare parts and technological knowledge."

"I think I heard someone say once," Evangeline said, "that this society had been totally static for centuries. That's true. The Eepera live for eating, sleeping, and fornicating. They're lazy, prideful to the point of being ridiculous, cruel, stupid, obnoxious, and very, very beautiful. They write poetry. If we could really get our teeth into the language, I think the poetry would be beautiful, as their works of art are, even though they have not progressed beyond the styles of the Old Kingdom of Egypt. I think we can work with them and maybe bring them up to date."

"Well, let's not go into that now, Evangeline," Rodrick said. He looked around the table. "Questions?"

The Egyptologist, Dr. Hiram Abdul, raised his hand. "I'd like to go back there with these two women."

"I was going to suggest that to you," Grace said. "I believe you'll be able to read the hieroglyphics easily."

"I'd like to suggest that everyone hold his or her questions until we've had a chance to check our translations and do some more work," Evangeline said.

"Sounds reasonable," Rodrick agreed. "Any information you find on this original Eepera empire, get it to us as quickly as you can."

"I think it's time we joined the party," Max suggested, rising, taking Grace's hand.

Most of the people left. Rodrick, Dexter Hamilton, Oscar Kost, and Harry Shaw remained.

"Well," Dexter said with a sigh, "it never seems to end, does it? We leave one planet where war has been the scourge of humankind for all history, and here we are, facing a powerful enemy who has been in space for thousands of years." He picked up his glass. "At least the *Spirit of America*'s gin mill does a good job."

"There's one little incident that Grace and Evangeline left out," Rodrick said. "Grace gave me a report on it a few days ago. She was talking with the high priest, Ahmes, and she suggested that all was not lost, that even if the Masters *had* detected the nuclear explosions, we could fight. Ahmes said, and I quote, 'what can *you* do against a fleet of a hundred thousand Master ships all equipped with weapons that can shatter a world?'"

Oscar Kost, looking surprisingly healthy, sipped his drink. "Still, we've got a few thousand years of history behind us, and they haven't been back to Earth. Maybe they've blown themselves up, like our fellow humans back home are threatening to do."

"Harry," Dexter Hamilton said, "wouldn't it be ironic

if you have to build a rhenium bomb after all to keep the Masters from eating us?"

Harry looked resigned. "We might be able to come up with a surprise or two."

"If there's one thing we understand and are pretty good at," Dexter said, "it's fighting. Lord knows we've done enough of it. And we've gone up against some pretty tough customers on Earth. I'm not ready to roll over and play dead. Not just yet."

"I thought I heard someone suggest that we join the party," Oscar said, rising. "There's one confrontation I hope I haven't missed." On the way off the ship, he explained to Rodrick about the robot, Sergeant York, who had been anticipating with eagerness a meeting with his prototype, the admiral. "If those two decide to fight," he said, "stand back. Waaaay back."

The meeting between the sergeant and the admiral did not take place. The sergeant, in fatigues, well-armed since his function was defense, stalked the streets of Hamilton City looking for a resplendent figure in navy whites. He did not even look twice at the handsome, graceful young man in the simple semiuniform of the colony who was dancing with Grace Monroe.

Another meeting had taken place. It happened by accident, when Derek Roebling came away from the show being put on by Clay and Cindy and the dragons to sample Omega's fall wine. He was pouring himself a glass when a dark-haired woman with romantically melancholy eyes came to the table and stood beside him, glass in hand.

"Fill 'er up?" Derek asked, smiling and looking into the woman's eyes.

"Thank you," Mandy Miller said.

Derek felt his face flush, for he was staring. He was falling into those sad eyes. He saw the woman's eyes widen slightly. It was one of those too rare moments when something, some force, some magnetism, some electricity in a man and a woman reaches out, meets, and is mutually recognized.

"Welcome to Omega," the woman said.

"I'm Derek Roebling," he said.

"Mandy," she said, extending her hand. Again her eyes widened in surprise at the sheer, delightful shock of the touch of his hand.